The Scouts of St. Michael

OPERATION ARCHANGEL

D1607915

On my honour I promise that—
I will do my duty to God and the King.
I will do my best to help others, whatever it costs me.
I know the scout law and will obey it.

—British Boy Scout promise,
sworn by all boys joining the BBS

In the presence of this blood banner which represents our Führer—
I swear to devote all my energies and strength to the saviour of our country,
Adolf Hitler.
I am willing and able to give up my life for him, so help me God.

—Hitler Youth oath,
mandatory for all German children
to pledge on their tenth birthday

St. Michael, the Archangel, defend us in battle—
Be our protection against the wickedness and snares of the devil.
O Prince of the heavenly host, by the power of God, thrust into hell Satan
and all evil spirits who wander throughout the world seeking
the ruin of souls. Amen.

—Prayer to St. Michael,
the Archangel

WAR OFFICE

10 May 1940

FROM: PRIME MINISTER, WINSTON CHURCHILL
TO: DR. HUGH DALTON, MINISTER OF ECONOMIC WARFARE
MAJOR LAWRENCE GRAND RE, Secret Intelligence Service

Gentlemen,

THE FOLLOWING HAS COME TO MY ATTENTION. IT IS A
TRANSCRIPT OF THE STATEMENT GIVEN BY EYEWITNESS YAS-
HAM HEITINGER REGARDING EVENTS THAT TRANSPIRED IN AND
AROUND THE TOWN OF FRANKFURT, GERMANY, ON THE NIGHT
OF 9 NOVEMBER 1938.

I was standing outside my shop, trying to get a
look at the commotion up the street as they are approaching. A gang of Hitlerjugend, a crowd cheering
them on. They stop at my shop. A tall, skinny one in
a dark uniform, the leader [CONFIRMED AS THOMAS PETER
HEYDRICH], he say, "You will no longer be allowed to
make money off the backs of the hardworking people of
Germany, Jew pig."
SMACK! He slapped me hard across the face. I
am too shocked, too afraid to cry out. The other
boys, some SA men too, in the brown shirts, they all
laughed. He points his skinny right finger in my face.
He say, "Listen filth, you are finished dressing the
German people in your Jew rags. Do you know why?"
SMACK! To the other side of my face. I was shak-
ing with fear. With each slap, there is uproarious

cheers. The police just stood by to watch, they doing nothing.

I could feel it. These youth wanted to rip me to pieces, beat me with their clubs, then God only knows what, maybe hang me from a pole in the street. I don't know why they do this to us Jews, but I instantly know what I must to do if I survive to the next minute. "WE are the new Germany," he says to me.

CRASH! This sound, from behind me, someone had thrown something through the glass door of my shop. The little tannins [monsters] rush in, smashing, tearing, shredding all I worked my whole life to build. They don't understand. I am a German. Born here—this is my home.

I knew many of these boys, I made their baby clothes and school outfits since they used to toddle underfoot. And now they blame me for Germany's ills, of somehow stealing my meagre living which I work so hard for. Me, a lowly tailor?

I say they were turned against me! Their minds poisoned by that little evil clown Hitler, feh!

After they rampage through my shop, they are flowing out of the door, smiling, laughing, giddy with their accomplishment for greater Germany. The last one out—it was Wilhelm Siegfried—his mother was a dear lady. His father was a baker. I look at him dead in his eyes, but only frenzied eyes look back, his eyes opened wide, his gaze was focused sharp with rage, but his vision, that was blurry—obscured by hate. Still, he paused for a tiny sliver of a second, his expression changed; then he went.

He saw me. As God is my witness, he saw me. Through the hate and the rage, he looked with his heart, and he saw me, his friend, the nice tailor who used to give to him lollipops if he hold still, who he used to call Herr Heitinger. I hope my face haunts his dreams forever.

Next, something orange goes through the air, through the front window where glass had moments before. The inside of my shop erupted in fire.

The mob cheered and moved on to the next shop. I crouch low and lose myself out of the back door of my burning shop, having time to grab the lockbox and a picture of my mother.

On the way to my house, I passed burning, broken shops of my neighbours, every Jewish shop smashed, burning synagogues, and worse, people beaten in the streets, kicked, spit on, called vile names.

These people were my neighbours, being beaten by children I knew. I saw one of my customers, an old lady of 82 years, dragged through the street by her hair, begging God to take her. It was just a boy, pulling this lady over the hard cobblestones and laughing, as a lunatic laughs. And there was no one to help her. The police just looked on. Some smiling, laughing. Bastard cowards.

I was able to make my way through the streets to my home, where my wife and I spent the long night hiding, locked in the basement. The next day, those same boys were back again. More looting and burning and beating. They were wearing street clothes, but we knew who they were. They were vermin Hitlerjugend and their leader who is called "the Prince"—nephew of SS Chief Heydrich himself.

That very day, we take what little money we have, and my wife and I sneak our way straight to the American consulate. They granted us immediate visas. We left the next day. We were lucky, but we were filled with so much sadness, leaving so many behind, forced to flee our beloved homeland that loved us no more.

AN ESTIMATED 1,400 SYNAGOGUES ACROSS GERMANY WERE BURNED ON 9 NOVEMBER AND THE DAYS THAT FOLLOWED. IT IS ALSO ESTIMATED THAT 1,500 JEWISH GERMAN NATIONALS WERE MASSACRED, WHILST THOUSANDS MORE WERE BEATEN AND TORTURED, AND HARSH RESTRICTIONS FROM MOVING ABOUT FREELY WERE IMPOSED. AN ESTIMATED 400,000 JEWS CURRENTLY RESIDE IN GERMANY.

THE HJ PATROL LEADER WHO CONFRONTED YASHAM HEITINGER HAS BEEN CONFIRMED AS HITLERJUGEND OBERSTAMMFÜHRER THOMAS PETER HEYDRICH, 16, NEPHEW OF SS-OBERGRUPPENFÜHRER REINHARD HEYDRICH, FOURTH IN COMMAND OF THE THIRD REICH.

THOMAS PETER IS ALSO THE "GODCHILD" OF ADOLF HITLER.

This marks a dangerous escalation in the use of the Hitler Youth.

Can we do something? Anything?

Winston S. Churchill

The Scouts of St. Michael

OPERATION
ARCHANGEL

A novel by

Dan Morales

ELM GROVE PUBLISHING
San Antonio, Texas

ISBN 978-1-943492-36-7 (hard back)
ISBN 978-1-943492-37-4 (soft cover)

Front cover photograph © 2018 by Kevin Kinert.
Back cover photograph © 2018 by Mark Jepsen.
Book and cover design by **designpanache.**

ELM GROVE PUBLISHING
www.elmgrovepublishing.com

CONTENTS

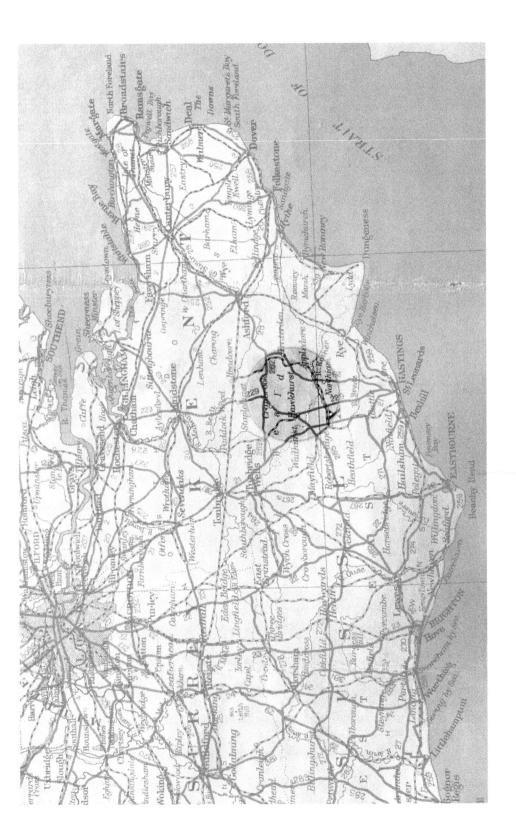

Chapter 1
Official Notification

Mr. Billings finally held in his hand what had transformed Katie and the boys into weepers. Today, like every day for the past two weeks, one of the tykes would undoubtedly be perched on the steps, awaiting his arrival—probably one of the little ones, most likely Willy, scooting about on his roller skates, or maybe Jack, picking off targets with his catapult.

After the first week, Mr. Billings had got used to pedalling up the road running along the stone wall surrounding the grounds and cemetery, through the iron gates, and up the short, tree-canopied path leading to the main house, then reaching in his postal pouch, pulling out the bundle sorted for St. Michael's, and shaking his head as he handed it over to whichever boy was there.

"Not today," he'd say, frowning and then smiling sympathetically. "But soon, you'll see." What he hadn't got used to was the reverse trip down that lovely winding lane, feeling miserable for disappointing the good boys of the home, who were waiting desperately for one particular correspondence. That was a feeling he hoped to never get used to.

In his hand he finally held that much anticipated communiqué from the Ronan Academy addressed to St. Michael's. He didn't dare bundle this post with the bunch. *No, sir*. Instead it would go in his special delivery pocket, where he carried only the most important post, to keep it from being lost in the mix of less important newspapers, form letters, and payment requests. That pocket had carried a lot in its time: hopes, dreams, fears, laughter, tears, sympathy when it was needed, and hardship when it wasn't. He kissed the envelope for luck, and with a silent prayer for good news, shoved it into his pocket.

There were always weepers on his round, especially now with the war on. Mostly, it was mothers, waiting for news that a boy, a husband—or both—had been called up for military service. Most would meet him with a simple hello or good morning—or "Afternoon, Dave," depending on the time of his delivery. The first indication that he was in for a rough day came at the morning sort. He knew, based on the envelopes alone, who would be called up that day, who would read the words NOTICE OF CALLING OUT UNDER THE RESERVE AND AUXILIARY FORCE ACT, 1939, and learn they'd soon be preparing for war and a very uncertain future. Like family, he shared in their anxious anticipation daily, and he dreaded the worried look that would spread across the addressee's face when he finally delivered the much anticipated post. Often first to hear the news, as a trusted member of the Royal Mail he was ever ready to lay aside his pouch and postal duties, to help folks absorb said news, good or ill, with an understanding word and warm cup of tea. It was his way and why the villagers on his round loved him.

Tossing his pouch over his shoulder, he rushed out of the door. No normal round today. *No, sir.* On his bike he hopped and away he pedalled, not up lovely Harcourt Lane as was his usual, but straight over to Moor Hill Road on a beeline for St. Michael's. If he didn't rid himself of it first thing, the weight of the letter in his pocket would drag him down all day.

***

St. Michael's Church and Home for Boys was situated in The Moor, the oldest section of the village of Hawkhurst, a short distance southwest of the village centre and home to only a handful of boys. Six, to be exact.

The first to arrive had done so via the church doorsteps, a toddler, Reggie, and his infant brother, Willy. The six-hundred-year-old church and attached building weren't constructed with the intention of being a boys home and school, but when old Vicar Davis, Sisters Noreen and Doreen, secretary Miss Goold,Maurice their cook, and caretakers Mr. McKenna and Mr. Greene decided that the responsibility of caring for this pair of brothers had been given to them by God, they set to work and quietly, over time, turned St. Michael's into a home and school for the boys.

In the months that followed Reggie and Willy's arrival, Freddie and Dougie each showed up unannounced on the church steps as well. Henry had been dropped off after being found abandoned, wondering in the East End, so said the note pinned to his small coat, and Jack was taken in after his parents, devout members of the parish, were tragically killed in a motor accident whilst on holiday in London.

Together for years, Freddie and Reggie were the oldest at fifteen and sixteen. Though younger then Reggie by a year Freddie was the biggest boy, with dark features, thick eyebrows and eyes of deep blue. Reggie, second largest, had red hair so bright it was almost orange, and was pale skinned with bright blue eyes. Henry and Dougie, both fourteen, had sandy blond hair with matching brown eyes. Although Henry was taller by an inch, Dougie outweighed him by a little under a stone. Jack — with his dark black, straight hair, and bright blue eyes — was the youngest at eleven. And lastly Willy, at twelve, had red hair to match his older brother, his most stunning feature being a piercing set of eyes that seemed to change colour from green to blue based on his surroundings. And whilst only Willy and Reggie were related by blood, all who knew the boys considered them—as they considered themselves—brothers. "Mike's Tykes" was the moniker used by the majority of villagers, who considered the six to be village mascots of a sort.

To folks who didn't care much for them—justly or not—they were unflatteringly referred to as "the fens" or worse, the "Hawkhurst Gang" after the infamous group of smugglers, highwaymen, and cutthroats who made the village itself infamous during the mid-eighteenth century.

***

Mr. Billings stuck his head into Katie Goold's office. She was a lovely young woman with pale skin and flowing red hair that today she wore pulled back from her face, wrapped with a bow.

"Excuse me, Katie, I hope you don't mind my letting meself in. There was no one out front."

"Hello, Dave, please come in." She glanced at the clock. He was very early. "Is everything all right?" she asked, stepping out from behind her desk.

"Well, now, I guess we'll be finding out." He pulled the envelope from his pocket. "I came straight over. I didn't want to leave it with any of the boys, you know, just in case."

She stepped from behind her desk and stood in the warm beams of the morning sun coming through the tall windows of her office. "Is that it?"

"I'm thinking it is, Miss. That's why I brought it straight over." He held out the envelope. She took it gingerly, as if the words might fall off the page inside if she handled it too roughly.

"I'm frightened to open it," she said. That phrase was something Mr. Billings of the Royal Mail had heard countless times in his thirty-plus years as Hawkhurst's postman. Without hesitating, he took her hand.

"I'm here, Miss Katie. We can open it together."

She smiled at the man in his weathered blue postal cap who had known for her entire life and he returned it, grateful he could be here for her now.

She grabbed the letter opener from her desk, an obnoxious thing—a long silver blade that looked like a sword. It was etched with the words "St. Michael ~ Protect Us." She inserted the blade and pulled it along the edge, and removed the letter. It was on stationery, the top decorated with gold leaf and an embossed fleur-de-lis arrowhead.

Mr. Billings watched as she read the note in silence, with no readable reaction on her face. Her lovely blue eyes started to glaze over, and a tear rolled down her cheek.

"Well, come on now, out with it! I've got to know!" Mr. Billings pleaded.

***

Miss Goold stuck her head in the classroom door. Sister Doreen was going over something about the Admiral Nelson and Trafalgar. "Excuse me, Sister, may I see Reggie for a moment, please?"

"Oh, what's he done now? If it's something you need my help on, Katie, you be letting me know." She eyed Reggie suspiciously. "I got you in my sights."

"Well," Reggie said. "I now know how it feels to be the dart board at the pub." The other boys in the room sniggered.

"I'll give you pub dart board, ya cheeky monkey, now go and be quick. Admiral Nelson is on the brink." She whacked him playfully across the backside with her pointer as he passed. Everyone laughed again, except Miss Goold. She simply turned and walked from the room. Reggie made eye contact with Freddie, who, judging by the look on his face, was also struck by Miss Goold's odd humourless demeanour and departure.

What's this about? Freddie asked Reggie by raising his eyebrows.

Reggie answered with a head shake and a shrug. Dunno. Freddie nodded in response towards the door. Go and find out.

Chapter 2
A Troop is Born

"After careful consideration, we *regret* to inform you that your request for inclusion in the Ronan Academy Boy Scout Troop has been denied." Miss Goold stopped reading and raised her eyes to his. "It goes on from there but the rest is unimportant. I'm so sorry, Reggie," she said.

"It's not so bad. Those Ronan boys don't care for us much anyway. I imagine it's not at all fun being part of a troop where nobody likes you." He said it as matter-of-factly as he could in hopes of putting up a brave front, but his heart ached nonetheless. Why aren't we good enough? He wondered silently. What had we ever done to make people dislike us so much?

"It's simply rubbish," Miss Goold said, her tone catching Reggie off guard. In his long years in her charge, he'd never seen her this agitated. Her red hair flashed in the sunlight, like flames dancing around her head as she fumed. "Silly snobs and their fancy school. I've a mind to march over there and let them know what I think of their *damned* decision."

Sister Noreen, happening past at just the right moment, heard the foul language, which at St. Mike's always meant trouble, good gossip or both, and she stuck her head in the door. "Am I interrupting something?" she asked.

"Yes, Sister, you are!" Miss Goold barked angrily. Her tone said *mind your own business lady* but she was making the *get in here* gesture, waving her hand about.

"Oh, good," Sister said. She stepped in quickly, shutting the door behind her. She enthusiastically and with only a slight of struggle, squeezed her oversized frame snugly into one of Miss Goold's office chair.

Funny, Reggie thought, all she needs for the big show are some sweets to snack on.

"Now, what's this about a—'decision'?" She asked, censoring the curse word.

"The *darned* snobs at that *darned* academy have decided that our boys aren't good enough for the British Boy Scouts—or at least not *their* crummy little troop, anyway." She crumpled the letter in her fist.

"Oh no, they did *not*!" gasped Sister Noreen. Her lips formed an 'O'. Her eyes widened. Reggie and Miss Goold recognised the signs; she was about to "hear the bell," as they all called it when Sister's temper overpowered her sacred oath. She'd start nervously rushing about the room, like an RAF fighter pilot who hears the bell to scramble, then lose her temper entirely. They didn't care. A little bit of Sister Noreen's temper might just be what this situation called for.

"How *dare* they say that about *our* boys!" she shouted, looking at Reggie through eyes starting to glisten with tears. She was a tough bird, but sensitive to the point of touchy about her boys. Her anguish turned to anger. "Have you seen *theirs*? That sorry little group of twits they call Scouts?" Sister Noreen asked. "Some patrol leader," she said sarcastically, "Victor Knoll, with his own Tweedledumb and Tweedledumber, Leonard Coxworth, Jr. and that Bennett boy."

"Well," Miss Goold continued, "they didn't exactly state it that way." She unrumpled the note in her hand and read aloud, "'Due to lack of parental support for each of the boys in question…' What the heck do they mean by parental support? Between me, you, Sister Doreen, the men, Vicar Davis, and Maurice, these boys have an entire staff of parental support!"

"Nope! No, they don't." Sister sat bolt upright in the chair, folding her large hands gently in her oversize lap, striking her 'I've-got-this-bit-worked-out' pose, the one she'd strike before expounding a suspicion, hypothesis, or synopsis. "They mean pounds, Katie, my dear. *Money,* plain and simple, is what they mean, but don't expect to hear it from their ungodly tongues. The root of all evil, that's what they mean. Well, if I weren't under sacred oath, I'd have a few choice words for those … those … *snobs.*" She glanced skyward whilst making the sign of the cross over her chest. "Judge only my good works and deeds, dear Lord, but forgive me my sinful words and thoughts." She kissed her fingers.

"The boys from that school don't care for us much anyway," Reggie repeated, reminding them of that which they were well aware, and that now it seemed was confirmed—by official notification. There had been "incidents" between the tykes and academy boys in the past, and boys being boys, some of those had come to blows. They were minor blows, still there remained bad blood between the two groups.

As usual, Reggie's first concern was for the his brothers. As the oldest, he was their natural leader so it fell on him to deliver the bad news.

"I have to tell the others. They were hoping for it more than I was," he fibbed. All at the home knew that being a real Boy Scout was a dream dearest to Reggie. He'd seen recruiting posters round the village, and now that the country and Empire truly needed his help, he, like most everyone, yearned to do his bit for King and Country. Miss Goold's younger brother Billy, a former Scout and current Royal Air Force Pilot Officer, had given Reggie his old Boy Scout handbook, and since then the boy was rarely seen without it. It was most often stuck in his back pocket, otherwise it was on his bedside table, where he studied it nightly as a monk studies scripture.

Miss Goold's eyes began to glisten and for a brief second Reggie thought she might be starting to cry. But when she spoke and there was only anger in her tone. "It's *preposterous* that you boys can't be Scouts because you're orphans and poor, two things completely out of your control or current ability to change." Check that, Reggie thought. She wasn't going to cry, she was just cheesed off.

"Since," she continued, a new defiance in her tone, "they've decided we aren't their kind of folks, they can just keep to their *snooty selves*." She made a point of stressing those last two words.

"Well, then," Sister said her voice filled with optimism and pride, "we'll just have do it ourselves, like we always have."

"What do you mean, Sister? Do *what* by ourselves?" Reggie asked.

"Where's that book of yours? Let me see it." Reggie surrendered his handbook and she delicately fanned the dry yellow pages with her generous thumb. "Well, where is it?" she asked, fanning the pages a second time. "It's supposed to be up front here." She opened the front cover, reading the first page. "Oh, that's why. It's not the BP version." She put the book down, and shimmying back and forth, she wiggled her backside out of the snug seat. "Sit tight, but not too tight," she said with a sneer at the chair, as if her girth were its fault. "I'll be right back."

She cracked the door, stuck her head out, looked both ways up and down the hall then gently closing it behind her, snuck away as if on a secret assignment. Reggie looked at Miss Goold puzzled. She returned an equally puzzled look. "Where do you suppose she's off to?" he asked.

"Not sure," she answered, shrugging for emphasis.

In a few seconds Sister returned with her own book in hand, only this one was a much different than Reggie's. It was an old, thick leatherbound volume tied with a leather strap, more like a journal. It was worn, and had the deep-brown patina that only many years of age can bring.

"This is what you'll be wanting." She handed Reggie the book.

"What is this?" the boy asked, handling the old book delicately. It felt heavy, as if the words themselves inside had weight. He began to unwrap the leather strap.

"This is what Boy Scouting is all about, written by the first Scout ever in 1908. It was Daddy's, God rest him. He knew BP personally. Served with him in the colonial forces during the Second Boer War in South Africa. They fought together to hold off the siege of Mafeking, they did."

Reggie's eyes widened as he opened the leather cover. Inside was a well-used first edition of *Scouting for Boys* by Lord Robert Baden-

Powell. It was signed by the master Scout himself and addressed to one Captain Clymore.

"Blimey," Reggie said with a breathy exhale. It was much different from the book Miss Goold's brother had given him. It was stuffed with folded maps, papers, newsprint clippings and old photographs. The pages themselves were filled with dozens of printed illustrations, and others drawn by the captain's own hand in pencil along the margins.

"That book dates back to when there were no Scout troops or patrols, no one to ask *permission* of to be a Boy Scout. Who ever heard of such hooey? Your version is just handbook, so you *need* to read this one." There was a tone of wonderment in her voice. "This book here is like the Bible for all Boy Scouts, filled with tales of BP's own life adventures, daring stories, camp fire yarns, and many lessons learned through his amazing experiences." She took the book from Reggie and started to riffle through the pages. He looked with excited bewilderment at Miss Goold, who wore a look just as bewildered.

"Aha! Here it is! 'Camp Fire Yarn Number Three' in black and white!"

"What are you talking about, Sister? What do you—"

"Pipe yourself down and listen." She said, cutting him off. "It says right here"—she started reading from the page—"'boys who belong to any kind of existing organisation, such as *schools*, football clubs, boys' or lads' church brigades, factories, district messengers…et cetera, et cetera, et cetera, can also take up scouting in addition to their other work or play.' Those are the words of Master Scout General Baden-Powell himself," she said with the passion of a pastor from the pulpit. She read on. "'But where there are *any* boys who do not belong to any kind of organisation, et cetera, et cetera, they can form themselves into patrols and become Boy Scouts.' It's right there," she repeated, "in black and white."

Sister looked at Miss Goold and smiled. Miss Goold's face broke into a smile of its own.

They sang out together but with different tonality, Miss Goold's of shear revelation, Sister Noreen's of utter conviction. "We'll start our own troop!"

Sister continued. "We're a church and a school and a home. Six boys is a patrol simply waiting for a scout master. It says so right there."

Reggie thought on it. It was a brilliant idea. There were six of them. What Sister Noreen had said was true. According to the master scout's own words, six boys made up a patrol, and they were six boys; all they needed were the uniforms and a Scoutmaster.

"But, Sister Noreen," he asked, astonished, "How did you know about all this?"

"Daddy made sure we were good scouts. Sister Doreen and I can sleep on stones and not miss a wink. I've read this cover to cover and back again." She said proudly. That was something Reggie never would have guessed about the good Sisters: they were daughters of a war hero captain who served alongside BP himself and were avid practisers of the scouting arts.

"But why have you never told us?" Reggie asked, puzzled that such an important detail of their lives would have remained a secret for so long.

"I've been waiting for the right time, is all," she said matter-of-factly. "And look, here it is!" She smiled warmly.

"Can we – I mean – do you think we could?" he asked Miss Goold, now sharing Sister Noreen's smile.

"Well, I don't see why not. Vicar Davis might have some reservations, but you know him. He's a pushover, too much on his plate as it is, and with war here, a group of Boy Scouts around the place will come in very helpful, almost necessary if we want to keep this parish going." Miss Goold answered.

"Don't you worry about Vicar Davis. I'll make sure he doesn't have any concerns," Sister Noreen said. Reggie half expected her to punch her hand with her fist, like those academy boys bullying someone for pocket change.

"Don't hurt him, Sister." Miss Goold said with a smirk.

"Oh, *yooou!*" Sister Noreen said, waving her off with a girlish giggle.

"I like this. You could be the 'Hawks of Hawkhurst!'" Miss Goold shouted, triumphantly thrusting her fist skyward.

"Or the 'Ravens of Greater Kent'!" shouted Sister Noreen like

Miss Goold, thrusting her own fist skyward. Those were good suggestions, Reggie thought, but not quite it.

"No." Reggie said. He began pacing, his finger and thumb rubbing his chin. "Those aren't right." He walked to the window. "I think it should be simple, not too bombastic, like who we are ... no more, but no less."

He glanced out the window, down into the courtyard below where stood the statue of St. Michael. It was a ten foot tall stone sculpture of the archangel, standing with his foot on the dragon, his sword raised, ready to strike. The boys had discussed many times what it would be like to be St. Michael, to have those mighty wings, covered in the armour of Heaven, the sword of Truth held tight in hand. It would be magnificent. That's when it struck him. There was no reason they had to select an animal as a troop mascot. They could select whatever they wanted, actually. That was it.

"We're the 'Scouts of St. Michael.'"

Squeals of delight erupted from both ladies.

"I love it!" Sister Noreen shouted.

"Brilliant!" Miss Goold cheered.

"Sister, might you and Sister Doreen help us make some uniforms?" Reggie asked.

"We'll turn you into the finest-looking troop of boys to ever wander the woods, if you don't mind my saying." She was rocking in her chair with excitement.

"And Miss Goold, you can help us ... help us ... well, what *can* you help us with?"

"Well, I'm not sure ... *wait*. I can start by coming downstairs with you and explaining to the others what's going on with the new troop and such."

Her suggestion instantly made him feel better. Perhaps if the others see how excited she is about this new idea, he thought, maybe it'll catch on and they'll go for it, too.

"Thanks, Miss Goold," he said, giving her a hug. She squeezed nice and tight. She smelled of sweet perfume.

"Ah, not so fast. Get over here." Sister Noreen sprang from of the tight seat and Reggie instantly found himself smothered and squished between two cushy breasts by big fleshy arms. She squeezed extra-tight, giving a right proper hug but she forever smelled of menthol vapour rub. While he was grateful for Sister Noreen's sentiment, he preferred Miss Goold's hugs.

***

Unlike the notorious orphanages and workhouses of old London, St. Michael's in Hawkhurst was a place of light, life, and much love. Having only six residents to care for, it was run much more like an actual home, rather than any dank, dirty warehouse filled with lonely, sad children, and infested with rats, bugs, filth, and disease. St. Michael's Home was clean; Sister Noreen saw to that by lording over old Mr. McKenna and Mr. Greene, her iron fist covered in a white glove, ready to test any surface at her slightest whim. Mr. Greene was always polite, but Mr. McKenna sometimes wanted to shove Sister's white glove where even St. Michael wouldn't dare tread. The boys did their part by daily completing chores that helped keep the place scrubbed and polished.

The walls held tall windows so that on the sunniest days, the light spilled through the rooms at almost every hour. Simply due to the sheer number, keeping those windows clean was the responsibility of everyone who lived or worked in the place.

Despite rationing, food was somehow always fresh and plentiful. Their French cook, Maurice, saw to that. All in all, from where the six of them had fallen, St. Michael's was as soft a place to land as they could have hoped for, and all involved were most grateful.

Chapter 3
Daddy's Girl

Sisters Noreen and Doreen Clymore, twin siblings and nuns of the highest order of the Anglican Community of St. John the Divine, were born when their father was off on an adventure, serving together with BP in the Boer Wars.

When news of Mrs. Clyborne's pregnancy with twins reached him, he so hoped their blessed union had produced a pair of boys. But when girls were delivered, he was not disappointed in the least, he simply decided to raise the beautiful girls with no consideration whatsoever of their sex. He would make sure his girls were prepared for whatever came their way, and set about to see to it.

Both Sisters were raised with a knowledge of Scout craft, but it was Sister Noreen who really excelled at, among other things, tracking, woodcraft, camping, first aid, and good deeds—all elements necessary to be a successful scout. Whilst at the time is was not considered at all lady-like to go traipsing through the woods in pursuit of such activities, neither girl particularly cared, especially Noreen.

She hadn't intentionally tried to hide that side of her life from her St. Michael's family. It was just that since taking her sacred oath upon entry to the Anglican Community of St. John the Divine, she had simply turned the page on that chapter of her life. Little did she realise those skills would come in so handy once again. Truth be told, she was delighted. Unwrapping Captain Clymore's version of *Scouting for Boys* after so many years had been like opening a time capsule full of memories from so long ago.

To get back out into the bush was an exciting prospect, but what really thrilled her was the idea of leading the boys and sharing her years of experience and the knowledge she had gained, all thanks to Daddy, God rest him.

When he returned from service, Captain Clymore, who had always been quite skilled at making and repairing his own clothes, took an apprenticeship in hopes of become a professional tailor. After working long hard hours, he was finally able to open a small shop, where he trained his two daughters to be seamstresses and mend clothes just as he'd been taught. In very short time, he had his daughters as skilled with scissors, needle and thread as they had become with their Scoutcraft.

***

Now that the boys had agreed to start their own troop, they needed a leader. After several days spent weighing the requirements of the task verses her current abilities to perform as necessary, Sister Noreen considered it her duty to step up, at least until a more suitable leader for the boys could be found.

"So unless you have some kind of objection, I'm offering myself as your new Scoutmaster," she proclaimed to Reggie proudly.

"That's very kind of you, Sister. Do you think you're up for it?" He asked. She easilydetected the hint of scepticism in his tone and was prepared for it.

"Daddy taught me everything in his book, and lots of things that aren't. He was a war hero, remember -- served with BP himself." The boy was well aware of that fact already but she figured it might help convince him if she dropped the master scout's name again. Truth be told, she hoped for nothing more in the world than to be a Scoutmaster for the boys. Over the past couple of days many vivid memories of happy times spent scouting with Daddy came flooding back. She so wanted to share what she knew, and her memories of Daddy's teachings with them.

Reggie remained quiet. His face registered no expression.

"You don't want me." She said, glumly. "It's written all over your face."

"No, Sister, it's not that. It's just—"

"It's just what? I'm too fat? A nun? Is that it?" she asked probingly.

"No, Sister, not at all. It's just—"

"Just what?" she asked again, becoming agitated. "Come on lad, out with it."

"Well, it's just … do you think you know how to be a Boy Scout? You're not even a boy." Her jaw dropped wide open, then snapped shut.

"It's because I'm a *lady?!*" She grabbed him by the ear and pulled it roughly. "Come on, you."

"Ouch!"

She continued pulling until they were standing on the steps in front of the home. She thrust out her hand and snapped her fingers twice.

"That hatchet on your hip. Give it here."

He reached down and begrudgingly pulled the ever present scout hatchet he carried on his hip from its holster, presenting it to her handle first. She held it up, closed one eye and studied its straightness with her open one. Satisfied, she glanced round and lined herself up with the nearest tree, roughly 10 yards away. Reggie's face now wore an expression halfway between confused and beguiled.

"Lady," she said curtly, "I'll show *you* who's a lady."

She brought the blade to her mouth, licked its length with her tongue, glanced quickly round for prying eyes, and finding none, she spit. Reggie watched her every move, growing more confused by the moment.

Reaching towards her face, she pulled her white coif down off her forehead so it covered both her eyes. She bent her arm at the elbow, and swung the hatchet in the direction of the tree. She repeated the move a second time. On the third, after putting her considerable weight behind the motion, she let loose the handle. To Reggie's amazement the hatchet sailed through the air, rotated twice then buried its head deep in the tree. A blind bull's-eye.

Sister lifted her coif off one eye and smiled broadly at the results.

"Welcome aboard, Scoutmaster Sister Noreen Clymore." Reggie said, extending his hand for her to shake. She took it and pumped it twice.

"Thank you, Patrol Leader Reggie," she said with a giggle. "Glad to be aboard."

Chapter 4

Uniform Discord

Days later they were gathered in the dormitory, the large common room where they slept side by side in two rows of three. Beside each bed sat a night table with a reading lamp on the left and a tall wooden wardrobe on the right.

"What in Mike's name is that?" Reggie asked, standing from his bed.

"It's splendid, innit?" Jack replied as he marched into the room.

Freddie looked up from his colourful comic to a sight nearly as comically colourful. Jack was dressed in a bright red, long-sleeved collarless tunic, over which was laid a brilliant white sash with a large red arrow patch pointing skyward, running from his right shoulder to his left hip. His deep green trousers ballooned at each hip, and tied laces ran up the side of each leg to the knee. On his ankles he wore matching white leggings that covered the tops of his shoes. A bright-yellow coiled cord decorated his opposite shoulder; and topping it all off, on his head was perched a well-worn, oversized khaki pith helmet, the type worn by turn-of-the-century colonial forces at the far flung edges of the Empire. At first glance he looked like a miniature doorman from a West End hotel.

"Dr. Livingstone, I presume?" Freddie asked, rising from his bed.

Reggie laughed. "The only things missing are the monocle and fluffy sideburns."

Willy giggled at the sight of Jack. A mix of awe and envy lit his face. "Wow," he said in a whisper.

"Is this what the Sisters had in mind for Scout uniforms?" Reggie wondered aloud. He stood leaning back on his heels, his arms crossed over his chest, rubbing his chin with his forefinger and thumb as he critiqued Jack's new look.

Jack, standing taller and straighter than Reggie had ever seen him, strutted across the room—as if he suddenly owned it—to the large oval mirror in the corner. Henry, Dougie, and Willy sat mesmerised. They slowly rose from their beds and gathered behind Jack, who stood enraptured by the reflection of his new splendour.

"It turned out so much better than I had hoped for." Jack commented gleefully. "Sisters did an amazing job, don't you think?" he asked, adjusting the helmet on his head so it sat with a slight tilt.

"It's all quite colourful," Reggie noted, "but not at all in tune with nature, as BP specified in his scouting manual."

"It is definitely a uniform," Freddie said. He had joined Reggie, standing, his arms also folded across his chest. "No doubt about that. It's just more classic, you know," he added, touching the fancy gold cord decoration hanging on the small boy's shoulder.

At first glance, Reggie thought it all a bit silly-looking on the boy, but once he took the time to look at it, really examine it, it was a very well-executed uniform. His blue enamel canteen matched his blue neckerchief. His white gaiters matched his white sash. Head to toe, he was covered in colourful kit. The Sisters even went so far as to add a leather neck lanyard to his catapult, which hung neatly tucked under his arm like a pistol in a shoulder holster. Every piece was thought through and in its place. And wearing it, the boy carried himself in a whole new manner. He seemed larger somehow, more assured of his own presence—like his outside finally matched the way he felt about himself on the inside.

"Sisters said since I'm first aid for the group I should stand out, to be seen at all times by everyone, in case you need me. That's why my tunic is red, and not green." He adjusted the hand-stitched red and white cross armband on his left bicep.

"Wow." Reggie raised his eyebrows as he considered, "That makes brilliant sense."

"Besides, this"—Jack did a spin turn with his arms out at his sides—"this is the original Scout uniform. At least that's what the Sisters said."

He adjusted his oversize helmet in the mirror again. "This was their father's helmet. Before he was a tailor, he was a scout for the Empire, did you know?"

"Wow," Dougie said. "Never knew that about the Sisters' father."

"Oh," Freddie said suddenly then snapped his fingers. "Don't you get it? It's like a Boy Scout version of their father's army uniform."

It clicked. Reggie smiled. "Now that is pretty splendid," he said.

"Will they make us each one?" Dougie gasped, suddenly filled with inspiration.

Reggie spoke up. "Hold on. This is great, it really is. Traditional, and it does look pretty stunning, true. But—"

"I want a cap like an artillery officer, with the chequered bits that hang down the back!" Dougie interrupted excitedly.

"I want a beret, like a commando!" Henry shouted.

"I want—"

"All right, shut up!" Reggie yelled, cutting Willy off. "There's something called Scout Law. The uniform is very important. It sets us apart, but it also draws us together, identifies us as being who we are and what we stand for."

They all slumped a bit in the shoulders, the wind knocked from their sails. Reggie noticed, but continued with his point anyway. "General Baden-Powell was very specific about it in his original Scouting for Boys handbook. The uniform puts us all on equal footing."

"Yeah, well," Freddie said, "since no one will let us be an 'official' troop, then we don't need to follow any 'official' rules, do we? If we have our own troop, we set the rules. We can have any kind of uniforms we want." The boys perked up. "And the Sisters have a good point." He continued, "This was the original scout uniform, you know, for the Empire."

Dougie quickly nodded his agreement, practically panting like a puppy.

Reggie's tone softened. "It was very nice of the Sisters to do this for Jack, sure, but—"

"Oh, come on. He looks snappy, don't he?" Freddie said in his ear, like a little angel on his shoulder. "Besides, we can't afford anything else. We'll have to make do with whatever the Sisters can come up with for us. We got nothing to lose."

"But what about our principles, the spirit of scouting, the rules of Baden-Powell," Reggie replied in spirited protest. "We follow the Scout Law for a reason. We listen to what BP teaches because it's our duty."

It was Freddie's voice he heard next in his ear, but it might as well have been BP himself. "It's not your kit that makes you a Scout, Reggie. It's your character." That was enough.

"Oh, all right, then. So be it." Reggie said, relenting. The boys cheered.

Freddie continued, "Besides, Jack *does* look rather snappy, don't he?"

***

So it went. Each boy was allowed to have as much say in creating his uniform as he liked. Instead of worrying about being official or trying to create some kind of conformity—not to mention because they couldn't afford new uniforms—they did as best they could with what they could scrounge up. Aside from always being clean and presentable (house rule number one, of course), each boy was free to create a uniform that was his and his alone.

Freddie was more partial to the blue uniforms of the Royal Air Force, and being a parish in Kent with its twenty-odd RAF bases, from Lympne in the east, to Hawkinge on the south coast, Trolley up north, and all the others in between, it made getting bits for his kit much easier. Aside from Katie Goold's brother being a Pilot Officer, many pilots and base personnel were regular members of the congregation. Any donation need only be mentioned to one of them, and in a short time it found its way from the base directly to the boys at the home, often delivered by RAF staff themselves.

"So Miss Goold's brother gave you this."

Freddie stood before Sister Noreen in the sky-blue fabric and brass buttons of an RAF tunic. It had a few holes, but it looked good on him, even if he was a bit large for it.

Sister Doreen elbowed Sister Noreen. "He'll have the girls buzzing about him, dressed like that."

Sister Noreen, not taking her eyes off Freddie, nodded her agreement. "It was very generous of Katie's brother to give you this now, aye?" Sister Noreen's tone said she felt the exact opposite.

"Yes, Sister. He gives us lots of his old things. Willy's helmet and goggles, this coat, and I think Henry's got a pair of blue trousers for his kit as well."

"Flies a Spitfire, does he?" Sister Noreen asked.

"Yes, Sister, he's one of their best Pilot Officers, so he got a new Spit."

"Well, then, if this was his, why does it have a Observer's wing brevet on it? Since when do Spitfires Pilot Officers wear an Observer brevet?"

"Well, Sister"—he folded his hands under his chin and batted his long eyelashes—"I don't really ask questions when the fine RAF lads donate items out of the kindness of their hearts for us poor, underprivileged lads. Those brave boys at the base give so freely to us wee ones who have so little and must rely on the handouts of good townsfolk—"

"I'll give ya good townsfolk across your backside. I'd have a serious issue with Billy Goold breaking one of the Ten Commandments, and you being the beneficiary. 'Thou Shall Not' is non-negotiable. BP doesn't out rank JC round here, and I'll tell him myself next time I see him. Pilot Officer or not, he's still little Billy Goold to me."

"Sister, Billy would never steal, especially from a fellow airman. He's too good for that." Freddie said in defence of Miss Goold's brother. Freddie batted his lashes over his pretty blue eyes once more and flashed her his sweetest smile, the one he knew she couldn't resist. All talk of broken commandments evaporated.

"Now get over here." He stepped forward. Sister Noreen grabbed his shoulder and whipped him round. Her finger traced a seam up the back of the jacket. "We can make that fit a little better across here," she said.

"Give more shoulder room, a bit more freedom to move without tearing." She traced another seam with her finger. "What do you think, Sister?"

"Hmm, open this seam"—Sister Doreen's turn to trace—"and we can expand it on the side." He felt like an unlucky patient being discussed by two mad surgeons.

"Okay, Freddie, off it comes so we can get to work."

***

"Where on earth did you find that filthy thing?" Jack asked Henry.

"Filthy? What you talking about, filthy? It's in rough shape, but it got *character*. That's what it got," Henry protested.

"It's got fleas," Jack said, "and if you keep wearing it, you'll have fleas, too."

Henry was dressed in his vest and underpants, and draped over his shoulders was a dark green greatcoat, undoubtedly a survivor of the Great War, though just barely. The green wool was moth-eaten, the seams around the high-necked collar were blown out, and there was so much dust and dirt embedded in it, its last cleaning must have been back around the time of the Treaty of Versailles signing. He was soon surrounded by the boys, gathered for a closer look.

"I found it in the basement among a box of old donations, I think."

"In the catacombs? Did you find a dead Tommie down there?" Willy asked. He slapped Henry on the back several times. A thick, odious cloud of heavy dust and dirt billowed from the coat.

Freddie coughed. "Ah, Willy! It's bad enough, don't spread it round," he said, fanning at the noxious cloud with his hands. Soon, all were coughing loudly enough to catch the attention of a passing Sister Noreen.

"There best be no smoking in the dormitory—best be no smoking at all." She stuck her head in the doorway.

The boys separated and there stood Henry.

"Ahahahaha!" She roared with laughter at his get up—undies, socks, and a decades-old greatcoat three sizes too large. "Where did you get that filthy thing?"

"It's not filthy! It got character. I like it." He stood up tall, proudly displaying the dishevelled coat.

"Yes, so will the rats when they come looking for a warm place to bed down." She shook her head. "Well, if that's what you want, the first thing it needs—and you along with it—is a good cleaning. Take that filthy thing off and get in the bath. No, better yet, leave that filthy thing on and get in the bath. That's its only hope."

The boys laughed, and several minutes later Henry was sitting naked in the bath under the ever increasing weight of a thirty-year-old wool greatcoat as it soaked up water like a sponge.

***

In the talented fingers of the Sisters, hand-me-down, haggard, and homemade became something brilliant. They cut, stitched, and cobbled together unique uniforms to each boy's exacting specifications but did so with details that would leave no doubt these boys were a single troop.

Aside from matching blue neckerchiefs, the only part of their uniforms that they had no say over were the St. Michael medals the Sisters had attached somewhere to each boy's kit.

"What's this?" asked Reggie, picking up his uniform after the Sisters worked their magic. His was the closest to a classic Boy Scout uniform, green long sleeve shirt, green shorts, and a sash filled with pins and old patches. The pin he was looking at was a simple oval medallion with the image of St. Michael, his wings spread, his sword pulled back for a killing strike.

"That is the symbol of who and what you are," Sister Doreen said. "It's to keep you protected as you go about your scoutly duties."

Reggie studied at it closely. "I think—"

"Nope," Sister Noreen cut him off. "You can hold tongue and your thoughts. We're not interested in hearing what you think," said Sister Noreen, wagging her finger in his general direction. She motioned towards Doreen. "Sister and I agreed to make you boys any uniforms you asked for, but you can't be the Scouts of St. Michael without an official symbol, and Sister and I decided it should be that. End of discussion. Full stop."

"It's within the rules, we looked it up in BP's book," added Sister Doreen.

"And it's non-negotiable. Each of you, at all times, will wear these medals to remind you of your mission and to protect you along the way. Blessed by Vicar Davis, those are," Noreen added.

As if on cue, Sister Doreen was crying, her hands coming up to cover her embarrassed face as tears fell from her eyes. "Please protect our boys, St. Michael, they're growing up so fast," she said with a sniffle.

"Now look what you did." Sister Noreen said to Reggie. "You set her off."

Reggie smiled compassionately. Sister Doreen was a hair-trigger crier. He knew it was all because of love. And he loved her back, just as deeply. "No," he said calmly, "I was just going to say how much me and the rest of the boys—we really like it, Sisters."

Doreen's blubbering stopped. "Wait, what'd he say?" She asked. She sometimes pretended not to hear what she didn't expect to.

"I said I think this is one of the most wonderful things you've ever done for us, Sisters. We're all very grateful."

"Ohh!" she bellowed out again. "You're such good boys."

"Actually," he continued, "I was wondering if you might be able to do one more thing for us. We need a troop pendant, so people know who we are when we're on patrol. I'd really like it if we could make one with St. Michael on it, just like on our medals."

Chapter 5

A Stranger in Town

The day their lives changed forever began as any other late spring day, except for the stranger who was making his way towards the village. He was walking up Highgate Hill Road, strolling and whistling as if he hadn't a care in the world, as if the country weren't on the brink of Nazi invasion.

Willy kept watch. He had been roller-skating round the village centre in his uniform, always a good place to find a good turn that needed doing, when he spotted the man a mile or so out of town. Willy, who knew almost everyone in the village, didn't recognize him—so he was a stranger for sure—but what was even more strange was what he carried. Most folks passing through town, if on foot, usually carried some sort of bag or bundle. If on a bike, it was tied to the back, or if in a car, lorry, or horse cart, it might be anywhere.

This particular stranger had nothing. Not a bag, box, or bundle to be seen as he casually made his way up the road.

Get Reggie, his brain chirped. No, he argued back. What business is it of mine? He's just a bloke on a stroll. But then it happened. Willy got one of his feelings. It usually started as a tingle in his toes that rose to his stomach and then his head. He would get dizzy to the point that he had to steady himself or fall over, especially if on his skates. It would last for a few seconds; then he'd get sweaty or a bit nauseated. Sometimes, afterward his mouth tasted like metal.

It was his thing. Vicar Davis called those his "episodes" because he preferred to think of them as a physical tic, not a metaphysical one, and they always seemed to come in a series over a relatively short time. The boys just considered these episodes "creepy".

Whilst Willy was the one who suffered these episodes, they were meaningless without Reggie's consultation. Like the priests and the Oracle of Delphi, Willy would experience the trancelike episode and it was up to Reggie to interpret the signs and figure out the meaning.

Truth be told, they all found it a bit unnerving, because he was always, *always* correct. That time part of the attic roof caved in. He had an episode, said something "didn't feel right." Sure enough, as they stepped from the attic, one of the old upper beams cracked and crashed to the floor, pulling two more and part of the roof with it, where they'd been standing seconds before. After it happened, Willy just smiled and snapped his fingers. "I *knew* it!"

And over the years the boys learned, sometimes the hard way— when Willy says something doesn't feel right, you trusted him.

Just like he was trusting his own feelings about this stranger. This simply dressed man, in work trousers and shirt, a blue jacket, and a cap. Nothing strange at all, but still. Maybe he should go fetch Reggie after all. What could it hurt? Except what happens while you're gone and this bloke disappears? He argued silently with himself. Really? This whole village isn't big enough for anyone to hide in. Besides he's probably just passing through to any place where the road leads, which is all of England.

The stranger had stopped a good half mile or so from town, and was speaking to Mr. Jessup, who was sitting high on his hay wagon.

Willy's 12-year-old imagination took over. This was his chance to get back to HQ (St. Michael's), grab reinforcements (Reggie), and be back to his post (skating circles in the village square) before the Nazi spy (the stranger) could cover even half that distance.

He turned and shot up the road, pushing as hard as he could. Right leg, left leg, right leg, left leg! His steel wheels bumped roughly along the stony surface. Past the bakery, past the pub, the glass shop, and the butcher, hard up the slight embankment … here comes the hill. He reached for the goggles that sat on the leather flight helmet that covered his head, pulling them down over his eyes and, like lightening, he raced up the face of the hill. He squatted low, crested the hill, then tucked into a tight ball for a speedy descent.

Sisters Noreen and Doreen were on their way back to St. Mike's from their Saturday morning stroll to the bakery and had just reached the bottom of the hill. Side by side their generous girth and black habits billowing in the breeze created a seemingly impenetrable black wall, blocking most of the path ahead.

Willy had only a split second to decide. Around, under, or through? His mind turned faster than the steel wheels under his feet. If he misjudged by even a fraction of an inch he would slam face-first directly into one of the four bulbous cheeks—or one of two very deep cracks—dead ahead. In the name of all that's holy, no!

"Comin' up from behind, Sisters! Break, break!" he shouted as loudly as he could, but between the steel wheels rattling and the wind howling in his helmet's ear holes, if he hadn't said it himself, he wouldn't have heard it. The Sisters heard him just fine.

Both startled. Sister Noreen, on the left, looked over her right shoulder, whilst Sister Doreen, on the right, looked over her left shoulder. The effect of two enormous nuns mirroring each other in fright caused Willy to break into hysterical laughter. He lost his balance, and began to whip his arms and legs frantically to gain it again.

"Ahhhh!" Sister Noreen screamed.

"Ahhhh!" Sister Doreen joined her.

Willy regained control and tucked himself into as tight a ball as he could manage, gritted his teeth and slammed shut his eyes. His brain screamed, *PREPARE FOR IMPACT!*

Reflexes bested them. Sister Noreen shoved Sister Doreen. Sister Doreen shoved Sister Noreen. The combined strength of the extra-large women shoving at the same time in opposite directions did the trick.

WHOOSH! He split them like an atom, getting a face full of billowing black habit for his troubles. *Whoa, that was too close!*

Looking back over his shoulder he saw them go down, crashing to the roadsides in unison, still mirroring each other, Sister Noreen to the left, Sister Doreen to the right, their feet up in the air. He thought to turn back and help the good Sisters up, but he'd already started a new round of laughing, so he let that thought pass. They probably wouldn't appreciate his take on the situation anyway. Besides, his brain screamed, the mission!

"Sorry, Sisters!" he shouted over his shoulder. It was the best he could manage for the moment.

"You're going to be when I get my hands on you!" Sister Noreen said, of course. She always had to have the last word.

He'd be sure to see each of them later and apologise directly. He'd probably be getting a special invitation to see Vicar Davis for that little encounter. No biggie. It was worth it.

***

"Reggie! It's me. Are you here?" His shout echoed through the main foyer of the home. It was a large building with school on the ground floor, the boy's living quarters on the first, and staff quarters and offices on the second.

Shouting into the foyer amplified the sound. It bounced off the wood floors and echoed into the cavernous space above. It could be heard almost everywhere in the building and was the easiest way for the boys to find one another. Whilst it was effective, it was also very disturbing to the whole place, sometimes even being heard in the church itself, which was connected to the home through the shared kitchen area.

"Reggie!"

"What the heck is it?" Willy looked up, and there was Reggie, leaning over the railing on the second floor.

"There's a stranger coming up Harcourt Road. About half a mile out, probably closer now."

"So what's the shouting about? Strangers come and go around here all the time." He raised his hand and scratched his unruly red hair.

A nap disturbed by a stranger. "Why should I care, Willy? I was trying to take a nap and—"

"I've got a *feeling* about him." Reggie's arm hair stood. Blimey, he thought. I hate those creepy things. "Get back. Keep your eyes on him. Watch where he goes and what he does. I'll grab my bike and join you. Are you alone? Any of the others with you?"

"No, I came straight to you."

"Okay, did he see you?" Reggie began to unbutton his shirt. He loosened his belt and pulled out his shirt tail.

"I don't think so. He was a good mile out when I first saw him. I just stuck to one place, watching. I'm sure he didn't see me, unless he was looking, like spies are trained to—"

"What do you know of spies?" Willy had a keen eye, but a keener imagination that often ran away with him. But this is also war, so he could be a spy, thought Reggie. Plus, he's had one of those creepy feelings.

"Change out of your uniform shirt and put this on." Reggie threw the shirt down to his younger brother. It would be a bit large, but it would be better than his Scout uniform, if his feeling was true.

"Now get back down there and don't let him out of your sight. I'll find the others. Go now." Willy threw his uniform shirt on the bench in the foyer, rushed out the door, vaulted over the three front stairs, and landed on the steel wheels of his skates as if they were his bare feet. He headed back to town.

***

Reggie dismounted his bike and joined Willy in front of the bakery. "Where is he?" Reggie asked, looking over Willy's shoulder and up the street. It was filled with the Saturday hustle and bustle of the quaint little village in the English countryside that it was. They were huddled, semi-hidden in the doorway of the bakery, looking up the street, almost staring at the front door of the pub.

"He's in the pub. But before he got there, he stopped in every shop along the way. Didn't skip one."

"Even the flower shop?"

"He was in there for some time. And when came out—*no flow-*

ers. Exactly like a spy would do," he added in a whisper.

"But if he were a spy, wouldn't he buy flowers? You know, to not stick out?"

"A little too late for that, I'd say. I'm going to go have a look-see." With that, Willy rolled to the middle of the road, spun, and with a graceful elegance, sailed up the street on one skate, the other leg outstretched behind him.

Reggie watched Willy roll up the road towards town centre like a figure skater. Even if that stranger is what Willy suspects he is, what were they to do?

"The police?" he asked himself aloud. He could bike over—or there was the phone in the church office—not exactly the most secure way. He supposed the best way would be to send Willy. On his skates he was fast. He could deliver the intel directly from the horse's mouth, so to speak.

Willy rolled past Mrs. Corbett and Mrs. Bucket crossing the road, headed towards the bakery. He gave them a friendly nod and wave as he passed. The ladies waved back. A car rounded the corner, forcing him onto the sidewalk where he had to avoid Mrs. Baker and the carriage with baby Baker inside.

"Morning, Mrs. Baker." He slowed almost a stop. "Lovely day, innit?"

Baby Baker giggled a positive response.

"Good morning, Willy. You're running about early this morning." Most of the townsfolk knew the tykes, at least in passing, and knowing they had grown up with no parents, everyone held a special place in their hearts for the boys. Well, almost everyone.

"No school today. I like to make the most of it," he replied with a smile.

Suddenly Baby Baker wailed from his rolling bed. "Oh, well, I'm off. Little Master Baker here is the boss. Say hello to the Sisters for me, Willy." And off she went down the sidewalk, pushing ahead of her what sounded like a mobile air raid siren. Willy watched her walk away, thinking that a stop in the bakery might be a good—

The mission! Focus, his brain barked. Back to the mission, right! His subject was in the pub, a place strictly off limits to 'the Hawkhurst

Gang' as the pub man, Mr. Coxworth, was fond of calling them. His pub was an official 'forbidden zone' for the boys. He had been given a warning from Sister Noreen —if any one of them boys were ever found even a wee bit tipsy, and not from church wine—he'd be the one she'd come looking for.

***

From his perch up the street, Reggie watched Willy duck an automobile and stop to chat with Mrs. Baker who didn't look at all like she had just recently had a baby. Her figure was very shapely. A flash of guilt swept him for thinking of things he shouldn't, but he couldn't help it. It was true. She was pretty and had long auburn hair that fell down over her shoulders. And she was so friendly. Mr. Baker was indeed a lucky man.

An automobile honked its horn, and startled Reggie out of his daydream. Across the street, Willy was tip-toeing on his front wheels, looking in the window of the pub. What the heck is he doing? Reggie wondered. He's not supposed to be anywhere near there. If he's seen—

"Hey, Reggie." He startled again. It was Dougie, dressed in his uniform, on his bike.

"Hey, Dougie. He's in the pub."

Dougie's eyes doubled in size. "Who? Who's in the pub? Freddie? It's out of bounds. Coxworth will have—"

"No, not Freddie," although that was a good guess. Freddie was always the first one to push the boundaries, or ignore them altogether. "The stranger. There's a stranger who's in town. Stopped at every shop on the way."

"Well, maybe he's on a shopping tour. Nothing wrong with doing a bit of shopping."

"Don't be daft. Who goes into a flower shop for ten minutes and comes out with no flowers?"

"No flowers at all, no plant, no bouquet?" he asked.

"Not even a boutonniere. Besides, Willy has had one of his feelings." Reggie returned his attention to the pub.

Dougie's eyes doubled in size again. "Oh, well. That changes everything." He started to hop off his bike when Reggie grabbed his arm.

"No, ride back and change your clothes. If he is who Willy thinks he is, I don't want him to know there are scouts about—at least, not us."

Dougie looked down at his homemade tunic. "Technically, there are no scouts about," he added. He motioned to salute Reggie, who grabbed his arm and held it down. "No saluting, it's a giveaway."

Dougie nodded, turned his bike and pedalled back towards the home.

***

Out in front of the Oak Yoke Pub, a small boy on rollers skates was bent over, looking at the small pane of glass closest to the ground. The windows, which Coxworth obviously kept low on his list of priorities, were so filthy he couldn't make out who was inside. It suddenly dawned on him, old Coxey might be more clever than he looked.

He glanced around quickly—no one watching—and rubbed the heel of his hand on the corner pane of glass. Bending down to a knee, he was able to see inside much better.

There sat the stranger at the corner of the bar, his back to the windows. He was chatting up Coxey. He also seemed to be pretty chit chatty with the patrons on either side. In front of him sat a pint glass, filled with clear liquid. Drinking water in a pub? Just like someone who needs to keep his wits about him … like a spy.

Inside someone must have said something funny, and everyone enjoyed a rousing chuckle. Coxey was talking a lot, gesticulating, and pointing in different directions. What was this stranger asking? And more important, what was old Coxey telling him? How to get to the RAF stations? Number of Local Defence bunkers about? Could be almost anything … this wasn't good.

He glanced back over his shoulder, looking at Reggie up the street on the opposite side of the road. He shook his head. This was bad. Just as he turned, he heard Reggie's whistle calling him back. Glancing one last time at the stranger sitting inside, Willy pulled away and rolled up the street towards the bakery.

"He's in there, all right. On the end. Old Coxworth needs to hire himself a window washer. Just filthy they are, inside and out—"

"I don't want a cleanliness report. Tell me about him."

"Well, he's in there, all right. On the end. And seems like old Coxey is giving the game away, pointing here and there. Surprised he didn't pull out a map and simply circle everything."

"Coxey was in the Great War. He'd know better. At least I hope he would." Coxworth was a kind fellow, but just as owning a pub had made him full in the belly and thick in the wallet, it also left him pink in the cheek and loose in the lips. And as the Home Office handbills constantly remind everyone, 'Careless talk costs lives.'

Being so focused on their huddled conversation, they failed to see the heavily carved, oak doors of the pub slowly open. They didn't notice the stranger cross the road to their side. As they were busy discussing Coxey giving the game away, they failed to realise that the stranger was now walking their way, was in fact, just mere feet from where they stood.

Willy turned to check the pub once again and instantly startled backwards into the arms of a startled Reggie, who instinctively wrapped up his brother, pulling him closer.

The stranger stood before them. He was a tall man, probably in his early or mid-thirties. His skin was rough and scarred with pox. A ragged stubble of three days growth clung to his chin. A deep scar ran across the man's face, from under his cap, down his forehead, and across the right cheekbone. He glared with searing eyes at the two boys huddled in the bakery doorway.

The boys remained silent, too startled to speak.

"Sorry, lads." He leaned in close to them. He smelled of cigarette smoke. He squinted as he spoke. "I hope I didn't frighten you … too badly."

"N-n-no, sir. Not at all." Reggie struggled to hide the quiver in his voice. "W-w-we shouldn't have been standing in the doorway, like that."

The stranger leaned in closer still. "What you shouldn't be doing is following around someone you don't know." He leaned in and hissed with a German accent, "Bad things can happen to little orphan boys who don't mind their own business." He leaned back, raised his hand, and rubbed the hair on Reggie's head, smiling. He laughed, opened the door of the bakery, and stepped inside. Reggie grabbed Willy's hand and pulled him quickly away.

"Did you hear that?" Willy gasped.

"Yeah, I heard it. He spoke just like a German."

"I told you I had a feeling about him." Willy said. Reggie was trembling. The man had walked right up on them. He knew they were orphans. That would mean he knew where they lived. "How does he know we're orphans? Did you see that scar? What are we going to do?"

"Willy, will you stop asking me questions? I don't know. All I know is he spotted us, so we'll need the help of others. I have to think."

"Should we alert someone?" Willy asked, to excited to oblige his brother's request.

"No, not yet. We're still six against one and I like those odds."

***

Assembled in the dormitory, perched on the edge of their beds, the others listened intently as Reggie and Willy told their tale. Both were speaking quickly, in short, excited bursts of words.

"He had a German accent and this huge scar," Willy said.

"He called us orphans. That means he knows who we are and where we live," Reggie added, anxiously.

"Blasted Coxey spilled the beans on everything," Willy reported.

"He must have seen you peeking in the pub window," Reggie surmised.

Willy frowned. "I tried to do it as secretly as I could."

"Stealthily," Jack corrected him. "You tried to do it *stealthily* as you could."

"That's what I said, *Jackie,"* Willy answered, saying that last word like a twist after a stab.

"Don't call me Jackie. You know I *hate* that," Jack snapped.

"Then don't correct me all the time, *Jackie.* You know *I* hate *that.* I can take you, ya know," Willy retorted.

Freddie spoke up. "Stop. If there's any taking to be done round here, I'll be doin' it." Well into his growth spurt, at fifteen he was already six foot one, eleven stone so he had the size to command all their attention, if he wanted it. "Now *shut up* and focus on Reggie's plan."

Reggie spoke, "This may be the most important job we ever have. Remember, we're scouts."

"Not really," Jack whispered annoyingly.

"Shhhh!" Freddie nudged him with his foot.

"Remember that we're Boy Scouts and it's our sworn duty." He paused. "Chaps, this could be a real Nazi. Not some pilot thousands of feet above our heads, but right here in our village. We need to be smart and do—"

"Excuse me, I don't mean to interrupt," Henry said. "But look out there, at the road." He pointed. All heads turned to the window.

A quarter of a mile away, standing in the middle of the road, was the stranger. He stood silhouetted against the morning sky for a few seconds on the crest of the hill, his hand brimming his eyes for a better view of the church and school. He started his way down the hill towards them. "Time for Plan B. Put on your full uniforms, now." They scrambled like fighter pilots for their wardrobes.

Once dressed, they rallied in the main foyer.

"If he's coming here for you two, he'd better be ready for a fight," said Henry. They all nodded and grunted in agreement.

"If he comes up that walkway, we move to the front steps," Reggie said. "Do it in this order: me and Freddie out front, backed up by Dougie and Henry on the first step, flanked by Willy and Jack on the landing. Got it? Nobody does anything till I do. Hear me, Freddie? Not even you."

"I hear you," Freddie replied.

Reggie smiled and winked at him. "Good boy."

***

"I say, aren't you looking spiffy this morning? Where are you off to? Is there a parade I don't know about?" It was strange to see all the boys in full uniform so early on a Saturday morning, unless there was an occasion or something, which even at seventy-nine, Vicar Davis was pretty sure there wasn't. Was there? "Good grief, if I've forgot something again—"

"No, Vicar. We've got a duty to do. You stay out of it," Freddie said.

"What?" the curious vicar asked, looking slightly confused. "Duty, what duty?"

"Look outside." The vicar glanced out the window of the front door. He saw a man standing at the end of the walkway, seemingly just staring at the front of the building.

The boys rushed passed him, in their prescribed order, and as Willy passed, he said "He's just a Nazi spy that followed us from town. Stay inside, Vicar, we can handle this."

Vicar Davis was instantly frantic.

"A Nazi spy? Good heavens. You're twelve!" He cried. "Did you forget you're twelve? We need a constable, or the army, not the Boy Scouts! Sisters! *Sisters!*"

***

Outside, the boys took their positions on the steps. The two biggest, Reggie and Freddie, on the bottom step, Henry and Dougie on the second step, and Willy and Jack on the landing. It created the impression that they all stood at the same height.

The stranger started up the path from the road to the front steps. As he approached, Reggie and Freddie stepped forwards. The stranger smiled broadly.

Reggie spoke. "That's close enough, mister. You're not particularly welcome here. You have ten seconds to tell us who you are and what you want or—"

"I beg your pardon?" the stranger asked, his smile fading. His voice had not even a hint of a German accent. He leaned back, looking over the group. "Might I inquire what exactly it is that—?"

"For Pete's sake mister, you're down to five seconds." Freddie said as he took two steps forwards. The man slowly put up his hands, palms out in a universal gesture of peace. With his left hand he reached inside his coat. Freddie pounced.

He sprang at the stranger, grabbing the arm inside his coat. Reggie was on him next, sweeping the stranger's legs with his own and taking both he and Freddie to the ground. Dougie grabbed his other arm and pinned it. Henry and Willy jumped on as well, each taking a leg. It would have been all but impossible for the stranger to move, had he tried. To Reggie's surprise, the large man was putting up no fight and offered zero resistance.

Jack calmly approached the stranger, reached inside the man's jacket, and removed the only thing he found there, a folded sheet of paper.

A still frantic Vicar Davis had joined the boys on the front steps. "Good heavens, lads! What are you doing?!" He flapped his arms as he fretted, like a bird that suddenly forgot how to fly.

Jack unfolded the sheet of paper.

"Congratulations, Reverend Hawkins, on your new assignment as curate of St. Michael's Church and Boys' Home in Hawkhurst, Kent, this year of our Lord nineteen-hundred and forty." He tilted his helmet back on his head, a look of confusion plastered over his face. His eyes met Reggie's. "It also says our address, VD's name and telephone exchange, plus all our names." He handed the sheet to Reggie. It was embossed with a fancy blue and black crest, topped with a crown. From the Archbishop of Canterbury.

"Boys, you're making a terrible mistake!" Vicar Davis shouted from the top step. "This is no Nazi spy! This is our new curate!"

"A pleasure to make your acquaintance, gentlemen. Now, if it's not too much trouble, might I get up?" asked the new vicar-in-training.

Chapter 6
<u>Stranger Still</u>

"Please forgive them, Father Hawkins, for being so wound up," Vicar Davis gasped, spitting out a phrase with each exasperated breath. "It was *my* fault. I wanted your arrival this morning to be a surprise, you see. I'm afraid just not as large a surprise, alas, as it turned out to be." The new curate raised himself from the ground, brushing dust and leaves from his clothes.

"I'm very sorry, Father, sir. I thought you were reaching for..." Freddie looked at the ground, his face flushed with embarrassment.

"It's quite all right, young man. You're the big one. You must be Fredrick." He stuck out his hand to shake Freddie's—his *left* hand, the traditional boy scout handshake.

Freddie looked at Reggie and raised an eyebrow. He reached out, smiled, and shook Father Hawkins's hand excitedly. "Freddie, if you don't mind, Father. Everyone calls me Freddie."

"Then Freddie it is. It's a pleasure to meet you, Freddie. A *rough* pleasure, but a pleasure nonetheless. I'm James Hawkins, but you can call me Father Jim, if you like." He smiled, smacking Freddie heartily on the shoulder.

"But you're not dressed like a reverend. How were we supposed to know?" Dougie asked, feeling foolish.

"And no bags. Where are your belongings if you're coming here to stay?" Henry asked.

"I don't wear my collar and coat when I travel because these days, with our boys off at war, it's hard to get anywhere without being stopped by so many poor mothers asking me to pray for their sons or daughters far away from home. It's not that I don't care. I care very much and pray for them every day. It's just quicker to travel in plain clothes." He smiled. "Not to mention the trip from the train. I wanted to walk it, to get a look at my beautiful new home. It's not a bad walk, without parcels or packages. I shipped my things ahead to make the trip easier."

"What about all the shops, going from one to the other, asking questions and not buying anything?" Reggie asked, trying to should more curious than suspicious.

"Ah," said Father Hawkins, extending his left hand to Reggie. "My shadow. If that one over there is Freddie"—he looked Reggie up and down—"and you're about his age, you're Reginald, yes?"

Reggie, not taking his eyes off the man's, first wiped his left hand on his pants, then extended it. The handshake was firm from both of them and duly noted. "Reggie, sir, if you don't mind, Father."

"Reggie, I'm the new village curate. I was merely making the acquaintance of my new neighbours and congregation. You can hardly blame a fellow for that."

"What about—"

He cut Willy off, laying it on thick. *"Zat accent?"* He leaned down and playfully pulled at Willy's neckerchief. "Simply giving a couple of amateur spy hunters something to do." He winked. "I knew you two were on to me from the moment I saw that one trying to get a look at me through the pub window. Mr. Coxworth filled me in on the lot of you. I was just having a bit of fun. After all this, I do hope you'll forgive me." Wow, Reggie thought, he's apologizing to us?

The man turned to Willy. "Wilfred, yes? You're Reggie's spy-catching partner and little brother, if I'm not mistaken."

Willy stood a bit taller and threw out his chest like a proud soldier. "I'm not that little. I'm Willy, if you please sir, I mean, Father."

"Very pleased, Willy." In a whisper, "Would you like to learn how to stalk—uh, *track*—like a *real* spy catcher? I can teach you." He winked at the boy again.

Willy glanced sideways at Reggie. This fellow certainly wasn't like any priest they'd ever met before, and they'd met a lot of priests in their time at St. Michael's. Most were far older, far more like Vicar Davis.

"So, I've met three. That leaves three. Who are you? Douglas or Henry?"

"I'm Dougie." He extended his left hand.

"I'm Henry." He also extended his left hand.

Father Hawkins shook one then the other. "Pleasure, lads."

He wandered and stopped in front of Jack. Because the boy was standing on the top step, they were practically eye-to-eye. "You must be—"

"Jack," he said. "And *please* don't call me Jackie." He sternly thrust out his hand, like an exclamation mark to his point.

Father Hawkins cleared his throat and stood up very straight. "Jack, it's an honour to meet you." He took the boy's hand, pumped it three times, snapped it to his side, and clicked his heels with a pop. "Curate James E. Hawkins reporting for duty." He then snapped a proper salute, which Jack promptly returned. The curate smiled warmly.

"I must say, this has turned out to be the best parish welcoming I've ever received." Everyone smiled at that. "I've never been met by an honour guard before. Were I a Nazi spy, I'd have steered as far as possible from this place and you lot. These uniforms are a particularly nice touch, though I must say, whilst they are splendid, they're not British Boy Scout regulation. If I remember."

"They're homemade, Father. We don't meet the qualifications to be 'real' Boy Scouts," Henry said.

"We're not British Boy Scouts, Father. They wouldn't let us in, so we started our own troop. We're the 'Scouts of St. Michael,'" Reggie said humbly.

Dougie spoke. "The uniforms are from the Sisters. They helped us put them together—"

"Wait a tick,"—he balled his fists on his hips—"what did you say?" His tone and expression turned sharply serious.

"The Sisters, they helped us make our uniforms. We put—"

"No, no, that other bit. They wouldn't let you in? That doesn't sound like the Boy Scouts I was a part of."

"That's not true," Dougie said softly. "Those academy folks just don't like us."

Hawkins rushed over and stood directly in front of the boy. "Well, I don't believe that for a second," he said. "Here, I've just met you, and already I like you."

"It's because we have no parents, they say. It's because we're lowly orphans, they call us," Henry added.

"Well," he said, flashing a half smile, "I have a few connections. We'll see what we can do about rectifying that." He quickly looked them over again in their fine kits. "I'd be quite proud to have you as my troop. You're a fine one, and so dedicated to your home."

"It's all we got, Father. Vicar Davis, the Sisters, and one another." Reggie put his arm around Jack's shoulder. "When you haven't got much, you fight extra hard for the things you do have."

"I know that experience all too well." Hawkins said. Reggie looked at the deep scar running down his otherwise handsome face, hoping a story might follow. It didn't. "Actually right now, what I'd love is a wash and a shave. It's been a long trip."

"Where'd you come from, Father? Your last parish, I mean," Reggie asked, not done digging.

"St. Mary's Church, Battersea in south London," he replied, without batting an eyelash. "I arrive by train in the wee hours just this morning."

"You must be famished from your journey. Would you care for some breakfast? Tea, eggs and bacon, if you like?" Vicar Davis asked.

"Sounds wonderful. I'll wash up and head down to breakfast. Gents, will you join me? I'd love to hear all about this place from the lads who live here, and maybe after breakfast you can give me the grand tour."

"We'd be happy to, Father. We'll get cleaned up, too. And again, we're awfully sorry about the mix-up." Reggie said.

"It's all right, lads. Now, go and meet me"—watch glance—"in, say, two shakes of a lamb's tail?" They looked curiously back. "Oh, twenty minutes then."

Chapter 7

A Stranger No More

The boys were silent as they changed from their uniforms into something more suitable for breakfast with the new curate. Wardrobes were opened and closed, shirts were hung and shoes tied, without a word being spoken.

Reggie broke first. "You and your stupid *feelings*."

"It's not my fault!" Willy shouted. "I said I had a *feeling* about him. I didn't say it was a bad feeling. I said I had a feeling about him that, when you think about it, was true. I had no idea who he was and here we are about to have breakfast with him downstairs in two shakes of a lamb's tail!"

Reggie rolled his eyes. "And for goodness sake, don't start talking like him."

Jack spoke up. "I'm with you, Willy. You had a feeling, and now he's here. Although you did *want* him to be a spy."

"Willy's trouble is his imagination. He wants everyone to be a spy or a Nazi on the run or some other exotic thing. As if living under the threat of real invasion isn't enough war for him. He looks to find Hitler round every corner," Reggie said. Willy frowned, but said nothing as he continued to dress.

"Well, I like him," Freddie insisted, changing the subject abruptly. "He seemed not like a Nazi spy at all when we met him, except for that scar—where'd you think that come from?"

That scar, Reggie thought. It had changed since he had first seen it—not the scar itself, but his perception of it. On a Nazi spy, it was sinister. Now that he was a curate, it was just curious. When we find out more about him, he thought, perhaps it may even become downright dashing. He was a handsome man, regardless. Still, Reggie couldn't help the sense of nagging dread he felt at allowing this stranger inside their home so quickly. One little piece of paper and Vicar Davis rolls out the red carpet. Paperwork can be faked.

"I bet he got that in the war. Unless it was a lorry crash or something."

"No, that's not from a lorry crash. I bet he's been round a bit, our new curate," Reggie said, "the way he mentioned 'stalking' and then corrected himself and changed it to 'tracking.'"

"What's the difference?" Henry piped up. Dougie shrugged.

"The difference is you stalk *prey*." Freddie uttered just as the thought registered. His eyes widened as they met Reggie's. He raised an eyebrow questioningly. "You think he could be an ex-soldier?"

"Dunno, maybe." Reggie replied.

"Well, either way, he's got to be a better Scoutmaster than Sister Noreen. He's a bloke, first off. Maybe now we can do some real Boy Scout stuff, like go on long hikes and overnighters," an already trusting Dougie added, not suspicious of the new curate in the least.

"Being a good Scout has nothing to do with being a bloke," Reggie reminded them all. "Sister Noreen is no mere Tenderfoot. She's more skilled than all of us combined."

"Yeah, well, if you'd seen him outside the bakery like we did earlier, you might think differently." Willy said to Dougie, then stopped himself for talking poorly of the new curate. "Is it a sin to mistake a priest for a Nazi?" Willy wondered aloud.

No one knew, so no one answered.

"And if so," Henry asked, thinking the question through to its logical conclusion, "what do you suppose the penance is?"

"Probably huge," Dougie surmised as he pushed button after button through hole after hole.

"He's got a signed, stamped letter from the Archbishop of Canterbury. Do you know what that means?" Reggie asked no one and everyone.

Freddie shrugged and shook his head.

Reggie kept on. "It means you can't get more holy in all of Great Britain. You'd have to go to Rome or Bethlehem or somewhere else. It means he could be the real deal."

"That paperwork could easily be fake." Dougie said. "The Archbishop probably has a whole room full of monks who forge stuff." Freddie and Jack sniggered.

Reggie's eyes rolled and he shook his head. "Poor Dougie," he said aloud.

"What," Dougie protested confidently. "I bet you he does."

"Actually, he's got a good point, well, kind of," Henry reminded Reggie. "Paperwork *can* be forged and spies *are* trained to be convincing."

Reggie stopped dressing. He'd heard enough. "All right, that's it. Listen, all of you. Keep your eyes open and more importantly keep your gobs shut about all this spy business. This man, whoever he is, is now living in our home. We don't know him, or his intentions, from Adam. He may be a real reverend, or he may not, so until we learn more we watch him like a hawk."

"Don't you mean *like a Hawkins?*" Jack asked, smiling broadly at his own cleverness.

Reggie was not amused. "I mean, *Jackie,* do not trust him." To the rest of them, "This goes for all of you. Keep your guard up until we know for sure about this Father Hawkins, that's all. That's it. End of discussion. Full stop."

"Well, I *like* him," Freddie piped up. "That's all I'm saying."

***

Much like sounds, the smells from the kitchen easily travelled through the entire building, eventually reaching every room in both the church and the home. Wafting up through the space this morning, the aromas included fresh sausages, fried tomatoes, fried bacon and eggs.

Every member of the St. Michael's family joined the new curate for his meet-and-greet breakfast, including the good Sisters; Mr. McKenna, janitor; Mr. Greene, groundskeeper; cook Maurice; and Miss Goold, house secretary. Of all the staff, at 27 years she was closest in age to the boys.

She saw it as her duty to keep things up-to-date, or as up-to-date as was possible during these difficult times. It was she who suggested to Vicar Davis that perhaps time had come to consider putting in for a curate. Seeing that the boys were quickly becoming men, perhaps another, younger set of hands might be helpful at drawing their reins. Not only for his sake, but for the sake of the boys. He needed an assistant. When she explained to him in those terms, his deep fears of being replaced dissipated.

"You aren't being replaced, heaven's no. We're just getting you some help, so you can take it a bit easier, that's all."

A letter requesting a new curate had already been typed up and was awaiting his signature. He signed it, and that quickly it was in the outgoing post. When it came to such matters, Miss Goold liked to work fast before the Vicar had a chance to change his mind, which he did often.

Now freshly cleaned, shaved and dressed in his official garb and looking as a proper curate should, Father Hawkins introduced himself after stumbling upon her as he passed through the kitchen.

"And you must be Miss Goold. I'm Jim Hawkins." He offered her his hand. "I'm very pleased to meet you." She took his hand and shook it, gently. "I understand you're the one I have to thank for my transfer?"

A slight blush rose in her cheeks, and she curtsied at the dashing young man. "Father, sir. It is an honour to meet you and serve—"

"Really?" he asked, taken aback slightly. "A curtsy?" He laughed heartily. "I'm not His Holiness or His Majesty. I'm just an ordinary man." She raised her eyes to his smiling face. "James, Jim? Call me whatever you like but please, no need for all this formality. It's one of the reasons I wanted a parish in the country."

She blushed again as a sense of great relief visibly washed over her from top down. "Oh thank goodness." She said. "I was so afraid we might end up with …" she trailed off and then laughed herself. "It's just you never know what you're going to get. Okay, how about Father Jim?

Or just Father?" she asked.

"I would be more than happy to answer to whatever you'd like to call me, dear lady. Besides, this is more your place than mine. I'm the new one here, don't forget."

"Yes, that's true. But remember, you're the vicar curate now. You're soon to be the boss of me and everyone else here."

"Oh, well, when you put it that way, I feel great pressure." He smiled again.

"No need. I'll help you." She smiled back.

"I have no intention of making any waves for anyone around here, I'll have you know. I swear it as my solemn vow." He crossed his heart.

"I have no intention of letting you, and that is my solemn vow, Father Jim. Yes," she said, "I rather like Father Jim. It's much nicer than VD."

"I beg your pardon?" he asked. "Did you say——"

"VD. Vicar Davis. It's the boys' pet name for him, and when the boys decide something——"

"They have a great influence over you—the boys." He looked deep into her eyes.

She didn't look away. "And I over them, I hope. They're my world." She glanced at the boys seated in the other room, at the long table, eating and laughing merrily. "And VD and the Sisters, the men, too. I love them all with all my heart and would protect them with my life. They're my family actually. Is that what you mean?" she asked.

"That's exactly what I mean. I can tell already how lucky they are to have you. How did you end up at this place?"

She turned back to him. He was very handsome. She glanced for a ring on his finger and saw none.

"I'd been babysitting for VD and the Sisters for years whilst I was still in school. When the time came for me to move on, I couldn't just abandon them to their fate, as so many in their lives had already done. I wanted to be part of their lives, to help guide them, at least until they became capable of taking care of themselves. Life is hard enough as it is, when you're alone"—she looked away—"and now with war here, they're close to the call up age, at least Freddie and Reggie are." She was on a cliff, close to falling into tears, yet only one escaped her eye, and it was brutally whisked off her cheek by an angry finger, an attempt to hide her embarrassment. He took her hand.

"Well as long as I'm around, neither those boys—nor you—will ever worry about being alone. I give you my word, Miss Goold." He gently touched her shoulder. She didn't pull away.

"Please … call me Kate or Katie if you like. Thank you, Father Jim. You're exactly what I was hoping for in a curate for the boys, and I think perhaps even more. Welcome to the family of St. Michael's." She took his hand and gently kissed his cheek.

"Hey, out of my kitchen! Get out there and eat my food when she's hot! This is your welcome breakfast, non?" Maurice shouted in his French-seasoned English, through his signature forced smile.

"Yes, yes, Maurice, and it all smells so delightful. I can't thank you eno—"

"Enough! I know! Get out!" He started waving his spatula.

Katie grabbed Jim's hand and pulled him from the kitchen, like a schoolgirl hurrying her best friend to recess. "Let's hope there's still some left," said Katie. "You have to be quick at mealtime around here, or you'll get nothing but the scraps. Wait till you see those boys eat."

Chapter 8
<u>Target Trouble</u>

Later that afternoon, Father Hawkins was busy arranging his new desk.

CRASH! Something skipped across the floor and bounced off the far wall. Rising from his chair, he looked out his newly broken window. Jack was standing in the courtyard below wearing his uniform, his slingshot in his hand, with proverbial smoke rising from its proverbial barrel. Jack was staring up at the window when Father Hawkins appeared. He tried unsuccessfully to hide his catapult, but there was no point. The window was busted, and so was he.

***

"Well, now, just what in heaven's name do you think you're doing?"

Father Hawkins was standing in the doorway, holding a rock in his hand. Jack had taken a bunch of dirty socks from the laundry, strategically placed each at a different spot on the statue of St. Michael and was firing at them unsuccessfully with his sling. Stones littered the courtyard.

Jack's tummy trembled. He was all alone and possibly about to experience the heretofore seen temper of the new curate.

"F-Father, I-I-" he stammered. "It was a ricochet off his head."

"Young man, I asked you a simple question."

"I-I'm sorry Father, I-I was … target practising. Sister Noreen lets me sometimes—"

"The reason you're missing those things consistently isn't your aim. It's your ammunition." Instantly Jack's previous concern vanished. "My ammo?" he asked, intrigued. "How could that be the problem?"

"Come over, and I'll show you."

Jack did as he was instructed, taking a sort of a skip step that turned into a trot. Soon, he was standing at Hawkins' side.

"Here now, empty your pouch, and let's have a look."

Jack flipped up the flap of the black leather pouch on his belt. Reaching inside, he pulled out several stones and opened his hand. Nestled in his palm were different stones and pebbles of all sizes and shapes, from smooth round ones to chunky sharp shards. Each was covered in dust from rubbing up against the others in the pouch.

"Ah," Father Hawkins said. "Just as I suspected."

He chose the smallest piece and the largest. "May I?" He pointed his open hand at Jack's sling. Jack removed the lanyard from over his neck, took the sling pouch off his shoulder, and handed it over, more curious than ever.

"Look here," Father said. "You're young so you have good eyes. And since you do, your aim should be very sharp. But there's more to good aim than keen eyes."

"I know that already, or I'd be Annie Oakley," Jack replied.

"You need to have the same kind of ammo to practice with so every shot goes just where you want it. This smooth little pebble will move through the air differently than this large chunky one, so you need to adjust the pulling power on your sling for the larger one." He demonstrated with the two stones. Both flew in drastically different patterns and landed in vastly different places. "Also, how old is the sling? How worn are the bands? What of the air? Is it a cool or warm day outside?"

Jack stared up at him, befuddled. "What's all that have to do with hitting those socks?"

Father Hawkins smiled at the boy. "Every one of those things,

51

and more, will affect your shot. Even gravity plays a part. Quite fascinating when you think of it, really."

"So I have to think about all that stuff before I shoot? That seems like a lot, especially if I'm just trying to bag a rabbit for dinner," Jack retorted. "Who's got time for that when trying to bag a rabbit?"

"Those are the things you think about before you ever even get to the field. You think it through, select the proper ammo, and make sure your bands are good and fresh. Then you're much more likely to actually come home with dinner, as opposed to empty-handed. All your projectiles should be of the same size and weight, or as close as you can get it." He sat down on the step. "Here, let's see that pouch."

Jack obliged, and soon Hawkins had picked out all the ones that would work well and tossed the others away.

"Hey, those are all my best ones."

"Rubbish," said the priest. "A Boy Scout makes his own shot, but we'll get to that." When he was finished, he had a much smaller collection of stones, all of them similar in size.

Father Hawkins took the slingshot and loaded it with one of the stones. He pulled back the sling, aimed, and let fly.

Fwap! The unmistakable sound of the catapult firing echoed through the courtyard. The sock that had been hanging off St. Mike's upraised forearm jumped and fell to the ground.

Fwap! The green sock on the sword hilt went down.

Fwap! The brown sock on his bicep.

Fwap! Freddie's dirty white one.

Fwap! VD's imperial purple one.

Jack stood, his eyes not on the falling socks, but on Father Hawkins, who was knocking them down like a sharpshooter in a circus. He stopped firing and stood tall, squinting at the statue, grinning at his success. He turned to Jack. The boy stood mouth agape, eyes staring at him, mesmerized.

Father Hawkins held out the slingshot to the boy, who didn't move.

"Blimey!" A whisper was all he could manage. Gingerly, he took the catapult from the man, as if it were now infused with some powerful magic he was afraid to disturb.

"You see, *consistency* is very important for success. Practice, practice, practice until you do it perfectly. Every bit of shot you fire should be the same size and weight. That way you get a feel for how to adjust your shot based on other factors, like wind and distance. Does that make sense to you?"

"Yes, Father, it does. But it will take forever to find that."

"That's why I'm going to teach you some woodcraft so you'll never be at a loss for ammo again. I'm going to teach you how to make your shot carved out of wood."

"Wow, that's like real Boy Scouts stuff, woodcraft. VD never taught us that, and Sister Noreen knows some—but not that, for sure."

"Then let's get started. You should always be with ammo. Until we have some, those pebbles will work. Keep practising, and you'll keep getting better." Jack was delighted beyond belief. "Now go and find Mr. Greene or Mr. McKenna and set about helping replace that window in my office."

Jack saluted. "Yes sir, Father." Father Jim returned it with a snap, shook his head, and smiled.

***

Father Hawkins made good on his promise, showing Jack how to select the right wood and use his knife to carve and whittle the selected branches and sticks into three different-size bits of ammunition, based on his target and other variables. What Jack liked best was he no longer caught any guff from Mr. Greene or the Sisters about using the St. Mike statue as his target holder.

Father Hawkins also let it be known to everyone in the home that rocks, stones and pebbles were no longer acceptable forms of ammunition on the "St. Michael's Catapult Range," and from that moment on, they were allowed to shoot only harmless wooden balls near the stone statue.

9 JULY 1940

FROM: LORD PRIVY SEAL CLEMENT ATTLEE
TO: DR. HUGH DALTON, MINISTER OF ECONOMIC WARFARE
    MAJOR J.C. HOLLAND RE, MI(R)
    MAJOR LAWRENCE GRAND RE, MI6

Gentlemen,

On 1 July, the War Cabinet agreed to the merger of several departments under a single umbrella organisation, namely Secret Intelligence Service's Section D, responsible for sabotage, propaganda and irregular methods, MI(R), Military Intelligence - Research section, and Foreign Office branch EH.

On 1 July, the War Cabinet granted approval to officially sanction the formation of a new single body to be chartered on 16 July, encompassing EH, Section D and MI(R), and entirely independent of the War Office, henceforth to be known as the SPECIAL OPERATIONS EXECUTIVE. As current Minister of Economic Warfare, Dr. Hugh Dalton shall be named Director of Operations. The purpose of this new body is to co-ordinate all covert action by way of subversion and sabotage against the enemy overseas. The Minister of Economic Warfare is to have Absolute Power of direction, subject only to Prime Minister, Winston Churchill.

Chapter 9
A Parish Prepares

One fine morning only several days after Father Hawkins arrival, the residents and staff of St. Michael's had gathered in the courtyard after breakfast to begin the monumental task of preparing the church and making evacuation plans for the coming German attacks.

There was a new anti-aircraft artillery installation being constructed on a far ridge overlooking the north fields, on an embankment roughly two hundred yards behind the church and school. It, along with a dugout, trenches, and tunnels, were being built to be used as a bunker for the army and Local Defence Volunteers.

"Must they build that thing so close?" Katie asked nervously.

"I'm afraid we've not much choice in the matter. The War Office is making those decisions. Besides, whether or not we like it, war is coming to our island, and every inch of it, including St. Michael's, is in the German crosshairs. The fact that we're a church, an orphanage, or a hospital means nothing to falling bombs. Those things will land on whatever they're dropped over." Father Hawkins answered.

"Besides," added Mr. McKenna, "it'll be nice to be able to give

back a bit of the fight to those dirty huns—if you'll pardon my language."
Mr. McKenna and Mr. Greene were both Auxiliary members of the LDV.

Father Hawkins turned to address his next comment directly to the boys, keying mostly on Freddie. "No one … I mean absolutely no one, is to lay a finger on that anti-aircraft gun at any time, under any conditions."

He turned to the Sisters. "So listen good, you two, no mucking about during your walks."

In his mind's eye he pictured the Sisters, sitting side by side on the AA gun, dark round goggles on their eyes, peering skyward with flat steel helmets covering their coifs, whizzing round, shooting at Luftwaffe bombers. "Not that you couldn't," he said. "you'd actually probably be pretty good at it."

Sister Noreen waved him off with one of her girlish giggles. "Oh, *yooou*."

"It's been placed there by Anti-aircraft Artillery Command and it's theirs to own, operate, and maintain. It can be as dangerous for the gunners as it is for whoever is on the receiving end of the ordnance."

"When the air raid sirens sound, our main job is to get anyone who shows up safely to the basement under the church as quickly as we can. Mr. McKenna and Mr. Greene, you get to the bells and ring like heck."

He turned to the boys again. "Each pair of you will be responsible for a floor of the school. I will cover the church. I'm going to break up the usual pairs that you boys tend to flock about in."

They glanced at each other. They usually flocked about paired up by size: Willy and Jack, Dougie and Henry, Reggie and Freddie. Usually.

"Dougie and Henry, you get the second floor. Reggie and Jack, first floor, including the dormitory. Freddie and Willy, you take the ground floor, including the kitchen." Father Hawkins turned to Maurice, who already had his finger raised in protest. "Maurice, you are in charge of the kitchen. The boys will back you up."

As a proud French cook Maurice liked the sound of that. He smiled, nodding his approval.

"Your first, most important job is to switch off the mains—gas, electric and water."

The Frenchman folded the arms across his chest, again nodded his approval. "Oui."

"Once every room has been cleared, gather in the courtyard and do a head count as each staff member enters the shelter. When everyone is accounted for, we lock down the basement."

"Reggie, I paired you with Jack, and Willy with Freddie, that way each of the smaller boys would have a larger, stronger partner, just in case. Of course, if you'd rather be partnered with your brother, that would work, as well." His voice had softened. "Does that make sense to you?" Father Hawkins asked.

"Yes, Father. It makes perfect sense." He glanced at Willy, who had already moved over to stand next to Freddie. He seemed so small and frail next to the larger boy. "Freddie is quite capable of taking care of your little brother." Freddie winked at Reggie.

"Don't worry, mate. He's my little brother too."

"Now, we also have to talk about how we handle an air raid in the very unlikely event it happens during service," Father Hawkins said. "Trying to move a lot of parishioners will take some doing, but if we move in orderly lines right down into the basement, we should be all right. Our main task at that time is to make sure everyone is cared for as best we can. Remember, they're always to be considered guests when in our home, especially when they're feeling frightened or vulnerable. It's our job to take care of them and remind them that if they're here, they'll be safe, even should a bomb fall through the roof into the great hall of the church."

"What a bloomin' mess that'd be," said Bob. "Here's to hoping."

Father Hawkins continued. "They'll be well protected in the base-ment and catacombs. Vicar, you will be in charge of the basement. You know the parishioners best. Because they trust you, they'll listen to you."

"Sisters," Father Hawkins said, "once everyone is below ground, it'll be your jobs to make sure no one leaves until the all-clear sounds."

The ladies looked at each other, nodded, and folded their arms across their chests. "No problem at all, Father. Once they're in, they're in to stay, or Heaven help them." If Vicar Davis was St. Michal's head, and Katie its heart, Hawkins thought, the Sisters were undoubtedly its muscle.

"Our most important responsibility is stocking the church basement so we can sustain people for a lengthy stay, should it be necessary. Folding beds, food, water, bags for sanitation, gas masks, and so on must be gathered and stowed for as many folks as we can."

"Wow, we have a lot of work to do, don't we?" Henry whispered to Dougie.

"Heck yes, we do." Dougie whispered back.

"First aid kits must be packed as well, so to extra blankets and pillows." Hawkins looked at his clipboard. "Our friends at the RAF and British War Relief Society have secured us medical supplies, bedding, and beds—lots of folding beds." He looked around, a bit worried. "Is there room down there for that? I've been through the basement, but haven't ventured into the catacombs."

"There's more room down there than most people have ever seen. We could secure the entire village population, with room to spare," Sister Noreen said boastfully.

"Well, from your lips to God's ears, we hopefully have room for all, even those who've built their own bomb shelters. I would much rather have the villagers here, as opposed to out there on their own during an air raid." Sister Doreen made the sign of the cross over her chest, offering a silent prayer.

Father Hawkins looked over his list. There was much to do.

"Okay, boys, after the all-clear signals, if Hawkhurst is hit, those folks who have their own shelters will need to be checked on as soon as possible. We'll draw up search areas on the parish map, areas for which each team will be responsible. If any bombs find their mark, we'll head directly to the blast scene in mass, as we may be the first team of rescuers to arrive."

"You know," Freddie said, "we could fix up our bikes so we can carry picks and spades, just in case we need them."

"Brilliant idea. Mr. McKenna, can you help with that?" Father Hawkins asked.

"Of course I can, Father, knock up something perfect for the job." Mr. McKenna looked at Mr. Greene. "Aye?" he asked.

Mr. Greene nodded. "I can already see the finished product in me mind."

At that moment, three blue RAF lorries arrived and pulled up in front of St. Michael's.

"Ah, they're here." Hawkins said.

Dougie rushed the lorry and jumped on the sideboard. "'Ello!"

"G'morning. Got some stuff here for Captain Hawkins," the driver said.

"Captain?" Dougie asked, confused. "You mean *Father* Hawkins?"

The driver looked at his paperwork. "Well, says Captain on here.'" He looked at his passenger, who shrugged and offered, "Maybe he's the 'captain' of the church."

"Sounds good enough to me." He turned his attention back to Dougie. "So where do you want these? Beds, tables, chairs, the lot."

"Dunno. Hey," Dougie yelled over his shoulder, "they got beds and stuff."

"Send them around back to the kitchen loading entrance. We can bring them in from there," Mr. McKenna answered.

"Right. I'll show you!" Dougie pounded his palm on the lorry's heavy bonnet. "Go right round the back—over there, mind the flower-bed." Dougie stayed put, standing on the running board of the lorry, holding the side mirror, pointing the way as the driver manoeuvred the large machine. "Perfect timing." Hawkins said. "Now boys, let's give these airmen a hand with those beds."

The second lorry was overloaded with sand. "What's this? We building a sandpit?" Willy asked.

"More like a sand castle, a giant, sandbag castle." Father Hawkins glanced up at the centuries-old stained-glass windows. It was going to take a lot of sandbags piled high to protect those.

"Say, Vicar," the lorry driver called incorrectly to Hawkins. "Where should I dump this for ya?"

"Follow that lorry and bring it round back. We can fill them there and move them to anywhere we might need them."

"Yes sir, Vicar." Round the back it went, spilling handfuls of sand with every bump it hit.

"Blimey, that's a lot of sand," Henry said, glaring at the heaped pile in the lorry.

"Yeah, and I bet they brought shovels for us all," Freddie added. "No need to get all mucked up." He undid his uniform shirt, and continued to work in his vest. The other boys followed suit.

***

It took several days, but once they finished shovelling, there were sandbags enough to surround all the ancient church's beloved stained-glass windows, well-protecting them from anything short of a direct hit. Sandbags also zig-zagged the courtyard where the boys had constructed a series of trenches ending at the statue of St. Michael, itself now also surrounded from sword tip to toe with heavy protective sandbags.

"He has spent so many years protecting us," Reggie explained to an astonished Father Hawkins, "the very least we could do is return the favour."

Chapter 10
<u>Into the Catacombs</u>

After the sandbags had been piled high and the exterior of the six-hundred year old church was protected, the next order of business was to prepare the basement and catacombs to handle villagers for the duration of an air raid. In the years that Vicar Davis was at St. Michael's, he had never once ventured into the catacombs beyond the basement—he simply had never needed to—so the conditions down there were unknown.

"Oh, I'm fairly certain no one has been down here in many decades," Vicar Davis said. He fumbled with a key ring that was as old as the catacombs themselves. The lock itself was very old, the thick iron kind one might expect pirates to use on their treasure chests. When he found the right key, Vicar Davis took the heavy padlock in his hand, inserted the key and tried to turn it. It didn't budge.

"Are you sure that's the proper key, Vicar?" Willy asked, flashing his torchlight at the key ring.

"Oh, yes, I'm quite sure this is the key. It's been so long since this lock has been opened. I suppose in this dampness its tumblers may have fused together."

"Let me have a go, Vicar," Freddie said. He was the strongest of all present, if he couldn't turn it, none of them would be able to. He took the lock and key from the vicar. Pulling out the key, he brought the lock to his mouth. First he blew in the hole hard, then he spit in it.

"A little lubrication helps a sticky situation." He paused and gave a little chuckle. The key slid in effortlessly. A couple of jiggles later and— *click*—the heavy lock sprang opened.

"Nice work, Freddie," Dougie chirped with a wink.

"Thanks, Dougie," he chirped back, also with a wink.

Vicar Davis pulled the lock from the door hasp and let it hang from the chain that secured it to the thick iron door.

"I wish Father Hawkins were here. Then at least we wouldn't have to go in there alone, I mean," Jack said, his voice sounding small. Reggie put his hand on Jack's thin shoulder.

"He trusted us to do it whilst he was out chasing down supplies. Don't worry. You won't be alone. We'll be with you. You should've brought your catapult." Jack was a pretty good shot with that thing and with Father Hawkins help was getting better. He'd already stacked up a decent count of church rodents he'd picked off. THOU SHALL NOT KILL on the plaque in their classroom did not apply to "disgusting, plague-infested, filthy vermin" Sister Noreen assured.

Jack had been genuinely relieved to hear that.

Freddie took the heavy door bolt in hand. He rolled the handle towards him, then tried to pull it back. It didn't move. He shook the handle a couple of times, and then, with a mighty pull, it slowly slid back and opened.

"Okay, here we go. Stand back." They all took a step back, their torch beams locked on Freddie. He pulled. The door didn't move. Wiping the sweat from his hands on his pants, Freddie pulled the large door handle again. Nothing. "Reg, step up and lend me your muscles."

Reggie did so, taking his spot next to Freddie. "Okay, on three. One ... two ... *three!*"

The heavy door opened with a creak, exhaling a groan of foul air, both musty and stale. Inside was nothing but blackness, as far as their torch beams could reach. "Ew, that smell," Dougie said, holding his nose. Henry smiled at him. "Now you know how we feel around you." They all laughed nervously, more to allay their fears than to acknowledge Henry's wit.

"Very good, lads." Vicar said, covering his nose and mouth with his handkerchief. "Now have at it and be very careful." He hung the keys on the hook and hurried away.

The boys gathered round the doorway and peered in, with none too eager to enter. The only way in or out was this door, and there was no telling how far or how deep the catacombs extended.

"Will there be rats?" Jack asked, "I really wish I had remembered to bring my catapult."

"I suppose there could be, but only if they have a key and can work that door, unless there's another way in." Freddie said.

"What about spiders? There are bound to be spiders," Dougie said. "And maybe snakes, so deep under the ground."

"How big is it?" Henry asked.

"Dunno," Reggie answered. "If there was ever a map of this place, it's long gone now."

"So, how do we keep from getting lost in there?" Dougie asked, his voice cracking slightly.

Somewhere deep inside the unnerving sound of water dripping echoed.

"You should spend more time with BP's manual and less time feeding your head with comics." From his pocket Reggie produced a large ball of twine. Freddie nodded, immediately recognising what he had in mind. Reggie approached the heavy door, and tied the end of the twine to its handle with a sturdy knot. He added a second. "Just in case," he said.

"We walk in, keeping a hand on the line at all times. Should we get turned round, the line will always lead to the way out." Henry nodded. Dougie nodded. Willy and Jack stayed silent and still, their default mode when they got scared, as to not miss something important.

"You want to take front or rear?" Reggie asked Freddie, knowing already what he'd choose.

"Rear," the large boy answered.

Reggie's his mouth fell open. "Wha—whaddya mean *rear?*

You're all about taking point and being first."

"Yeah, well, maybe it's better this time if I take the rear, you know, keep an eye on our six, and all," the large boy replied.

"Great," Reggie said, spitefully, "I suppose *I'll* take point then."

"Good on you for volunteering." Freddie said. "We'll be directly behind you." They bunched closer together.

"I'll take second rear—you know … be Freddie's backup … just in case," Dougie chimed in.

"Perfect," Reggie whined, "another hero."

"Me too," Jack said. "I'll take third rear."

Starting to feel betrayed and abandoned, Reggie turned, his arms akimbo. "Seriously, would you lot like me to go it alone? It's just dark and kind of stinky. There's nothing to be afraid of."

"Maybe Jack and I should double up." Willy suggested. "You know, he is so small, and I could help keep an eye on him." Normally one to take umbrage at his lack of size being noted, Jack's rapid nodding signalled that, in this instance, he was just fine with it.

"I can't believe what a bunch of cowardy custards you've all suddenly become. Where is your sense of—"

From the deep darkness behind him, there came a low moaning. It echoed through the darkness for several seconds. Reggie jumped, joining the others, gathered in a tight bunch, regarding that blackened doorway as if it were the gateway to hell itself.

"You were saying something about cutting mustard?" Freddie said, glaring into the darkness.

"I'm sure that was just the wind, passing over a hole. From the other side. Maybe a draft or s-s-something."

"Or *something,*" Dougie repeated.

"Oh, for Pete's sake, let's go," Reggie said courageously, before whispering to himself "St. Mike, protect us." With torch in one hand and twine in the other, he entered the dank, dark chill of the catacombs.

***

As Reggie stepped into the blackness, he kept his eye on the circle of light from his electric torch shining on the ground, so he missed the large spider web that was hanging across the interior of the doorway. He walked full face into it, then commenced the unmistakable dance of someone who has just walked full face into a spider web. He spat, huffed, and waved frantically at the unseen, yet clearly felt webs that covered his face. "*Bahaaa* I hate that!" he shouted.

Dougie and Henry broke up, Willy and Jack jumped and grabbed each other's arms, and Freddie silently congratulated himself for wisely choosing to take the rear.

It was at least twenty degrees colder inside than out. Freddie shone his torch down the long walls on either side. Each was lined with vaults that had been covered up very long ago. There was writing and inscriptions on each. "There must be hundreds of people in here." Reggie said.

"Where?" asked Dougie. "I don't see anyone."

Henry shone his torch on the wall next to Dougie. "See those vaults?" He pointed his beam at the lighter-coloured horizontal patches. "There's a body behind each one. This is where they used to bury folks before the cemetery was built."

Reggie moved forwards down the long passage, feeling slightly more at ease as his eyes became accustomed to the dark. It was just an old place, with lots of dead bodies, that's all.

At some point in the distant past, the catacombs must have been used regularly. Here and there about the vaults were wooden barrels, melted candles, ceramic pots, and small piles of dust that at one time were probably offerings of flowers.

"It's just a bigger part of the basement, lads," Reggie said aloud, trying to reassuring himself as much as the others; however, speaking louder only made his voice echo, which made the situation that much more creepy, as if voices were calling from out of the darkness.

"Yeah, the cemetery part. Who puts dead people in their basement, honestly?" Dougie added.

"Hawkhurst used to be a bad place. Dead bodies had value, especially rich dead bodies," Henry said. "They're probably here so they didn't get dug up and robbed."

Hearing that, Willy became instantly intrigued. He was suddenly feeling like Howard Carter, sure that each vault he passed held a Tut-ankhamen-like treasure trove of gold and jewels. "Does that mean there could be treasure behind those things?" he asked.

"You'll never know, because we're not here to disrupt the graves of the dead. Sister Noreen would have your hide if she knew you even suggested such a thing," Reggie said. "So just forget it."

Willy's visions of fame and fortune evaporated like his breath before him.

"Besides," Reggie reminded him, "there was a curse on Tut-ankhamen's tomb, remember? Each one of these crypts has a ghost behind it just waiting to come out and haunt anyone who disturbs its slumber."

Dougie swallowed hard. "Need we speak of such things now?" he asked, his voice quivering.

Freddie smiled and shook his head. "It will be easy to string electric lights in here, and if we find another exit of some kind, we can get some ventilation going. No one can stay in here until we do that." His eyes were beginning to adjust to the darkness, but it did little to alleviate his general discomfort. "It's too damp, cold and smelly the way it is now.

Reggie reached the end of the first passage, which turned to the right. He continued laying out the twine, and the boys followed, torch beams sweeping from side to side as they moved. Looking about, Jack failed to realise Reggie had stopped and ran smack into his back. He shone his torch at Reggie, who was standing with his fist up, giving a visual signal for the column to stop.

Jack turned to the rest of the boys. "Hold up. Reggie's stopped."

Freddie left the line to join Reggie. "What's up, buttercup?" he asked.

Reggie placed his index finger over his lips. He lowered his torch and pointed at the floor.

In the middle of the passage, there was a set of fresh footprints that disappeared into the darkness ahead.

Chapter 11
<u>Savvy Spooring</u>

Freddie's stomach flipped. He turned and grabbed the boys behind him. *"Shhh!"* He clicked off his torch. The boys followed his lead. He leaned in until his lips were touching Reggie's ear, whispering as softly as possible. "Those look fresh."

Reggie nodded in agreement.

Willy moved forwards, knelt down, and clicked his torch on. He leaned in close and studied the track. Without a word, he tugged Reggie's shirt and made a circle with his finger, signalling for them to regroup back where they'd started.

No one spoke. They just turned, grabbed the twine and hastily moved back to the heavy door. Once outside, Reggie and Freddie pushed the door closed, but not sealed.

"A man made those tracks," Willy said. "From size and the stride, he's a full-size man," he said with complete confidence. "Definitely a man's shoe, with distinct characteristics I could easily see in the dirt."

"But VD said no one's been in there for decades. Who would make those?" Dougie asked.

"Maybe the same person who made that sound we heard."

"We know for a fact that this door was locked from the outside when we came in," Henry said.

"Then there's no way anyone could be inside, is there?" Jack asked.

"Well, someone made those tracks," Reggie said. "We should find out where they lead."

"I'm not going in there again—not without my catapult, that's for sure," Jack piped up.

That was a good idea. "Agreed," Reggie said. "Dougie, you stay here and watch that door. Make sure no one goes in or comes out."

"I ... umm, I don't know—"

Freddie cut him off. "I'll stay with him. Grab my compass and map case. I want to sketch the floor plan whilst we're in there."

Reggie turned to Willy. "You go and get your notepad. A drawing and measurements of that footprint should come in handy. Also grab a lantern, and make sure it's nice and full." Willy took off like a shot. "Okay, everyone. Just long enough to grab our gear, then back here. Go now. And mum's the word." They scrambled out of the basement, leaving Freddie and Dougie behind.

***

On their return, each was wearing his Sam Browne belt.

"Miss anything?" Reggie asked, handing Freddie his belt and case, and Dougie his belt.

"Not a thing, in or out," Freddie said. Dougie just shook his head, his eyes still fixed on the door.

They quickly secured the cross straps over their shoulders and buckled up. Freddie put his map case across his chest. Dougie wore his belt mirroring Reggie: slung low on his dominant hand side, hatchet in leather tool holsters at fingers' length. They looked like gunfighters from the American Old West, but packing hatchets instead of six-guns.

Willy wore his blade strapped to his shin guard. Jack, as always, carried his catapult slung over his shoulder, its handle hanging under his arm.

"That's better. Now we can handle anyone we run into," Henry said.

"Or any*thing?*" asked Dougie with a hard swallow.

"Stop it," Freddie said. "The only thing you need to be afraid of is me if you don't shut it." Dougie shut it. "Focus on the task at hand. We need to find out who's been prowling round our basement."

Once equipped with their belts, they attached their torches to the shoulder cross straps, which gave them a free hand. Willy handed Reggie the lantern. It was heavy, which meant it was full of fuel. He lit it. White light flooded their faces. The surrounding darkness became an even deeper black.

"Okay, lads. Let's do this." The long twine could easily be seen leading off into the darkness. Reggie gave two good tugs on the knot, which held firm. He stepped through the doorway with the lantern light and twine leading the way.

Willy moved forwards, second behind Reggie. Standard patrol formation outlined in BP's book wouldn't work here because the space was too cramped. Willy pulled his torch from his chest and began to examine the prints on the floor. "Try not to scuffing up these tracks," he whispered. "I need to find the one that's the clearest."

As he walked, Freddie counted his measured steps, as each of the squares on his map grid sheet represented a single yard, and he could mark them off as he went.

Reggie moved forwards down the line, the lantern casting much brighter light to a much larger area than their torches had done. Huge shadow forms followed them, creeping along the walls, wavering against the movement of the lantern and the light pattern it threw.

"No good," Willy said, studying the ground closely with his torch. "We fouled these up with ours. I can't find the one we saw."

"Well, we didn't go all the way. There should be some clear ones up ahead," Dougie reminded him. Willy rushed up to join Reggie in the lead. When they reached the end of the passage, it turned ninety degrees to the east, as far as they had made it into the catacombs before they stopped. Freddie took notes. Ahead of them laid unexplored territory.

Reggie picked up the ball of twine from where he had left it on their last trip in. Willy rushed a few feet ahead, careful not to muck up the tracks already there.

"Got it. Here's where they start again." He dropped to his knees. "Oh, here's a great one." He pulled out his pad and ruler and started to measure, draw and document the track, as best as he could. Spooring was one of his favourite scout activities, and among the boys, his skills were the most highly regarded.

Reggie rounded the corner and entered the second passage, which was longer than the first.

"Hey," Willy called out. "Look at this." The boys gathered round. Bordering the strange footprints were two long tracks. "Those look like tyre tracks. Whoever was in here was pushing or pulling something with wheels."

"What about the last person buried here?" Jack asked. "Maybe they used a cart to get the body to its hole ... vault ... thing."

"No, Jack. Look closer."

Jack moved in. "Those long tracks have a pattern or a tread that you can still see. These were made by tyres, air-filled rubber tyres. I'm pretty sure there weren't rubber tyres with treads six hundred years ago." He thought again. "Wood, maybe stone, but surely not rubber."

"Look over there!" Henry shouted. "Another set of tracks, heading out."

Willy rushed over, shining his torch on the ground. "Same shoe prints, but no tyre tracks." The group gathered to confirm Willy's report.

"That means whoever came in went out again. We're the only ones in here," Freddie said. "Come on, let's see where this ends." Taking the twine and point from Reggie, he checked his compass bearing and moved forwards down the passage. After several dozen feet, another, third passageway opened on his right hand side. Shining his torch down it, he froze.

"What the bloody hell is that?"

Reggie held the bright lantern above his head to cut the glare. Willy's head began to swim. He reached for Reggie. He was instantly sweating and trembling slightly.

"Something doesn't feel right," he said aloud, causing gooseflesh to rise on all of them.

Against the wall sat a large wooden crate, its side opened. Inside was a shortwave radio and transmitter. Behind it sat a two-wheeled trolley with fat, air-filled rubber tyres. "Those tyre tracks end right at those wheels, don't they?" Dougie asked.

"Oh, you're a right proper Sherlock Holmes, you are," Henry replied.

Chapter 12
Radio Silence

They stood in stunned silence, just staring at the radio: three separate components covered in dials, knobs, and switches, still bolted in its shipping crate. Reggie, feeling a bit sick to his stomach, cautiously stepped closer. The wooden crate had no obvious markings, place of manufacture, or origin of delivery. Nor did it have an addressee.

There was an attached pair of headphones, a crank handle, and a slide-out Morse Code key. The front of the machine was marked.

"Wireless Set No. 19 Mk 3, RAC," Henry read aloud.

"What's RAC?" Dougie asked.

Reggie shook his head. "Not sure, but all the writing on these switches is English, not German."

"Maybe so," said Freddie, "but be it German or English, the bigger questions are who does it belong to, and what's it doing here?"

"Or who are they talking to, and what are they saying?" Reggie raised his eyebrows. "The range on this—it might be able to reach ships in the Channel."

"Or U-boats under it," Henry added. "Great way to tell a roaming wolf pack where and when to find the convoys."

"Well, I know one thing," Reggie spoke up. "Whoever put it down here went to the trouble of hiding it deep off the main entrance and round two corners. It wasn't meant to be seen by just glancing down either passageway."

"Do you think it belongs to—" Freddie stopped himself before he said the name and raised an eyebrow back at Reggie.

"Dunno. But I suppose anything is possible. Look at him." He nodded his head towards the crypt wall, where Willy, in the middle of an episode, had dropped to his knees to steady himself. Jack handed the woozy boy his canteen for a swig.

"Maybe Willy's been right about our new Father Hawkins all along."

"Patrol, form up round Willy," Reggie ordered. They did so. "We don't know who put that here or why, so until we find out, mum's the word. Forget you saw it. Forget we were even in here for now. All hands in."

They put their hands in, and Reggie squeezed them together. "On our honour to St. Michael, we promise to keep this information as most secret. Talk about it to no one but each other, and only when you're sure there's no chance of being overheard. To this we swear."

They all nodded.

"Good. Now let's get out of here ... before someone comes along." He didn't need to specify the someone he was referring to.

**

They gathered in the dormitory, trying to process what they had just found. "I suppose you know what to do next," Reggie said to Willy as he studied the sketch he'd drawn in the catacombs.

"Getting a look at the bottom of some shoes ought to come first," Willy said.

"Yes, but you know whose shoes you should check first, don't you?" Dougie asked, then the answer. "Mr. McKenna."

They all looked at him with the same blank stares he'd seen from them so many time before. "What?" he asked.

"Mr. McKenna?" Jack repeated. "Are you daft or something?"

"Well, he is the caretaker," Dougie said, "so it makes sense that he might be the one who's been walking around down there."

"That's not bad thinking, Dougie," Henry said. "But the first question you should ask is what need old Bob would have for a new transmitter and radio receiver?"

"The bigger question is why would he—or anyone else for that matter—hide it in our catacombs?" Freddie spoke up. "We were sent down there to make the place ready for villagers, so whoever put it there would have to know we'd eventually find it."

That was sound logic to Reggie's ears. "So then, it would have to be someone who didn't know the catacombs would be used as an air raid shelter." Reggie said.

"But everyone knows that, it's been in the planning for months," Henry replied.

"Or is that why it's there in the first place?" Freddie asked. "To keep it safe from air raids."

Reggie wanted answers, but they just kept coming up with were more questions.

"Okay, let's keep this simple, focus on what we know and not speculate." Reggie instructed.

"What does that mean?" Dougie asked Henry in a whisper.

"Guess," Henry answered.

"No, just tell me."

"Speculate means 'guess'," Reggie answered him. "Let's not guess but instead focus on what we can support with evidence, like that shoe print. That's where we start looking. If we find that shoe, we find the person who brought in that transmitter. Once we know that, we can start working out who's on the receiving end."

Chapter 13
<u>Meeting Miss Lucy</u>

It was just past dawn the following morning. Sunlight was starting to creep into the darkest corners of the room.

POM-POM-POM-POM!

Their beds shook. Bright light flashed outside. Concussions rattled the tall windows in their frames. Each boy sat bolt upright in bed, their heads turned towards the windows, bewilderment and fear in their eyes. All but Freddie, who remained curled up under his covers, an unmoving lump.

"What in Mike's name was that?" asked Dougie, eyes-wide on Reggie. Reggie moved to the windows that faced north. "Are we under attack?"

POM-POM-POM-POM!

The pounding noise sounded again, and as it did, the northern sky flashed with light.

"I don't hear any air raid sirens. Maybe it's a surprise attack," Henry guessed nervously.

"It's the AA gun," Freddie said from under his warm blankets. "Why are they firing that thing now?" He rolled over with a huff, pulling his pillow over his head as he did.

The other boys joined Reggie at the window, waiting for the next volley. They didn't have to wait long.

POM-POM-POM-POM!

"Wow! Did you see those streaks?" Jack asked, his hands pressed full against the glass. Reggie smacked him on the head. Remembering himself, Jack removed his hands, then lifted the front of his shirt and began to wipe his hand prints off the window, only smudging them, making the mess worse.

Reggie shook his head. "You're cleaning that later."

Willy raced to his wardrobe and started dressing quickly.

"What are you doing?" Dougie asked. He already knew the answer, but he never let that stand in his way of asking a stupid question. "You're not going to the gun—are you?"

"I want to see what's going on," Willy responded.

Reggie turned to the small boy. "We've been given direct orders from Father Hawkins to stay away from that thing. You heard it, too. I was there," Reggie reminded him.

"No," corrected Willy, "what he said was not to lay a single finger on it, so I'm just going to watch. No harm in that, is there? Besides, I'm sure the gunners and army men will take good care of me."

"Is that why you're wearing your uniform?" Dougie asked.

"Yes," he answered excitedly, "maybe if they see I'm a Scout they'll let me get closer." He gave Reggie a quick glance, expecting to find a look of disapproval. He wasn't disappointed. Reggie stood shaking his head, his arms locked across his chest in disgust.

"Brilliant idea Willy," Dougie agreed.

"I don't want to pull rank," Reggie threatened, "but I will. We were given a direct order. That thing is dangerous and off limits."

"Let them go." Freddie growled in his rough early morning voice. "Better yet, why not join them so I can get back to sleep?"

POM-POM-POM-POM! More shaking, more window rattling.

"Fat chance of that," Reggie said. "That gun is loud."

Willy finished dressing and grabbed his roller skates. "Well, I'm going. Anyone else coming with me?"

"Wait for me, I'm coming," Dougie said. He sprang into action, rushing from the window to put on his uniform.

"Well, if you two are going ..." chimed in Henry.

"Mutiny in the dormitory, aye?" Reggie asked. The lump that was Freddie started shaking with laughter in his bed. "Fine, just go then," Reggie said. "But when Father Hawkins has harsh words for you, I'm going to say 'I told you so' and not feel the slightest bit bad about it."

The other boys carried on dressing, as if they hadn't heard a single word of his warning.

"Fine, fine. Go if you want—"

POM-POM-POM-POM!

Like the Pied Piper, the artillery fire echoed again.

"What's the fuss?" Freddie asked. "There are obviously gunners manning the thing. Do you honestly think they'll allow any of you to get in harm's way? I'm sure Father wouldn't mind, knowing there are trained professionals on duty," he added, still unmoved from his bed.

Reggie reconsidered. Freddie was right. No way would any of those men let the boys get anywhere near the deadly weapon.

"Fine." Reggie relented with a huff. "If you're all going to go, then I better go with you. A squad of dolts, you are."

"Now that sounds like sense," Freddie said. "And when you get there, tell them to bugger off and shut it down. People in this village are trying to sleep!"

***

There were multiple ways out of the home, the front door being most direct but also most likely to get them noticed, which, for this excursion, Reggie preferred they not be. That way no one would bother to ask them where they were off to. They left via the kitchen back door and started their short trip to the anti-aircraft artillery installation.

The installation was being constructed as a flak gun position and had several small underground bunkers that were connected by tunnels. The boys climbed the slope of the embankment that surrounded the first platform. That's when the gun came into view. It was a big thing—black steel with a single long, fluted barrel pointing skyward. It had four wheels used to haul it, but they were raised off the ground as the gun was set in a stationary position, supported by four heavy steel stabilising extensions.

Two gunners sat in rear seats close to the ground, one on either side of the thick barrel. Each had their hands on a crank and were working them independently of each other. One of the men in the gunner's chair cranked his arms to raise or lower the gun vertically from 0 to 90 degrees, and operated the foot trigger. The gunner seated opposite him used his crank to rotate the gun horizontally, allowing 360 degree movement. Between them both, there wasn't a spot in the sky below 15,000 feet the gun couldn't cover. In front of each was an identical, large round web-like sight through which to aim at a target. Behind them, three more men worked to keep the gun supplied with ammunition, handling full magazines of four rounds each that would be dropped into the top of the breech as quickly as they could manage.

The concussion from each burst of fire slammed them hard in the chests. The blast of fire from the barrel flashed white against the dark morning sky. Adrenaline flooded their veins. The five stood slack-jawed at the heavy war machine before them.

Without warning, the boys found themselves being dragged down off the embankment backward by their neckerchiefs. When they reached the bottom of the embankment the pulling stopped.

They scrambled to their feet and turned. Before them stood two men, wearing khakis and green berets, one with a submachine gun and the other a rifle, slung over their shoulders.

"Sweet Holy Mary! What're you trying to do, get yourselves killed?" It was Mr. Benedict and Mr. Steeves, both villagers who knew the tykes.

Reggie stammered. "We were just trying to—"

"I know what ya was just trying to do, and the way ya went about it makes no sense a-tall!" Mr. Steeves was yelling. Muffler's the size of tin cans covered his ears. "You never approach the exterior embankment of the gun platform when the crew is firing! Always approach from the bunker or the dugout, through the open doors!" He pointed at the skull-and-crossbones DANGER: KEEP OFF signs the boys hadn't paid any attention to.

"What are you lads doing here? You know, we've got strict in-

78

structions from Father Hawkins. This place is off limits to everyone, especially you lot," Mr. Benedict said.

"We're just curious," replied Reggie. "You gents woke us up with all the noise."

"Yeah, sorry about that, but it can't be helped at present. This is only temporary until this battery is complete." The boys stared up the embankment at the large gun. "This is the latest in triple A. Can fire almost as fast a machine gun, it can. We're just working on getting the hang of it. If you promise not to mention it to Father Hawkins, I can give you scouts a closer look. Would you like that?"

"Would we?" Dougie asked, glancing at Willy.

Smiling, Willy answered for them all. "You bet we would."

***

Mr. Steeves lead them down a short tunnel and into the dugout. Though incomplete, it was already stocked with crates of small arms, flat Brodie helmets, and gas masks. There was a table with a radio, a crank field telephone, and various maps and charts hung from the concrete walls. Stores of rations, water, and first aid supplies were neatly stacked on shelves. A dart board hung on one of the walls.

Although most of the installation was still under construction, with various equipment and building supplies scattered about, there was already a portrait of the prime minister hanging next to a framed photo of the King, in his full military dress uniform.

"Blimey," Dougie said. "This place is like a war zone."

Henry laughed. "This place is a war zone, you pea-brain."

"You lucky lads are just in time. We're going to do our first timed test, loading and firing for a full 30 seconds, as fast as she can. That don't happen often because ammo is in tight supply. Here"—he handed each a pair of mufflers—"stick these on your ears, or you're in for a nasty headache." He also handed out goggles for their eyes, and round Brodie helmets for their heads. They felt like kids in a candy shop.

Once dressed in their safety gear Mr. Steeves said "Come on, I'll show you our pride and joy." He led them out of the dugout and up a narrow tunnel towards the gun platform. Reggie eyed the sub-machine gun the man carried over his shoulder. It was like the kind he had seen in pictures of gangsters from America. It had a wooden front grip and a round drum magazine. "Mr. Steeves, is that a gangster gun, from America?"

"This?" He unshouldered it and held it up for the boys to see. "Aye, this here is a Thompson submachine gun. It is American indeed, Reggie. Made famous by blokes like John Dillinger and that Al Capone feller from Chicago. This beauty can spit out eight hundred rounds a minute, if you got an eight-hundred-round magazine, that is. This drum here"—he tapped it with his fingers—"only holds fifty. And when it starts spittin' 'em out, it clacks out one hell of a *rat-tat-tat*. That's why it's also called 'the Chicago typewriter'."

At the end of the tunnel, they exited into a small concrete trench which led to the gun platform. The steel behemoth was now silent, smoking, and ticking, with helmeted, gloved, and goggled men crawling all over it.

"Now, lads, let me introduce you to the Bofors Quick Firing 40 millimetre Mark III two-pounder anti-aircraft gun, also known as 'Miss Lucy'. Ain't she lovely? She's all by her lonesome here until they install the large four-and-a-half inch flak guns and Predictor for this installation."

When the time for the test came, the six members of the gun crew dismounted and retreated into the dugout. Mr. Steeves moved the boys to a safe distance. "Stand back and get ready," he said.

At the designated time, Mr. Steeves started blowing his whistle and pressed the start button on the stop-watch in his hand. The gun crew rushed from the dugout, up the trench and literally jumped onto the gun, each in his designated position. In less than half-a-second the gun fired its first volley.

POM-POM-POM-POM! POM-POM-POM-POM!

Again and again the gun fired and recoiled, fired and recoiled. The men operating the weapon looked well at ease, as if they had done this hundreds of times before. Far from being the clunky machine they expected, this anti-aircraft gun was a finely tuned piece of technology. The gunners were spinning cranks quickly, causing the barrel to effortlessly rise and fall and turning the entire rig smoothly on its axis. The recoil from each shot was absorbed by the barrel so there was no rattling from of the large gun. The loaders moved as fast as they could to keep the steel machine spitting as much hot lead skyward, as fast as a Bren gun, with heavy spent shells dropping all around.

From behind their round goggles the boys watched with unblinking eyes. Another surge of adrenaline coursed through their veins. Their hearts pounded. Sweat broke on their skin. The powerful display was as frightening as it was thrilling. The sound assaulted their ears, the smell burned their nose, the concussions rocked their innards.

When time was up Mr. Steeves blew his whistle again.

The gun fell silent but for the steady ticking of the hot metal barrel expanding.

The boys were trembling slightly. They were covered in soot, cordite and machine oil. Reggie realised the jig was up. There would be no way to keep this little field trip a secret now. Their smell alone would give them away. That's when he noticed the gunners were all wearing coveralls.

"40 shots in 30 seconds. Not bad. So, what do you think?" Mr. Steeves removed his mufflers, pulled off his goggles and letting them dangle around his neck. The boys did the same with theirs.

"I think I'm glad not flying for the Luftwaffe right now," Jack answered. His ears were ringing, regardless of the mufflers that had protected them. "Aren't those shells going to come down somewhere?" Willy asked.

"Four miles effective range, as the bird flies. That puts them down in the fields miles north of here." He gestured in that direction. "The whole area's clear o' folks, marked as one giant no go zone," Mr. Steeves said. "So you boys best remember to say far away from that area—no camping or getting overly curious, like today." He looked at them sternly. "I might bend the rule here at the gun and let you come up, but all you'll find out there is trouble. Now you best be on your way, and remember, mum's the word on this to Father Hawkins, aye?"

"Yes, sir." Reggie answered. The others nodded their agreement. No chance they'd risk Mr. Steeves's neck when he'd been kind enough to extend it for a private show with Miss Lucy.

Chapter 14
Operation Bob-a-job

Because Willy would be making the call on matching the shoe prints, he felt it was his duty to figure out a way to make that happen. He couldn't just walk up to a bloke and ask to look at the bottom of his shoes. That would be odd. But he could walk up to a bloke and ask, "Bob-a-job, gov'na? We're in need of some money for overnight supplies. Would you like a clean and shine?"

"Oh, I say," Vicar Davis said. "This is a pleasant surprise," he pushed himself away from his desk and inspected his black shoes. Willy could see they were scuffed, scrapped and in need of some attention indeed. VD kicked them off and waved Willy over.

"I'll have these shined up for you in no time, Vicar." He picked up the man's shoes.

"Do stop in my room and grab my other pair if you like, and there's a second bob in it for you." Unbeknownst to the Vicar, he had just willingly handed over possibly incriminating evidence, and did so with a smile. Easy-peasy this, Willy thought proudly.

***

He repeated the scene just as successfully with each of the other men at the home. Mr. McKenna, Mr. Greene, Father Hawkins, even Maurice, all sat or worked in only their stocking feet, as a very pleased Willy gathered up their shoes with not a single questions asked or suspicion raised.

Back in the dormitory, all the collected pairs of shoes were lined up, ready to be examined by Willy's talented eye. He had eliminated the Sisters as suspects outright, as their shoes were simply too small to make the large prints. For large ladies, they had very dainty feet.

"Not to mention" Willy informed the others, "those black shoes they wear with the big chunky heels leave very distinctive shoe prints."

What he was looking for was a man's shoe, roughly eleven to twelve inches long, with an exact nail pattern on the bottom. One of Willy's drawings showed a right shoe print missing a nail third from the tip. The other shoe print showed a smear.

"This," Willy surmised, "is probably caused by the bloke walking funny, pulling his leg to the left slightly. His shoe should be worn away on this outer edge here." He pointed at the edge of VD's shoe as an example. "This shoe isn't worn on this edge, so Vicar Davis is a no go, or at least this pair of his shoes is cleared."

Freddie went straight to Father Hawkins shoes and flipped them over. "Worn edge? Check. Other shoe missing nail? Check. It's Father Hawkins."

"Wait," Willy protested. "We have to eliminate the rest of the pairs of shoes to be sure!"

"We haven't time for all these Bulldog Drummond games, Willy. Here, look for yourselves." The group gathered round Hawkins' shoes.

Willy took them and laid them out next to each of the drawings he had made. It was a perfect match. The nail was gone, and the edge was worn away.

"We should put a new nail in there before we give them back," Dougie said.

"Seriously, you care about the nail?" Freddie asked.

"Well, yeah. Any job worth doing is worth doing well, I say. 'Sides, we're not supposed to even know about the"—in a whisper—"you know what in the you know where. We still need to pretend we know nothing."

"That shouldn't be too hard for you to pretend, Dougie," Henry said. The boys laughed.

"Freddie's right, Willy. Maybe you should have started by checking Father Hawkins's shoes *before* we collected everyone else's." Reggie said. "Now we have a pile of shoes to polish. Serves us right, I suppose." He picked up a brush and one of the shoes. "At least we're being paid."

Jack spoke up. "Yes, so it's worth it. Most importantly, we now know who owns that radio."

"Indeed," Willy said, proud his plan had worked, though his head was still filled with troubling questions. If Father Hawkins was in charge round here now, and if he was a German spy, what would he do when he found out they were on to his secret? Who could they tell without putting everyone in danger? They had to sleep under the same roof with the man. For the love of Mike, they were at his mercy.

Chapter 15
Best-Laid Plans

"Right. So who's interested in taking an overnighter?" They startled. It was Father Hawkins.

Since they all were heads down, noses buried in their school books, none had seen him stick his head in the dormitory doorway.

"Really?" Dougie asked. "As in camp out in the woods all night? Alone?" He swallowed hard. "With you?"

"Well, it is called an overnighter for a reason, isn't it?" He stepped in the room. All studying of books gave way to studying Father Hawkins. They eyed him suspiciously. "And yes, we'll all be together."

"Tonight?" Reggie asked. It was already well into the evening.

"No, not tonight. There's planning and preparing needs to be done. Haven't you ever been on a proper overnighter before?"

"Well, once VD let us set up some blankets, and we made some tents and slept in the courtyard," Henry answered. "But by morning we were all back in our beds. It was ghastly cold that night."

"No, that doesn't count," Father said as he took a seat on Reggie's bed. "If we're going to have a successful camping trip we need to plan for it, prepare for it. We need tents and sleeping rolls. We need to plan a menu for meals, secure the provisions and cooking gear, and pack up rucksacks. There's a lot that goes into a proper outdoor excursion. Let's make it three days hence."

"Maurice can handle that. He's a great cook." Jack said.

"Nothing doing," spoke up Hawkins. "This is your trip, so it's your responsibility, not Maurice's. As a matter of fact, I'm going to instruct him that he's not to help you in the slightest. Being a proper Scout is about being self-sufficient, figuring things out for yourself, and then following through. Maurice already knows how to prepare a menu. None of you boys do."

"But I bet we could," Willy said optimistically. "Yeah, course we can. We eat every day. All we need is food for each meal—meat and veg and such."

Freddie added, "We've been eating three meals a day for our whole lives—well, most of them. If we can't come up with meals for two nights, we're a pretty sorry lot."

"Two nights?" asked Father Hawkins, catching the switch.

"Well, if we're going to go on a proper expedition, it should at least be for a couple of nights. Seems not worth all the trouble for one silly night in the woods," Freddie argued, sounding as if the decision was to be taken for granted.

"Two nights?" Father Hawkins asked again, eyebrows raised.

"Oh, yes!" Dougie shouted.

"Please? Can we?" Willy begged.

"Well, I'm fine with one night. I like my bed," Jack added.

"Two nights, eh? Well, in that case, we've just doubled our work." Father Hawkins said with a wink and smile at Freddie. The boys broke into an enthusiastic cheer. It had been his intent all along to let the boys stay an extra night, so they ruined their own surprise, but no matter, he had others up his sleeve.

After Hawkins left, Reggie spoke. "Listen, I know we have to act like nothing is going on, but ease up on the enthusiastic cheers until we know he deserves the fanfare. Especially until we find out more about the you-know-what in the you-know-where."

***

The next day was spent planning a menu for the two-night outing, packing meals and filling backpacks with extra socks and rain gear they'd never wear, utensils, meals, sleeping rolls, and tents, all that would never be used.

As Father Hawkins had instructed, they planned a six-meal menu on their own, with Maurice diligently watching to *oui-oui* or *pooh-pooh* their epicurean choices, based on their cooking skill and ease of preparation over a campfire. Through it all, he stepped in only when needed, as when he showed them the proper way to wrap and tie the food for storage. He also approved their final selection of cooking pots and utensils.

The mess the boys had created in the kitchen was immense, with open cupboards, piles of pots, and bits of spilled mess everywhere Maurice laid his eyes. Though his kitchen was a disaster, he couldn't have been more thrilled; it was a joy to see his boys so excited for their trip. And when their two-hour menu-meal-planning exercise was complete, they returned his kitchen to the exact condition in which they had found it, not a spoon out of place or a speck of flour to be seen.

***

In the dormitory, their rucksacks leaned against their beds in a state of partial readiness, filled with things they would need to make it through two days in the wilderness, although truth be told, they were only venturing three-quarters of a mile to a wooded area a bit beyond The Moors; at least, that was the plan. They were preparing for bed when Father Hawkins joined them. He had heard good things from Maurice. "*Ils sont préparés, oui.* They will not starve."

"I'd love to take you boys farther, on a nice march, a real hiking trip, good and far, but with the situation being as it is"—he pointed up—"Hitler's bombers are on the prowl, so we need to stay close to the village." The news diminished their excitement not one iota. "Should we hear the sirens start, we'll need to hightail it back to the church in a big hurry. We'll be sorely needed." The sirens would give them ample time to make it back to St. Michael's as the bombers always took some time to reach this deep.

"Duty first," Reggie reminded them.

"'Sides, who wants to be stuck in the open when bombs are falling?" Freddie added. Everyone nodded, Father Hawkins included. "We can cover that distance very quickly, if need be."

"And Willy'll beat every one of us." Henry laughed.

"All right, well, get some sleep. We've got more work tomorrow." They hustled to their beds. "Good night, lads. Don't forget to say your prayers." He clicked off the light and closed the door.

***

"Do you think he knows about the you-know-what yet?" Dougie whispered from his bed. "I mean, that we found it?"

"Who knows?" Jack replied. "But if he has found out, this camping trip might just be his way of getting us away from home, to someplace deep in the woods, where he can get rid of us for good," Jack whispered.

Reggie shivered in his bed as a cold chill ran up his spine. Jack could be right. It was true, once Hawkins got them away from the Home they would really have to keep their guard up. Out there, anything might be possible.

Chapter 16
Mixed Signals

Late the following afternoon, Jack made his way through the village to spend some of their earned bobs on supplies for the overnighter. He rounded a corner, shortcutting through the empty lot between the bakery and Dr. Garrett's office. There, three boys in identical Boy Scout uniforms had two smaller children, a boy and a little girl, up against a wall, rifling through their pockets. Jack was instantly incensed at the sight. "Hey! Leave them alone!" he roared.

The scouts startled and turned, backing away from their victims.

Jack approached the small children. "Are you all right?" he asked, his face aflame.

"Blimey, what have we here?" One of the scouts asked at seeing Jack dressed in his full kit. "Looks like a Little Orphan Annie commando out begging for scraps." Whilst all attention was on Jack, the children saw their chance to run away and promptly took it.

Before he could turn round, Jack was shoved hard from behind at his shoulders. His head snapped backwards and his helmet was sent flying. He spilled onto the ground, arms forward to break his fall, but both knees were scraped and torn against the hard ground. He scrambled fast to his feet and turned to his tormenters.

It was Victor Knolls, patrol leader of the Boy Scouts, Ronan Academy Troop, dressed in his full kit, minus his round-brimmed campaign hat. Beside him were two taller boys, Leonard and Christopher, both dressed similarly. Leonard bent down, picked up Jack's pith helmet, and put it on his own head. The three large boys surrounded him. Their number, not their size, gave him pause.

"What the hell"—a shove to his chest—"do you think you're playing at?" He looked Jack over, paying attention to the assorted collection of badges and ribbons on the small boy's white sash.

"There's one Boy Scout troop in this village, and we're it," Victor said.

As Victor spoke, Leonard started grabbing at Jack's St. Michael medal. "Here, what's this rubbish?" he said with a sneer, pulling at it. Because it was pinned to his sash, Jack was pulled forwards along with it. Victor leaned in. "St. Michael, protect us. Aw, isn't that cute?" He laughed. "Protect us, St. Michael," he whimpered in the mocking tone of a weakling—or as Jack heard it—a begging orphan. That only stoked his anger.

"Don't you dare touch that." Jack sneered, and shoved Christopher's hand away—

SMACK!

Victor's slap to his face caught Jack by surprise, but had the same effect as pouring petrol on a bonfire. Heat rose and his ears burned purple with hot blood. Full-on rage blew away the last remaining bit of care he had for his own well-being. He gritted his teeth and wrinkled his nose. As hard and fast as he could, he smashed his shin into Christopher's groin with such force the tall boy instantly doubled over, his pained face now level with Jack's. Seizing the opportunity, Jack full-fisted Christopher square in the nose. There was a sickening *POP* when the cartilage in Christopher's nose gave way. Blood splattered Jack's fist as it gushed from both of the larger boy's nostrils. He dropped to the ground at Jack's feet. Useless sack, Jack thought, proud he'd pulled it off. He was trembling with anger. Two left. Now that's more like it, he thought, suddenly emboldened. It was no longer three-on-one. And two-on-one were odds he'd faced and beaten before.

"You little shit!" Leonard grabbed Jack, threw him to the ground, then leapt on top of him. Jack scrambled for his whistle, but before he could reach it, Leonard's strong, teenaged legs pinned his arms to his sides.

Taking stock of the quickly changing situation, Jack realised it wasn't good. There's nothing worse than being small, he thought. He felt defenceless, but his rage still burned, so he felt far from hopeless. Rage might cloud one's judgement—but in a fight—it's a lot more useful than hopelessness.

Christopher was in a heap next to him, bleeding, coughing, unable to speak, tears flowing. His red, watery eyes bulged, and he rocked slightly back and forth in the dirt, hands cupping his aching groin as the pain radiated across his face in waves. Now it was Leonard's turn to slap Jack.

SMACK! A stinging palm across the left cheek.

SMACK! A knuckle-filled backhand across the right. He felt his cheek bone start to swell.

"You don't mess with us, especially with no guardian angels around to protect you."

Leonard leaned directly over Jack's face, and let a long string of spit drip from his tongue right onto the smaller boy's mouth. The sun glinted off Leonard's dangling whistle, catching Jack's eye. It was hanging mere inches from his lips. A new strategy sparked in his head. If it was going to work, he needed Leonard's unwitting help.

"Mmmm, yummy." Jack said as he licked the boy's spit from his lips.

"Ewww!" Disgust washed over Victor's face, but Leonard just laughed.

"Hahahaha! Oh, you like that, do you, little boy? You're going to love this." He snorted hard, then hocked up a generous ball of phlegm into his mouth. Jack focused his attention on the boy's dangling whistle. Just a little lower.

"Bugger off!" Jack taunted.

"Well, you're not very bright," Victor said, "but you sure got guts, I'll give you that."

Leonard leaned over, closely lining up his mouth directly over

Jack's. The whistle was as close as it was going to get. In a flash, Jack raised his head from the ground and he locked his teeth and lips around Leonard's whistle. He huffed three sharp blasts as hard as he could, and then three more before Leonard slapped the whistle out of his mouth. "Ahh, right in my bloody ear!" Leonard howled, putting his hand to his buzzing ear.

He hit Jack again—harder—just for fun. Jack shaped his lips and tongue and blasted out a whistle of his own making, sounding exactly like a song bird only much louder—an eardrum-piercing song bird.

"Shut up!" Leonard yelled, cocking his hand back.

SMACK!

Jack stopped whistling.

***

Not far away, Dougie asked Henry, "Did you hear that?"

"Of course. It's Willy." His eyes opened wide.

"Where was he going? What was he doing today?"

"Dunno. But wherever he is, that was him."

"Go get the others. I'm going towards the direction it came from," Dougie said.

"Don't do anything stupid," Henry reminded him.

"Well, that's not possible, is it?"

"Yeah, right." Henry tore off down the road towards the home. Dougie headed for Jack's trouble signal.

***

Jack watched Christopher struggle to find his feet. His knees wobbled. He wretched a couple of times as if he were going to throw up. His nose was bleeding. Blood and tears streaked his cheeks. He still hadn't said anything or collected himself, but Jack knew as soon as he did, a retaliatory kick in the balls was coming his way, as payback.

"This is an ace lid, Jackie-girl," Leonard said, adjusting Jack's pith helmet, now perched on his own head. "I might have to keep this as a trophy." He reached for the St. Michael medal and started to unpin it from Jack's sash.

"No!" Jack yelled. He kicked and shifted, rocked and rolled. Leo was forced to hold on, like a rodeo cowboy trying to break a bucking bronco.

"What right do you *lowly orphans* have to your own Scout troop in our village? None. We're the only scouts round here, the Boy Scouts," Victor lectured from behind Leonard. "We were first in this village. It's ours, and until you stupid orphans realise it, I guess we're going to have to keep reminding you."

"St. Michael's beat the Boy Scouts by six hundred years, you bloody moron!" Jack corrected him.

***

Dougie, feeling every bit the coward, heard it all from safety, hidden around the corner of Dr. Bennett's building. He'd peeked round to the empty lot and saw Leonard sitting on Jack, slapping away at him. He wanted to rush in, but he also saw blood. He didn't know whose, but there was blood, and a lot of it. Mostly on that bloke Christopher on the ground. Bet Jack did that, he thought, it's why he's getting slapped.

Victor was there, too, going on about Boy Scout this and that whilst beating up a little boy. What does he know? He doesn't deserve to wear that uniform anyway. Come on, tykes, hurry up.

SMACK!

That was enough. Regardless of what those others would do to him, he wouldn't let Jack get slapped again. He stepped round the corner when from behind—

"Dougie. You found him?" It was Freddie—and Reggie, Henry, and Willy—dressed to the nines in their kits. He smiled at such a fine sight and gave silent thanks. Atta boy, St. Mike!

***

Angrily Leonard ripped the St. Michael medal from Jack's sash, tearing it. Jack watched horrified, as he tossed the small medallion to Victor. "Here. A trophy for you, too."

"Great." Victor replied. "One down, five to go." He pinned it to his own shirt. "Now St. Mikey can protect me." Victor said. Leonard laughed.

93

"Oh, I wouldn't bet on that anytime soon, if I were you." It was Freddie's voice. It sounded like the Heavenly Hosts to Jack ears. Leonard stopped laughing and let his grip relax for a split second. Instantly, Jack sensed an opportunity to gain the upper hand and snatched it, freeing his arms and shoving the bigger boy off of him.

Victor turned.

Before him stood the other five medals for his taking, each accompanied by the Scout of St. Michael it was pinned to.

***

"Did you hear that?" Boy Scout Spencer asked his troop mate Richard.

"What? The whistles? Yeah I heard 'em."

"We should go check it out. Who do you think it is?"

"Dunno. Victor, Leo, and Chris are running about somewhere. Let them do it."

SMACK! Across the back of the head.

"Oww! What'd you do that for?" Richard asked, rubbing his head.

"Because we're scouts and that signal means trouble, three short blasts on the whistle is a call for help! What's the point of having these stupid things if we don't use them?" Spencer replied.

"Well, you don't have to hit me. Boy Scouts are supposed to be kind, you know."

***

Christopher tried his best to stand yet again, but crashed back down to the ground. He attempted to wipe clean his face of the blood and tears, but all he really did was smear himself into a bloody, snotty mess. Jack must have had a go at him before the others jumped him, Reggie surmised. Ah Jack, our terrier. He's small, but he's vicious.

Jack stood menacingly over Leonard, who was now cowering at his feet. Reggie watched as Jack kicked dirt in Leonard's face and snatched his helmet back. Returning it to his head, he leaned in with a pointed finger. "If you ever touch that helmet again," he pointed at Christopher, "you'll get what he got. And *don't* call me Jackie!" he growled.

That's our Jack, Reggie smiled.

Jack marched over and took a spot between Freddie and Reggie. "Guess you're all right then," Freddie said, not taking his eyes off Victor. "Yeah, fine—I think." His face was red from the slapping assault, but it was hard to tell because he was also flushed from his racing heart.

"What'd you do to the big one?" Reggie asked, already guessing as he watched Christopher holding himself. The large boy on the ground was cloaked in the pain, vulnerability and humiliation that every boy the world over works very hard to avoid.

Reggie looked Jack over; dirt, scratches and scrapes, but all the pieces basically still there, minus one small, yet hardly insignificant piece of kit.

"I got a good one in his bits. I think I bruised my shin." Jack said with a grin. Freddie, still eyeing the other boys, smiled too.

"That's not fighting fair, Jack." Freddie reminded him. "That's a low blow."

"So is three-on-one." Jack replied, "One good turn of unsportsmanlike conduct deserves another. Eye-for-an-eye, straight from the Bible."

"I hope when he slapped you on the right, you offered the left." Freddie said.

"I didn't offer, but he sure took." Jack replied, rubbing his swollen, throbbing cheekbone.

"Where's your medal?" Reggie asked. Jack turned and pointed his finger at Victor. Reggie squinted and fixed his gaze, like a radar beam, on Jack's shimmering silver medal dangling off Victor's left breast pocket.

***

As Spencer and Richard were making their way towards the distress signal, Boy Scouts Seymour, Oscar, William, and Simon joined them at an intersection. They now numbered six.

"Did you lot blow that signal?" Oscar asked.

"No, none of us. Did you?" Simon asked.

"Would I have asked you if we had, stupid?"

Simon shrugged.

"We heard it, too," Richard replied.

"Well, if it wasn't you, and it wasn't us…"

"It's got to be Victor, Christopher or Leonard. Come on, let's find them."

"Why don't they blast again? To give us another fix."

"Maybe they can't," Spencer said.

"Let's head off. It'll be dark soon." Simon said. They headed in the direction of the whistles.

***

"Victor." Reggie approached him slowly. He was face-to-face with the 14 year-old boy who was wearing Jack's medal on his pocket.

"Patrol Leader Victor, if you please," the boy spat. It was easy to tell he was one of those academy boys. The way they talked was a dead giveaway. "We're the real Boy Scout patrol in this village, not some fake, orphan-made-up rubbish. It's not our fault you have no parents." Victor said with a sneer.

"That's right," Reggie replied, "haven't you heard of us? We're the 'Hawkhurst Gang.' No parents to tell us what we can or can't do. No one to punish us for our misdeeds. We can do whatever we want and no one can stop us. And right now,"—he leaned in close and whispered threateningly—"we want *you* to take off that medal and put it back where you found it."

At that moment, six Ronan Boy Scouts rounded the corner into the lot. Everyone startled but Reggie, who didn't so much as flinch. Suddenly outnumbered by three, the tykes instinctively took up to a defensive position: semicircle facing the nine Boy Scouts. Jack covered Reggie— his catapult suddenly loaded, and drawn to let fly—with a bead on Victor's forehead.

"What's this?" asked a confused Scout Seymour, pushing his thick glasses up his long nose.

"This," Victor replied with a sneer, "is called being outnumbered, and"—to Reggie—"I think I'll be collecting the rest of those medals from you lasses now."

It took Reggie exactly half-a-second to size up Victor's reinforcements; Too Tall, Birdlegs, Chunker, Pretty Boy, Nose, and Goggles. His concern at being outnumbered instantly evaporated: no sweat, this crew.

"But you only have nine," Reggie taunted. "You'd better wait for the cavalry to arrive."

"They are the cavalry, you idiot," Victor snapped. "Don't they teach you anything in that so-called school of yours?"

"*This* is the cavalry?" Reggie asked, a smile spreading across his face. "In that case, Patrol Leader Victor," he laughed, "you'd better wait for the armoured division to show up." On cue, the tykes burst into a fit of laughter. Victor's face boiled.

"*Attack!*" Victor yelled.

FWAPP! The sound of Jack's slingshot echoed through the air.

***

Victor's head snapped back as the wooden ball connected directly above his right eye with a resounding *CRACK!*It split the skin, and a thin trail of blood trickled down, his eyebrow being the only thing stopping it from seeping into his eye.

The Ronan Boy Scouts not only did not attack, but actually took a step backwards.

Reggie and Dougie fingered their hanging hatchets, ready to draw. Willy had already drawn his. Henry twirled their troop banner flag like a bow staff, showing all that he was ready to use it like one, if need be. Jack reloaded his catapult and dropped to one knee, ready to launch at Victor's already bleeding forehead.

"This isn't what we want," Reggie said calmly, suddenly seeing the danger in this situation. Fifteen boys, boiling tempers and sharp weapons could easily lead to a very bad outcome; blood had already been spilled, and Jack had been the one to spill it - twice. "Three-on-one isn't a fair fight, especially when the *one* is our smallest. Where's the honour in that, Patrol Leader?" Reggie asked Victor. "Since when did being a Boy Scout and doing good turns include beating up outnumbered smaller boys?"

"We're the British Boy Scouts!" Victor screamed, his voice cracking. "This is our Scout district, and you can't join! It's as simple as that! The decision wasn't ours!"

No, thought Reggie, it was your snobby, rich fathers who decided.

"And we're the Scouts of St. Michael." Reggie said calmly. "We aren't here to steal your territory, or take your glory, we just … we want to be scouts and do our bit."

"Your *bit,*" Victor spat, "is to remember your place as orphans."

Jack made a chirping whistle: *incoming!*

"Oh, Vic, wrong answer," Reggie replied.

FWAPP!

CRACK! Another ball bounced off Victor's forehead.

"Ow! Stop it!" Victor screamed.

His reinforcements took a second step back.

Reggie glanced over his shoulder at Jack, who was kneeling with another ball loaded and ready fire. He winked at Reggie. Reggie gave him a pointed look that said, excellent shot, really, but come on, I'm trying to accomplish something here. He turned his attention back to Victor.

"Jack did not like that answer," Reggie said. "Since," he continued, "the cavalry over there seems a bit reluctant to join the fun, and my guess is the armoured division won't be arriving any time soon, maybe you should stop talking and just listen."

He stepped closer. "I'll tell you what. Let's do a swap. You put that medal back where it came from, and not only will Jack stop using his shot to pop your pimples, but I'll also have him dress you and your boy's wounds. Trust me, that's a good deal. He's deadly accurate with that thing."

Dougie and Willy smiled and nodded their agreement. Freddie continued to stand his ground, ready for anything.

Victor looked over his cavalry standing there, still grossly unaware of what they'd just walked up on.

"What an embarrassingly pathetic display." Victor conceded. "Nine of them and not a pair of balls in the lot. Well, except for Christopher, and look what they got him. At least you St. Michael's scouts have each other's back—like a real patrol—or like brothers would."

Victor glanced at Jack. He was crouched low to the ground, seated on one bent leg, the other stretched out in front of him. Whilst one eye was closed, the other was locked on his forehead through the gap of the wooden 'Y' held in his outstretched hand. The sling was pulled back with another one of those hard wooden balls ready to fire. He opened his other eye and winked at Victor.

Victor looked straight into Reggie's unblinking eyes. His hands went to his breast pocket, and he began to unpin Jack's medal. Reggie glanced over his shoulder. "Jack, bring your bag. We have wounded scouts here."

"Right," Henry said, "you broke 'em, you fix 'em." Dougie and Freddie sniggered.

As if the entire previous incident hadn't happened, Jack followed as ordered, unloaded and threw his catapult over his shoulder, and trotted fearlessly to where Reggie and Victor stood. Jack reached into his bag and pulled out a small bottle, a roll of gauze, and some pads.

 "Willy, here, take these pads to that one over there. Put them under his nose. Hold it until I finish with Patrol Leader Victor here." Willy rolled over to Christopher to do as he was told.

"Drop down—on your knees—so I can reach." Jack said. Victor did so. The British Boy Scouts now began to mill about each of the injured boys, watching Jack wipe, clean, and dress Victor's cut forehead. As Jack tended him, Victor reached up and pinned the medal back onto Jack's sash, exactly where it had been when this mess had started. Quite accidentally, he jabbed Jack's chest with the pin. "Sssss, ow, that hurts!" Jack said.

Victor smirked. "Sorry."

Jack poured alcohol on Victor's open wound. "Sssss, ow, *that* hurts!" Victor said.

Jack smirked. "Sorry."

"Oh, shut it, you big baby. That's just rubbing alcohol. It cleans it," Dougie said.

"I know what it's for. I have my first aid merit." Victor said. His vitriol was quickly evaporating. "Do you have one?" he asked, only slightly sarcastically.

"No, we don't have any badges. Just a handbook, but we all know that thing backwards and forwards, eh, lads?" Jack said.

"It's practically worn out," Henry added.

"We got it from Miss Goold's brother, Billy. He flies a Spit."

Dougie informed them. They all murmured their impressed approval.

"Is that where you got your kit?" Victor asked Freddie, admiring his blue RAF tunic.

"Yes, the lads at that base take pretty good care of us when it comes to things. All we have to do is ask," he said. "It helps having Miss Goold is about. They're keen on her, the lot of them."

"And sometimes we don't even have to ask, blokes bring stuff by all the time." Just then Willy rolled past, a pair of Mk III flying goggles perched atop his leather flying helmet, both also gifts from Pilot Officer Billy Goold.

"So you didn't steal any of it?" Coxey Jr. asked. "My father says folks in town think you lot got sticky fingers."

Jack applied more alcohol to Victor's head at the comment.

"Sssss, *ow!*" Victor cried. "*He* said it, not me!"

"Heavens no!" Dougie answered. "If we got caught stealing, Sister Noreen would skin us, hang us out to dry, and sell our hides for shoe leather. She's a tough bird, that one," he said.

"Aye, she would," the others agreed. All the Ronan Boy Scouts laughed.

"It's true," Reggie said. "If you think it's bad having two adults watching after you, try six sometime. Bloke can't take a leak without someone knowing."

"No fibbing?" Christopher asked, his voice squeaky through the gauze and his newly rearranged nose. "I thought you lot were the 'Hawkhurst Gang' and got the run of the mill."

The tykes chuckled. "Are you kidding?" Reggie asked. "That was nothing but a lot of blustering and bluffing."

"The only time we get the run is when there're errands to do or to get away from the Sisters when they're looking for a good-night kiss." Freddie said to Victor with a smirk.

The entire group laughed. "Really, you lads should come visit and see for yourselves sometime." Reggie said, extending an olive branch to the Ronan Boy Scouts. It was then that a distant air raid siren began to howl through the darkening sky.

WAR OFFICE

NOT TO BE COPIED OR REMOVED FROM THIS OFFICE

11 July 1940

FROM: PRIME MINISTER WINSTON CHURCHILL

TO: DR. HUGH DALTON, D.O.O., S.O.E.

    MAJOR GENERAL COLIN GUBBINS, S.O.E.

    AIR VICE MARSHAL KEITH PARK, R.A.F., S.O.E.

ANOTHER CHILLING REPORT. THIS IS THE TRANSCRIPT OF
A STATEMENT GIVEN BY POLISH NATIONAL WOLFRAM SPENGLER
REGARDING EVENTS WHICH TRANSPIRED IN THE TOWN OF KRA-
KOW, POLAND, ON 4 NOVEMBER 1939.

It was dark. I was sleeping. I do not know what
the time was. I hear a deep thumping, far in the distance. I sit up in my bed. It was getting closer. I
jump from bed und look out the window. My blood—it
went cold. I froze on that spot.

Up the street, I see walls of the houses flicker
with orange light, the thumping sound getting louder,
closer. Then I see them. They round the bend up the
street. He was at the head of a column of marching
boys, the flag bearer on his right. The thumping was
the pounding of their drums; und the flicker came from
their Fackeln—how you say—fire sticks? Torches!

I hear that before, but I don't believe it—if you
not send your boy, they will come und take him. But
I say no. No Nazi pigs will get mein boy. But I know
the truth already. They were coming for Joachim.

BOOM! BOOM! BOOM! [SOUND HEARD IS WITNESS POUNDING
ON THE TABLE] That pounding came on and on, like my
beating heart in my ears, a snake slithering up the

street, to my very own home, to devour mein boy. What could I do? Where could I hide him? These thought break my trance. I turn from the window and rush to his room.

Was ist es? My wife, she ask me. She was sitting up in the bed now too. I tell her, you stay and do not come out this room. To make sure, I lock it behind me so she cannot.

I rush into Joachim room. He is standing, looking out the window. Vater, he say. I never before see him look so scared—then the thumping halts—in front of unser Haus—our house. I clutch him to my side. He is trembling.

He start to cry. I bend down, and I hold his face and look at him strong. I say, Joachim, you listen to me. Kein Weinen—no crying—keine Tränen—no tears. If they see this, du bist tot. Do you know was das means? You are dead. No tears. Do not let them see. Nien. Never.

CRACK! CRACK! CRACK! Es klang—it sounded—like a rifle butt slammed on the door.

Joachim startled, and his eyes grow large. Do not be afraid, my son, I say. Be brave, do as they tell you, and all will be okay. I wipe away his tears, then my own. I take his hand and lead him down the stairs.

CRACK! CRACK! CRACK! So hard—the door, it rattled in its frame.

I moved to door. Joachim, he stand behind me.

Joachim Spengler! I know that voice. It was the Bastard.

In the name of the Führer, Adolf Hitler, open up!

I open the door a crack and look outside. My God, I say, then I open all the way. In front of our house they stood three lines deep—a large Halbkreis—how you say—half circle of boys in brown uniforms, bent-cross banners, flaming torches, drums, knives on each of their belts. There also was a group of big boys; they have thick wooden clubs.

Joachim Spengler! On the basis of the Second Execution Order of Article 4 of the Law of the Hitler Youth, you are hereby requested for duty, someone says.

I pushed Joachim back behind me more. Nein, no, I say, you cannot do this.

Oh, I can do many things, the Bastard, he say. Why was not he registered? As his father, guardian, and good citizen of the Reich it is your duty. He step closer to me. He screams in my face: WIE IST DEINE ANTWORT? SPRECHEN! WHAT IS YOUR ANSWER? SPEAK!

I need not explain my choices to you, boy, I say. I am the parent of this child, er gehört mir. [THUMP- ING SOUND IS WITNESS HITTING HIS OWN CHEST] He is mine.

Not anymore, Father. The Bastard say, and he laugh. He now belong to the Führer. Do you know Sec- tion 12 to Article 4? It is my favourite section. He stepped forwards again, glaring into my eyes. He shouted at my face. It was for everyone to hear, the neighbours who gathered at the Aufregung, ah, the commotion.

Whoever malevolently prevents or attempts to pre- vent a juvenile from serving in the Hitler Youth will be punished with prison!

There was no sound but for the flapping of their torches.

Now, the Bastard say, young Joachim come to us, he say, or we come in and get him. At this he jerk his head back, behind his shoulder. In back, the large boys—with the clubs—took a step closer. Choose,

Father.

That was when Joachim step out from behind me. "You did your best to protect me, Vater," he say. "Now I must do the same for you, mein lieber Vater und meine Familie."

[Sobbing] Forgive me; I promised Joachim I not cry. I—I grab his arm. I not want to let go. I was filled with nothing but fear and pain.

Joachim, he take my hand. Es ist okay, Papa, he say to me, it is okay. A tear falls from my eye. He smile at me so I won't be afraid, so beautiful, my boy, and wipes away my tear. No more tears, Papa, he say to me. Don't let them see you cry. He kissed my lips. I turned away when he stepped out the door.

The band starts to playing and the other boys began to sing as they took my boy away. I see him no more.

THE BODY OF A BOY BELIEVED TO BE JOACHIM WAS FOUND IN AN OPEN FIELD LOCATED ON THE OUTSKIRTS OF BOSTLIN-GEN, WHERE THE COLUMN HAD APPARENTLY CAMPED FOR THE EVENING. THE BODY WAS FOUND TIED TO A TREE, AND BEAT-EN AND BURNED BEYOND RECOGNITION. A PIECE OF WOOD WAS NAILED TO THE TREE WITH THE GERMAN WORD FOR COWARD, FEIGLING, WRITTEN IN THE VICTIM'S BLOOD.

EIGHT OTHER BOYS TAKEN FROM BOSTLINGEN ON THE NIGHT OF 4 NOVEMBER ARE STILL UNACCOUNTED FOR; THEIR WHEREABOUTS AND CONDITIONS REMAIN UNKNOWN AT THIS TIME.

We must find a way to end this madness.

Winston S. Churchill

Chapter 17
<u>Teamwork</u>

They turned, glaring towards the southern sky. The sirens wailed, increasingly joined by others far in the distance. It would be dark very soon.

Like rolling thunder, squadrons of RAF Hurricanes and Spit-fires—their powerful Royal-Royce Merlin engines pulling them towards their fate—raced skyward from the west towards the still unseen enemy, so low Freddie thought he could reach up and touch their bellies.

At the flash of the red, white, and blue roundels on their wings, pride swelled in the boys hearts. Another surge rocketed through their veins. Their fear forgotten, they sprang up, fists pumping in the air, shouting cheers and wishes of good luck to the men not much older than themselves heading into battle.

In the distance, the bells of St. Michael's began to ring.

"We've got to go, now. What are you going to do?" Reggie asked Victor, who was up on his feet, his head bandaged, looking skyward as well. "I-I don't know. We have to get back to the academy and to the shelter."

"There's not time. You'll never beat the bombers. Come with us. St. Mike's is closer."

"Are you sure it's all right? Have you room for nine of us?" Victor asked.

"We've room for nine hundred plus nine," Dougie assured him. "But we also have our duties."

"Let's get moving, Scouts. All of us. Now!" Reggie said, taking command as he always did. This lot was no different than his. They just needed a leader. Up the road they raced, in the direction of St. Michael's, Willy on wheels, leading the way.

"Remember your jobs? Freddie and Willy, me and Jack, Henry and Dougie—those are the teams." They had rehearsed, but not done it under actual air raid conditions. There's a first time for everything, thought Reggie. "Do you boys have duties?" he asked.

"No," came Victor's reply. "Our parents won't allow us to join the Scouts War Service. Said it was too dangerous, those things should be the job of the ARP folks and wardens, not the Boy Scouts."

"That's rubbish!" Jack said, racing along. "We make perfect ARP and wardens. We'll take three with us," he said, speaking for Reggie. They were still a hundred yards from the school. The sound of aeroplane engines was growing louder from the southern sky.

"Right brilliant, Jack!" Reggie turned to Victor, running at his side. "We have to break into three teams," he said. "That means you have three groups of three, one for each of our teams of two. Three teams of five is what we'll end up with. Who goes where?"

Victor was on it. "Pence, Dickey, and Seymour, you go with Freddie. Lenny, Chris, you come with me. Billy, Simon, and Oscar, you're the third group."

"That means you're with us," Henry said, moving alongside and in time with Dougie. Billy, Simon, and Oscar joined them.

Victor's heart pumped fast as he spoke with bated breath. "If we were back at the academy ... they'd have been hustled us to the basement for safekeeping by now ... not have us running about whilst it was going on ... this a lot more exciting ... what duties do you have?"

"It's our job to make sure the buildings are empty, three levels, three teams. We each have a floor we're responsible for clearing. Then we do a head count as we go straight for the basement, where it's safe,"

Reggie replied. "Think you're up for it?"

"Are we?" asked Victor, smiling. "This is what being a Boy Scout is supposed to be all about! Lead on!"

***

The church bells clanged loudly from above as they reached the courtyard. Some villagers, mostly Moor residents, were already making their way into the church basement with the help of Vicar Davis and the Sisters.

"What's this? You've picked up reinforcements?" Vicar Davis asked as his boys, along with nine uniformed Boy Scouts, suddenly appeared in the courtyard. Reggie moved past him without stopping. "We'll introduce you later, Vicar. Got a job to do. Where's Father Hawkins?"

"He and Katie haven't yet returned from an earlier trip they took to the village." Vicar Davis said, his voice shaky.

"That means we'll also have to check the church to make sure it's empty. Come on, lads." He headed into the foyer and up the staircase, with three new boys in tow. Willy kicked off his roller skates and raced up the stairs to join his team.

"Good heavens, boys! Get your search done then hurry to the basement!" Vicar Davis shouted, rushing to his position, and his duty.

***

Each team performed their assigned sweep, giving their Ronan guests a hurried tour of each respective floor and their home. When all were found to be empty, the boys gathered in the courtyard, per the established plan, eyes up, watching the show in the sky as the night fighters were attacking the bombers, the gunfire buzzing overhead sounding like zips being pulled. The bells continued to ring. The trail of villagers had stopped, with everyone who was coming now there.

VD was waiting at the door, helmet on his head and the Shelter Monitor armband over his cassock. "Very good work, lads, now let's head down to basement quickly."

"Not yet," replied Reggie, turning to VD. "I'm going to get the men. The sirens are blaring, and everyone who's coming is here. They needn't stay up there."

"Take someone with you," VD insisted.

Reggie turned to Victor. "Want to come?"

"Who, me?" Victor asked surprised, pointing at his own chest.

"You're a Scout. You're perfect for the job, am I right?"

"Yes," Victor said, delighted at the revelation. "I suppose you are."

"Good. Let's get to it." Across the courtyard they ran, through the kitchen door, almost crashing into an evacuating Maurice. "Where do you go?" he asked, stopping the boys in their tracks.

"We're going to get the men off those blasted bells," Reggie shouted.

"Qui est-ce?" he asked, looking Victor over.

"This is Victor. He's a friend."

"Hello, sir," Victor said, tipping his head.

"What you mean, 'hello, sir'? Get to it! Hurry fast! The bombs! She's coming!" He rushed out into the courtyard.

"He likes you!" Reggie said. "Come on!"

Into the church, behind the altar, and up the stairs to the first floor they ran, the bells growing louder with each step. They entered the bell tower, and there were Messrs. Greene and McKenna, pulling on their respective ropes with all their might, one going down, whilst the other was up, then reversing. Their backs were to them, so calling out was useless. Reggie ran to the old men and tugged on their shirts. Both jumped. Reggie dragged his hand across his throat in the international sign for "cut it".

Bob stopped, stooped over, and started breathing very heavily. Mr. Greene leaned back to get as much air into his lungs as possible. As the sound of the bells faded, it was replaced with the sounds of engines overhead, exploding flak, and air raid sirens howling.

Reggie hustled Victor and the men along. Freddie and the others were waiting for them at the door to the basement. "Go with Bob below, he'll show you the way, you'll be safe there," Reggie reassured Victor, who simply nodded, wide-eyed, and followed the men inside. Reggie paused.

"What's wrong?" asked Freddie, seeing the concern in Reggie's eyes, which were fixed on the northern sky, not the southern from where the bombers were coming. "I think there's a problem. Tykes," he said, getting their attention, "mount up."

Chapter 18

Duty Calls

From all directions the blood-chilling wail of air raid sirens announced the coming bombers.

Reggie looked to the gun installation on the hill. "Where's that crew? Why aren't they firing? Come on!"

"Boys! Boys! Come back here!" Vicar Davis protested. His cries fell on deaf ears.

Up Harcourt Road towards the installation they ran, Reggie and Freddie leading, with Henry, Dougie, Willy, and Jack in tow.

First up the embankment and into the bunker, Reggie yelled, "Hello?" No answer. He picked up the receiver of the field phone, wound the crank handle on front and tapped the button twice. The other end rang in his ear.

"Come on, pick up." With each ring, he grew more anxious.

The other end of the line clicked. "FCHQ." Thank You God.

"Help! We're under attack!" he screamed into the receiver.

"Who is this? What are you playing at? We're a bit busy here at the moment."

"I'm a Scout from St. Michael's. We're at the triple A installation in Hawkhurst but it's unmanned! The Germans are on top of us!"

"That's an incomplete battery installation, it's not ready for action yet."

"Well, ready or not, we've got action!" he screamed into the line. "No one is here!"

"Well, who am I talking to?" barked the voice back at him. "You're someone! Now get off the line and get about your duty, Scout! We'll send help when we can!" The voice on the other end was right. They were here; they were somebody.

"Yes, sir!" Reggie replied, his voice cracking a bit. He hung up the receiver. His eyes met the stoic portraits of the prime minister and King George VI. He removed his campaign cap and let it fall across his back. He swallowed hard and ran his hand through his red hair. When he turned back, he was met with nothing but fear painted on the faces of the other boys.

Reggie pulled a flat, heavy helmet, one of many lining the walls of the bunker, and tossed it to Freddie, then others to the rest of the boys. Strapping his under his chin, he rushed up the dark tunnel to the elevated gun platform outside. The others followed his lead.

When they exited the bunker, they froze. The sirens wailed over the sound of the approaching aircraft.

Before them Miss Lucy's long barrel rose skyward. She was a deadly sleeping beast they'd have to rouse. They were scared. None but Reggie made an effort to hide it. "Steady, lads," he said, trying to encourage them. "We can do this."

Being largest, Freddie jumped in one of the seats while Reggie mounted the other, each grabbing the rotating hand cranks in front of them. Steel bars, tubes, wheels, pedals, levers, and gears surrounded them. Freddie's hands instinctively found their place on his own hand cranks, as he eyed the round pancake-sized steel webbed sight directly in front of him. Reggie so wished Freddie hadn't stayed in bed the other morning. He'd need help if they had any chance in hell.

"What do we *do*?" Freddie shouted. Reggie was twisting and turning, his wide eyes darting all over the deadly machine. His brain clicked rapidly back to the day they had visited Mr. Steeves and Mr. Bennett.

"See this?" Reggie yelled, grabbing a heavy lever. "Do *this*!" He pulled it and locked it into place. Freddie did the same on his side.

"They're getting closer!" Dougie warned, standing atop the sandbag bunker, his eyes riveted to the now dark sky. Spotlights danced across the horizon. "Get this thing going!"

Reggie hustled as best he could, trying to acquaint himself with something he'd only seen operated once. Henry yelled to Dougie. "Get over here and help me! These are heavy!" He was struggling to lift a heavy magazine of four shells to the ammunition port. Together they hoisted it into place. *CLUNK!*

"It's in!"

Reggie to Freddie: "See *this?* Go like this!" Reggie arms frantically worked the crank. The platform began to rotate.

Freddie did as instructed. He moved his hand crank forward and the gun barrel began to sink. He rotated the crank back towards himself and the barrel began to raise.

"Got it!" Freddie yelled.

Dougie was close to panic, as the rumble of engines roared thick from the southern sky. "Here they come!"

"Are we loaded?" Reggie shouted. Dougie slapped him on top of his helmet and flashed thumbs up. "Fire!"

"Like *this*!" Reggie bellowed, raising and lowering his right leg.

Freddie spotted the foot trigger and slammed his right foot home.

All of them yelled out of pure fright, rocked by the raw power of the war machine. As every two-pound shell fired the concussion slammed like a thunderclap against their bodies, stabbed like a dagger to their ears as it left the barrel. Freddie kept the foot trigger depressed.

The sleeping beast was now wide awake, and angry to be so. Reggie cranked, traversing Miss Lucy right and back left, her barrel blasting away wildly, recoiling, blasting again. Jack stood shocked speechless, trembling in awe.

POM-POM-POM-POM! POM-POM-POM-POM!

The ground around them flashed with each blast, regardless of the flash suppressor. Red glowing shells raced skyward at hundreds of feet per second. Their teeth rattled in their heads. Hot spent casings spilled from the front port, like water from a spigot, piling up at a feverish rate.

SSSS. TICK. TICK. TICK. TICK.

As instantly as it exploded to life, the gun fell silent, except for the eerie tick of the hot expanding barrel. Trembling. Nausea. Sweat. Burning. Buzzing.

"What happened?" Freddie panicked. "What did I do?"

"We're out of ammo!" Willy yelled. "Reload!" As the boys moved for anther magazine, Dougie heard it first. He tilted his helmeted head to the sky.

"Listen!" He pointed straight up. His bladder let go.

***

After an anti-aircraft gun emptied itself into the sky below him, Wing Commander of SK3 I Gruppe followed the trajectory of the glowing shells streaking skyward back to the source, directly below. He glanced through his bombsight window in the cockpit floor at the glowing shells approaching from the ground.

Perfekt.

He pushed his plane's stick forwards as he closed its coolant caps. The nose of his Stuka dive-bomber swept right as the pilot began its steep dive sequence. As it did, the siren fixed to the aircraft for no other purpose than to induce terror began to do its job, howling in dual tones, as it advanced on its intended target below. Hearing that siren always made the Luftwaffe captain's heart race as the plane inverted and swept to full vertical. He pulled his goggles down over his eyes, licked his lips, and moved his thumb to the trigger button. His other hand held tight to the bomb release

***

Like the screech of an angry dragon, the bloodcurdling terror siren of a Stuka dive-bomber screamed at them from above, its pitch rising ever higher as it streaked ever closer.

"GET THIS THING LOADED!" Willy screamed as he never had before. It scared them into action. Reggie leapt from his seat to help

hoist a magazine. It slammed home. He grabbed for another and handed it to Willy. The terror siren grew more piercing as the diving bomber picked up speed: 450, 500, 550 knots.

"Hurry!" Dougie cried over the deafening wail.

"It's in! Go!" Freddie heard none of it. Willy slapped the top his helmet.

Reggie grabbed his crank and pumped his arms. Freddie did the same. The barrel rose to a few degrees shy of vertical. "Steady… steady!" Freddie shouted. His hands were sweaty. He wanted to wipe them on his pants and reseat his grip—there was no time. He held fast.

His world faded to that round steel sight, and the diving black aeroplane.

The underbelly and wings of the diving plane suddenly lit with flames, as the pilot, intently focused on his own sight, pressed his gun button. The screeching dragon began breathing fire down upon them. Two machine guns and two heavy 37-mm cannons unleashed hundreds of hot bullets and glowing tracers, creating long red streaks that ripped and whipped through the night sky, headed in their direction.

Glowing bullets slammed everywhere seemingly at once. Splinters of wood, chucks of concrete, deadly shards of burning metal ripped and ricocheted in all directions.

The boys screamed again, diving for cover. Like Dougie's earlier, the rest of their bladders emptied.

Henry's attention became fixated on his untied right shoelace. It made zero sense, but the impulse was so strong that he was sure if he didn't tie it—that instant—it'd be his demise. Dropping to his right knee, his brain started the mental instructions it always repeated as he tied his left shoe: loop both laces first, then wrap around the—

WHOOMPH! A string of glowing 37-mm shells slammed into the platform, exploding on impact—one exactly where Henry's chest had been a millisecond before. The blast flattened him and Jack to the ground, crushing the air from their lungs. The concussion knocked Willy down and blew Reggie from the gun. Sand and debris rocketed in every direction. Henry's clothes were on fire.

"Henry!" Dougie screamed.

When the diving bomber's siren reached a crescendo, the boys threw themselves to the ground and curled up as small as they could manage. This was it. Willy raised himself up on his elbow and screamed, *"Freddie! Fire!"* Freddie slammed the foot trigger. *POM-POM-POM-POM!*

The diving plane's starboard wing exploded into bits of blazing wood and metal.

Stunned, Freddie watched the burning plane start to roll violently, its siren wobbled sickeningly as it went over and over again, spraying burning fuel in all directions mere feet above their heads.

Willy was up instantly, arms raised, two-finger salute held high. "Welcome to England, Jerry!" he spat through bloody tears at the burning plane. It tumbled over a distant tree line, and buried itself with a thundering crash deep in the woods beyond. There was no explosion.

The boys celebrated with cheers as if they'd just won the most important match of their young lives, because they had. Dougie broke away from the others and rushed to Henry.

The boy laid in a ball, semiconscious, the back of his shirt on fire. Dougie jumped atop him and began to use his own body to extinguish the flames. Everyone joined him, pulling shirts and beating out flame best they could.

All but Freddie. He sat, still stunned and expressionless, hands on the gun, breathing heavily, sweating, trembling, and staring at nothing but that round sight before him. Tears ran over his cheeks, streaking the dust, dirt, soot and grease that covered them. Cordite fumes from the spent shells burned his nose and throat. His pants were wet.

Dougie helped a groggy, still smouldering Henry to his feet. "Are you badly burned? Still got all your pieces?" he asked. His hair was smoking, and one eyebrow was singed nearly completely.

"No," Henry answered, not entirely sure. "I mean, no, I'm not burned. Just my clothes." He looked at his hands, wiggled his fingers, pulled his belt out, and saw his penis. "Yes, I still have all my parts. You saved me, Dougie."

Willy, amazed to see he still had it with him, handed Henry his canteen.

"Cracking good shot, Freddie!" Reggie yelled.

"You knocked the bastard down!" Dougie chimed.

"We're in *sooo* much trouble!" Jack cried. "'Never touch that thing,' Father Hawkins said." He surveyed the burning carnage surrounding them. "We did, and look what happened!" That broke Freddie.

"No one's in trouble but that plane's crew. We need to find them," he said. There was no nonsense to his tone.

"What about the gun?" Dougie asked. Jack pointed to the air raid wardens rushing up the road in the distance. "It'll be fine. They're coming."

"But should we leave it? What if another Jerry comes?" he asked no one in particular and everyone at once.

"Do you really think we'll shoot down *two* planes tonight? Honestly?" Jack asked.

"I didn't think we'd shoot down any planes, but Freddie and Reggie did it." Dougie elbowed Freddie on the shoulder.

"We *all* did it," Freddie said over the thundering rumble of battle in the distance. The Jerries seemed to be focusing their attack on the nearby RAF aerodrome. "You're bleeding."

Henry touched his forehead. His hand came away bloody, and he suddenly felt woozy again. They were all bleeding from a nick or cut somewhere, but none too serious.

"We need to find that plane," Reggie said. He looked them over—dirty, sweaty, anxious, cut, bloody, smoking and bruised, but still together and ready for duty. "That crew may need help."

"So what do we do now?" Dougie asked. "Get guns and head out?" he asked, answering his own question with another.

"Guns. Grab two Enfields—and here." Reggie tossed Jack a piece of canvas gun cover. "We'll make a stretcher of that. Someone has to stay and let the ARP blokes know."

"I'll do it," Jack said. Normally, that'd be fine, since he was one of the smaller boys, but not in this case. "Good lad, Jack," Reggie said, "but it should be Henry. He got knocked up pretty bad. Besides, that crew, if they're alive, is bound to need your help."

Jack nodded. "You're right. Henry should stay."

Henry wasn't about to argue; his head throbbed, and his ears were useless. "Send for Father Hawkins. We don't need to be out there with Nazis and no backup," Freddie said. He tore a strip from his undershirt and handed it to Jack, who tied it around Henry's bleeding forehead.

***

Their selection of small arms included Lee-Enfield rifles, shotguns, and Webley pistols. Freddie took an Enfield and handed another to Reggie. To Willy, Jack, and Dougie, Reggie issued revolvers.

"What am I supposed to do with this?" Dougie queried, holding the Webley by its lanyard ring.

"You point that part with the hole at your head and pull that trigger thing. What the hell do you mean, what do you do with it?" Reggie asked.

"Well, it's just a tiny thing, innit?" At .455 calibre it was plenty big enough to put a hole in anything, especially a person.

Reggie took the revolver, handing an Enfield to a smiling Dougie. "Here. Satisfied?"

Dougie took the rifle and almost dropped it to the floor. His smile disintegrated under its weight. "You're with Freddie on point." Dougie snatched the Webley back, thrusting the heavy rifle to Reggie. "No, no, this little one's just fine."

"Good, now you can take up the rear."

"That sounds just fine to me," Dougie replied.

"That's where you find all the heroes," Henry commented groggily, his head clearing.

All sniggered, but Freddie. "No more stooging. Remember your duty. It's not over." They fell silent. Freddie slid back the bolt and chambered a round in the Lee-Enfield. Reggie did the same. Gooseflesh rose on his arms.

"Let's move." Leaving Henry behind, they followed Freddie towards for the forest's edge.

***

They stopped where the field ended and the woods began. "This is it, lads." Freddie looked each boy in the eye, ending with Reggie. Only then did he allow his gaze to betray his courage. "You got my back,

116

right?" he asked Reggie.

Reggie gave him with wink, a nod, and added an affirmative tongue click. "Always."

"Scouts, follow me." Freddie stepped past the tree line and disappeared into the darkness of the woods. In the distance the air raid sirens wailed; ACK ACK explosions flashed like lightening and thundered in the night sky. Reggie took a deep breath and followed Freddie. Jack and Willy did the same. Dougie paused.

Deep in the woods, he could see an eerie orange glow. He thought about that fairy tale, the one with the witch who lived in a clearing deep in a haunted forest and tempted lost children with her gingerbread house. She'd lure them in with sweets, and then after she caught them, she'd cook them in her oven. I bet her house glowed just like that, he thought. He stepped beyond the tree line, taking up his position at the rear.

Chapter 19
Above and Beyond

"Where on earth are the reinforcements?" Henry asked no one, aloud. Only a few moments had passed since the boys had headed out to find the plane, but to Henry if felt like hours. He was completely unaware that his perception of time had been knocked completely off kilter. That hit, back at the platform, had jostled him something fierce. His trousers were wet, but he hadn't remembered wetting them. Must have happened when I was knocked out a bit, he thought. That someone might notice he wet himself was the least of his concerns.

His head was still spinning, and those blasted sirens weren't helping. He wanted to be with the others. Perhaps a note would suffice? Yes, why do I have to be here to deliver a message? He sat at the desk and frantically began to scribble a note to whoever might find it first.

***

As they made their way through the woods, no one spoke. The younger boys seemed to bunch up close together. "Standard patrol form," Reggie reminded them, and they fanned out to form a proper patrol, minus one.

"Hey, be careful back there," Reggie reminded Dougie, who had bumped into Willy ahead of him. "Safeties off, but no fingers on triggers. I'm talking to you too, Freddie." Freddie pulled his finger off the trigger.

"I know, I know," he whispered back.

Just beyond the tree line, they had stepped into an all-encompassing dark, a deep blackness but for the distant eerie orange glow of the burning plane. As they drew closer, drops of burning fuel had set the forest canopy alight in spots, the forest floor aflame in others. Here and there, the trees dripped burning fuel, as if weeping tears of fire. Reggie couldn't help but think they were following a path left by the devil himself. He whispered to Freddie, "Wow, this is creepy."

"Yeah," Freddie said, "it is. Steady, mate. We're all together."

***

"There," Henry said aloud, barely hearing his own voice in his buzzing ears. His note sat neatly on the table. It read: Gone off to find downed plane. Send more help. Follow the trail and the light in the forest. Henry, SOSM.

He grabbed a Webley pistol and pulled a holster from the wall, strapped it round his waist, then started out after the others. The belt had an ammo pouch filled with extra cartridges, not that he hoped to use that many, but just in case. One never knows, does one? Yes, do your best and always be prepared! And keep your shoes tied at all times!

"The others," he said out loud. "Focus and find them!" He took to the grass, following the path the boys had cut through the clearing on their way to the downed plane.

***

When they found the Stuka, it was burning, buried nose first, its prop blades broken, bent, and twisted. It was leaning on its side, the one from which Freddie had shot off its wing.

Freddie, in the lead, made a fist with his hand and raised it, and all the boys instantly stopped in their tracks. He opened his hand wide, and the boys silently fanned out behind him, crouching down into the brush, their weapons at the ready.

He couldn't see anything in the cockpit because it was tilted away from his line of sight. Under the belly of the Stuka, a heavy bomb was still attached to the metal sled that held it out beyond the line of the propeller when dropped in a dive. The sled was bent and twisted, the fuselage resting directly on the unexploded bomb itself. All in all, it was not the kind of situation that Father Hawkins, or anyone with sense, would approve of them being near.

Freddie spoke to Reggie. "Cover me."

Reggie took a knee and raised the Enfield, ready to pop anything that moved in Freddie's direction.

Freddie raised his own rifle to his shoulder, and began to slowly make his way from tree to tree. When he got within a few feet of the plane, he glanced back and forth and then broke into a mad dash.

He sprang forwards, bounding up, one foot directly onto the unexploded bomb, the other onto the stump of the right wing that remained. Dougie's heart leapt, as did Reggie's. "Did he even realise that was the bomb he just jumped on?" Dougie asked Reggie. The older boy simply shrugged in bewilderment.

As Freddie stood on the aeroplane, rising heat and smoke burned his eyes, making them run, blurring his vision whilst it choked his lungs. Fire was wrapping up the back side of the fuselage and licked up towards the unexploded bomb.

The windscreen was shattered, and the pilot's canopy was slid back up in the open position. In the rear seat the gunner was leaning against his closed canopy, his dead eyes open, looking skyward. His lower jaw had been ripped away from his face. The horrific sight made Freddie's stomach flip and he instantly vomited.

Flames were spilling from under the engine cowling, now buried several feet deep in the muddy forest floor. The cockpit glowed by the light of burning fuel. Freddie looked around as quickly as he could. No pilot, no papers, no maps, nothing of strategic value at all. As a matter of fact, the only item that let him know a person was ever in the thing was the picture a young blonde girl smiling at the camera from behind a basket of flowers. That and the blood all over the interior.

The pilot might have escaped, but he was not unscathed. Freddie grabbed the picture and jumped from the wing, the flames now licking at him from that direction.

"Keep down behind those bushes. The gunner is dead. The pilot – he's not there. It's empty."

Each instinctively turned, putting their backs together, peering out into the surrounding darkness, their guns pointed in various directions.

"He's out here somewhere." Chill and dread gripped each of them. "We need to find the pilot." Freddie moved forwards and couched low to the ground. "Look for a trail, a path though the grass ... he has to be around here. He couldn't have got far. Blood," he whispered, "there's blood all over in that thing."

"He got away, but he's hurt," Reggie commented. "That's good for us."

"That should make him easier to find. We can follow the blood right to him." Willy said.

Jack spoke up. "Not now, it's too dark and too dangerous. We need daylight."

"By then he could be long gone," Reggie said. "With a head start like that he could make it back to Germany."

"Not if he's wounded. He won't get very far. Besides, he's likely got a Mauser." Jack speculated.

"Or a P-38," Henry said.

"Luger," Willy added.

"Shhhh!" Freddie stood and motioned for the others to follow.

"Don't you think we need to stand guard around it or something?" Jack asked.

"We need to get away from here, away from that bomb." Reggie said. In the distance the sirens still wailed ominously. Explosions could be heard, as well as the planes flying high above. "We need to get back to that gun. This isn't over. This Jerry can wait," Dougie protested.

"No, Dougie, we follow this blood trail where it leads. Enemy or not, there's a bleeding man at the end of it who may need help." Reggie nodded in full agreement, lifesaving must be the their first order, as Freddie had said, enemy or otherwise. "They're not just words we say, Doug, old boy. They have to mean something, or we lose everything."

Jack nodded. "If he's bleeding, he's in trouble. He needs me." He slapped his first aid bag.

Dougie moved round to the other side of the plane, seeing the smear of blood down the fuselage. He followed it down to the grass, where he instantly lost sight of the blood, but he could make out a track. It looked to him like this pilot fell, but then he was on two feet, walking upright, but dragging his left—no, his right foot. Dougie was sure of it. "Willy, look over here."

"What is it, Doug?"

"I think our pilot went this way, towards that other tree line. On two legs, but one is hurt. Check out these tracks." Reggie was on one knee, scanning the area, his Enfield still at the ready. Freddie and rest studied the trail Dougie had found.

"Good show, Doug," Willy commented. "You're right. See the print from his boot on this side every few feet, and look how this grass is trampled between steps. See the blood? I'd say he's this way. Leg wound, I bet ya."

"A tanner. You're on!" Dougie said back, spitting in his hand. Willy spit in his, and they shook on it.

"Okay, we move out. No need to stay here," Freddie said. "We don't know how wounded he is, but let's assume he can still fight, he's armed, and he's hiding out here somewhere, because some part of that"— he swallowed hard—"maybe all of it, is true." What else? What else? His young mind whirled with things to tell them.

"Also, remember, there are going to be town folk coming through this area very soon. Don't shoot anything that moves. Use your senses, know your target. Do you all understand?" They all nodded, including Reggie, who was still on one knee, rifle at the ready. "Uh, the bomb is cooking," he reminded them.

"Okay, lads, let's move," Freddie ordered. "Two by two. One watch left, the other right." They scrambled away from the burning crash and its unexploded bomb as quickly as they could.

***

Henry reached the edge of the dense woods. Beyond he could see the glow of the burning aircraft against the trees and the smoke column that rose in the sky. Fear ran cold up his back, or maybe it was just the night air, as his clothes had been burned away and his sweating back was exposed to the cool breeze. He reached into the holster, pulling out the Webley. It was a strong enough gun to stop any man, but it did little to calm his nerves. Actually it did quite the opposite, as the idea of having to use it was far more unsettling.

Alone in the dark, dense woods of the English countryside hardly seemed ideal conditions to look for a downed Luftwaffe crew. He wasn't sure what kind of night would be perfect for that, but he *was* sure he wished he had at least Jack with him. Dougie would be first choice, but even whiny Jack would be better than going it alone. Alone can be a very hard place to be sometimes.

That's when he heard a gun cock close behind him, felt a cold steel muzzle against the back of his ear. P-38? Luger? Mauser?

"I will take that," a voice from him behind spoke, as a hand in a black leather glove closed around the Webley. Alone can be a very hard place, indeed.

***

Mr. Hopkins and Mr. Williams were the first of the air raid wardens to reach the bunker. It had been firing moments before, even knocked down a Hun into the woods not far from the Maloney farm. But now, it was just smoking, shot up, silent, and empty.

Williams said, "There's no one here."

Hopkins replied, "Well...I can see that with me own eyes. Where ya think they went?"

Hopkins swept his torch on the table. "Well, I dunno. Here's a note."

Williams asked, "Well...what's it say?"

Hopkins answered, "Well...I dunno. I haven't read it yet."

"Well...what are ya waitin' for? Read it."

"I am readin' it."

"Well...read it out loud, ya darn fool." Williams wondered how he and Hopkins had remained friends for so long. "It's hard to make out,

but says something 'bout a plane…down in the woods…and send help."
Hopkins eyes were big as saucers. "We need the navy!"

"No, no we don't need the navy, but we need more than you
and me." He pointed to an opened gun crate and empty slots where rifles
should be. "At least they're armed," he said. "Look, two are missing."

"Well, I guess the boys must've taken them. The boys, out there
alone. We need to tell Father Hawkins directly. I'll ring up the HQ."

"Right. You stay put and wait for reinforcements. I'll run and
get Father Hawkins." And off Williams hustled up the road towards St.
Michael's.

***

Henry felt a fresh flush of warm liquid fill his pants, again. He
gave up his Webley without a fight. "Please don't shoot me." His hands
were in the air. He ducked his head down.

"I try not to make a habit of shooting young boys in the back of
the head. But make the wrong move, und I will. Understand das?"

Henry nodded. He understood very well indeed.

He heard the pilot tuck the Webley into his waistband. "Come,
we go to that house."

With that the pilot leaned almost his full weight against Henry.
He was injured, pretty badly, with blood running thickly down his trouser
leg and onto his knee-high leather boot. Henry observed and noted so he
could be a good witness—if he made it out of this.

"Vat us yur *name*?" the pilot asked.

The boy figured he wasn't giving out national secrets by telling
this pilot his name. "Henry."

"Henry." The pilot repeated. "How many years?" he asked. His
breathing was becoming very laboured.

"I'm fourteen years old," Henry said.

"Vierzehn? You are brave for only those many."

"What's your name?" Henry asked.

"Horst."

"I think you're brave for flying that thing."

The pilot smiled. "This ist mine job. This is not for hate of Eng-

124

lish."

I wish I could say the same for you, Nazi bombing bastard, the boy thought.

As they made their way through the thick woods towards the Maloney farmhouse, Henry was sure Horst wasn't going to make it. He was slowing, and his breathing was bad. Henry stopped and looked at the pilot. "Let me look at your leg. You're bleeding badly."

Horst stumbled to his knees and fell over, dropping his gun to the ground. Here he was, laid out in all his glory for Henry to admire. Black boots, red-piped balloon pants, black leather jacket with shiny buttons, and even a silk scarf.

Henry took the scarf from around Horst's neck and made a tourniquet, stopping the blood from the long gash in his leg.

He took the Webley from Horst's waistband and placed it back in his holster. The pilot was close to losing consciousness now. He took the captain's pistol, a sleek Mauser, and stuck it in his own belt. He had just captured a German pilot. The German had practically no blood left in him, still he thought it might count. But, if he didn't do something fast, Horst would die a very painful death. He couldn't let that happen.

Pulling Horst's Mauser from his belt he fired three shots in rapid succession.

***

"What the hell was that?" They turned in the direction of the shots. "Those were gun shots!"

Then very faintly: "Help! Help! I found him! Lads! Over here!"

They tore off through the underbrush like a pack of wild boars, heading for the sound of Henry's voice. "Keep yelling, Henry, we're coming!"

Henry heard them, thank God. "I'm here! I'm here!" he shouted. "This pilot is in poor shape! Hurry! His leg is bleeding badly!"

"Ha! You owe me a tanner, Dougie!" Willy shouted.

"Tourniquet!" Jack yelled to Henry, now in a full sprint.

"Already done, but he's passed out!"

When they got there, they sprang into action, with Henry reporting the whole time. "I thought I was done for. He came up behind me. I didn't even hear him. His gun—right behind my ear—I couldn't do anything."

"What are you talking about?" Freddie asked. "You captured him by yourself. You should be proud."

"Well," Henry said, "I'm not. It was loss of blood that got him captured."

Reggie spoke up. "Well it's going to be his death if we don't get him to an ambulance. Willy, you go and get to the road so you can show them where we are." The boy did as told, rushing off towards the road.

Jack touched his finger to the man's blood soaked pants. He then made a cross of blood on the pilot's forehead.

"Are you giving him last rights?" Dougie asked. "Is that what the cross on his head is for?"

"That's not a cross, Dougie." Jack answered. "You know, you really should read the first aid section of BP's book. That's a 'T' so at hospital folks know he has a tourniquet on his leg. You always mark the forehead."

The pilot began to stir a bit. "Relax, Horst. We'll help you."

Freddie's eyes grew big. "Did you say Horst, as in—"

"Yah…mine…Horst Ademeit. Tri-tri-un…" he faded back into unconscious. His name was one Freddie recognised.

"You captured Horst Ademeit?He's number one on the RAF's most wanted list," Freddie said.

They quickly removed their belts and secured Horst so he would be safe from falling off of their make-shift stretcher. There was no escape to worry about, not in his condition. Dougie and Henry covered him to keep him warm, whilst Freddie and Reggie carried his limp body between the two rifles. Reggie was beginning to fear they were too late when the burning plane ignited the attached 550lb. bomb, sending an explosion, blast wave and razor-sharp fragments of shrapnel and aircraft pieces ripping through the forest around them.

***

Willy arrived at the road to await the coming ambulance. What he found was a mass of townspeople, including Father Hawkins, constables, and officers from the nearby RAF base heading in his direction.

"Over here!" he yelled, waving his arms. "Over here!" He grabbed his whistle and gave three blasts then three more, elated to see help on the way. Just as the first men arrived, the Stuka's bomb cooked off and exploded, as did Willy's heart with fear for his brothers. "No!" he screamed. Dear St. Michael, please let them by okay, he prayed. He tore off through the woods again, towards the scene of the blast.

***

"Come on, lads! Who's hurt? Are you okay?" Willy was in a panic, seeing all his brothers laid out on the ground, not moving, possibly dead. He moved from one to the next, touching their necks, feeling for a pulse, a breath, any sign of life. He ran his hands over their chests, feeling for wounds or blood. He rubbed each extra hard on their sternums, trying to illicit the slightest moan or groan. Each was like music to his ears. "Ha!" He pulled his canteen, giving them each a mouthful. "Come on lads, you're all alive. You're all still with me."

Freddie shook his dazed head, and grabbed Willy's arm as he was just about to start rubbing his chest.

"I'm good, Willy. Water." Willy hugged him and squeezed hard.

"Oh, thank you, St. Mike." He handed Freddie his canteen. The boy took a big swig of water, spilling most of it from his mouth. The others were slow in coming round. "This pilot is out. There's an ambulance at the road. Let's get to it, Scouts! Come on!" Willy said taking command, pulling at each boy to help get him to his feet. The boys rose wearily, hoisted their patient and stumbled towards the road.

***

When they finally arrived, onlookers watched as six lads, the youngest merely eleven, wearing Brodie helmets, exited the woods carrying a makeshift stretcher on which lay one of the most feared men in Goering's air force.

The crowd broke into a spontaneous outburst of clapping and cheers. Reggie and Freddie only gave up their improvised stretcher when an actual, more suitable one had been presented, and even then they loaded the pilot themselves into the back of the ambulance for the trip to Hawkhurst Hospital. Freddie trotted to the cab of the ambulance.

"He's got an open leg wound, and we've put a tourney on it and stopped the bleeding. We marked his forehead," he said to the driver. "But be quick. He's lost a lot of blood." He reached into his shirt pocket and pulled out the blood covered picture of the young blond girl. "This belongs to him," he said, handing it to the driver. "Please see that he gets it."

"Yes, sir," the driver replied. Freddie stood tall and saluted. The driver shot one back and the ambulance raced away up the road, bells ringing.

Father Hawkins arrived in time to see the boys load the bandaged pilot into the ambulance. The other boys stood together, their clothes tattered, wearing helmets, covered from head to toe in mud, soot, sweat, and what he feared most, blood. Lots of it. He counted only five of them, until Freddie jumped from the back of the ambulance and went to talk to the driver. As the ambulance pulled away, the large boy turned and walked back to join the others.

Those are my boys, Hawkins thought, overjoyed at seeing them all alive. They turned and saw Father Hawkins standing at a distance, his expression one of grief mixed with relief. They broke for him in a sprint, huddling and hugging as they had never before. Henry let loose with a heart-wrenching sob, which they all soon joined. "Come on, my lads." Father Hawkins said. "Let's go home."

Down the road they walked, arm in arm, wiping away tears from overwhelmed emotions, and simple utter exhaustion. Dawn was breaking, and the all-clear sirens were sounding through the early morning sky.

Chapter 20

A Fine Catch

"What's his main injury?" the ambulance driver asked the assistant in back.

"Deep lacerations to the leg and face, possible facial skull fractures, broken ribs. He's a blooming mess, he is." The ambulance assistant replied.

"Them boys pulled him out that plane. Shot it down and then went into the woods and pulled this one from the fiery wreckage."

"Blimey! Those *boys* did that?"

The German stirred. He seemed to be floating between awake and out.

"Should've shot the bastard right then. I'd have. Ain't it just his luck to be get shot down by a lot of bloody Boy Scouts. They musta been down on their good turn quota for the day," said the driver.

"Did a pretty good job patchin' him up, between them scarves and the belts they used. Stopped the bleeding. Probably saved this bugger's life."

"One of 'em lads, he gimme this—musta pulled it out of the cockpit—picture of Fritz's girl. They make 'em pretty over there." He flipped the blood covered photo. "Mein dearest Horst" he read as the ambulance sped up the road.

"Dearest Horst?" the assistant asked through the hole. "You don't think this chap is ..." He looked again at the bloody man on the stretcher. His face was bruised and swollen, but that uniform. As if a couple gongs, bull boots, puffy pants, and fancy silver buttons on his fancy black leather jacket weren't enough, he even had them li'l flashy doohickeys on his collar. I may only be a body snatcher, he thought, but I know who's in me rig when I got him. And right here in our very ambulance. This'll make us famous, he thought.

"Say, know who I think we have here?" He leaned in and whispered in the driver's ear. The driver whipped his head back, wide-eyed as a doe in headlights, looking at the man on the stretcher through the little window.

"Forget Hawkhurst Hospital. We're takin' this one straight to Biggin Hill. They got a hospital there. Plus, if it's him, they're gonna wanna hold on tight. Here, take this pistol. Don't take no chances." The pilot was passed out and turning a ghostly grey colour.

"I don't need that. He's barely breathing, let alone puttin' up a fight. Just hurry." The ambulance turned at the next right and headed west to the HQ base of the Royal Air Force.

***

At Biggin Hill it was confirmed that, yes indeed, the boys had shot down and captured Horst Ademeit, one of Hitler's top aces and current number one on the RAF's most wanted list for creating havoc over the channel. Not taken down by an RAF Hurricane or Spitfire, Goering's best was bested by six boys, who'd never before fired a shot in anger, the oldest being no more than sixteen years of age.

Both body snatchers—the unflattering nickname for ambulance drivers—were seriously disappointed when commanded by the base doctor not to mention a word to anyone about whom they had or whom they even *thought* they might have transported to hospital that night, under the penalty of treason. The doctors could do what they needed to save his life, but everything else about this new POW definitely had to be run up the chain before any action being taken. This was a strategic-value target beyond their wildest dreams, a safe's worth full of intel and a big dog out of the fight for good.

Still, they hoped the news would find its way out, perhaps through a leak, so their fame might still be secured. They wouldn't say a word about it, however, because when command says keep your lips sealed, they meant it, and those who chose not to do so during wartime could find their last memory to be that of swinging at the end of a short rope two sizes too small for their neck.

So while the ambulance attendants were put under strict orders to say nothing about the POW they transported that night, nobody had said anything in regards to keeping quiet about who did the shooting down. The six orphans from St. Michael's Boy's Home in Hawkhurst shot down a German Stuka dive-bomber during an air raid last night. And in Hawkhurst, that was front page news.

***

"We need a cover story that'll make sense and not let Jerry know we have their man." The air marshal glanced out of his base office window. He liked to glance out of the window when he thought, to let his mind run free across the rolling green fields. "First, no press. Of any kind."

"Why do we need a story at all?" asked his wing commander. He was seated at the side of the AM's desk, taking notes. "Why not just release numbers and let it stand at that?"

"Because you know how these things work, Commander. We say one thing on this side, they say another thing on theirs, and back and forth it goes."

"Yes, sir, all the more reason to say nothing," he insisted. "Even if he'd been killed, why should we call him out as special? To us, he's just another check mark on the plus list."

The air marshal frowned. Wing Commander Weber instantly realised what he had said, how it sounded. "I'm sorry, sir, that does not reflect the way I feel about these men, it's … just … it's a way of …"

In his most compassionate tone: "I know what it is, Commander. It's a bloody shame."

He knew it was, but the battle was happening in England now, or at least above it. Hitler's forces were gathering on the shore across the Channel, building their invasion force continuously. The RAF had been doing a fine job of stopping that from happening. Without the sky, they couldn't take England. With the RAF, they couldn't take the sky. But the pace of attack on the RAF bases was pressing them towards trouble. He'd forbidden himself to think of defeat. *Trouble* was the best he'd give them. Still they were being pounded down, day after day, the under the hail of German bombs.

"We can't let them know we have him until we can talk to him, and based on what condition he's in, Lord only knows when that will be. Let them stew about him for a bit, yes?"

"Yes, sir. Very wise, sir." the wing commander replied.

***

Back at home the boys received heroes' welcomes, filled with sloppy kisses, endless hugs, a few harsh words from who else, the Sisters Clymore, and a private shot of brandy for each, provided by Bob McKenna, allowed by Father Hawkins.

"Here's to a fine bit of work, boys." He tossed it back. The boys did as well, with Willy, Dougie, and Jack promptly coughing as the harsh liquid burned their throats.

Exhausted, they could barely make it up the main stairs to the dormitory. As they climbed the steps, they stripped off their dirty clothes. By the time they reached the top of the stairs, six grubby underwear-clad boys walked into the bath room, not caring who saw, including St. Michael himself.

Reggie glanced at Freddie's yellowed undershorts. "You wet yourself?"

"Couldn't help it." He looked at Reggie's. "Uh huh, looks like you had a spot of trouble yourself." Reggie turned and looked at rest of the boys. Each was wearing a pair of yellow stained undershorts. He looked at Freddie, raised his index finger over his lips. "No need to embarrass the younger boys about it."

"Ha! Henry *wet* himself!" Dougie shouted. So much for inconspicuousness. Henry looked down. His short were indeed drenched and stained. "Shut up. So did you!"

Dougie ripped off his wet pants and threw them at Henry, but missed and hit Jack square in the face. Everyone had a good laugh, except Jack.

Chapter 21

Number 10

Dinner at Number 10 proved to be a low-key affair, yet with just the touch of highbrow expected from an invitation to dine with the prime minister. It included all the fine china, gleaming silver, and glittering crystal of the state dining room, but instead of the cold vastness of that space, it was served to the three diners within the warm, inviting, oak-covered walls of the small private dining room.

After a meal of beef Wellington with fresh asparagus and carrot purée paired with a classic '28 Bordeaux Merlot, the men retired to the white state drawing room to continue their discussion. The PM loved visitors for dinner, especially military men. They rode the tip of the sword, and he needed their counsel more now than ever before, and he didn't care who knew it.

The general and air vice-marshal followed as the prime minister led them into the dim room, lit by glow of the crackling fireplace. The PM took his favourite, leather, high-back chair opposite it. He stoked his after-dinner cigar with a few brief puffs to get it started. The general offered the other high back to the air vice-marshal, who refused and offered it back with an open-palm gesture. The general took the seat. "Thank you, sir."

A tuxedoed butler brought in a silver tray with three champagne flutes, an ice bucket, and bottle of the PM's favourite Pol Roger.

The air vice-marshal continued with his point from dinner, "Do you honestly think it wise to use Boy Scouts? What you're suggesting is nothing less than creating a squad of boy soldiers."

"Yes, sir, if they'll best do the job, I am. They're already more versed in field-craft than most agent recruits, even if they are only boys. They are British subjects none the less."

"That does not make it morally right. The idea of sending children to war is unconscionable." It was the father in him coming out.

"With all due respect, Air Vice-Marshal," the general continued, "we created the Special Operations Executive to be unusual, unexpected and unconventional. This is *exactly* the type of mission the section was created for. And, begging your pardon, we are not sending them into the field as combat soldiers. Combat is the last thing we're hoping for."

"Still," the air vice-marshal spoke, "it is immoral, the whole idea of sending boys on a potentially suicidal mission." The faces of his own young sons flashed before his eyes.

"Again, sir, with all due respect, we're beyond the point of a morality discussion. We're almost beyond the point of discussion entirely. Across from us is a mainland filled with men intent on slaughtering us in our homes. And they're coming." It was true, and they were keenly aware of that fact.

"War is here. It will certainly sweep up these boys as well, so let's prepare them for what is already on the doorstep. Better they die doing their part than killed in some bloody air raid. These lads have dealt with hardship and disappointment their entire lives. At least give them a fighting chance at their own fate." It was the same argument he had made repeatedly over dinner.

The general looked away from the air vice-marshal directly into the eyes of the PM, who sat motionless, riveted by these two officers as each presented his most impassioned arguments for consideration.

"But if they succeed, surely people on this island and the mainland will be saved. Hitler's storm troopers *do not care, will not stop*, and *must be met.* If by these boys, so be it. They've proved a willingness to accept their duty and see it through," the general reiterated.

"This is preposterous. We're talking about sending children to war, a violation of the Geneva Convention, everything we stand for," the air vice-marshal said. "And, if I may remind you, should they be found wearing enemy uniforms, they will be instantly shot as spies, if not tortured first."

The general spoke. "Right now, Thomas Peter Heydrich is acting commander of a *Hitlerjugend Streifendienst,* a sort of junior Gestapo unit of the *Einsatzgruppen,* the barbaric units of secret police and SS security service that move in after a town is captured and the invading shock troops have moved on. They are ultra-loyal to Hitler, acting as an internal political police, controlling the streets with violence, ferreting out disloyal members, and reporting anyone who criticises Hitler or the Nazis up to and including, in a few instances, their own parents. They use terror and fear to keep the new territory in line."

He turned to the prime minister. "It's rumoured they kill anyone who resists in the slightest. Men, women, children, Jews in particular, gypsies, psychiatric patients, homosexuals, anyone they've deemed undesirable who might 'pollute' the Aryan gene pool of Germany. Prime Minister, MI6 confirms reports of mass kidnappings. Heydrich is operating under no one's command because his uncle is chief of the SS, as you well know. And young Thomas Peter is doing his damnedest to show his uncle he has a strong hand and a stomach for the job. He leads a pack of child murderers who are murdering other children."

"And you think *six boys* will be able to pull this off? A mission of this complexity calls for the army or more specifically the Special Intelligence Service, not the bloody BBS," the air vice- marshal said. "I don't care if they did capture a pilot. This calls for a special team."

"Beg your pardon, Air Vice-Marshal, but you haven't read all the reports I have," the general replied. "They are the special team this mission calls for."

"How's that, General?" asked the PM.

The general continued. "Well, sir, ironically, being orphaned 'brothers,' if you will, has given them a leg up. They've had to learn to be resourceful, to work together since a very young age. It's quite amazing, actually. They observe, think, and then act in the best interest of the group, learned by way of looking out for themselves and one another." The PM's ear perked up. He nodded and puffed his cigar.

The general continued. "They can hold entire conversations with tongue clicks and whistles. They sometimes finish each other's sentences. It's extraordinary."

"Tongue clicks and whistles? That means they're soldiers?" snapped the air vice-marshal.

"No, sir, that means they're brothers. You've been in a foxhole; it's not for King, it's not for country." He met the PM's eyes. "No disrespect intended, sir."

"None taken, continue," the PM retorted with a shake of his head.

"A man fights hardest for the man fighting next to him: his brother, blood or not. These boys already possess a natural cohesion far beyond anything we could hope to instil. They've been fighting for one another their entire lives, as short as those may be." He fell silent. A lump formed in his throat, as the unforgettable faces of the "brothers" he'd lost to battle flashed through his mind. Composing himself, he returned his eyes to the PM's.

"As you know, before founding the Boy Scouts, Baden-Powell was a stellar officer who became a stellar field agent for MI6. He thinks with the proper training, our Boy Scouts would be more than a match for anything the Hitler Youth can produce. They already possess the skills of map reading, field craft, and basic signalling, and they're already more field ready than most adults whom we recruit. We simply add weapons training, unarmed combat, and demolition, and these boys will become a formidable foe." That was a half-truth. Thomas Peter was vicious. Hopefully, these boys had his constitution for the nasty business. Captain Fairbairn and Sergeant Major Preston-Downey would see to that.

The PM drew in and puffed out. "One more time, General. Explain this 'Operation Archangel' from the top."

***

"Prime Minister, it seems BP has been working on plans to activate the Boy Scouts for two much larger wartime roles. One, as a subunit

137

of the Home Guard and two, just as the SS uses the Hitler Youth as a pool of so-called talent, he suggests using the Boy Scouts to find and select the best candidates for the commando branches, SIS, our new SOE, the special air service regiment in the works and so forth."

The general reached for a flute and raised it to his lips for a sip. It was amazingly light and effervescent. The PM watched for his reaction. When the general took a second swallow, he noticed the PM watching. He offered his approval and gratitude by raising his flute to the PM with a quick nod. The PM's round cheeks and nose tip glowed orange against the tip of his cigar. He nodded back, winking. These two men genuinely liked each other. The entire exchange went unnoticed by the air vice-marshal.

"He's been working on a new programme of his own, something a bit more in line with Fairbairn & Sykes's training." William Ewart Fairbairn and Eric Sykes were magnificent bastards, self-taught creators of a style of hand-to-hand combat that saved their lives on hundreds of occasions as they worked as beat coppers on the notoriously dangerous streets of 1930's Shanghai. Creating commandos from cadets was their specialty.

"Fairbairn? And Sykes?" repeated the air vice-marshal, his tone conveying his objection. "You needn't worry about the Nazis. Their training alone will kill those boys."

The general ignored the comment. "Well, Prime Minister, as things would have it, a perfect convergence of situations will soon take place, making now the perfect time to put elements of BP's plan into play."

"As you know"—he flipped open a folder from his attaché case and began reading—"at zero-three-thirty hours, Tempsford, at Bedfordshire, received a call requesting an ambulance to the countryside just outside of Hawkhurst. They found a downed German pilot, one Captain Horst Ademeit, who was assumed to have been shot down by UK defence forces. It seems a troop of six Boy Scouts, aged eleven to sixteen, shot down the Stuka and then hiked into the forest. They found the pilot, administered first aid, and carried him to the waiting RAF ambulance."

He pulled a silver cigarette case from his jacket pocket. "May I?" he asked the PM.

"Please do."

He lit a cigarette, flipped closed the file, and laid the silver case on the top of it. "At hospital, the surgeon said they likely saved his life." He raised his eyebrows. "They did all of this on their own initiative, with anti-aircraft artillery they hadn't been trained on."

"Splendid. I wish we had six hundred—no, six thousand—more just like them." the PM commented. "How did they pull through?"

"Without a scratch—well, so to speak. They were fired upon by Ademeit and were a bit banged up, but nothing worse than scrapes, cuts, and bruises."

"And Ademeit?" the PM asked. He hadn't moved from the edge of his seat.

"In hospital at Biggin Hill. He's in sorry shape, much worse off than the boys," the air vice- marshal reported. "It will take some time, however, he is expected to survive and make a full recovery."

The PM nodded. "A very good turn of events indeed. Leave it to the Boy Scouts to provide a good turn."

The general continued. "BP wired the moment he heard, recommended considering these boys sight unseen. My contact at MI6 reports the build-up prior to the annual Hitlerjugend Rally at Nuremburg coming soon would present our best opportunity to capture Heydrich, as well as time enough to adequately prep the boys."

"I thought they ended those Nuremburg gatherings in 1938?" the PM commented.

"Yes sir. The massive full-party rallies are no longer held, however the Hitler Youth continue the tradition on a smaller scale with their members."

"I must protest, yet again. Something of this magnitude and complexity belongs to agents already in field," the air vice-marshal said. "Bomber Command is already strained to the limit, minus the added burden of shuttling in and dropping a handful of operatives. Seems hardly worth the risk of an aircraft for such an implausible"—he bit his tongue as the word "scheme" tried to pass his lips—"*operation*. Is it worthy to risk the reputation, the very existence of the new branch, this SOE, with such an implausible mission?"

The general leaned forwards in his chair, elbow on knee, closing the gap between himself and the PM. He gestured, with pointed thumb.

"This is exactly the type of mission the SOE was created for and precisely why it needs to be boys. They'll be least expected, or *suspected*, as the case may be. They're already a boy scout troop. We run them through the special training schools, dress them in Hitler Youth uniforms, and they'll blend in with, and disappear among, the tens of thousands of other boys there." He sat back in his chair again, took a sip of his drink. "There's more."

"More?" the air vice-marshal asked, surprise raising his pitch. "More, you say, General?" The general noted the man's tone and not wanting to embarrass his counterpart in front of his boss, he quickly replied. "Yes, Air Vice-Marshal, I apologise, but this new intel came in from HQ just before I hopped in my car for dinner, and I didn't have adequate time to brief you prior. I do apologise."

"Go on," the PM said gruffly. He took a sip of champagne.

"The new curate at St. Michael's isn't exactly what he seems."

***

"A former SIS operative, a captain, who's seen his share of action. Captain James E. Hawkins. I won't read them all, but the first two letters that follow his name are V and C."

"Why the bloody hell is a Victoria Cross winner 'converting' during war time?" the PM asked.

"Well, sir, after a narrow escape and being wounded in France, he retired himself. But with war just offshore, he joined up with the GHQ Auxiliary Units. It was just lucky happenstance that the current vicar, a man named Davis, is up in age, and the parish filled a paperwork request for a younger man to act as his curate. Hawkhurst and St. Michael's had already been selected as one of the places for a covert Auxiliary base and weapons depot. Their request for a new curate cemented it. It allowed us to get a man in there with the perfectly logical cover story. The boys just happened to come with the place."

The PM grumbled. "There are no lucky happenstances, General. Hawkins of Hawkhurst? I think not. If it seems too good to be true, in this case, it's the hand of Providence."

The general drew another drag, exhaling as he spoke. "As far as Hawkins goes, I trained with him, served with him. I can personally vouch. My guess is he's already teaching those boys things you won't find in any Scout handbook. He's smart. If he's the Jim Hawkins I know, he's preparing them already, at least to be Auxiliary Unit members. He's a good man, Prime Minister."

The general fell silent, letting the PM digest this new information. After a few moments of quiet contemplation, the PM spoke. "Continue, General."

"We'll send the boys to Arisaig House in Scotland to start the Special Training Schools immediately, no different from any other man preparing for work behind the lines, except slightly abbreviated due to a short time table. But that's okay, as they won't need to be fully trained in wireless, resistance organising and such. When they're ready, they'll be sent to Europe where members of the local resistance will be waiting to help them. They shall make their way through Germany posed as a Hitler Youth squad, joining the annual march of Hitlerjugend to the rally at Nuremburg; infiltrate, capture, and escape with Thomas Peter Heydrich; and then evade their own capture whilst they smuggle him back here." The general paused and took in a breath. "That's it in a nutshell, Prime Minister."

The PM was again silent, as he was after the last time the general paced him through it at dinner. But he was now on his second flute.

"You make it sound like child's play, General, which I assure you, to the Nazis it is not. What of this chap Hawkins? A captain, you say? If he's served in France, he might not want those boys anywhere near war, especially this one. He could sink the entire plan if he's not on board," barked the PM. "What then?"

"Sir, he's a realist. He knows grim times are in their future." He looked at the floor, trying to wrap his mind round this entire idea. Ludicrous, and yet here he was, pitching it. Suggesting a plan like this undoubtedly put his competence on display for the PM to judge, just as the AVM was doing. It was a gamble, and by the time this conversation was over, so might be his military career.

The general turned. "Prime Minister, as orphans, these boys are Crown wards, they belong to His Majesty. As such, there's no need for the captain's or anyone's permission. Those boys are ours to do with as we please, regardless of Hawkins' protest, should he have any."

Brutally unfair, this whole business sounded to the prime minister's ears. These brave lads, already dealt a raw deal in life, being lined up for the same probable offering in death. Apart from the unpleasantness of that possible outcome, there was something about this initiative that intrigued him. England needed a bold plan, and although this bordered on foolhardy, it was also undoubtedly bold. If executed properly—and that was an enormous *if*—it might work. Regardless, he could dissolve the entire operation with a snap of his fingers if he so chose. Still, should it not succeed, it could scuttle his newly formed SOE before it even set sail.

"Does there need to be a conversation about the good they could do as recruiting tools?" considered the PM. "Say for the Home Guard, or Local Defence Volunteers?"

"Our active members now number one and a half million, with Hitler still across the Channel," replied the general, although the more, the merrier was his true sentiment.

"Yes," the air vice-marshal said, jumping on this new idea with vigour. "Think of the moral boost it would give the suffering masses of Great Britain. These young boys—heroes each—could do wonders for the fighting spirit of the British people."

"Hmm," grunted the prime minister. "I hate to think of those boys as tools or pawns, but they're no use to us, for good or ill, if they're dead. Consider hard, gentlemen; six orphaned Boy Scouts sent to their deaths by our hands, all before their seventeenth birthdays. If found out, the people *will* demand our heads and rightly so."

"Yes," the air vice-marshal said, swallowing hard and suddenly noticing the stiff collar around his throat. "I suppose they would."

"Gentlemen," the general said, "I think you're missing the forest for the trees. If the Nazis make it to this island, millions of heads will roll. This is a matter of survival, and with an invasion mounting, those boys may be safer undercover on the mainland than here." He looked at the PM. "Begging your pardon, of course, sir."

The PM nodded. He, too, was a realist. The RAF were doing their finest, yet they stood alone, and this bloody Battle of Britain, as he had coined it, was just getting started, with victory not yet a spec on the horizon.

The general continued. "If we put those boys on recruiting posters, we may as well title them WANTED." He paused, sipped his champagne. "If Hitler gets to this island, he'll hunt those boys down and use them as propaganda to achieve the surrender of the British Isles and enslavement of the British people." He took a long last drag of his smoke. "When he finds them, he will hang them in Piccadilly Circus by their heels, naked and bloody for the Empire and the world to see." He crushed out his Woodbine and exhaled.

The PM took another sip of his champagne. He puffed his cigar, set it in the ashtray, and stood. The general followed his lead. Pulling back his shoulders and standing straight upright, the PM spoke.

"May I offer an opinion with regard to this operation?" asked the PM. "It seems foolhardy, redolent with danger, and doomed to failure; otherwise I can find no fault with it," he barked out, quoting Dickens. "It is actually so preposterous, our enemy would be foolish to expect anything like it, and our enemy, gentlemen, are no fools. Permission granted. Proceed as you see fit, General."

"Yes, Prime Minister." He thought to say thank you but settled for "Very good, sir."

"But hear me very clearly, gentlemen. If by the end of Special Training Schools, these boys don't prove conclusively that they are thoroughly prepared as field agents, the mission is dead, for if not, those boys most certainly will be." He crushed out the cigar burning in its tray. "If after these three months, even *one* of them is not up to snuff, the mission is scrubbed. Is that clear, General, Air Vice-Marshal?" the PM asked.

They nodded

"I want to hear it."

"Yes, sir. Very clear."

"Agreed. Very clear, Prime Minister."

When the PM stuck out his hand, the general took it and gave it two solid pumps. The PM continued to hold it. "Oh, and by the by, next time you speak to BP, do give him my best. Let him know I'd like to take tea with him sometime very soon, won't you?" The PM released his hand.

"He's been ill, Prime Minister. He's recuperating in Kenya at the moment, so it may be some time, but I will do so. Thank you for being such a gracious host, Prime Minister. Please share my sentiment with the kitchen and staff as well." He stepped back and saluted the men. The PM returned it. The air vice-marshal did the same.

"General, good evening."

***

That night the air vice-marshal awoke with a start, drenched in a cold sweat. He had been having a horrific nightmare. In it, he stood and watched as six dead children—naked and bloody—were strung up with steel cable through their heels to swing in the centre of Piccadilly Circus. The six children were the two girls and four boys who called him "Daddy."

16 July, 1940

FROM: PRIME MINISTER WINSTON CHURCHILL

TO: MAJOR GENERAL COLIN GUBBINS, S.O.E.

AIR VICE-MARSHAL KEITH PARK, R.A.F., S.O.E.

DR. HUGH DALTON, D.O.O., S.O.E.

RE: OPERATION ARCHANGEL

Gentlemen,

As discussed over dinner, I would like to be kept
informed on any and all developments, good or bad. As
discussed, this matter should be treated with the utmost secrecy and given attention at all times.

Chapter 22
Gallant Effort

When news of the capture reached Buckingham Palace and ears of King George VI, he instantly thought the boys deserved recognition for their bravery and gallant effort.

"Perhaps the Victoria Cross?" he asked Mr. Abbey.

"Your Majesty, you know they would never qualify for that honour. They aren't members of the armed services."

"W-well," the King continued, "they were acting as Boy S-Scouts, in u-uni-uniform, in the de-defence of our island, s-surely they deserve some sort of rec-recognition. Why not the V-Victoria Cross?"

"Again, Your Majesty, as you know the top brass would never allow it. The criteria are extremely demanding. Many obstacles would stand—or be placed—in the way, by many upper-echelon commanders who wouldn't want to get their feathers ruffled." He continued, "Granted, the boys' actions did constitute extreme acts of bravery with little or no concern for their own lives in the face of the enemy. For shooting down an aeroplane and capturing a POW they deserve something, but presenting them the VC would likely be considered most inappropriate by those to whom it has already been awarded."

The King rose and stepped to the window.

"Well," he considered. "p-perhaps the time has come for another m-medal, a gallantry award for those not in the service, but s-still doing their duty for the c-country."

Mr. Abbey silently considered the plan. "Surely, Your Majesty, there will be more acts of heroism performed by Britons not in uniform. Yes, it does make great sense. Good for the will of the people."

The King turned from the window. "I propose a medal, in the spirit of the Victoria Cross for th-those who d-do their duty in the face of the enemy but are not part of the Armed Forces. We can c-call it the George Cross, after S-St. George of course. It should have an image of S-St. George, with a b-blue ribbon. I've always b-been partial to blue."

Mr. Abbey spoke up. "Well, Your Majesty, I know you would never approve, but I think the medal should also have your likeness, perhaps on the reverse. You are the originator of this new award after all."

"No, too presumptuous. This is about St. George, not me." The King considered. "I do like this idea i-immensely."

"Actually, I think it's quite fitting, Your Majesty."

"Then so b-be it. These six scouts shall be the first recipients of this new award. We need six of them as soon as humanly possible." Mr. Abbey was already scribbling in his little book.

"Very good, Your Majesty. I'll set the jewellers to work on new proofs immediately."

"No, there's not time. I'm rather partial to that fellow who did such a s-smashing job on the c-coronation medal."

"Percy Metcalfe," Mr. Abbey said. "He's very familiar with engraving St. George. He did the 1938 Crown with St. George on the reverse. If ever there was an artist for the job, it's Metcalfe." Abbey scribbled away in his notepad. "I'll dispatch a messenger for him at once, Your Majesty."

"V-very good, Mr. Abbey." the King replied.

Chapter 23
A Grateful Nation

For nearly three days following the downing of the Stuka, the boys were out of sorts, sleeping at odd times, eating very little at one meal and far too much at the next, expressing many types of behaviours that come with surviving a traumatic event. On the third day, a postal delivery arrived by special carrier, addressed to the Scouts of St. Michael.

"We got another set of boxes delivered addressed the same way yesterday, Father." Bob said. "Came in from London, I think, but I didn't go poking about to see what it was. Put 'em in Miss Goold's office I did." Odd, Father Hawkins thought, why two deliveries? Why not just wait until it's all ready to go and make a single delivery? London is half a day's journey.

Father Hawkins trotted up the foyer staircase. He skidded to a stop before reaching Miss Goold's office doorway, just in case she was in there. He stuck his head round the door frame. No one. He rushed in, immediately spotting the boxes Bob had mentioned. "Henry Poole & Company, Ltd. London."

Henry Poole & Company was the finest men's shop in London.

Now what are these? There was a packing slip attached to the outside of the box. From the Ministry of Defence to the Scouts of St. Michael. Six complete British Boy Scout uniforms. Brand spanking new. Hawkins smiled. "As a gift for your gallant efforts against the enemy, you are hereby awarded the rights, benefits, and perks as official Boy Scouts of the Highest Order. Chief Master Scout Lord Baden-Powell."

"Oh, St. Michael, you outdid yourself. Thank you." He opened the smallest box, and it was a beautiful plaque with their official troop name, under glass. He flipped open the larger box. This was all too good to be true. His brain started ticking. This will make a fantastic surprise, if he could pull it off.

There was no way he'd be able to get these downstairs without the boys seeing. He looked at the boxes and lifted one to consider its weight by curling it up and down a couple of times. He shrugged. It wasn't like china or nitro-glycerine or something; it was just shirts, trousers, a few scarves, some socks. If he threw them over the banister outside the office—just drop the box over the railing—it'd land right next to where Bob and VD could hang the plaque—close, anyway. The point was to surprise the boys, right? The box with the plaque he set aside, as not to damage it, then he gave a quick look to make sure the coast was clear, and over the edge of the banister he tossed the box.

As it fell, it gained speed, so by the time it reached the floor thirty-five feet below, it hit with terminal velocity and the sound of the exploding box echoing loudly through the foyer. Not exactly the stealth he had hoped to achieve.

"Jesus, Mary and Joseph!" Mr. McKenna shouted as he and VD jumped together, startled as the box hit the floor loudly behind them, splitting, spilling Boy Scout uniforms all over the foyer floor. So much for surprises, Hawkins thought. On the floor at their feet, Bob and VD saw an obliterated cardboard box, with new Boy Scout uniforms scattered in all directions. They looked up.

Over the second-floor railing, stretched over as far as he could reach, was Father Hawkins, wearing his own startled look. He nervously smiled, signalling with two thumbs up. Suddenly, on the floor below him, six heads sprang over the banister, one for each boy, glaring wide-eyed at the floor below, soon joined by Miss Goold's red haired-head. They all stared down at Bob and VD, who stood in the middle of the green fabric mess, looking confused.

"Well, uh, looks like we got ourselves a surprise delivery," Bob stammered, not knowing what to say now. "Surprise!"

"Are those—?" from Henry.

"They are!" Freddie shouted. "Official, really?"

"Wow!" Reggie couldn't believe it.

"Real uniforms!" Willy shouted.

"Blimey! They are, neckerchiefs and all." Dougie licked his lips.

Six mad boys stampeded down the staircase to the ground floor, creating a ruckus unheard in the home, except on Christmas morning. Miss Goold looked down at the floor below, very confused.

Three seconds later Father Jim raced past, plaque in hand, almost knocking her over in the process. "Come on. You'll not want to miss this."

As they reached to the ground floor, the boys were already knee-deep, digging through the piles of new clothes strewn across the floor. It *was* Christmas morning. They kept picking up each article, holding it out in front of them, holding it up against themselves, studying each stitch and seam. They looked so official and sharp, as Boy Scout uniforms should.

"They're named! Everything has name tags!" Jack shouted.

"I should hope so," Hawkins said. "Otherwise, I've created quite a mess." He beamed, watching them sort through the clothes, each more excited than the next.

"Without tags, you'd have a devil of a time sorting out the wash, don't you think?" They all noisily agreed. Bob stood by, actually hopping from foot to foot, doing an odd sort of jig, as excited as the boys he was watching.

Noticing it on the floor, Vicar Davis picked up a sheet of paper that had spilled from the split box. It was another packing slip. "Contents of this parcel includes official Boy Scout tunics, two large, two medium, two small. Official Boy Scout trousers, two large, two medium, two small. Official Boy Scout leather belts with braiding, six of various sizes. Six official—"

"Caps! We have caps! Official Boy Scout Caps!" Dougie shouted.

"Caps, six count. Twelve pairs of knee-high socks, green, twelve pairs of undershorts, boxer style, white. Six official Boy Scout neckerchiefs, navy blue."

Henry stood mesmerised in the middle of the mess, slowly pulling one of the new silk scarves through his fingers. It felt so smooth against his skin. The curate beamed. "That will keep your neck from getting chafed by the wool collar of the blouse, same as the RAF pilots." Henry beamed. "I've never felt anything so smooth before … it's like silk."

"'Tis silk, according to this here paper," Bob said, glancing over VD's shoulder. "Six official Boy Scout silk neckerchiefs, navy blue, six official Boy Scout wood-wobble neckerchief three-hole slides. Wow, them sound fancy."

Each of the boys was helping to sort out the gear, trading back and forth items that belonged to someone else based on the tags. Miss Goold just watched, as stunned as the boys, a smile and look of bewilderment painted across her lovely face. Father Hawkins winked at her.

She mouthed to him silently 'How did you do this?'

He shrugged, raised his eyebrows, shook his head and mouthed back 'It wasn't me.'

"Boys, boys. Attention. This was supposed to be a surprise—and I suppose in some way it did turn out to be one, just not as I had hoped—but I have something else I'd like to show you." Father Hawkins said. They didn't hear him over one another, still buzzing in their heads and jabbering in their jaws, and he knew this was going nowhere fast.

"Oh, for the love of Mike. Atten-*SHUN!*" Father Hawkins shouted.

Everyone, including the adults, froze and stared at him.

"By your reaction I can see we're not going to get anything else accomplished today until you try them on, so go and try them on."

The boys gasped together as if it suddenly dawned on them that they owned these things; these were all theirs.

***

They scurried like scavenging church mice, grabbing up their new shirts, shorts, trousers, belts, and all. If their coming down had been a racket, going up was worse; each now carried large armfuls of clothing, dropping pieces as they went. Freddie took his and Willy's things so Willy could follow behind, picking up the odds and ends as they fell, Henry's neckerchief on the sixth stair, a pair of boxers dropped by Dougie on the eighth. By the time they got to the dormitory, Willy had his own entire armful, as did VD, who was following behind Willy, picking up his droppings.

Before climbing the stairs, his arms as full as the rest, Reggie stood before Father Jim and Miss Goold. "I don't know how to thank you for all this, for all you have done." He looked at the floor, hoping neither saw the tears of joy forming in his young eyes. Too late. Miss Goold reached out and gave him a hug.

"You don't need to thank me, Reggie, you've all earned it," Father said. "Besides, I had nothing to do with it."

Reggie raised his head and looked straight into the Hawkins' eyes, and saw the man was telling the truth. "But how? This must have cost a small fortune." Jim turned to Miss Goold. "Katie, will you do me a favour and go and check on how the boys are coming along? I'd like to have a word with Reggie man-to-man, if you don't mind."

"Of course I mind," she snapped back. "Just send me away because I'm a woman." Her false indignation did nothing but make both of them smile. She kissed Reggie on the forehead and whispered in his ear, "Congratulations." As she did, he inhaled deeply. Her scent was as fragrant as her face was pretty. He smiled in return.

"But not too long," she reminded him. "You have muster in fifteen—" She checked her watch. "No, twelve minutes. Twelve minutes? With this lot and all those uniform pieces, fat chance of that. It'll take twenty just to get it all sorted out." She then reached out and took the armful of items away from Reggie. "I'll drop this on your bed." And away she went, leaving the two of them alone.

"Reggie, when I first came here you didn't trust me much, and I understood that. You're very protective of the family you have, as you should be. You're the biggest of the big brothers."

"Freddie is bigger than me, by half a foot almost," Reggie corrected him.

"That's not exactly what I mean. I mean, you're the oldest one,

152

regardless of age. Just like Willy is wise beyond his years, you are as well."

"I guess when you grow up like we have, you think about things differently. At some point you realise that you're all you've got. And until the others realise it, I have to be what they've got. Does that make sense to you, Father?"

"It does, Reggie. More than you know." He took Reggie's hand and gave it a pat with his other hand. "I think you have a very good heart, Reggie. But I think you carry around a lot of ache in that heart."

"Sometimes at night, Father, I get so afraid … of so many things. My mind gets going, and I can't stop it. All I can think about is Willy and how I will take care of him, especially with war coming. I'll be called up. What will happen to him?"

"Reggie, you don't have to be the big man around here anymore. How about you let me handle that for a time? How about you just worry about your schoolwork, and your scouting work, and as my promise, I won't let anything happen to you or your brothers."

They sat silently for a moment. It had been so long since he hadn't worried about something or other. It's one of the curses of growing up, he thought. Learning that the world is a bigger, more cruel place. And it seemed to get more so as each year towards adulthood passed.

"Father, I can't thank you enough. This is amazing. We've never all got something brand-new at the same time. The Sisters and VD— sorry, Vicar Davis—do their best. The townspeople are very kind to us at Christmas"—his tone changed—"always feeling sorry for the poor or- phans at Christmastime. That's when we really make out."

Why you crafty little con man, Father Jim thought. "Are you playing at poor little orphan?"

Reggie looked at him, all cheeky like. "Spare a penny for a poor orphan, gov-na?" he said in his best quavering Artful Dodger voice, eyes sad and fluttering for effect.

"And here I was feeling compassion for you," Father said playfully.

"When you grow up like we did, Father, you learn quickly to use what you got. We got dealt this hand, so—" He smirked and shrugged his shoulders.

"Well, if I ever catch you or your brothers pulling that nonsense around town, I'll have your hides. Now go and get changed."

"Yes, sir, Father." He stood, and again his tone changed. "I'll do my best to just try and be a kid for a while, but"—Reggie raised his finger and shook it in the curate's direction—"I'll be watching you, so if you mess up …" He winked and smiled.

"Go, you cheeky little—just go!" Father Jim said.

Away Reggie went in a trot.

"Bob!" Father called out. "I've a job for you. We need to get this up."

Chapter 24
Fit for a King

The boys came down the stairs in their usual order, in pairs, large too small. Father Jim was standing at the entrance of the foyer, where the large portrait of St. Michael had previously hung. It was gone and in its place, a white sheet hung, covering something hanging on the wall.

"Nice touch," Father Jim commented from the side of his mouth, just loud enough for Bob's ears. Bob grinned bashfully, and turned his eyes to the floor.

"Weren't nothing for those boys." He didn't receive many compliments, and when he did, his way of accepting them was usually to become embarrassed.

"Father," he heard Reggie say behind him. "I think we have a problem."

Hawkins turned and broke into a fit of laughter. Before him stood six Boy Scouts, in new uniforms that were unfinished. The sleeves were all too long, the trousers extended well past the length of their toes, and raw-edged fabric was everywhere. They held up their trousers with their hands, as the belts that had been delivered didn't have any holes. The only things that seemed to fit properly were the neckerchiefs.

"Ha-ha," Freddie said, a look of disappointment across his face. "How are we supposed to be a troop like this? They forgot to finished these. We look ridiculous."

"You just need a little bit—or maybe a lot, actually—of fitting and tailoring. I bet the Sisters can turn those into amazing pieces in no time at all." He started up the stairs. "Just sit tight, and I'll go and find the Sisters. Don't look so glum. We can fix this."

***

The telephone started ringing the same moment Father Hawkins stepped through Katie's door. She raised her finger, indicating him to hang on, as the telephone took higher priority.

Well I never, he thought, feigning outrage by indignantly folding his arms across his chest and pouting.

She rolled her eyes. "Yes, this is she. Who's on the line please?" She tried to be her pleasant self, but she was truly tired of all the same questions she'd heard herself answer over and over since the boys took down that wretched plane. Word spread like wildfire, faster even because it was such good news. The place had been inundated with visits from well-wishers, just wanting to check on the tykes, and telephone calls—dozens, it seemed. The pace of the last couple of days had been exhausting.

Hawkins waited, watching Katie's expression turn from curious to befuddled to finally excitement. "Well, yes, it would be fine, yes. Are you sure?" She picked up a pencil and started scribbling madly on a pad, nodding as she did, agreeing with someone who couldn't see her. She nodded anyway. "Of course. I will make sure everything is ready for you." She looked at Jim, shrugging and pointing at the telephone. "Yes, sir, thank you again." She returned the receiver to its cradle.

"You're not going to believe this one."

"Who was that?" he asked. He unfolded his arms.

"That was Buckingham Palace."

***

The front bell rang. Like puppies, the boys wanted to scramble

156

for the door, but their oversize, unfinished clothing prevented them from doing so. Miss Goold rushed down the stairs to the main door. As she did, she caught sight of the boys in their ill-fitting garb, and she too started to laugh. They did look funny, and all so small, especially Freddie.

"Hardeeharhar," Freddie said, rolling his eyes.

When she opened the door, Katie was greeted by a short, bald, smartly dressed man in tails and a vest. He was extending his arm, thrusting a card in her direction.

"Good day, madam. I am here. I understand you are in dire need of my services."

Katie accepted the card. She read it and it said:

"By appointment to His Majesty, King George VI, Livery Tailors Established 1806, Henry Poole & Company, 15 Saville Row, London".

Flabbergasted and flustered, Katie's jaw dropped—literally speechless—when the finely dressed man turned towards his van and gave two very crisp, very curt claps.

Six men marched from the back of the van with assorted bits of tailor craft. Sewing machines on wheels, box after box of assorted bits and bobbins and whatnots, mirrors and standing blocks, all came out of the van and were carried into the home.

"Normally I would prefer to do this down at the shop, but time is an issue, and we've much to do. Where might we set up?"

"What is it exactly you are here to do, Mr.—?"

"Wilson, Archibald Wilson, master tailor." He took a notebook from his coat pocket and placed the armless gold spectacles that hung on a cord around his neck on the tip of his nose, where they stayed in place, seemingly held by magic.

He looked over the spectacles. "My staff and I are at the behest of the Palace. We're here per His Majesty's request to properly fit the uniforms we've created and sent for the six brave Scouts of St. Michael's. Now, dear lady, where might we set ourselves up?"

He looked past her to see the boys, wearing the very uniforms the man and his staff had made over the previous two days. "Ah," he said, charging past her, "I see you are all ready for us. Excellent." Two more sharp claps. "Come, come. We will do it right here, in this large space."

The men set up six workstations, one for each uniform that needed tailoring.

The staff and residents of St. Michael's watched in awe as the men, like busy elves in Father Christmas's workshop, began to practice their craft.

***

The Sisters, whilst brilliant with a needle and thread, were nowhere near the calibre of the men working before them. Each boy was standing on a box, as men circled then with measuring tapes, pins and chalk sticks. Lines here, dashes there, off with a shirt, on with a pair of trousers.

They worked with extreme efficiency, not a stitch too few or even one too many. The Sisters hovered, taking in the whole process, nodding approval when the craftsmen did something they liked, gathering in hushed consultation between themselves when things weren't going to their liking.

"All in all, these gents are alright," Sister Noreen whispered to Sister Doreen, who nodded her agreement. "But Daddy would have brought the boys to his shop." Doreen again agreed with a stern nod.

The front bell chimed out again.

"Door!" the boys sang out simultaneously, startling the tailors only slightly.

"Good Lord, what's all this?" Mr. McKenna asked, signing paperwork for the several boxes and bundles that were being delivered.

"Oh, very good, just in time, as ordered." Mr. Wilson said, snapping shut his pocket watch and returning it to its proper pocket.

Assisted by Bob, the deliveryman hauled in box after box, addressed individually to each of the boys. Reggie, clad only in undershorts—his uniform was under the machine's needle—was done with his measurements and helped carry in and place the boxes in piles for each of the boys. He opened the largest one, a hat box, with his name on it. Inside was a campaign styled hat with broad round brim. He put it on his head. It was a perfect fit.

"See here, you can't be a proper Boy Scout without all the accoutrements that go along with it," Mr. Wilson said.

As Reggie opened another box, his face lit with glee. "Wow," he said, "a genuine Boy Scout pocketknife. Is this for real?" He removed it as if it were a delicate piece of crystal, instead of the rugged scouting tool it was.

Mr. Wilson and the rest of the tailors smiled and laughed, delighted to be serving the boys.

"If all of our clientele were this grateful, every day would be a dream." Mr. Wilson said to Father Hawkins, as he worked pins into Henry's uniform. "The high-powered, highly paid men we're used to serving never express the level of gratitude these dear boys are for the simplest of items."

"When you have nothing," Hawkins reminded him, "everything is a gift."

Wilson looked over the top of his spectacles at the priest. "When you have everything, nothing is special," he replied, shaking his head.

"Boots! We've got new leather boots!" Dougie shouted.

"All matching, I bet," Henry added from his perch.

"Please, Henry, if you don't hold still, I can't—oh, forget it," Mr. Wilson said, signalling surrender. "Boys, go and get your packages. Nothing will get done until you do."

It was like another frantic Christmas morning. As packages were opened, the contents were loudly shared with the group. "A canteen, cover and everything!" Jack shouted.

"A compass!" Willy yelled.

"Whistles!" Freddie laughed. "We even got matching metal whistles!"

"You have everything a proper British Boy Scout needs to be prepared. These are all gifts for you, courtesy of His Majesty. We make his uniforms and suits as well. Did you know?" Mr. Wilson mentioned as he smiled broadly. He handed Sister Noreen one of his embossed cards.

"Whoa," Sister Noreen said, rubbing the raised crest with her finger. "They dress the King himself."

She looked at a smiling Katie, who stood, shaking her head, again speechless.

"Now," Mr. Wilson said. "everything has arrived. We will work to have these finished for you in two hours. We must be ready by two p.m."

"What happens at two?" Reggie asked, looking to the Father Hawkins.

The curate simply shook his head and shrugged.

***

The boys were gathered in the dorm at two o'clock, as instructed, dressed in their newly tailored uniforms. They sat anxiously on their beds, waiting for Father Hawkins. Jack, never one to sit still long, and wearing his favourite new boots, decided to take a walk.

"Hey, where are you going?" Willy asked.

"Just for a walk out in the hallway. I'll be right there in case Father Hawkins comes. He'll have to pass me."

"Well, don't wander too far," Willy said. His tone was such that he caught his brother's ear.

"What's that, Willy?" he asked, again already guessing at the answer. Willy answered matter-of-factly, "I've got a feeling is all."

"One of *those* feelings?" Reggie asked.

"Yes, but only a little. A bit queer really." It always was when he had those feelings.

"I'll be right here, you can see me through the glass." Jack walked out the door and started down the hall, listening to his wonderful footsteps echo through the great open space. These hard-soled boots, he thought, they're really something. They actually made him want to walk around loudly. People can hear you coming, so best to make every step strong and lively.

Lost in his thoughts, he continued down the stairs, listening closely to each, and how it made its own particular sound against his soles. He listened, head down, as the tone changed with each step.

He was stopped at the front door when he ran chest first into a pair of crossed rifles. "Hold on, just where do you think you're going'?"

Startled, Jack stumbled backwards and looked up. Two young soldiers were standing in front of him and the door, with crossed rifles blocking his way. "I-I-I'm sorry. I was just going…" He noticed the big shiny black cars parked outside, and several police wagons.

"Nope, sorry lad. Orders are no one in or out until further notice." They both smiled, lowered their rifles to rest.

Jack, thinking of Willy's episode, turned and bolted up the stairs in a flash, down the hall to the dorm. He burst through the door.

"There are two soldiers guarding the front door! They said no one in or out until further notice. The police are here, too. Lots of cars and such." Willy snapped his fingers and winked. "I told you I had a feeling."

Freddie now joined the group by Willy's bed. "What did they say?"

"I was walking, and they stopped me with their rifles," Jack said.

"Rifles?" Dougie asked. "They have guns?"

"Yes, big Enfields."

"Wow. Guards with rifles, and police are here, and we can't leave," Freddie said, rubbing his chin, eyeing the window. It would be the quickest way out of the building, if they weren't two stories up.

"I told you we were in trouble. You never should have touched that gun!" Jack yelled, pointing directly at Freddie.

"Me? Reggie was the one who worked out how to use the thing. I just followed his lead," he said, pleading his defence.

"Yeah, they'll buy that. Reggie told you what to do." Jack snapped.

Now it was Reggie's turn to protest. "I did tell him what to do! Without me, he'd have been—"

Freddie spoke up. "Are you calling me stupid, you—"

"All of you stop, now. Don't be daft," Henry said. "We just shot down a German Stuka and captured one of the most wanted Nazi pilots. They probably want to question us, give us the debrief or whatever they call it."

"Yes," Dougie said, "but we did do a lot of things we shouldn't 'ave done. Touching that gun was the first." He spoke the truth. They had done many things that under normal circumstances would've got them in a lot of trouble. But under normal circumstances, they didn't have an AA gun parked practically in their backyard.

"Maybe that's why they gave us new uniforms," Dougie said. "Maybe they want us to look like soldiers when they line us up against the wall—you know, blindfold, last cigarette, and whatnot."

Reggie hadn't thought of that. He did now. "It could be anything we want it to be, so stop making things up. We'll know soon enough."

161

The sounds of footsteps coming up the stairs sent each dashing to their own beds, where they sat stiffly. This was it.

***

Father Hawkins stepped into the room with a man they had never seen before. "Boys, this is Mr. Abbey. He's got a few instructions for you, so pay close attention, and you'll do just fine."

"Do? What do we have to do now?" Henry whispered in Dougie's ear.

"Dunno," Dougie whispered back. This whole day had been surreal, so he was ready for just about anything, or so he thought.

Mr. Abbey stepped up. "Hello, gentlemen. Let's line up." He referred to a sheet on a clipboard he was carrying. "Reginald?" he asked. Reggie raised his hand. "Good, you're our patrol leader, correct?"

Reggie nodded.

"Splendid. Let's get you up front here." He physically grabbed Reggie and pulled him roughly to the front.

"Very good. Now, Fredrick, the corporal, you're next." Freddie moved behind Reggie.

"Now, where are…ah, Henry and Douglas, you two are next. Then let's follow up with Wilfred, and smallest, Jack, you can take the spot on the end."

Now that they were in proper order, he started looking each up and down, paying attention to the smallest detail: hat just so, not a scarf, tie, or button out of place.

"Now," Mr. Abbey continued. "We will march down the stairs in this order. Reginald, you continue walking and stop at the X marked on the floor. When you come to your mark, face the foyer and stand at attention."

Reggie nodded.

"Now, when it's your turn, you should bow your head, salute, wait for him to return it, then drop yours. If he extends his hand, which he will, you are to grasp it firmly and give a solid shake. Don't speak until addressed. No personal questions, please. If he asks your name, or any question, you may answer freely," Mr. Abbey said.

It sure would be nice, Reggie thought, if they told us who we were supposed to be receiving.

"However, most important, whatever your answer is, you should address the King as 'Your Majesty.' The Princess you address as 'Your Grace.'"

***

Mr. Abbey led them single file from the dormitory. Never before had they seen the bright foyer filled so many people: village officials and dignitaries, prominent parishioners, photographers, constables, RAF officers, and army brass in dress uniforms.

Father Hawkins and Vicar Davis, Messrs. Greene and McKenna, the Sisters Clymore, and Miss Goold were also there, standing separately from the boys but all together, never looking more proud. Sister Doreen was already wiping her eyes.

Henry Poole's men had worked a miracle, completing six brilliant Boy Scout uniforms in under four hours. Each boy was dressed in full kit: hat, canteen, electric torch, and rucksack complete with sleeping roll, pocket knife, shiny whistle, socks with tassels, and shiny black boots. They beamed with a pride they'd never felt before in their young lives.

When Reggie reached the tape 'X' on the floor, he stopped, turned, and faced the crowd. His stomach was doing nervous flips. He felt a little dizzy.

King George VI entered the room, followed by his daughter, Princess Elizabeth. He looked simply dashing, dressed in his full army uniform, his chest covered in ribbons of every colour of the rainbow and more. Round his waste and over his shoulder he wore a brown leather Sam Browne belt. Princess Elizabeth wore a pretty powder-blue wool coat and a matching beret. She seemed very excited to meet the boys. The King approached the podium Bob had hastily assembled per Mr. Abbey's request.

"Well, I-I must say. You present yourselves as the b-best and brightest Britain has to offer. Th-thank you…for your w-warm congeniality at such short notice. I'm honoured to m-meet you all." Mr. Abbey nodded in silent agreement.

"I heard of your actions of several evenings p-past, that without thought for your own safety or well-being, you mounted an AA gun whilst under d-direct enemy fire and proceeded to down and capture one of the most deadly Luftwaffe pilots our b-brave boys have ever had to t-tangle with. By this c-course, you undoubtedly saved ma-many of our brave flyers."

Mr. Abbey handed the King a small polished-mahogany box. He opened it, displaying a lining of blue velvet, holding a cross the colour of silver, suspended from a ribbon of deep blue. The crowd gasped.

"N-normally, criteria m-must be met before receiving an award for valour, the m-main sti-stipulation being that one is a s-serving m-member of the armed forces, which, of course, y-you lads are n-not. However, at the time of your g-gallant actions, you were in uniform, w-working in defence of the realm. Th-that's close enough for m-me. And, after all, I am the King." There was no stammer in that sentence.

Abbey nodded again. The boys looked on in stunned disbelief.

"You did, however, fulfil your d-duty by performing an act of most conspicuous bravery and extreme devotion to duty in the presence of the enemy." He looked at the boys. "Lads, it is my honour to present you, the Scouts of St. Michael, our nation's newest, highest award for civilian valour, the George Cross, so named for our patron St. George, not for myself." The foyer filled with the sharp echoes of clapping, and Sister Doreen's cries of pride.

"However, there is one s-small bit of business that needs address-ing. Let's m-make it official. It g-gives me extraordinary pleasure to pro-claim you official British Boy Scouts, St. M-Michael Pat-trol."

Mr. Abbey signalled Mr. McKenna, who pulled the tablecloth from the plaque. It was beautiful—gold leaf and all. It had a crest in the corner, and best of all, a handwritten note at the bottom next to the stamped red ribbon.

> *To the Boys of St. Michael's,*
>
> *You are now Boy Scouts. I trust you—on your honour—at all times to do your best to carry out your duty and to do a good turn to somebody every day.*
>
> *—R. S. Baden-Powell, Master Scout*

"Boys," the King continued, "please raise your right hand in the Scout salute." They raised their right hands, pinkie tucked under thumb in the official Boy Scout salute. Father Hawkins did the same. His Majesty spoke a line, paused, and waited for the boys to repeat it.

"On my honour, I promise that—"

"On my honour, I promise that—"

"I will do my duty to God and to King."

"I will do my duty to God and to King." Their voices rose through the space like a choir in the church.

"I will do my best to help others, whatever it costs me." The King said.

"I will do my best to help others, whatever it costs me." The boys repeated.

The Sisters, taken by the moment, blew their twin noses.

"I know the scout law, and I will obey it."

"I know the scout law, and I will obey it."

"Congratulations, you are now official Boy Scouts."

He stepped round the podium and approached Reggie, with Princess Elizabeth and Mr. Abbey following a step behind. When he stopped in front of Reggie, he was saluted by the handsome red-haired young man.

"Reginald, it is my honour." He shook Reggie's hand firmly. Abbey carried six small decorative boxes, one of which he handed to Princess Elizabeth. She grasped it gently in her white-gloved hands, opened it, and removed and handed the medal to her father. The King took the ribbon with the dangling silver cross and pinned it to Reggie's left breast pocket.

"Thank you, Your Majesty,"

Elizabeth smiled at him. She had bright blue eyes, and brown curls fell from under her powder-blue hat, not at all how he had pictured her from her voice on the BBC radio broadcasts. "You're very brave," she said. The thirteen-year-old princess touched his arm, leaned forwards and slightly up, and kissed him gently on the cheek. Camera clicks and flash pops echoed through the room at the un-princess like act that all who were present thought was simply charming, even if a bit out of protocol.

She smelled of lavender. Her eyes twinkled.

"Thank you, Your Grace."

The scene was repeated with Freddie, Henry, Willy, and Jack. As the King pinned Dougie's medal to his shirt, the boy forgot his place. "For real? I don't even have a gardening merit yet, sir, um, Your Majesty, I mean." Everyone in the room laughed heartily, none more so than the King himself.

"After this, Douglas," he said, smiling at the gathered military brass, "you needn't w-win another badge again, if you s-so choose. Like the VC, this merit beats them all." The men laughed. His Majesty smiled and winked at the Father Hawkins, who looked at the floor and struggled to swallow a smile. Reggie noted the exchange.

When he had finished with Willy and Jack, the King approached Father Hawkins and the rest of the staff. "You've a brilliant group of boys here, Father. You should b-be proud."

"Yes, Your Majesty, very proud, but I'm late to the party. If not for Miss Goold here, and the Sisters, and the men, everyone really, even the villagers of Hawkhurst—"

"Ah, the good S-Sisters. I've heard a lot about your work with these l-lads. Run a rather t-tight ship, and not too shabby round a needle and b-bobbin." Sister Noreen giggled and curtsied. "Your Majesty, I'm Sister Noreen." Star struck, she shook his hand and smiled from ear to ear. Sister Doreen, standing next to her, was having a hard time keeping it together. She stood, sniffling, trembling slightly, her right hand extended.

"Then you must b-be the dear Sister Doreen I've heard m-much good of." His Majesty gently took her hand in his. That overwhelmed her completely. She burst into tears and fled from the room, leaving the King standing empty-handed with Noreen.

"Now ya done it, Majesty. You set her off. Excuse me, Your Worship." Away went Sister Noreen giving chase, leaving the King, now standing alone, looking more confused than ever. Bob leaned in to him. "Don't worry, Your Majesty. She'll be back," he whispered. "There's cake."

His Majesty leaned in and whispered, "Well, at least she d-didn't faint. It might have taken all m-my horses and a-all my m-men to get the d-dear sister on her feet again, aye?"

Bob sniggered. "Yes, indeed, Sire. Yes, indeed it would."

The King sniggered as well. Sire, he thought, how quaint.

"I like this place, Father," Princess Elizabeth said. "Perhaps Margaret and I could come visit together. I'm sure she would like to meet the boys as well."

"Oh, that would be wonderful, Your Grace! We're a lot more fun when there's not so many important people around," Jack said. All the boys hastily agreed, with wide eyes and excited nods.

"Well, I can't m-make any p-promises, but I can talk it over w-with your mum." He glanced at the military brass again. "She's the one in charge, you know." Another laugh. Abbey pulled a pad from his pocket and took note.

Maurice spoke up. "Come, we have cake for Your Majesty."

"I do wish we c-could, but unfortunately, our time is q-quite limited, and we've another appointment to m-maintain. But I do so k-kindly thank you for all your efforts."

The King turned to Abbey. "You'll remember to bring back a piece of cake for the Queen and send a-another for Margaret, won't you?" Maurice didn't wait for an answer. He ducked and turned, trotting off to the kitchen to pack pieces of cake for the royal family.

"The Queen begged me to offer her expressions of regret that she had to miss meeting you boys. So much so, she asked me to invite you to Buckingham Palace, that she might have the p-pleasure of making your acquaintance. Would you like that?" Abbey immediately nodded with more scribbling in his pad.

Miss Goold looked with awed disbelief at Father Hawkins. This is all a big deal, isn't it, her glance asked.

Bigger than you know, sweet lady, he thought. Big enough to swallow us whole.

***

They were halfway back to the palace when the King finally spoke. "I'm very pleased we've created this George Cross," he said. "Those fighting fires, the neighbours d-digging one another from rubble, the everyday f-folks who are s-suffering, yet r-rise ab-above to act when called by their fellow citizen." He glanced at the countryside, his countryside, as it passed outside his window.

167

"Yes, Father," the princess said. "It is a fine award. I think people who do daring acts to help others inspire more people to do the same. It's very encouraging."

"There've al-already b-been good p-people, like those brave boys, who have d-done a great deal."

As Abbey listened he reached for his pad.

"When Hitler m-makes his move, that number will undoubtedly grow, and s-so will the numbers of recipients beyond six," King George VI decreed. "This is s-something we shall d-do for every country of the Empire."

Chapter 25
All the King's Men

An hour before the King arrived, Dr. Dalton, General Gubbins, Air Vice-Marshal Park and Father Hawkins were taking tea in Father Hawkins' office unbeknownst to the boys; however, unlike the rest of the gathered celebrants, the reason for their visit was more than a social, congratulatory one.

"General, if you please." The air vice-marshal offered him the floor.

The general spoke. "Several months ago in Portsmouth, a young French lad arrived in town. Said he stowed himself away on a freighter from Spain after escaping over the mountains from France. He headed directly to the local base there and asked to speak to the commander." He took a sip of his tea.

"After giving him his due attention, the base commander contacted Home Office, who contacted up and up and up the chain until it landed on my desk. The Secret Intelligence Service doesn't usually get involved in something as seemingly insignificant as the Hitler Youth, but after I explain, you'll understand why, after all this time, we're seeking your help." Another sip of tea. Father Hawkins took a sip of his, trying to calm the butterflies that felt like bats flopping in his stomach.

"This boy, it seems, had been a member of a Scoutisme Français, a new scouting federation formed just prior to the invasion of France. Not only did the Nazis come, but they brought with them some particularly nasty contingent of the Hitler Youth. This confirms field reports we've collected from agents and local witnesses," the general said.

"They move in, ban scouting in any form, and then force native troop members to swear allegiance to them under threat of broken limbs or worse. They're used to terrorise the local population, act as spies, and in general be a reinforcing arm of the Nazis."

"This seems like a problem large enough to be taken on by agents already in the field," said Father Hawkins. "What would you need with an old man like me?" There were already, all over occupied Europe, young, fit, eager agents working covertly. Bombing trains, cutting power lines, blowing up bridges … the sort of things one does when one works undercover in occupied territory during wartime. It literally came with the territory.

"If you please." The general held up his teacup. Hawkins topped it off and re-cosied the pot. "According to intel field reports we've been receiving for months, there's a person of particular interest taking part in this Nazifying of the scouts of Europe, a nasty little bloke who goes by Oberstammführer Thomas Peter Heydrich, to be exact. Senior Unit Leader of a sixty member unit."

"Not *the* Heydrich?" the curate asked.

"The very one, same family. Thomas Peter is Reinhard's nephew, and a godson of Hitler, whom he also calls 'Uncle.' They call him the Nazi Prince. And unfortunately for Europe, he's living up to his name," said Air Vice-Marshal Park.

"Yes, he is. The stories of violence perpetrated by these boys seem too horrific to believe," General Gubbins said, shaking his head as he did so.

Hawkins was as confused as he was intrigued. "But again, what has any of this to do with me?" he asked.

"Jim," the air vice-marshal said, standing and taking the curate's arm, "we need your help. Or more specifically, we need your boys help."

"My *boys*?"

"In the guise of a Hitler Youth unit"—the general cleared his throat—"your boys, with Resistance and SIS support, of course, will cross into Germany, infiltrate Heydrich's unit of Hitler Youth and as soon as possible subdue Heydrich."

"Subdue as in kill?" the priest asked.

"Kill? Heavens no." the general laughed. "He's far too valuable to us alive." He shook his head. "Torture doesn't work and he most likely hasn't any useful intelligence to wring out anyway. It's just the very fact that we have would him, that we went in and were able to snag him from right under their noses. It sends a strong signal, not to mention, at the very least, it would create an added psychological burden on the minds of his merciless uncles."

Father Hawkins' head was spinning. Did these men actually expect him to agree to this hare-brained scheme? Did they really want to send his lads into the lion's den to capture some other lad and smuggle him out of the most dangerous country on the planet? It was a pipe dream.

"Dougie, Willy, Jack?" he asked, his voice getting louder as he did. "They're just boys."

"Boys," the general countered, "who shot down an enemy aircraft, under fire, and captured one of the most deadly pilots of the Luftwaffe, all on their own. They met danger, and they acted accordingly, facing bombs and bullets, yet carrying out what they saw as their duty." He looked the curate in the eyes.

"Those sorts of things—initiative, adaptation, courage under fire, cohesion—can't be taught, and are a great foundation upon which we can build even more skills into them. They're already a unit. We'd like to send to them to the School."

"The School? Are you serious? They wouldn't survive that. Grown men wash out of the School regularly." He knew because he was one of few who had actually been trained there, and made it through to graduation. That seemed so long ago now. "I can't agree to this plan. I know I have a duty to this country, but I swore a duty to protect these boys, and what you are proposing would be a difficult enough task for fully grown—fully trained—men, let alone a group of Boy Scouts."

"Really?" the general interrupted, "Because after hearing of what your boys did"—he lit a cigarette, took a long drag, and exhaled as he spoke—"BP himself suggested this might be the troop for the job. He wrote the first version of the *Scouting for Boys* handbook based on what he learned as a Secret Intelligence Service agent."

"Right. He just left out all the nasty bits about the hand-to-hand combat, demolitions, interrogation, and assassination—all the things the boys will learn at the School, if I agree to let them do this." Hawkins replied sarcastically.

That was a very big *if.*

"Jim," Park said, "we've already run it past the powers that be, and they've agreed."

He'd been bypassed. They had already made the decision.

"But how can you?" he asked, feeling dizzy.

"Wards of court, or His Majesty. As orphans, they have no parents to grant permission. They belong to the King, and the PM has approved." He paused, adding weight to his next statement. "Jim, they all think this plan could have an enormous positive impact on the war."

"The war? What about an impact on them? They're just children. They've been downtrodden their whole lives, and now you want to throw them to the wolves? Where is your compassion for these boys? Have you none? Were the scout uniforms gifts or a recruitment bribes?" He felt his face getting hot.

"They were almost killed the other night defending this country from attack. You say they're too young to fight, yet were they in the military, their actions would have won them the Victoria Cross," the general reminded him.

"But instead, you reward them with another opportunity to get themselves killed?" Hawkins snapped.

"Better to die fighting than by a stray bomb in the night. At least give them the chance to do their duty. Let us give them the tools that will *help them survive* these times."

"Has the decision been made?" he asked, knowing if it hadn't been they wouldn't be here.

"It has, but Jim, we'd"—Park said—"*I* would still like your blessing, if you'll pardon the expression."

The general added, "If not for the mission, at least for those boys."

"I'll have to tell everyone at the home." He had the least seniority, but now the most responsibility. The rest of the St. Michael's family had cared for and loved those boys for far longer. How was he going to tell them their boys were to be sent away, perhaps never to return?

"Jim, as you know, this conversation must stay here. We also have a cover story …" he trailed off.

Jim nodded, raised his fingers to his lips, twisting the invisible key that locked his lips.

"The 'official' cover story to be told is an extended scouting adventure in Scotland, a gift from the King, which isn't too far from the truth," the general explained.

They were going to do what they wanted. His mind flashed with the idea to take the boys and run away to someplace where they couldn't be found. But as quickly as it sprung up he dismissed it as ridiculous. Desertion during war time equates to a death sentence, even if his own sense of duty would allow it, which it wouldn't.

"You'll get my blessing, on one condition …"

The general looked Father Hawkins square in the eye and nodded for him to continue.

***

Father Hawkins wasn't sure his boys could kill, but no matter. He'd help teach them, not because he was particularly good at it, but because they'd need that skill where they were going, just in case. God forbid they should need to use it. Still, their Boy Scout motto was "be prepared." So, they'd learn the importance of killing quickly, quietly, and without remorse, just as he'd been taught.

"Captain, it was a pleasure to meet you." The general saluted and held out his hand. Father Hawkins returned the salute and shook his hand. Captain, he thought. It'd been a long time since anyone had called him that.

Chapter 26

For God and Country

Once the King and Princess Elizabeth had taken their leave, the majority of the crowd went with them, but others, mostly military men, stayed behind. Hawkins told the boys to gather in their room, and he would be up in a bit with a few men who wished to meet them.

When he walked in the dormitory, Father Hawkins was accompanied by three men, two in uniform.

One they instantly recognised as Royal Air Force by his blue tunic, Air Vice-Marshal Park, his cap with gold oak leaves covering the brim held neatly under his left arm, a silver-tipped swagger stick tucked neatly under his right.

Next to him was another commanding figure, dressed in the khaki uniform of the Army, a general. The third man was dressed simply in an unremarkable black suit.

The boys jumped and snapped to attention.

"At ease, Scouts," Father Hawkins said. They snapped from stiff attention to stiff parade rest, legs shoulder-width apart, wrists crossed behind their backs. The three men were impressed immediately.

"Boys," Father Jim said, "I'd like to introduce you to three of gentlemen. This is Skipper, also known as Air Vice-Marshal Keith Park, commander of His Majesty's RAF Eleven Group. Those are his planes up there every day flying overhead. Sometimes he's even in one of them." The AVM nodded.

"And this is Dr. Hugh Dalton, and Army General Colin Gubbins." The boys stood still, looking forwards but dying to get a better look at the visitors from the War Office.

"Oh, for goodness sake, boys, you're scouts, not soldiers. Come over here and greet these men the way we greet guests of St. Michael's." With that they all broke, and rushed to the dashing Air Vice-Marshal, Dr. Dalton, and General Gubbins, falling into their accustomed order of single file, tall to short.

"Congratulations on your GCs," Park said, "and the fine job of capturing Captain Ademeit. Come boys, sit on these beds. Make yourselves comfortable. As I'm sure the Captain *hasn't* told you, since it's a secret of the highest magnitude he wasn't privy to until now, our visit here was only partially to give you these well-deserved medals." He removed a silver cigarette case, with the RAF crest emblazoned across it. He took one out and began to tap it on the case.

"BP and the prime minister himself sent us to have a look at you." He paused. "So far I like what I see very much."

Dr. Dalton nodded again in silent agreement.

"Military intelligence has been working on a plan for several months that, if successful, could possibly shorten the course of this war." The boys' minds started racing. "After your encounter with that Stuka, Lieutenant General Baden-Powell thinks you may be the group for the job." They glanced at one another. BP himself suggested them?

"What is it you'd like us to do, sir?" Freddie asked.

"First things first. There's a small matter of 'technicality' before we proceed any further. Boys, please raise your right hands and form the Scout salute," the AVM said. They did it. Dr. Dalton stepped forwards and spoke.

"On your Scout's honour and as winners of the George Cross, you acknowledge any and all information revealed to you here and now is classified most secret, and you understand it is not to be discussed or disseminated in any fashion—to anyone—*under penalty of death.* Please state 'I do.'"

Freddie glanced again at Reggie, saucer-eyed. *Did he say...?* Yes, was Reggie's silent retort, we're in it deep now. Reggie looked at all the boys, their eyes on him for guidance. He simply nodded assuredly. For King and Country, lads.

"I do." They spoke it together, as they did so many things, their words echoing through the dorm and into the large space beyond.

***

For the next two hours, the boys hung on General Gubbins every word. He called it OPERATION ARCHANGEL. He spelled out Phase One of the plan as it stood, sugar-coating nothing. These boys were now George Cross winners and that meant something.

"It means you deserve the truth," he explained, "because you possessed a raw courage that could, in the right hands, be turned into something special. But," he explained, "what would be expected of you would be very dangerous, and there is a chance you could be killed, but that's what comes with the territory of being a covert agent. Good men are already risking their lives as part of teams performing secret work for the Empire across occupied Europe," the general said

"If you accept this mission, you will be designated as Team Archangel." Dr. Dalton added.

The general answered all their questions as best he could, never once mentioning he had the option to take them, even if they chose not to accept. He hoped they would willingly and of their own accord. But if they didn't he still had the unimaginable option of loading them at gunpoint into the lorry outside and speeding them away like a kidnapper, something he most certainly had no intention of doing, yet it remained an option.

They had until morning to decide, as did he.

***

Later that evening, Hawkins joined the boys in the dormitory

176

away from the ears of the Special Operations Executive commanders. He was met with a less than receptive audience.

"So are you even a curate then?" Freddie asked bluntly.

"Well, I suppose in some ways I am, yes, but no, I'm not an official reverend." He lied about being a priest, what else had he lied about, Reggie wondered angrily.

"For Pete's sake! Is your name really even James Hawkins?" Reggie asked, his tone speaking volumes. This entire day had taken his grasp of reality and turned it on its head. Everything he'd thought of as solid ground was quickly crumbling away under his feet. He felt foundation-less for the first time ever in his life at St. Michael's. And it made him spitting angry.

"Yes, Reggie," Hawkins answered, he reply calm and resolute. "My name is James E. Hawkins. E is for Edward. Before being given the title of curate, I went by Captain Hawkins. I was an SIS officer —Secret Intelligence Service—working undercover in places and on operations I'm not allowed to discuss."

"I knew it!" Willy said as he snapped his fingers. "Spot a spy a mile away, I can."

"I retired from duty after being wounded." That partially explained his scar. "But lucky for me, they don't like to see Victoria Cross winners sitting around swapping stories about the last war when there's one on, so I volunteered and was granted a commission with the Local Defence Volunteers, which had the good sense to put me in with you boys. Vicar Davis needs all the help he can get."

"Blimey," said Dougie. "a VC winner." He looked at the scar on the dashing man's face.

"So your being here has nothing to do with us, it has to do with your mission with Local Defence Volunteers?" Reggie's anger caused his voice to shake as he spoke. Here he'd finally let himself trust this man, and everything he had told them was a lie. Shame on me, he thought bitterly.

"My being placed here had to do with England's best interest, not yours, I'm sorry to say. But"—he tried to make it sound more soft than sobering—"being here has made me think of you as the most important responsibility I have, not my Auxiliary Unit of LDV."

"My duty at St. Michael's is to act as a sleeper agent. Should the Nazis invade I'm to monitor and report everything the Germans in the area are up to via a radio hidden in the catacombs. If instructed, I'm to carry out covert operations making life as much a living hell for the invading forces as possible, hampering conveys, blowing up rail lines and such. My intention was, over time, to include you all in these covert operations, should it have come to that. A village vicar and his alter boys makes an ideal cover for an undercover unit such as that, wouldn't you agree?"

Reggie did, or rather, they all did, as each nodded his head silently. They might be young, but they understood the dire situation their nation now faced.

"So you are a trained SIS officer," Dougie said, sounding more intrigued with this man than ever before. "Espionage and explosives and the lot?"

The curate nodded. "Hand-to-hand, knife fighting, evasion, distraction, demolition. Yes, I know it and have used it all. That's why"—he paused and took a deep breath—"I have decided that if you choose to accept what has been asked of you,"—he swallowed hard—"I'm going with you."

Reggie's visibly slumped in his shoulders, as if the weight of the world had just rolled off, which of course, it had. His eyes welled with thankful tears he tried his best to hide.

"Brilliant! This is better than ever!" Henry and Dougie sat up in their beds. "Is it really true?"

"Yes." He nodded. "I will go with you and take you as far as I can. The rest will be up to you. I'll be waiting for you upon your return to help get you back home. You have my word." He paused and looked steely-eyed at Reggie. The boy returned the steely gaze through his tears.

"Now, it's been an *eventful* day to say the least, and you've a big choice ahead of you. You have until morning to make your decision. But I want you to remember, whatever you decide, no one will judge you and you'll always have a home here." He stood and walked to the door. "G'night, lads. Don't forget to say your prayers."

"Good night, Father."

***

They sat in silence, each lost deep in his own thoughts about the evenings events and what they had been asked to undertake. "It would mean we might not come home." Reggie said. "One or all of us."

"It sounds like a great adventure, if you ask me." Dougie spoke.

"A dangerous adventure, but the best adventures are always dangerous, in some way or other." Henry added, "Of course, I don't care one bit for the idea of never seeing St. Michael's again."

"But," Freddie said, "that's only if we fail. There must be a chance that it could work, otherwise, why would those military men spend their time and effort to attempt it?"

"Could be they're desperate, after Dunkirk," Henry said. "Desperate times call for desperate measures."

"Or desperate missions." Dougie added.

"Well, Father, *eh,* Captain Hawkins did agree to go with us, so he must have some faith in the plan, or at least what he knows of it." Reggie said. "He was in the SIS. after all."

"And they will be sending us to that school they kept talking about," Henry commented, "so we'll be prepared, or at least as prepared as we can be in three months."

"That doesn't seem like much time to learn how to be a covert agent, let alone to learn how to speak German." Jack said, sceptically.

"Well, at least now we know for sure Father Hawkins is not a Nazi. Quite the opposite," Dougie said. "He graduated from that same school they'll be sending us to and he ended up with the Victoria Cross. What reason would we have to not trust him now?"

"Because *now* we're talking about our lives, get it? This isn't a game we're playing," Jack said most seriously. "You were all at that AA gun just like I was. We should have been blasted to pieces. Those were real bullets and could've —should've—cut us to ribbons."

"Yes, they were," Henry agreed, rubbing his still sore shoulder.

"But we weren't, and instead they gave us medals. Strange how that worked out, innit?" Dougie added, glancing at his GC as it dangled off the left side of his nightshirt.

"And remember," Jack pressed his point, "if we're caught in the uniform of the enemy, we'll be shot on sight. We may be gone for a very long time or never see home, this place, ever again. We best think long and hard on that." He fell silent.

"Well, I'm ready to take the risk," Freddie replied, discounting all Jack had just said. Jack rolled his eyes.

"Me too." Dougie said, of course. Whilst Dougie loved all his brothers, he idolised Freddie to the extent that he'd follow him anywhere.

"Me too," echoed Willy. It was at the tipping point. With three in, it would be very difficult for the last three to stay out. All for one, after all.

"I guess so," Henry said, somewhat reluctantly. Reggie figured since he'd got the worst of it at the gun his apprehension was understandable. But Dougie had already agreed, and it was always Henry and Dougie, Dougie and Henry. Being the same age and size, they came as a matched set, like bookends or quality luggage.

Reggie smiled proudly at his brothers, then stood to his feet. "I'm ready, too. What do you say, Jackie?" Only Reggie could call him Jackie and get away with it, because he used it only as a term of endearment, *rarely* sarcasm.

Jack sighed deeply. "I swore an oath to my King and Country. Of course I'm in."

Reggie was pleasantly surprised at how quickly it went, how matter-of-factly and simply the whole decision came to be that fateful night in the dorm. No laboured debates, no hours of side conversations, no need to argue points pro or con. Their baptism by fire at the AA gun gave them a far better grasp of what might lay ahead than any words the air vice-marshal or general could ever convey.

"Gather round," Reggie said. They did as instructed, forming a circle. "Just as King Arthur called his Knights of the Round Table to duty, so have we been called by our own King, George VI. Let it be known, here and now, that we answer his call to duty of our own free wills. Put your hands in." They reached into the centre of the circle, each hand on top of the other. Reggie squeezed them all between his two.

"If you want to change your minds, now is the time. No judgements or ridicule. We're all scared. Say the word, and we forget the whole ordeal." No one moved. He squeezed their hands together tighter. They looked at one another and smiled. "Then it's done." Reggie said. "Scouts of St. Michael: mission accepted."

"Mission accepted." They repeated in unison. "Stay here," Reggie said.

He gathered a piece of paper and pencil. He reached over to Dougie and unpinned the George Cross from the boy's nightshirt. "Don't worry, old boy. I'll give this right back. Everyone, come stick your hand in again."

***

Reggie, dressed in his night shirt and robe, stepped into Father Hawkins office. The curate sat behind his desk, a bottle and a half glass of whisky before him. Reggie walked to the front of the desk. The curate leaned back in his chair and smiled compassionately.

Reggie laid a piece of paper on the curate's desk. "Here you go, Father. This is our decision. Have a good night." With no more to say, he turned and walked from the curate's office.

Jim sat and stared at the folded sheet of paper on his desk, in no hurry to look at its contents.

He grabbed the glass of whisky and drank what remained in a single swig.

He set down the glass, and picked up the piece of paper Reggie had laid there. One sheet, folded once in half. Inside was their answer and their future as they wished it.

He unfolded the sheet.

Across the top, were written only two words: Mission Accepted. Beneath it were six dabs of blood, each the impression of a thumbprint. Underneath the blood stains it said simply Team Archangel. Jim leaned back in his chair. They had accepted and signed the commitment not with their names, but with their blood. In so doing, they had acknowledged the duties expected of them, and affirmed their willingness to undertake those duties regardless of a positive outcome. These lads, Hawkins thought, so very brave indeed.

He reached in his top drawer and removed a medal of his own, the Victoria Cross he had been awarded from the King for his own act of valour performed in the face of the enemy. He unclasped it, jabbed the pin into his thumb and squeezed a drop of blood to the surface. Once pooled, he placed his thumb firmly to the page.

It was done.

***

Upon returning to the dormitory after delivering their acceptance letter Reggie expected to find his brothers awake and waiting for a full report. Instead, he found the rest of the boys fast asleep in their beds. Turning out the light he crawled, exhausted, into his own.

Even though there was no way of knowing where this path would lead, it was now accepted as their duty and their destiny. Whatever future faced them, like the past, they'd meet it together.

Chapter 27
We Each Must Play Our Part

Father Hawkins knocked on her open door frame and stuck his head into Katie's room. "Miss Goold, can I see you in my office in ten minutes? Alone please." That last bit struck her as odd and rather cryptic. Everyone was down for the night. It had been a very long day and exhausting day, what with a visit from the King and all, so she desperately wanted to go to bed. "Of course, Father." By the look on his face, she knew something serious was on his mind. She stopped what she was doing. "Is everything alright?" He said nothing. He just looked in her eyes and smiled. "Ten minutes, please," he said, then he was gone.

She stood, as strange thoughts of all kinds began to creep from the dark corners of her imagination. Is this a surprise, like the boys with their uniforms? She looked at the clock and patiently began waiting through ten minutes that had the feel of ten hours.

When she walked into Father Jim's office, he was seated not behind his desk, but in one of the two high-back leather chairs in front of it. He stood when she entered. "Thanks for coming. Close the door, please. And have a seat, won't you?" Reluctance washed over her. Thanks for coming? Seriously?

"Father Jim," she said, "what is it?" She sensed he was being distant, which was also very odd. "Have I done something wrong?"

"No, but I think I very well may have."

"Does this have something to do with that visit from those three men earlier?" For all his pleasantries and openness, Father James Hawkins was a man with a lot of secrets, some she didn't want to hear, of that she was sure. She had a feeling, as Willy would say, that she was about to hear one of those now.

"Would you care for some tea? Maurice sent up a fresh pot. It's still piping." The tone of his voice unsettled her. He was stalling, and stalling was not in his nature and didn't come naturally. She saw right through it.

"No, Father, I don't care for any tea, thank you." She watched him move to the pot.

"Well then," he said, trying, and failing spectacularly, to sound cheerful. "I believe I'd care for some." He took one of the two cups off the serving tray, walked behind his desk, opened the bottom drawer and pulled out the half-full bottle of whisky, poured a bit into his cup, and drank it down in a quick mouthful.

She stood. "Jim, what is it? What's wrong?"

Father Hawkins poured a bit more, walked around the desk, and poured a bit into Kate's waiting cup.

"Well, if I didn't want tea, I'm surely not in need of that."

"You will be." He gestured. "Please sit." She sat, perched on just the edge of the chair. The curate sat on the edge of his desk. He looked at the floor and then slowly raised his eyes to meet hers. Even looking fearful, how beautiful her eyes were.

"Do you trust me?" He asked her.

"Of course, Father. You're the curate."

"No, Kate, I mean do you really trust me, not a curate, but as a man, Jim Hawkins? Do you trust me to care for you and the boys and St. Michael's?"

Was that it? Is he having a moment of doubt, questioning his faith? "Implicitly, Jim. I trust you with my life and the boys' lives. You're a fine reverend and a wonderful man." She spoke her true feelings, unafraid for him to hear. "The things you have done for all of us are beyond what we could have ever hoped for. We're looking at a better future, unless of course..." She glanced skyward.

"Well," he said, taking another swig, "the only way to do it is to come out with it." He stood and walked to the matching chair across from her. "I'm not exactly who I appear to be."

A flock of birds invaded her stomach. "Jim, you're frightening me."

He flashed as warm a smile as he could manage, although since the general's visit, he hadn't felt much need for smiling. The fear was now visible on her face.

"I'm not a curate, as such. That is, I am a curate, or hope to actually be a vicar someday. Before I put on the vestments, I went by the title captain." Her face didn't change. "My name is James E. Hawkins, I was a captain working for the Secret Intelligence Service behind enemy lines, covert work."

She looked at the scar on his face. It said all she needed to know about his prior service to the country.

"When I retired, I thought nothing more of leaving it behind to serve this higher calling, in a village just like this one, small, quiet—in the country. Because of my past service and the things I knew, saw, what have you, I was 'volunteered' a rank in the LDV Auxiliary Forces. If the Nazis invade, which they're preparing for as we speak, I'm to be the eyes and ears of the Home Guard, and as a commander in the LDV, raise as much hell for the invaders as possible. Under the guise of their Boy Scout training, I've been getting the boys ready for doing their bit in the LDV, as well."

Katie sank back in her chair, a bit more relieved and a bit more grateful. He's not here to save souls, he's here to save St. Michael's, the village, Britain itself. "Jim, why didn't you tell me earlier?"

"Because just by this very conversation we're having now I'm jeopardising the entire plan and your life." He reached out, took her hand, and gently held it in his. "But you deserve to know the truth. You must swear upon all that is holy in life, that you know nothing of my purpose here, to no one, not VD, not the Sisters, Maurice, no one. Not with the

Nazis standing on our doorstep. Do you understand that, Kate?"

She did. Yesterday, the fighters scrambled several times, with her brother at the controls of one. This was serious business; lives hung in the balance day to day, sometimes minute to minute.

"The boys ... they don't know?"

"I suspect they've had an idea for a while. Too clever and intuitive they are, that silly Willy and his creepy feelings. He's like a little sideshow attraction. I've been doing my best to get them ready for what's coming, if not in our future, definitely in theirs. I suspect Freddie is already itching to get in the fight. He and Reggie will be called up first. And as you can tell from their dealing with that plane and pilot, the boys can handle... well, the boys can hold their own."

He let go of her hand and stood, turning his back to her, again looking outside his window at the dark night sky.

The relief Kate felt was enormous. To know they had a professional soldier watching over the family made her very glad indeed. As he'd already displayed, he was certainly a very capable man. She assumed he had a few medals to go along with that dashing scar on his face. "Well, I for one, Father Jim, am very glad you're here. And I know the boys have come to love you, or at the very least, respect you as a man, and maybe even as a father."

"Please," he said, raising his hand to quiet her. "There's more."

***

By the time he had finished explaining about the general and air-vice marshal, BP's suggestion, and the Prime Minister's approval of the plan, and about how the boys, *her boys,* were to *play* a crucial part in the mission, the bottle of whisky was empty. "Play" was the word he used, as if they had just advanced to the semi-finals of some cricket match, but it was no game, nor would any playing be taking place.

"I think I'm going to throw up." She raised her cup to her lips once more, but the smell of the alcohol only made it worse. Her head was swimming.

"So there it is. That's the truth as best I can give it. You deserved to hear nothing less," he said. He had left out most of the mission details, but she got more than the gist.

"I wish I didn't." She sat, wavering between anger, confusion, sadness, and back to anger. "Isn't there another way?"

"I brought up all my objections and offered other ideas, simply because I knew I'd have to have this conversation with you. The cover story is coming in a few hours, when the general will be back to pick up the boys."

"A few hours?" She shot to her feet, only to find her legs wobbling beneath her. She sat back down.

"Yes, 0800 tomorrow morning."

"I won't allow it. They are just boys. The youngest of them is only eleven years old. How can you think of sending them off alone to do something grown men should be doing?" There was a begging element in her voice, as if she'd already given up the fight.

"I'm not sending them off alone," he said. "I'm going with them." On that she gasped and began to sob. He went to her and lifted her from the chair. Hugging her was all he could think to do. She was trembling with each sob. "Oh, Jim. Please tell me this isn't true." He looked deeply into her blue eyes. Sparkling with tears, they looked even more beautiful.

"It will give them the best chances for coming home, so I must go. For you, the Sisters, but especially for the boys. They'll need the best support they can get. And for that I'd send no one but myself." He hadn't told her they would be heading into Germany alone, without him. Just that they were going to be behind enemy lines. If she assumed it was to occupied France, he was more than willing to let her assume so.

"And my boys"—her bottom lip trembled again—"you will bring them back to me, won't you?" Tears streamed over her beautiful young cheeks.

"You have my undying promise."

She buried her head in her chest and sobbed again.

"Come now. This is no way for a proper English lady to behave," he said, his tone consoling.

She raised her head from his chest. *"Psssh* proper."

He laughed. "This is a national security matter. I could be shot for doing what I just did, telling you what I've told you. And you could be

187

locked up or worse ... and then you'd surely never see the boys again."
He paused to reinforce the seriousness of what he was saying. "You
can't—mustn't—mention this to another living soul. You can't act as if
you know anything about it around the rest of the staff, or anyone else
for that matter. Their lives depend on this being kept as secret as possible. Leave this room in the manner in which you entered it, cheerful and
happy, and forget every word you heard. Can you do that for me, Katie?"

"Stiff upper lip and all that?"

He smiled. "That's right, my dear. You were strong enough to
raise these boys, and you must find the strength to let them go do what
must be done, for all of us."

"The Sisters will miss them terribly," she said, regaining her
composure. "And VD, he'll be lost without them."

"It's your new job now to be strong and get them through this,"
he said. "There will be enough for everyone to do in support of St. Michael's. Remember, just because you no longer have these boys to keep
track of, there's an entire village of people who will need your help in my
absence."

Funny, she thought, he's not even a vicar, and he was thinking
about the parish. Although, she rethought cynically, for the best disguises
to work, one must live them.

"They'll be sending another curate to take my place, one who's
also an Auxiliary member and qualified to run the radio hidden in the
catacombs. Should the Jerries invade, he'll be here, just as I was to be.
Promise me you won't fall for him," he joked and actually managed to
work a smile from her face.

"About this radio," she asked. "Can you teach me how to operate it?"

"That's my brave Katie girl," he replied. "Of course. I can and
I will."

***

Reggie awoke in the middle of the night, feeling extra warm.
Willy must have crawled into bed with him, as he sometimes did, when
the dormitory got cold. Reggie usually just carried the sleeping child back
to his bed and tucked him in tightly. But this wasn't Willy. It was Jack,

188

curled up against him, sleeping soundly.

He let the boy sleep as he watched the clouds outside the window move past the bright moon. The enormity of to the blood oath they had just signed was beginning to sink in.

Please, St. Michael, he prayed, protect me and guide my thoughts and actions. Be with me always and help me, for I know not what I'm doing. Not for me, St. Mike, but for them, please protect us. A tear rolled down his cheek. Amen.

He closed his eyes and fell into a deep, dreamless sleep.

**

At 0700 hours the boys were woken up by Father Hawkins and given a small bag. They were told to pack and had just enough to space to carry a set of clothes and a few personal items. They were hustled downstairs, still half-asleep, and paired up. Under the cover story of a surprise three-month extended scouting adventure to Scotland as a gift from the King, they were hustled out, without even having breakfast.

There were no long tearful good-byes, no promises to write or say prayers. There was no last good-bye meal from Maurice with all their favourite dishes. As the Sisters knew it, they'd see the boys again in three months. In reality, as Katie and Father Jim knew it, they may never be back again. They were now part of a secret military mission, and were simply along for wherever the ride was about to take them. The military isn't very forthcoming when sending boys off to war, especially underage boys on an illegal covert mission behind enemy lines.

A hug and quick kiss on the cheek from Miss Goold, and Sister Noreen, a few tears from Sister Doreen, a hug, handshake and a kiss on the forehead from Father Hawkins, and out the door they went. Each pair was packed into a separate black automobile. Katie hugged Father Hawkins and sobbed quietly as she watched the automobiles pull away.

"Please," she prayed, "St. Michael protect them and bring them back to me."

Each automobile took a different route when leaving the home, arriving at a different RAF station, where planes were waiting to carry each pair of boys to the rendezvous airstrip near Isle of Skye, Scotland.

18 July 1940

FROM: MAJOR GENERAL COLIN GUBBINS, S.O.E.

TO: PRIME MINISTER WINSTON CHURCHILL

DR. HUGH DALTON, D.O.O., S.O.E.

AIR VICE-MARSHAL KEITH PARK, R.A.F., S.O.E.

RE: OPERATION ARCHANGEL

Prime Minister,

I have been informed by Captain Hawkins that his scouts have agreed to accept their assigned roles in the mission noted above. They have already begun their trip to their first Special Training School, Arsaig House. They are to begin training upon their immediate arrival.

The operation is still dependant on successful completion of each STS assignment and individual assessment of each agent candidate. Due to the abbreviated time table involved, some elements of their training maybe shortened or eliminated based on mission requirements.

Chapter 28
<u>Far From Home</u>

Dougie and Henry reached the aerodrome fifteen minutes after leaving St. Michael's. Their automobile, pulled directly onto the airstrip, stopping mere yards from an aeroplane which sat waiting, its engine already running.

"Are we going … in that?" Dougie asked, his eyes wide on the small plane sitting in the large mist covered field.

"Blimey!" was the only response Henry could manage, his face plastered against the glass of the window. They were suddenly filled with an excitement that had them bouncing in their seats.

The driver exited and opened the back door. "Don't forget your bags, lads."

Dougie and Henry literally spilled onto the grass, then scrambled to their feet again, only to stand in stunned silence, staring at the loud aeroplane.

Living near an RAF base they'd seen lots of planes flying overhead, but they'd never had the actual experience of being this close to one, of climbing aboard, strapping in, and leaving the ground. Henry had always hoped his first flight might be in a Spitfire or Hurricane, but the fact that it was a different type of aircraft was no less thrilling. Neither of the boys had ever seen a Lysander Mk III aeroplane before. It had enough room to carry the two of them and a pilot, so it served the purpose well. At least Henry hoped it did.

"This flying stuff is for the birds," Dougie said nervously, ribbing Henry, who managed a nervous laugh.

The driver walked them over to the plane, slid the canopy back and helped the boys climb inside.

"Morning!" the pilot shouted. It was very loud behind the large engine. "Welcome aboard. We've a long flight ahead, so if you buckle yourselves in, we can get underway."

The driver helped each boy fasten and secure his seat belt and then gave them a salute. He slid shut the canopy, and secured it. Slapping the pilot's window twice, he gave a thumbs-up and waited for the pilot to return it. When he did, the driver turned and was gone.

The feeling that they were all alone dropped on them like a ton of bricks. Dougie anxiously reached out and took Henry's hand. Henry squeezed back.

The pilot pushed his throttle forwards, and the Lysander began its take-off roll.

***

The plane touched down on a remote airstrip on the rugged coastline of the island, 3 hours and 58 minutes after wheels up. Unlike their take-offs, which had all been from separate fields, all three planes landed within a half hour window of each other at the same airstrip. As with their departure, a car pulled directly up to the plane upon their arrival. Exiting the automobile was a tall, thin lad of about 20 years old, wearing a khaki uniform of the army. He had a light brown hair and a boyish face, and wore round framed spectacles.

"Hello, I'm Corporal Fleming. Welcome to Scotland. I'm here to collect you and the rest of the team and escort you to your new quarters at STS-21, Arisaig House." He stuck out his hand. Not knowing if he should salute, Reggie just reached out and shook it. "Hello, sir, I'm Reggie. I'm patrol leader of the Scouts of St. Michael, this is my brother Willy."

He shook their hands. "Very pleased to meet you both."

As he spoke, a second aeroplane was dropping in for a landing on the grass field. "Ah, a few moments behind but still right on time." The pilot landed the plane with a bounce, then a second, and finally taxied it to within several yards of where they had gathered. The door opened and Dougie and Henry climbed out.

"Blimey!" Dougie yelled, unable to contain his excitement. "Wasn't that just brilliant?" Henry came following up behind, carrying both his and Dougie's bag, as in his excitement to get out of the aeroplane, he had forgotten to take it. "Here you dolt, you forgot this." Henry shoved the bag at Dougie, who was still working to catch his breath. "That was the best three and a half hours of my life." Dougie exclaimed. "Now I know the RAF is right for me."

"Yes, but you are far from right for them." Henry quipped. "You're far from right, full stop."

Corporal Fleming introduced himself.

"I'm Henry, sir."

"I'm Dougie, sir." And a quick hand shake. "Very nice to meet you both boys." As if on cue, the sound of the third and final aeroplane reached their ears. They all turned to watch the machine land.

"So then, if you're all here, that must mean Freddie and Jackie will be joining us shortly."

"Jack, sir" Reggie corrected the corporal.

"I beg your pardon?" he asked.

"He doesn't like to be called Jackie. He much prefers Jack."

"Very good to know. Thank you, Reggie. I hate to make a poor first impression."

"Oh, don't worry, if you forget he'll be the first to remind you," Henry added.

The third plane landed and joined the other two parked on the airstrip. Freddie and Jack climbed out of the aircraft. Fleming was taken by the size difference in the two lads. One was huge, the other slight.

"Hello, Freddie, I'm Corporal Fleming. Very pleased to meet you." Strong hand shake.

"Hello, Jack," Fleming said, offering the small boy his hand to shake. Jack was pleasantly surprised. "Corporal Fleming at your service." All six of them had arrived, so they were ready to go. "If you'll all hop in the car over there, we should be able to make it to the School by tea time."

***

Between tea and supper they were taken to the Quartermaster store where each was issued two sets of khaki battle dress uniforms, belts and boots, socks, undershorts and vests, with even the smallest sizes being too large for Willy and Jack. Bedding for their mattresses was passed out, as were pillows, towels and wash kits. They then went to the barracks that would serve as their home for the next several weeks. The barracks were arranged much like the dormitory back home, with a bed, night table and wardrobe for each boy. After supper, it was back to the barracks where Corporal Fleming instructed them on how to unpack, set up their wardrobes, make their beds and do it all according to army regulations. By 2100 hours, the exhausted boys were grateful for lights out.

Chapter 29
<u>STS-21, Commando School</u>

They were awoken with a click and flood of stark white light that sent their dreams scattering and dragged them back to the cold reality of the barracks. Standing at the doorway was Corporal Fleming, his fingers on the switches. He turned them on and off, creating a strobe effect and then left the switch in the on position.

"G'morning," he said in a tone that was far too chipper for this ungodly hour.

It was still dark outside, and moving from under the warm heavy wool blankets was the last thing any of them wanted to do. Freddie moaned, as did Dougie. Henry, Jack, and Willy remained motionless lumps.

Only Reggie managed to roll over and raise himself on his arm. His eyes struggled to adjust to the harsh onslaught from overhead. Suddenly realising where he was, he jumped from his bed, and saluted the man with the stripe.

Corporal Fleming looked about the room at the other boys still in their beds, and switched off two of the lights, returning the room to a state more conducive to this early hour.

Under his right arm, he was carrying a box, so as a return salute he simply waved his hand at the boy. "No need to salute me. I'm just a lowly corporal."

"I'm sorry, sir," Reggie said. Dressed only in his underwear, he stood hopping from one bare foot to the other, trying to escape the cold floor. "It just—what time is it, anyway, sir?" He scratched his ruffled hair and yawned.

"Don't worry, it's day two. You aren't like regular troops here, no matter how much they say they're going treat you just like everyone else. The fact that I've been named your batman instead of giving you lot a FANY is proof enough of that. You boys are heroes. Put on your dressing gown before you catch cold."

"FANY, sir?" Reggie asked. "Batman?"

"First Aid Nursing Yeomanry. They're the ladies who work as assistants to the new recruits here, kind of like a nursemaid. You'll see them round. As a batman, I'm kind of the same thing, really. To keep an eye on you and help you assimilate to life in the programme. And to answer your question," he glanced at his wristwatch. "it's 0430 hours. You have your first training session with Captain Fairbairn this morning at 0530 hours."

Reggie opened the wardrobe next to his bed, pulling out a khaki dressing gown (everything here seemed khaki) and put it over his cold shoulders. He instantly felt better. He was surprised at how much the place reminded him of the dormitory back home.

As Fleming had said, they were special, so they lived in their own private barracks, which was laid out like their room at St. Michael's—to help with homesickness, Reggie guessed.

"Got something for you boys—new toys, direct from the Captain himself."

He set down the box he was carrying. Reggie sat back down on his bed, glancing at the lifeless boys in the other bunks. Wow, this was early, he thought, which led to another yawn, a big one, which set off Fleming yawning.

"See here," the Corporal warned. "That's one of the things you'll not want to be doing in front of any officers. If they see you do that, they're liable to think you're not interested in the pearls of wisdom they're spouting and slap you with a beasting, like run a mile or do 50 press-ups, so none of that, if you're wise."

"Yes, sir. Sorry, sir," Reggie replied.

"Listen, whilst we're about it, I'm just a bloke like you. I only made corporal a short time ago, once they said you boys were coming and needed a batman of your own, one who could speak German—which I can—so forget that whole sir-this and sir-that bit." He nudged Reggie in the ribs. "I'm a just a corporal, not a bloody CBE. You address me as corporal. Just plain corporal. Or Corporal Fleming, if you like."

"You can speak German?" Reggie asked.

"*Ja.*" Fleming answered. "That's German for yes. And I also speak French, Italian and Spanish as well. Language was my speciality at university before I was called up." Fleming answered.

"I have to wake the others. Willy finds it tough in the mornings sometimes, he's a deep sleeper."

"I got the thing for that. One manual and one Hitler Youth knife." He reached in the box and pulled out a knife, with a red and black swastika on the handle. He handed it to Reggie, along with one of the thick books. "Happy Christmas in July."

Reggie read the title aloud. "*Get Tough!* by William E. Fairbairn? Is that our Captain Fairbairn?" he asked.

"The one and only, thank God. He's the man who literally wrote the book on this stuff, and that's it in your hand. You'd be hard pressed to find a better instructor."

Reggie thumbed through the book. On one page was a short written description explaining a hand-to-hand combat move, and on the page opposite were illustrations of two men fighting, with step-by-step instructions of how to perform the move on an enemy combatant. It was much like a comic, with none of the humour.

"One tough bloke, Captain Fairbairn is. He used to walk a copper's beat on the tough streets of Old Shanghai, and streets don't get any tougher. Gangsters, pirates, thugs, you name 'em, he's fought 'em. Over six hundred confirmed fights he was in. Stabbed dozens of times. He was even shot six times once, and they still couldn't kill him. He's got sixteen lethal ways to silently kill a man. You're here to learn them."

"Saints, preserve us!" Reggie said, borrowing Sister Doreen's favourite and only expletive. "Captain Fairbairn sounds like some kind of superman … or maybe a ghost." Reggie said.

"He actually invented that." Corporal Fleming pointed at the knife.

"He invented Hitler Youth knives?" asked Reggie. He picked up the sheathed blade.

"That isn't a Hitler Youth knife—well, not a regular kind anyway." He watched in the dim light as Reggie pulled the blade from its black metal sheath. It was a double-sided blade, tapered to a point at the end. It was black, thin, and sleek. It may have had a Hitler Youth handle, but that was where any resemblance to a single edged Hitler Youth knife ended. This was a double-edged metal dagger.

"Wow," he said, as he turned the blade over in his hand, "It's beautiful."

"Him and another fella, Captain Sykes, designed it to be the perfect commando blade. In that box is a manual and knife for each of you." He stood and walked to the light switches again.

"Now, you get them up and pass those manuals and blades out, one each. Then grab your wash kits and head over the Ablutions. You have fifteen minutes to wash up. You're to muster in the battle dress uniforms you were issued by the Quartermaster yesterday when you arrived. This is the uniform to be worn every day during working hours." Fleming said, sounding like a training manual. "This is for security, and to save your civilian clothes the wear and tear of training activities, many of which take place outdoors." He took a deep breath and continued. "There is no objection to your wearing whatever clothes you please for relaxation in the evening."

"Also," he continued, "each of you should have your FS blade hanging from your belt." He turned on the remaining lights to a collective moan.

"A few brief reminders for you lads. Meal times are the same every day. 0815 breakfast. 1245 lunch. 1630 tea. 1900 supper. It is particularly requested" he continued, again sounding as if he'd spoken these words before, "that you observe these times. Kitchen accommodation and staff are limited. Considerable inconvenience can be caused through unpunctuality. Not to mention," he continued. "that it's just plain rude. But

I needn't tell a group of Boy Scouts that. We've got a long day ahead, so bring your appetite to breakfast."

Reggie snapped to attention and saluted him properly. "Thank you, Corporal Fleming."

The corporal smiled. "I suppose I should start getting used to that, aye?" he said with a wink.

"We'll get used to it together, Corporal," Reggie said and returned the smile and the wink.

"Right. Now look sharp." Fleming said, "You don't want to keep 'Dangerous Dan' waiting."

Chapter 30
Getting Tough

"Right," the captain began. He was a very slight man, fit, yet also very thin, with nothing that set him apart as the world's best commando, which he was, except for his battle dress and black combat boots. On his head sat a black beret with crest, the thin face below it looking older than its fifty-eight years.

All in all, with his little round wire spectacles, he looked more like a librarian, or worse, a schoolteacher. "My name is Captain William Ewart Fairbairn of the Royal Marines. You may refer to me as Captain Fairbairn, or sir." His voice was squeaky. He looked them up and down. "You're here to get tough. I don't know what you *expect* to learn here, but I can guarantee what you *will* learn, and very well, if I may say. You will learn unarmed hand-to-hand and knife-to-hand combat the way it was meant to be taught. I'll see to that."

The boys stood in a line, tall to short.

"Now, the way we're going to learn is just like a dance class." Unlike other officers who liked "walked the line" when addressing his troops, the captain stood motionless as a statue, his hands locked behind his back. "Why a dance class, you ask? Because out there"—he used a jerk of his head for emphasise—"when you find a willing partner who wants to do this kind of dancing, you best know the fancy footwork, or you'll find yourself in a very bad spot indeed. I'm going to make sure your feet know how to finish the dance before your ears even hear the music."

The sun slowly began to rise. They were dressed as instructed in boots and wool battle dress uniforms issued on their arrival, yet still, they shivered in the cool pre-dawn.

Captain Fairbairn pulled his fighting knife from its sheath. "This is your new best friend. It's called the Fairbairn-Sykes Commando Blade for myself and my partner, Captain E. A. Sykes. It's a weapon we designed for the commando forces, except, you'll notice, the handle. Whilst mine"—he held up the sleek, double-sided combat blade for them to see—"has a round handle, the one you will be carrying will have the handle of a Hitler Youth dagger, same as every other Hitler Youth member. That way, when Jerry gives you a quick once-over, all he'll see is a regular dagger in your sheath, not an FS commando blade."

He winked, making a clicking sound with his mouth as he did.

"You'll notice the FS blade is thin, almost flat. That is purposely to allow it to slip easily between the ribcage and into the vital organs beneath without getting stuck. You will also notice it is sharpened and tapers to a point on both sides. This makes it the perfect blade for cutting a sentry's throat, because when done correctly, it will sever both jugular arteries with a single run through." He demonstrated with the pantomime of sticking it in, and then punching it forwards. "But that will all come later."

"Now, there's no reason a smaller man is at a disadvantage, if he knows what he's doing. But before I show you how to handle someone larger, we're going to start simple, especially since you come in various sizes. So, find someone your size and pair up."

They glanced at each other and didn't move. They were always paired up by size, whenever they stood abreast, simply by force of habit.

"Right. Now that you've found your size partner, let's get started. First thing any good commando needs to learn is how to fall down properly. You're asking yourself, 'There's a proper way to fall?' There certainly is." He stood, hands clasped behind his back, his glasses reflecting the lightening sky in their lenses. "The secret to falling down is not letting it happen in the first place, as the ground makes a less than ideal fighting platform. Key is getting back on your feet as quickly as possible. And, for the next few days, you boys are going to be finding yourselves down on the ground a lot."

Dougie leaned into Henry. "He's talking to you," he whispered.

"Douglas!" The captain shouted. "Step two paces forwards." Dougie immediately snapped to attention and stepped two paces forwards. When he did the captain walked over, stepped behind the boy, and wrapped his lean arm around the boy's neck. Dougie's face instantly turned beet red as the captain's bicep and forearm easily stopped the flow of blood to and from the boy's head.

Dougie's hands instinctively went for the captain's arm and grabbed it, as if his young hands had any possibility of breaking the vice-like grip round his neck. Air could no longer move into his chest as he tried to inhale, instantly causing him to panic. His open hands became fists, swinging and punching at the man's arm, but like battering rams against boulders, they had little chance.

None of the boys liked watching Dougie being treated this way but no one moved. This was a lesson for Dougie, taught the way they teach things round this place, Reggie reasoned. When someone else's mouth is moving, especially Captain Fairbairn's, yours had best not be. It was a lesson Dougie, a chronic interrupter, had needed to learn for a very long time.

"This is known as the Japanese Strangle hold." Captain Fairbairn said. "Notice where I place my arms, one squeezing the neck, one pushing the head into the crux of my elbow."

Dougie's arms dropped to his sides as his eyes rolled back in his head. "As you can see, it's quite effective for subduing an opponent from behind."

The captain released him, and Dougie flopped to the ground, like a large sack of dry flour. "Killing at close quarters demands extreme concentration." The boys stood silently watching Dougie—motionless—facedown in the grass.

"The reason that looked so easy is because it was. He was expecting I'd come over and tell him he should shut up and not interrupt.

Instead, I did what he wasn't expecting. I closed off the blood and oxygen to his brain, and shut him up myself. That's called initiative, and we look for that from our agents."

Dougie was beginning to stir on the ground as the blood refilled his thirsty brain. He slowly raised himself to his feet, wobbling slightly. "It's a good thing I'm not a Nazi or we'd have to find Henry here a new partner. Good show, Douglas."

"Tha-thank-you, s-sir," he said, feeling dazed and slightly confused.

Freddie locked eyes with Reggie, questioningly. This is the real thing, innit? A saucer-eyed Reggie responded with a simple nod, it's time to get tough.

Chapter 31

Into the Gutter

"Now as I was saying, this is your new best friend." He held up the steel dagger balanced between his fingers. He began tossing it continuously from left hand to right and back again, rolling the handle with his fingers as he did.

"In a knife fight," he said, "you keep moving the blade from one hand to the other. That way your enemy doesn't know from which hand to expect the attack." He worked the dagger between his fingers displaying his complete control of and comfort with the sharp weapon. "With a mere 1/16th of an inch of this blade into an enemy's back I can make him go anywhere I choose. Or I can dispatch him with silence and speed, two things necessary for ultimate success. I know it works because I designed it, and I've used it to kill." Three of the boys were looking at the ground.

"Excuse me, gentlemen," the captain said sternly. "Are you not interested?"

"No, sir, it's not that, sir. We've never really talked about …" Reggie spoke what the whole group was feeling.

"Killing? Oh. Well, see there? Already you've got it wrong. My job is to teach you how to keep living, not how to kill as such. Killing is just something you may find yourself having to do to stay alive. Make no mistake. Your enemy has been trained to kill, even if it means giving up his life. However, your will to live will always overpower their willingness to die. It's the way of war. If you've been trained to keep living, you will succeed. Your only duty from this moment forward is to learn what you're here to be taught. It will serve you well and keep you alive. That's the truth, best I know it. And gentlemen, that's the truth of your future, of what's ahead of you."

He looked at Reggie. "I was about your age when a 'generous' recruiting officer forged papers saying I was old enough to sign up. Truth be told, I was but sixteen years old, looking for adventure. And I sure found it. In the form of aeroplanes that would drop gas bombs on us." The captain said, glancing skyward.

"So, when I talk about fighting and dying, all you're going to get from these lips is the truth as I've lived it. I've seen and done things in my life I'd never tell me mum." He winked. "And so will you." The boys smirked.

"If you're looking to survive this coming mission, then give these lessons more attention than you've ever given anything before." He leaned forwards, in front of Willy, bent, and looked in his eyes. "Because make no mistake, your enemy *has* and he's out there waiting—for *you*." Every eyeball was riveted to the captain. He turned crisply.

"I've got only weeks to teach you what took me thirty-five years and a lot of pain to learn. So forget all you know about fighting, and you'll be in a much better place to start learning to keep living."

The boys stood silent.

"I'm going to teach you to encounter a brutal enemy up close and live to tell the tale. Understand that the Boy Scouts and the Hitler Youth are two entirely different types of groups. The Hitler Youth is a paramilitary organisation, a primary school for Hitler's newly christened Waffen-*SS*. Ever heard of them? These units consist mostly of pre-selected Hitler Youth members. These boys have been training for military action from an early age so when the they turn 17, the armed wing of the SS comes looking to recruit them directly into their ranks, They are fanatical and reported by intelligence sources to be responsible for brutal atrocities and the massacre of civilians as well as captured British and Polish troops, in both occupied Poland and France."

The boys had indeed heard of the much feared SS. The *Schutzstaffel*, Hitler's private force of black uniformed bodyguards had grown beyond that assigned role to become a fanatically loyal tool of terror, which he unleashed against any and all who dared stand in his way. British newspapers were filled with reports of their murderous exploits against the allies and civilian populations.

"These are the types of boys you must be ready to encounter. And you will be. Mark my words."

Like everything else the captain said, they had no reason to doubt him.

"Sergeant Major!" he called out. A giant of a man wearing a similar beret came striding through the morning darkness. He was dressed in a short sleeve shirt which barely contained his bulging arms, and around his waist hung a tartan kilt. He carefully studied each of the boys as the captain spoke. "This is Sergeant Major Burns Preston-Downey. He will be your training instructor, and I shall oversee him."

"Sergeant Major, these are our newest operatives, selected by the prime minister himself."

"Oh, you don't say, sir. Sounds fancy," replied the sergeant major in a Scottish brogue as thick as the hair-covered forearms currently folded across his wide chest. Red stubble lined his head under his beret. His presence only made the captain appear that much more bookish, at least that was Reggie's initial impression.

"They have less than the usual six weeks to learn 'defensu' handto hand as it needs to be known."

"I'll have them ready in four weeks, sir. Tops." The large man answered, his voice strong and tone confident.

The boys could practically feel the sergeant major's eyes heavy on them.

The captain spoke with the utmost seriousness. "You are not allowed to kill them, Sergeant. They've been selected for a very special mission, so they must survive school."

This was definitely not the Boy Scouts, Reggie thought. Even if they were kidding, which he truly hoped they were, that was not an appropriate joke for children.

"Oh, now don't you go worrying one bit, sir." The sergeant major said. "They're in my charge now. In a few short weeks their own mothers won't recognise them."

Freddie stepped forwards, out of line. The sergeant major smirked. He stepped forwards to meet the large boy, who stood almost eye to eye with him. The sergeant major, at six four, had a couple of inches on Freddie. The big man unfolded his arms and rested his balled fists his hands on his hips.

"My word," the sergeant major said, looking at the large boy before him. "How much did they feed you at that place?"

"Not enough, sir," Freddie answered.

The sergeant's jovial expression melted instantly to one of displeasure.

"I'll let it go this time, because you haven't any sense yet. The rest of you would do well to listen closely." The sergeant major said, addressing all the boys. "You do not call me sir. I'm a Sergeant Major so work for a living." He turned his head and winked at a smirking Captain Fairbairn. "You are to refer to me as Sergeant or Sergeant Major, not sir. If any of you calls me sir again, I might just have to rearrange your testicles. Do you understand?"

"Yes, Sergeant Major." Freddie answered.

"Let me hear the lot of you!" the big man barked.

They answered in unison. "Yes, Sergeant Major."

"Well, lad," to Freddie, "here you can eat as much as you like, and go back for seconds. You'll need all your strength and more for what you'll be doing over the next three months. Now, would you like to share with me your reason for stepping out of line, lad?" he asked the boy.

"Yes, Sergeant Major," he said in a stern, yet respectful tone. The sight of the man's thick arms covered in scars made him second-guess his objection. He paused.

"Come on then, let's have it." The sergeant major prodded.

"Well Sergeant Major, it's about our mothers."

"Your mothers?" he asked, glancing over his shoulder at the cap-

207

tain, who nodded.

"Yes, Sergeant Major. You and the captain have made remarks about our mothers. I'd like you to know Sergeant Major, that we have no mothers, we're orphans." The boy's voice trembled slightly. He lowered his volume so only the sergeant major could hear him. "It doesn't bother me, I can take it. But I don't like to see the younger boys reminded in such a rude manner. If you don't mind, Sergeant Major." The large man nodded, considering the boy's comments.

"Hmm. Initiative. Not afraid, also not combative, asked like a true gentlemen not to be confrontational, but to spare the feelings of your men, or in this case, your younger brothers. For a first meeting, that took some serious balls," Sergeant Major Preston-Downey replied. "I like this one already," he remarked over his shoulder to Captain Fairbairn. He turned back to Freddie. "Well spoken, lad. And since you have been so kind to inform me of that which I am already keenly aware, from this moment on I want you to think of me as your mother. And that goes for the rest of you lot." He leaned in closer, lowering his voice so Freddie alone could hear him. "Also, if you ever have something to say to me or any other NCO again, ask permission first. This is a conversation the captain does not need to waste his time on. Do you understand, Scout?"

"Yes, Sergeant Major!" Freddie shouted, snapping to even sharper attention.

"Louder!" The sergeant major yelled.

"YES, SERGEANT MAJOR!" Freddie screamed.

"Fall in!" The sergeant major barked at him. Freddie jumped two paces back and re-joined the line.

The sergeant major spoke. "Now, let's pair up. Freddie and Reggie. Henry and Dougie. Willy and Jackie."

Jack visibly slouched and frowned, which didn't escape the attention of their new instructor.

"Is there a problem, Jackie?"

"Yes Sergeant Major!" the smallest boy shouted, trying to make his voice sound less childlike.

No! Reggie's brain screamed. *Don't be daft Jack, not now, not with this man.*

The sergeant major slowly strolled over and stood in front of the small boy.

"Please don't call me Jackie. I much prefer Jack, Sergeant Major."

"You prefer Jack do you? Very well, Jack it is. Take two paces forwards, *Jack*."

"Now boys, Jack here has been good enough to volunteer for our first demonstration. Can I get another volunteer?" Freddie stepped forwards out of line.

"Ah, Freddie. Perfect. Now, fight."

They looked from the sergeant major to captain and back again, confused.

"Did you not hear me, Scouts? I said *fight*. Come on, get at it."

Jack lunged at Freddie, wrapping the larger boy up in his arms. Freddie looked down, twisted round, and easily escaped Jack's grasp. He swung his leg, and Jack fell to the ground. He sprang up almost instantly, and Freddie easily put him in a headlock and felt foolish. Jack swung his fists in vain. The mismatch in size made the exercise almost comical. Jack managed to trip Freddie to the ground, where they rolled around a bit more, kicking up dust and pulling at each other's clothing, but in the end they looked more like a couple of dogs tussling together in the dirt.

"Alright, that's enough. Back in line." The sergeant major commanded.

"Is that what you call fighting? That might be fine for the school-yard, but this isn't a playground anymore, lads. This is *war* and war means kill or be killed." The captain said in his squeaky voice.

"He's so big!" Jack yelled at the captain, picking himself up off the ground, forgetting his place. "How am I supposed to do anything against someone so big, sir?"

"You think size matters, do you?" Preston-Downey smiled, winking at Jack. "Cochran!" The sergeant major barked out. A monster of a man, two heads taller than the sergeant major and twice as wide, trotted across the field. Reggie, having never seen a fellow that large, thought he could actually feel the ground shake with each of the man's steps.

"This is Cochran. He's one of my best and definitely my biggest. Cochran, I'm trying to teach young Jack here that size doesn't matter.

May I?"

"Of course you may, Sergeant Major."

"Captain?" The sergeant major offered. Captain Fairbairn approached Cochran, making himself look like a frail old man in the process.

"Cochran, I see we meet again," Fairbairn said with a smirk. He extended his hand for the man to shake. The larger man took it.

"Yes, sir, good to see y—oof!" The tiny captain grabbed the larger man's hand, and pulled him in close as his shin rocketed up between Cochran's legs, his calf making full contact with the large man's testicles. Cochran found himself, as he knew he would, powerless against the lightning-fast onslaught. The violent blow forced the large man to involuntarily bend forwards at the hips, causing his head and chin to protrude at the perfect angle for the captain to thrust his open palm full-force into the man's jaw. The giant man's teeth slammed together with an audible *crunch*.

Fairbairn's fingers became a claw which he ruthlessly gouged into the huge man's eye sockets. Holding Cochran's head in a vice-like grip, the small captain slammed him to the ground with tremendous force. The captain's open free hand smashed against the giant man's throat, as his other hand pressed hard over his victim's eyes, nose, and mouth. Like a bolt of lightning, the brutal assault was over almost before it began, as David had beaten Goliath.

"Don't stop or give up on your opponent just because he is crippled. Crippling him only makes him that much easier to kill," the captain remarked.

"Blimey," Dougie whispered.

"All blows are struck with the side of the hand, fingers and thumb locked and extended, like so." He held up his hand to show them, emphasising the proper chopping style of a proper blow. "Never a fist, or you'll end up with broken fingers."

The captain released Cochran, who methodically, slowly, struggled to his feet. His face was deep red, tears streamed from his eyes, the arteries in his neck visibly pulsed with each beat of his pounding heart. He bent slightly at the waist. The boys stood in awe.

"Very good, Cochran. Are you alright?" The captain helped the large man steady himself on his feet. Cochran leaned his head forwards and spit a bit of vomit from his mouth.

"Yes, sir," Cochran managed to say between coughs brought on by the testicle blow. "Always my pleasure, Danny Boy, sir."

"You see, by knowing the right points of the body to attack, size means nothing." Cochran stood. "Now, I want you to strangle me." Cochran put both of his massive hands around the captain's neck. With a free hand, the captain reached up to the large man's face, and grabbed one side of Cochran's jaw with a thumb and two fingers, a seemingly dainty hold compared to Cochran's two-handed grip on his throat. The huge man's face contorted in pain, and he instantly dropped his hands from the captain's neck, and as the captain increased his pressure by the slightest degree, Cochran dropped to his knees.

"Pressure points." The captain said. "See how easy it is when you know how?" he asked, releasing the massive man. "Thank you again, Cochran." The captain said. The sergeant major nodded his approval.

Cochran stood and trotted off with a tad less trot than he had when he joined them but seemed no worse for the wear. Reggie surmised that, as one of their finest, he was tough enough to handle a full-speed kick to the balls, and quarter-speed smash to the throat. It was now clear to them why Fairbairn's nickname round camp was 'Dangerous Dan'.

"That, lads, is how you keep living'. I call it 'defensu'— or 'gutter fighting'—because it's how you'll beat your enemy. It's eye gouging, it's ball kicking, it's down, it's dirty, it's from the gutter, and it *will* save your life."

The sergeant major spoke up next. "This is the level of training you will undergo for the next three months. It's rough, it's violent and it will hurt. But if you are not willing to train to this level, then you should not be going to war, because this is war. It's rough and violent and it hurts." The boys were intrigued, yet, after seeing the blunt display, also more apprehensive than ever.

"Now is a good time to forget all about fair fighting, and good sportsmanship, and all that cock-and-bull about Queensberry rules, being a good Scout, and being kindly and helpful to all you meet. There's not too many old ladies to help cross the street where you're going."

The captain reiterated. "This, my lads, is *war*. Your object here is to learn how to kill. Since this course is meant to teach you to kill, its methods are dangerous. You will, however, get no credit if you damage or kill your sparring partner." Again, there was no humour in his tone. Reggie swallowed hard. "You must never disregard the two tap submission signal, as that means you should stop what you are doing instantly. It is the one rule here that is never broken. Is that understood?"

Together: "Yes, sir."

"Good. Make no mistake, when I'm done with you, you'll have no equals your age, except each other. Now, the sun is joining us, so it's time to begin. Sergeant Major, I leave these boys in your capable hands."

"Thank you, sir. Now, lads, let's start the morning off with some Physical Training, shall we?"

***

That first morning they went on a seven mile run which culminated in various field exercises including dozens of press-ups, dozens of pull-ups and a run across an obstacle course with dozens of stations designed to make them jump, climb, swing, balance, hop then crawl up, over, down, under and through. That first morning set the timetable they'd keep every morning, between 0530 and 0700 hours, for the next three months. It was a far different timetable than they had been used to living at St. Michael's, and it would take some serious adjustment.

Upon return from their morning calisthenics, they broke into pairs and spent an hour rehearsing over and over the sixteen lethal hand-to-hand combat moves developed by Captains Fairbairn and Sykes. It took many days for the boys to reset their minds and adjust their bodies to the violent, painful "gutter fighting" style of training which often brought them to tears. But Captain Fairbairn and Sergeant Major Preston-Downey assured them they could handle the beating they were enduring under the guise of training. "You are far tougher and more resilient than you know."

"Pain is temporary," they preached, "but defeat is forever."

They trained to take a throat chop and brush it off, how to be thrown hard and roll to get up again quick, how to take a blow to the balls and accept that, whilst uncomfortable for a time, it rarely caused death.

"This isn't something that can be learned from a book, even one written by a living legend like Captain Fairbairn himself. It must to be taught by doing, and learned by suffering." The Sergeant Major reminded them. "This is the regimen that will prepare you to survive your trip to the gutter."

Chapter 32
<u>Saints or Sinners</u>

Every minute of every day was filled with something to do, learn, or practice. Each morning training consisted of the sergeant major running them ragged for an hour and half, then hand-to-hand drills, until 0815 breakfast, then classroom instructions until lunch at 1245 hours. Afternoon drills of some sort were held outside until tea time at 1630, then classroom language lessons until 1900 hours when supper was served. The rest of the evening they could spend as they wished, as long as it was spent on base. Lights out was officially 2100 hours, but the boys were often in bed well before then, using sleep to help them adjust to their new lifestyle.

They were all lying in their bunks, dressed only in their underwear and vests, as lights out was quickly approaching.

"Have you looked through this massive thing?" Dougie asked no one in particular. He was sitting on his bunk flipping through the 400 plus page binder that made up their training manual. He read the first page. "OBJECTS AND METHODS OF IRREGULAR WARFARE."

"I read about demolitions," Henry chimed in as he twisted the handle on an imaginary detonator he held in his hand. "I can't wait to blow something up. Maybe a bridge or a train or some such thing."

"I guess all that stuff they tried to teach us at St. Michael's can go right out the window," Jack said. "The commandments don't seem to mean much around here. They talk about breaking them like they're eggs, and no one say a thing about it."

"I don't think I want to kill anyone. I mean, that's the biggest one, isn't it?" Henry asked.

"Thou shall not kill," Dougie stated what they all knew by heart.

"So who's in charge?" Henry asked, genuinely concerned. "I mean, if God says no, who are these chaps to be telling us yes? He's their God, too, and won't that make Him angry?" he asked.

"The only one any of us should worry about getting angry is Captain Fairbairn," Reggie reminded them. "This is about staying alive, and sometimes killing has to be done to make sure that happens. If we die, the mission fails. Which means they either send more like us to finish it, or they scrap the plan. Either way, we're dead."

"Then they outrank God? How can you say such a thing?" Henry asked, almost in a whisper, as if Jesus himself were listening in on a headset somewhere, writing it all down, like a master spy, *the* master spy.

"Then we die for nothing, and go straight to hell." They fell silent. It was true; they'd been raised by priests and nuns, who spoke of nothing but God's love, and the giving grace of the Lord. Now, their countrymen were operating off a completely separate list of commandments, it seemed.

"Perhaps the Lord is a Jerry. What then?" Dougie asked, genuinely concerned.

Reggie pondered this previously unconsidered angle. If they thought that God was on their side—God, King, country and all that—then surely the Jerries thought the same thing. Seeing the way they took over most of Europe so quickly, perhaps they were in God's favour.

"I wish Father Hawkins were here," Willy said in his child's voice. "He'd have an answer that would make sense of all this madness," or at least he would know what to say to the boys, Reggie thought. He had nothing to offer.

"Listen." Freddie said. "I know you're scared, I am too."

Henry looked at Freddie hard. Even after admitting it, the larger boy didn't look scared.

"But," he continued, "it's like they've been telling us. This is a new world, and we need these skills if we want to stay alive in it." He looked directly at Henry. "If you have a problem with 'Thou shall not kill,' just turn it around, and that will keep God happy. Get it? 'Thou shall not die.' After all, if God gave you your life, who is some dirty Nazi to take it from you? You have a godly duty to kill, if someone is trying to kill you."

"If he hits your left, aren't you supposed to offer him the right? 'Turn the other cheek,' Jesus called it." Dougie said.

Jack commented. "Yes," he said, "But dying isn't a sin. Killing is a pretty big one."

"You don't think about it when you squash an insect, do you? Or swat a fly, crush a spider?" asked Freddie. "When you see a spider and squash it, didn't you just kill?"

"Yes, but that's just a spider," Dougie said, not helping matters. "It's not a person, you know, a human being, with parents, like you and me."

"The commandment doesn't say 'Thou shall not kill people, but insects are just fine.' It says 'Thou shall not kill.' Full stop. You've already killed one of God's creatures. And if so, you're already damned to hell, so why not take some Nazis with you?" Freddie said flippantly, as if he'd rationalised this all through before. "Like the captain said. Kill or be killed. It's that simple. I'll deal with God when that time comes, but for now, the Nazis are far bigger threat to us than the wrath of God or the fires of hell."

"I don't want to go to hell. It's seems like such a nasty place," Willy reminded everyone.

"Do you see anyone else around here worried about it? They're all too busy preparing to live," Freddie said, now sounding tired of the conversation. "All this talk after a long painful day only serves to made it longer and more painful," he said, rubbing his tired eyes. There had been running, and fighting, and running, and climbing, and running, and crawling, and more running. He was beyond exhausted. "As long as these people say it's okay, I'm going to do whatever I have to do to *keep living.* We have a duty to fulfil, we need to be prepared. These men are going to teach us to take care of one another better than we ever have, understood?"

He looked to Reggie hoping to see some kind of reassurance in his eyes. Instead all he saw was more uncertainty. Unasked questions seemed to be stuck just inside every mouth.

"I don't think I can do this," Dougie said from his bed. "What if they kill us?" His whisper was trembling, as if on the verge of tears.

"They can't kill us," said Henry. "They need us."

"What makes you think so? There are plenty of replacements out there. Plenty of Boy Scouts to choose from." Jack said.

Dougie persisted, "It could happen by mistake. Sergeant Major's hands are awfully strong. He can crush bone with that grip."

"We have to jump out of a plane," Henry added. "We've only gone up in one once and they want us to jump out of one. What if the parachute doesn't open?"

Willy smiled and rubbed his sweaty hands on his underpants. "It's perfectly safe, and they'll teach us to do it. Although it does sound a little scary."

"A little?" Reggie said to Freddie quietly. "I practically wet myself just thinking about it."

"There'll be no wetting yourself allowed," Freddie said, imitating the sergeant major and his heavy brogue quite well, "as it'll make you bludy cold on the way doon which could led to duble pneumonia, disarientation and death in minootes." They had a good laugh at that. Freddie turned beet red.

"Oh, stop," Henry said, laughing hard.

"Just keep doing what you're told, keep your eyes open and your gob shut, and everything will be fine." He moaned, rubbing his temples. In a Cockney dialect, like an old man, he said, "Me head hurts summink awful."

"My everything hurts," Reggie said from his bunk. "Let's get some sleep. Tomorrow will be here very soon. Don't forget to say your prayers."

Chapter 33
Making Memories

The next day began with a start that literally flung Reggie from a warm bed onto the ice-cold floor. A terrifying racket filled the room. The boy leapt to his feet and snapped to attention.

He struggled to open his eye against the harsh overhead lights. When he was finally able to, he was treated to the sight of the sergeant major trotting up and down the centre aisle of the barracks banging two tin garbage can lids together. "Let's go! Let's go! Let's go!" he shouted at the top of his lungs.

"Drop your cocks! Grab your socks!" he shouted. "Out of those toasty beds. Time for some PT." Reggie scanned the room and saw his brothers, also standing at attention next to their beds, also barely awake. Standing there shivering together in the morning cold they looked like a pathetic lot.

The sergeant major was trotting in place. "Let's get moving! Good for the blood!" He marched towards the door like a raving lunatic playing a set of cymbals. He clicked the lights off as he trotted out the door. This place, Reggie thought as he shook his head, it's an asylum.

All six boys collapsed back onto their warm beds, scrambled undercover and were back asleep as quickly as they'd been awoken.

***

Reggie was roused again, this time by a gentle nudge. He instantly remembered—PT! He must have fallen back asleep. He bolted upright in his bed, about to jump and start waking the others, when he felt a hand on his shoulder. It was Corporal Fleming.

"Good morning, sunshine," he said with a slight smile, quiet enough to not wake the other boys.

"We've overslept—the sergeant major—" he stammered.

"Shhh, you'll wake the others." Reggie glanced the room. Nothing but wool-covered lumps on each bed. "But, the sergeant major said… physical training…"

"No, no PT for you lads today. He was just giving you lot a bit of what soldiers get in boot camp. Consider yourself lucky. Loads of fun you missed there." He punctuated his remark with a roll of his light-green eyes.

"Well, they did say we would be treated just like everyone else. It does seem a very labour-intensive way to wake people, though, when the same could be achieved with a simple alarm clock."

Fleming smiled. "Right you are. Sergeant Major came to me after he tried to wake you. Taking one look at you pathetic lot, he said PT means 'probably tomorrow,' so get ready for that. He might go extra hard for giving you a day's rest."

Reggie slowly began to notice pain reporting in from all parts of his body. Instinctively he started rubbing his shoulder.

"Sore, aye? That's Captain Fairbairn. He doesn't fool around."

The intensity of their training with their partners had increased during the past several days. "Dancing, he calls it," Reggie said aloud. "I've never been so sore from dancing in my life." He wiggled his skinny toes, then bent his legs and began to massage his sore feet.

"Pain, or being sore, is pretty much how you're all going to feel for the next three months or so. Better get used to it. It's kind of the general state of everyone in this programme, so at least you're not alone, eh?" he said, elbowing Reggie in his other shoulder, which was also aching.

"I didn't know it was possible to feel this—this ruddy." Almost everything they had done was in slow motion, until recently. Once they had the movements down, Fairbairn stepped it up a notch in speed. "We're getting better at the moves but the ground never gets any softer."

"You're muscles are starting to remember," Fleming said. "That takes training."

Reggie lay back down in bed, pulling the covers up to his neck.

"The way all this stuff works," Fleming whispered, his words mixed with the snores and breathing of the boys sleeping around him, "it's all muscle memory. That's why some of these blokes are so fast and deadly. They don't have to think about it, just let their muscles take over." It was a concept new to Reggie, muscles that remember.

"If you say so."

"Oh, believe me, it works. Very soon Captain Fairbairn will have you doing those moves like lightning. Learn what these blokes have to teach, and you'll never lose another fight in your life."

"Actually, *we've* never lost one. With six of us, we always have back-up." He raised his hand and began to scratch at his orange hair, more for soothing than any actual itch.

The corporal snapped his fingers. "See, just like that." He pointed at Reggie's hand. "You didn't think about raising your hand and scratching your head, because you've done it a million times. I've seen you do it dozens since you've been here." That struck Reggie as odd. "When you're tired or thinking, you play with your hair. That's muscle memory."

"You've noticed I scratch my head when I'm tired?" Reggie asked.

The corporal smiled. "Both you and Willy. Might be a brother thing. Freddie bites his nails—not all the time, only when he's nervous, or plotting. Dougie has a hard time with eye contact, except with Henry, who grabs at his own groin constantly, and Jack...well, Jackie boy is a whole other pickle. That lad's got some quirks."

Reggie raised himself on his elbow, his other hand still playing with his hair. "You've noticed all that, in only this short time?"

Charlie leaned in close, lowering his voice to a whisper. "I'll tell you this because you're the leader." He glanced around again to make sure no one was looking, or more important, listening.

"Part of my job as batman goes beyond language lessons and general assistant. I'm also to observe and report everything you lads do. The brass are trying to figure out the natural order of how you work together as a group." Taking another glance around, he said, "It's my job to keep daily reports ready to give them, on how it's all going, any injuries, weaknesses that need addressing, homesickness, all that sort of thing. I have to work up a psychological report on each of you."

Reggie smiled. The revelation had made him feel better. "So you're not just a babysitter for the brats?"

"The brats? Now where did you hear that?" His tone changed instantly.

"Yesterday, on the way to the mess hall. We passed a group of men, and one made a comment about 'There go the brats'. His mate then said, 'Yeah, that's a good name for them, the brats.' I didn't really didn't think anything of it. We've been called far worse."

"I'm sorry about that, Reggie, I truly am." And he sounded it. "Every man here is preparing for a secret mission, but yours is very special, extra secret, let's say. It's why we put you in separate barracks. No man here knows what any other man's mission is, same with you boys. Well, they'd be idiots to not know you were here for special training, but as George Cross winners, you and the rest of the boys deserve a bit more respect."

He glanced at his watch. "All right, I want you to rouse them, grab your wash kits and head over to Ablutions. Make sure the younger boys wash their armpits thoroughly and don't miss their undercarriages. Then dress in your battle dress and head over to the mess for some breakfast. Eat well, you've another full day ahead of you."

Chapter 34

Close Combat

"All right lads, I'd like you to meet Fritz One through Six." Captain Fairbairn said. He was standing next to a long rack that held fifteen life sized dummies, consisting of thick burlap stuffed with hay. Like a person, each had distinct arms, legs and a head. Each was suspended by two ropes connected at the shoulders and one connected to the ground at the bottom of each leg. The first six of the dummies had newly painted ascending numbers on them.

"Each of you are to have your own Fritz, it doesn't matter which you get, they are all the same and each serves the same purpose."

"What you will do to Fritz is not very friendly, but we're not here to learn to make friends."

He stepped to Fritz One. "Because we don't want you killing each other, you will practice lethal strikes and knife attacks on Fritz." Suddenly, he stuck Fritz One with the butt of his left hand hard across the base of the neck, whilst also jabbing the five extended and locked fingers of his right hand directly into the base of Fritz's throat. He performed both strikes with extreme speed and utmost violence. Had Fritz not been made of straw, Reggie thought, he'd be in very serious trouble, indeed.

"You must learn to really let him have it, always striking with the outside base of the opened hand, fingers and thumb extended and locked. This strike can be delivered with the utmost power from almost any angle." He showed them again, displaying the edge of the hand.

"Remember the vulnerable points, the best places to deliver a blow that will hopefully bring him down." He approached poor Fritz One again. "The groin, or fork." Quick kick. "The chin." An upward palm strike. "The forearm, bicep, or back of the arm." Three quick hand blows to each. He moved round behind Fritz. "Back of the neck." A chop. "The kidneys and base of the spine." A hard quick strike. "Either side of the neck." One forehand blow, one backhand delivered to each side. Crossing to the front again, this time he used his hand to strike. "The Adam's apple. And finally,"—he kicked out—"the shin, and," with a heel-first hard stomp, "the instep." He stopped and turned to the boys. "Did you catch all that? Any one or a combination of those strikes will take your opponent to the ground where you then kick and stomp him until he's done. Of course you can't do that to Fritz here because he's strung up, like all good Nazis should be." The boys laughed. "Now, each of your pick a Fritz and let's begin."

For the next four hours they delivered blow after blow with the side of their hands, to all the most vulnerable spots of Fritz until the idea of using a fist in a fight was washed away completely. After several days of training, Corporal Fleming wrote his report.

"Whilst Reggie and Freddie, being closest in size to their straw adversaries and able to cover all attack points most effectively, Henry and Dougie present cause for concern due to a bit of struggle managing their foot coordination, something not un-common for boys of their age. Moving from front to back of the target and back again was hindered by their footwork. Further scrutiny and more training will be necessary to ensure they can overcome and perform as needed. Willy and Jack, at their small statures, had challenges in delivering blows against body areas that were simply out of reach, a square shot to the side of the neck, for instance. Where they excel is in their still youthful grace, physical coordination and ability to deliver powerful rear body blows and lower limb kicks."

"Even with these difficulties and complications," Fleming wrote, "the empowerment instilled in them at learning these new techniques has been quite exhilarating and they have taken to the task with great vigour, eager to engage each and every time. My personal impression: they have finally started to feel like commandos. And like the Scouts they are, they've had a taste and want more."

***

After several more days of extensive practice attacking a single Fritz, they graduated to the next level: learning how to deal with more than one opponent.

"As you will come to experience first-hand, one of the favourite activities of the Hitler Youth is violence. They love boxing, but they adore brawling even more. They have no problem with gutter fighting, so you'd best not either." Captain Fairbairn led them to another kind rack containing a group of six dummies that were hung in a close circle, all facing each other.

"Today, you're going to start learning to fight against a group, because when they hold one of those brawls they're so fond of, you will be set upon by more than one boy at a time. This exercise is designed to show you how to do so, hold your own and come out in one piece. Broken bones are not uncommon from these brawls. Should that happen to any of you, it would have very serious repercussions for the mission, I need not tell you that." The captain stepped inside the circle of suspended hay dummies.

"The key to fighting a group of opponents is to keep moving at all times as to not be struck yourself. If you are constantly in motion your attackers don't have enough time to set up for a proper strike, because they must constantly adjust to your movements. But remember, you know how and where to strike, so as you move you can do considerable damage."

On that note, he stepped inside the circle of dummies and began to move about the circle, stepping from one to another, striking at will, chopping at arms and kicking at shins, all the whilst maintaining a perfect fluidness, moving with an elegant grace from target to target. He kneed forks and poked at throats. At one point he even head-butted a Fritz in the solar plexus. His every move was precise and every strike exact.

"Don't just go forwards and back, but remember to move laterally, and bend at the knees, so to bob and weave, moving at different heights and causing your attacker even more confusion. Evasion of a group attack is your goal. Remember to stay off the ground, at all cost."

He continued to dance around the circle of dummies, attacking one then bounding across the circle to attack another. As a final demonstration, he did a short spin round one of the dummies and escaped from the middle of the circle.

"As you can see, the goal is to escape the group, not to try and fight them all but to make an escape route from which to remove yourself from a situation that has you outnumbered." He spoke as if he had done it hundreds of times, which he had, and against real enemies who wanted him dead.

"Now, it will be your turn. Each of you will get 30 seconds in the circle to attack your opponents with any and all strikes, kicks and attacks we've learned, and on my whistle you will make your way out of the circle. Freddie, you're up first."

Freddie stepped into the circle of Nazi mannequins. "Hello, lads," he said with a smirk. The captain blew his whistle. Freddie began to copy the dance he had just watched the captain perform, but at a much more feverish rate. He would move to one, perform a swift kick to the fork, pivot and deliver a throat blow to the dummy next to him. Ducking low, he stepped across the circle to the attack the dummies there. An elbow upper cut to the groin, whilst a finger stab at the throat. A skip hop behind him and he was across the circle again, delivering a hammering blow to the abdomen of one dummy, and a neck breaking chop to another. He was moving with greater speed than the captain had, but his attacks were clumsy. They would improve greatly with practice, a lot of which was in their near future.

The captain blew his whistle. Freddie hunched low, and rolled out of the circle centre. He stood, breathing heavy, sweat dripping from his forehead. Reggie hadn't seen him that exhausted since they did their first seven mile run on morning one.

"You alright?" Reggie asked. "You seem a bit winded there?"

225

he said.

"Okay, you just give it a go then," Freddie said between deep breaths. "That's bloody exhausting."

"Reggie," the captain called. "Let's go, lad. Into the circle." Reggie soon learned what Freddie was talking about, as did they all. The 30 seconds in the circle felt like three minutes and it took an enormous amount of effort. For the next several hours they each took their turns in the middle of that ring, fighting off and escaping from the outnumbering, hay-filled Nazis.

***

They next learned how to use of their FS knifes to silently sneak up on an unsuspecting sentry, and instead of thrusting the knife into Fritz, reach round, cup the mouth and nose, and simply pulled Fritz back onto their waiting blade. After it slipped easily into where Fritz's kidneys would be, they were instructed to "stir it round a bit", which would cause the nervous system to fail and the sentry to collapse instantly in a heap. They learned the nasty business of how to properly cut a throat, again from behind and silently. Again, this presented the most problem for the smaller boys, who had some trouble with the height of the dummies.

When sparring in pairs they used rubber knives to practice striking, parrying and disarming each other, both whilst armed and unarmed. Over days and days they practiced, until much like Corporal Fleming had promised, their muscles remembered every step and swing, and much of it became second nature.

Chapter 35
Shaping Up

As intensity of their training increased, so too did their appreciation for mealtimes. The extra physical activity drastically affected their already ravenous teenage appetites. They were already being fed a hearty all-they-could-eat diet of horsemeat, vegetables, and more horsemeat, but their vigorous training regimen always guaranteed a gnawing hunger before the next mess time.

Besides their exhausting combat exercises with the captain, they were still subjected to daily Physical Training with the sergeant major which still consisted of an early morning run, then field calisthenics, then just for fun, a quick run through the obstacle course. There was also the constant hustling from here to there they seemed always subjected to.

The physical changes were most noticeable first on Reggie and Freddie: their arms began to thicken, their shoulders widened, even their chests showed strands of muscle that a mere month ago seemed not to have been there at all. They had also fallen into the habit of constantly sparring with each other, even in their evening, off hours, with the goal of being able to execute each of Captain Fairbairn's lethal dance steps as quickly as the captain himself could.

Both Dougie and Henry had always been rather pudgy boys (Dougie slightly more so than Henry), thanks to Maurice.

"Ah, 'Enri, help me with this, she is man-e-feek!" he'd croon and then shove a mixing spoon covered in some kind of frothy goo, always a delicious frothy goo, straight into Henry's waiting mouth. "Hmmm, merci beaucoup, Maurice." The boy would sing.

If Dougie heard any moaning coming from the kitchen, he'd be there right quick, just in time for his spoonful. "Avez-vous pour moi?" he would ask. "Of course, I have one for you," Maurice would answer, shoving a gooey spoon in Dougie's mouth. Mousse au chocolat was Henry's favourite. Dougie's was the crème brûlée.

Here, there was none of the fluff, just meat, veg and more meat.

As the weeks passed, Henry and Dougie had turned this change in their bodies into a game. They had both lost a layer of fat, and were now feeling lighter, running faster and finding it easier to do just about everything. They were long-winded and could run far without tiring, plus there was extra room in their waistbands that hadn't been there when they first arrived. It was now a race between the two of them—who could reach the next smaller hole on their belts first. Dougie, with the most to lose, was in the lead.

As for Jack and Willy, they found themselves competing daily to see who could do the most pull-up and press-ups, and who was growing taller fastest. Willy was in the lead, because he had started ahead, but Jack was gaining quickly. As all their bodies grew ever stronger, so too did their confidence in their newly gained abilities.

Chapter 36
Machine Carbine Course

As a change of pace, one morning after breakfast they were ordered to muster at the firing range instead of the classroom. "Why do we need firearms training?" Freddie asked Reggie at the beginning of their week-long instruction into the use of allied small arms. "I thought we were just going in as a Hitler Youth pack. The only weapons they carry are their Hitler Youth daggers."

"I'm not sure," Reggie answered. "I suppose there's a chance we may have to use them, so better we know how. At least, I'd rather know how and never have to use them than have to use them, and not having a clue as to how," he said. "Remember, it's all part of being prepared." Freddie nodded. "Good point," he said. "It's always better to know more than less."

The sergeant major joined them carrying a weapon they all instantly recognised.

"Gentlemen, allow me to introduce you to the Thompson Model 1928A1 submachine gun." The sergeant major lifted the heavy weapon easily with one hand. "It's made in America and goes by the name of —

"The Chicago Typewriter!" Dougie yelled. "Ah, Sergeant Major," he added, in a far more hushed tone.

"That is correct Douglas. But I was going to call it by its more 'official' unofficial name, the Tommy gun. It's also called the Chicago Organ Grinder, after you fire it, you'll know why."

"Wow, between the typewriters and organ grinders that Chicago sounds like a rough place," Henry said.

"One of the roughest," the sergeant major replied. "This is the preferred weapon of gangsters and commandos alike."

On the table before the sergeant major laid two magazines filled with ammunition, a round drum and one rectangular box clip. It was the gun that they had seen Mr. Steeves wearing when they visited the AA gun that fateful morning.

"Now, as you can see, we have the fifty round drum, one straight magazine, one holds twenty rounds. This model Thompson is capable of handling either type of magazine without any modification whatsoever. Yes, Henry?"

"Does it make a difference which is used?" he asked.

Dougie smacked his arm. "Of course, the drum is better. Of course," he said again.

"And why would you say that, Dougie?" the sergeant major asked.

"Because Sergeant Major, it holds more bullets," he answered. "And the more bullets, the better."

"First, let's remember our lessons and call things by their proper name. A round is what gets loaded into the breach from the magazine. When fired, the bullet comes out of the muzzle and the casing gets ejected from the ejection port. Now, do you care to rephrase your answer, Dougie?" the sergeant major asked.

"Because it holds more rounds, Sergeant Major. And more rounds means more bullets, and the more bullets, the better." Dougie answered, beaming.

"Very good lad. And so it does, but it's also heavy, rattles when carried, is oddly shaped and a bugger to reload, so you will not find these magazines being used in the field. I have them here for training purposes only," the sergeant major said. "With his advanced knowledge of the subject, Douglas will help me with the first demonstration for the day. Now, it is true that this," he held up the round magazine, "does hold more cartridges. Thirty more to be exact. Douglas, take this gun and load the magazine. Mind the slots and it should slip on just fine."

Dougie did as he was told and took the 10 pound gun from the sergeant. He grabbed up the long rectangular twenty round clip and carefully lined up the magazine groves with the guides on the gun's trigger guard that hold the magazine in place. "Good show, lad. Now how does that feel?"

"It feels okay." Dougie answered, although he wasn't sure exactly how it was supposed to feel, except a slight weight increase with the charged magazine attached. The other boys watched, itching to get their own hands on the gun Dougie held.

"Now," said Sergeant Major, "remove that magazine and add the drum. You push that release on the side and the clip should fall away." Dougie did as he was told, and indeed, the heavy clip slipped from the port as soon as he touched the release button, landing on the table with a thud. Reaching for the drum, he was instantly struck by its increased weight. Thirty more rounds made a big difference. He brought the drum to the port and began to affix it to the bottom of the Thompson. When he was finished he looked like a gangster from Chicago, all he was missing was the felt hat and cigar.

"How does that feel, lad?" the sergeant major asked. "It's very heavy, Sergeant Major."

"So, now, do you still think more rounds are better?" he asked, raising a single red eyebrow.

"Not if I have to carry them, Sergeant Major," he said. "I think I like those other clips better."

"Just remember, chaps, the more rounds the heavier the gun." He motioned Dougie round in front of the table. Down range several metal targets were waiting.

"So, we're going to shoot this from the hip first, to get a feel for it. Tuck the wooden butt against your side, and hold it tight with your left arm. Like so." He moved the gun into position, making sure Dougie held it where he was supposed to. "Your left hand goes on the grip, very good, and your right hand holds the wooden hand grip out front. Keep your finger off the trigger until you're ready to shoot." Dougie stood as instructed, his finger outside of the trigger guard.

"Now, with your right hand, grab the bolt on the top and slide it back to chamber a round and cock the hammer." Dougie was trembling slightly. He was nervous to be holding the deadly machine in his hands. He grabbed the slide as told and slid back the heavy bolt, locking it in place.

"That's it lad, now your cocked and ready to fire." Sergeant Major stepped behind Dougie, ready to help the boy if need be. "Just point the muzzle towards the target, unlock the safety and squeeze the trigger." Dougie nervously looked down the long range. The target consisted of a large oval shaped bag of hay with a round white spot in the midsection. He aimed at the target and squeezed the trigger. Nothing happened.

"Take off the safety," said Freddie, wanting to jump in and take over for him. "Sorry, Sergeant Major."

"You'll get your chance Freddie. Douglas, take off the safety." The sergeant major reminded him. Dougie held up the weapon towards his face, looking for the safety switch. He turned towards the sergeant major, and as he did the muzzle of the gun swung towards the boys gathered behind him.

They all dropped to the ground instantly to avoid the business end of the loaded .45 submachine gun that Dougie was carelessly swinging about. The sergeant major grabbed the gun and pointed the muzzle down range. "The safety is here." He clicked it off. "And always mind your muzzle. That goes for all of you. Keep it pointed down range at all times. Knowing you lot, you'll probably put a slug in your own backsides." The boys slowly raised themselves from the ground.

Dougie squeezed harder on the wooden grips of the heavy gun. Again, butt braced against his hip, he aimed at the target. He squeezed the trigger. This time the gun roared to life in his hands. It bucked and jumped, catching him off guard. He squeezed harder, desperately trying not to drop the powerful gun. With each shot, flame erupted two feet from the muzzle. Five, ten, 15, 20, 25 rounds pumped from the gun. The front end began to rise quickly as Dougie wrestled to keep it down. The *rat-*

tat-tat was deafening, and actually did crack like a clacking typewriter. Once the barrel of the gun started skyward, the sergeant major stepped in and gave Dougie the cease-fire signal, which of course, Dougie didn't see because his eye were shut as tight as he could get them.

The sergeant major slapped Dougie on the head and the boy released his grip on the trigger.

He had emptied the drum of its fifty rounds in a single burst. The gun's barrel smoked and a smell of gunpowder filled the air.

"Blimey," Dougie said, his heart racing, "that was brilliant." He surrendered the hot gun to the waiting sergeant major.

"It would have been a lot more brilliant if you had kept your eyes open," sergeant major barked. "Listen closely, all of you. Your chances of hitting your target increase dramatically if you keep your eyes open when you shoot. Trust me on this. Now, I know this was Dougie's first time, and in so being, he provided us with an excellent learning opportunity. When shooting," he tapped Dougie's forehead with his pointed finger with each word, "always keep your eyes *open* and on the target. Is that clear?"

In unison. "Yes, Sergeant Major."

"Is that clear, Dougie?"

"Yes, Sergeant Major," the boy answered.

"You may also have noticed, when the Thompson is fired, the barrel tends to rise up vertically, which means always make your first shot low, say at the fork, as the following shots will be higher, like in the gut or in the chest. Do remember to fire in controlled three round bursts, not all in one long spray of bullets. That only wastes valuable ammo and makes you a target for return fire. Three round bursts help conserve rounds and control the muzzle rise."

"How many times did I hit the target, Sergeant Major?" Dougie asked.

"None, but don't worry. You'll do much better with open eyes. That I promise," he said with a wink. "Now," the sergeant major asked, "Who's next?" Every hand went up.

***

Of course, Freddie and Reggie did best with the Thompson. Dougie and Henry held their own, but Willy and Jack had the most trouble, as expected. It wasn't impossible for the small boys to operate the heavy gun, once they had their shoulder straps adjusted to take some of the weight, they did fairly well for their sizes. Practice included firing the gun from prone, kneeling, the hip, and standing positions, with a focus always on three round bursts.

Dougie redeemed himself on his second go round, when they fired the thirty round clip from the shoulder, aiming down the site. The sergeant major explained "You need to adjust this rear site for distance." Once done, Dougie hit his target with fifteen of his 20 rounds, still having a bit of a struggle controlling the muzzle rise. His first and second round would score a hit, but his third bullet was always too high. "Luckily these guns shoot a .45 slug, so the first two should do the trick. At least, for your sake Dougie lad, I hope so," he remarked.

***

Along with more Tommy time, over the course of the next two weeks, they also spent classroom and range time with the Bren .303 Light Machine gun, the Colt Model 1911 .45 pistol, the .455 Webley revolver and .303 Lee-Enfield rifle, with all the boys but Dougie receiving average or above marks for accuracy on each. And they loved every minute of it.

At the end of the two weeks of allied firearm training their marks rivalled those of any adult agent who had ever passed through the school.

15 AUGUST 1940

FROM: DR. HUGH DALTON, D.O.O., S.O.E.
TO: PRIME MINISTER WINSTON CHURCHILL
   AIR VICE-MARSHAL KEITH PARK, R.A.F., S.O.E.
   MAJOR GENERAL COLIN GUBBINS, S.O.E.
RE: OPERATION ARCHANGEL

Gentlemen,

I received a field report from Corporal Fleming at STS-21 regarding the above mentioned operation. Training is proceeding at an accelerated pace due to the candidates previous experience with field craft and their performance on tasks thus far.

Although this is the case, we seek to extend, not reduce their time spent at STS-31, specifically to maximize time for the boys German language lessons, which are well underway. They are already well versed in French, which has hence proven to be quite helpful in strategic planning for the mission.

I suggest we follow this recommendation, as Captain Brown agrees and he has a particularly unique understanding on the level of competence required to make ready the candidates.

Chapter 37

Station XVa, Kensington

"We want your ladies." The general said.

"I beg your pardon?"

"We want your ladies. Specifically the Sisters."

"How's that?" Hawkins asked.

"We've a covert sewing operation that they'd be perfect for."

"Covert sewing? For the Barn?" Hawkins asked.

"No, we've a new Station, we're calling it XVa, it's much closer-by, in London. Design section for camouflage, disguises, costumes, and should the good Sister's agree, Hitler Youth uniforms, French schoolboy clothing, et cetera. Can't be sending the boys over in their Scout uniforms, now can we?" The general asked.

Hawkins was familiar with Section XV, the special group of English and foreign tailors, weavers and craftsmen from occupied countries who worked on behalf of MI6. Their job was to create appropriate attire for agents in the field, to match their country of operation. For an agent to be successful they needed to blend in, and could be picked out instantly among a population of Frenchmen, simply by wearing an article of clothing made of the wrong fabric. No tags could be included, or false ones need to be provided. All materials had to come from the appropriate country, or be created to look as though they did. Proper disguises would then be fit for agents to wear whilst on assignment. The 'Thatched Barn' was the Stations unofficial name, based on the building in which the group did some of its work. But he knew nothing of this new London 'shop'.

"Why not just run them through The Barn? Surely the folks there have the ability and know-how to put together everything the boys need." Hawkins asked.

"Yes, but what the folks at Station XV don't have is knowledge of this particular mission," he said. "As you know, due to the circumstances, we'd prefer to play this as close to the chest as possible—not to mention, if we give the Sisters a larger part to play, they'll be more likely to keep it hush-hush. As a bonus, in London they're not so far away from their home."

"Oh, they already operate under an oath more sacred than any we could ask them to take, believe you me. They won't talk. I mean, at times they won't stop talking, but never about this. Last thing those ladies would do is jeopardise the lives of their boys."

"Do you think they're too close? I mean, should something happen to the boys …" he trailed off at the thought.

"No," Hawkins answered. "I actually think they'll be a perfect addition to the new Station. It would keep the number of people involved to a minimum. And they do have a lot of experience making clothes, including uniforms, for the boys."

The Sisters, Hawkins thought. This will be right up their alley, especially Sister Noreen. Were he to ask her, she'd probably strap on a parachute and make the jump with them.

"If you provide them the opportunity to join the team I'm certain they'll do a bang-up job, no doubt, sir." Hawkins answered.

"Good. It's settled then. Once we swear them in, they can get them to London. Splendid."

237

Chapter 38
Sheep in Wolves' Clothing

"Sisters," Father Hawkins started, "I want you to know that I greatly appreciate everything you've done for the boys. They have amazing guardians in you both." The Sisters smiled and a warm flush blushed their cheeks.

"Well," Sister Noreen said, "we just do what Jesus would have, and sometimes a bit more that He might not approve of, but He's forgiving. Sometimes a firm hand needs to be a swift kick."

"Spiritually speaking, of course, Father," Sister Doreen added.

"Yes, well, the boys are growing up fast and I'm concerned Vicar Davis might not be up to the challenge for much longer. You two provide great support."

"Support nothing, Father Hawkins. Between you, us and the walls, we're the ones who really keep those boys in line round here. No disrespect to Vicar of course, Father." Sister Noreen said.

"Of course, Sister Noreen." He winked at her. "The thing is," he said, "I have a sort of special favour I need to ask you both. And it will require you to go away for a while."

"Ohh," Sister Doreen cried out, startling Father Hawkins. "We knew it, didn't we Sister? *Obsolete!"* She raised her hands to her face, crying into a hand that already held a lace handkerchief. "You don't need us anymore, so you're sending us away." She blew her nose.

"Obsolete, Sister Doreen? Are you joking? That's the last thing on my mind. I need you and Sister Noreen now more than ever," he answered.

Doreen instantly stopped crying, looking up as if she hadn't heard exactly what he had.

"What'd he say?" she asked her sister.

"I said, dear lady, that I need you both now more than ever, and I need you in a way that you've never been needed before." They sat, stunned. No man had ever said those words to either of them, let alone to both of them at the same time.

He moved to the door and quietly pulled it shut. Once done, he move to the window shades andpulled each down in order. "I need to ask you to keep secret what's about to happen. No one must ever know what went on here." He locked the door. "What I'm about to ask of you is quite serious."

Their eyes grew large. Both ladies moved to the edge of their seats, leaning in as not to miss one juicy word. He sat on the corner of his desk.

"I need your skills." He paused. "The boys need your skills," he paused again,"well actually,to be quite honest, the British Empire itself, needs your skills." Father Hawkins said.

"Our skills?" Doreen asked, perplexed. "What skills might those be, Father?"

Noreen's expression mirrored her Sister's.

"Seamstress. Of course."

"The British Empire needs our seamstress skills? What in blazes does that mean?" Sister Noreen asked.

"It means, ladies, I've been deceiving you." He stood, walked behind his desk, took out a new bottle of whisky and cracked the label. Both ladies looked at each other, then simultaneously their eyes moved straight to the wall clock. It wasn't even yet noon.

***

After they each had a small nip, after he had them swear to national security on their sacred oaths, after he revealed that he was actually 'Captain' Hawkins and told them of his time in the SIS, after they told him of Daddy's and BP's heroic escapades at Mafeking, he came to the heart of the conversation.

"And so, the Empire—and far more directly, the boys—need your help."

"The boys? Aren't they away in Scotland? We won't be seeing them for another three months." Sister Noreen said.

"On holiday." Sister Doreen reiterated.

"Not exactly." Hawkins said. "You see, that pilot they shot down, he was a bit of a bigwig in the Luftwaffe."

The Sisters listened intently to his every word and were keeping up in spite of the whisky.

He continued. "When those three visitors came by the other day—"

"RAF brass, I saw all the gold decorations on his cap brim," Noreen said to Doreen, who nodded. "And Army, a general at that."

"Yes, well," he continued, "they're considering the boys for a special mission for a new branch of the Intelligence services. Special Operations Executive it's called. Chosen by the Prime Minister himself, they were."

"Blimey, no!" Sister Noreen shouted. "By Winnie himself?"

Sister Doreen hushed her, whispering loudly, "*Shhh!* It's top secret."

"Yes, Sister, blimey indeed. You did that. You"—he pointed to Sister Doreen—"and you."

Doreen's bottom lip started a new round of quivering.

He continued, "And VD, Katie, everyone here at St. Michael's did that. You raised six George Cross winners. Congratulations. That takes some doing."

Doreen sniffled, and a single tear of pride ran down her cheek. She brushed it away with her handkerchief.

"I really can't divulge much more, but suffice it to say that as we speak, the boys are undergoing special testing and training by MI6." He was hitting all the right notes, as with each bit of info he revealed the

Sisters sat up a little straighter in their chairs.

"I know you're the right ladies for the task, based on the fantastic job you did creating their original Scout kits, which were much better than the ones from those Henry Poole fellows, I don't mind telling you."

Noreen waved him off. "Oh, weren't nothing for those boys. We'd do it all again if we had to, and without the help of that fancy London shop."

"Well, that is good to hear, because if I had to go to them, I'm not sure they could be trusted to keep it utmost secret. You ladies on the other hand, I know can be trusted." Hawkins said. "Besides General Gubbins himself wants you. Requested you directly,"

"Oh, my, General Gubbins." Noreen swooned at the high-ranking officer's mention. "Well, then, we have no choice in the matter. It's our duty."

"We would be so honoured, Father." Doreen sniffled.

"That is so very good to hear." Father replied.

"So," Noreen asked, "what exactly is it you'll be needing us to do for you, Father?"

"Well, for starters, I have a picture I'd like to show you." He unlocked the top drawer of his desk, slid it open, and pulled out a folder. He opened it wide and laid it across on the desk.

Sister Noreen looked at the open folder and the photograph inside. She blinked hard and looked into Father Hawkins eyes. She let her glasses fall around her neck, wiped her eyes, then put her spectacles back on the tip of her nose. Her jaw dropped.

"Is that a—?" she pointed, her exasperation building.

"Yes, Sister," he said cutting her off in as calming a voice as he could manage. "That is a swastika, and that is a Hitler Youth uniform. I need six of these, in various sizes that you ladies are already very familiar with. To create them, you've officially been assigned as agents to secret Station XVa, in London. Congratulations Sisters. Welcome to MI6. You leave at sun up."

Sister Noreen finished her drink in a single swallow. She then took Sister Doreen's drink from her hand and finished it in a single swallow.

Chapter 39
STS-51, Parachute School

Special Training School-51, Number 1 Parachute Training School at Dunham House, Altrincham near RAF station Ringway, had been put into operation to train thousands of pilots and paratroopers but also covert agents who would be, or already were, parachuting into France to covertly organise resistance against the occupying Nazis forces.

The sergeant major stood on the ground, looking at the six anxious boys standing above him. They stood in line, waiting their turn to jump off a 10 foot high platform into a sand pit below.

"Right. So once again, before we learn to fly, we have to learn to fall."

The boys let out an audible groan.

"Atten-*SHUN!*" The boys snapped to it. "I don't want to hear another sound like that come from you lot again. You're here to do a job, and today the job is jumping off this 10 foot high platform into this pit of sand, and learning to land so you can walk away from it. Is that clear?"

Together: "Yes, Sergeant Major."

"Very good. Who's up first?" Freddie stepped forward. "Ah, Freddie. Give it a go, lad. Just jump off the platform and when you land, keep your legs together and bend at the knee, letting your whole body roll forwards."

Freddie jumped as he was instructed. His feet hit the sand, he bent his legs at the knee and rolled onto the ground. Each of the boys followed, each with his own unique style, but all achieving the same end, landing without breaking either ankle. After they had each jumped once the Sergeant Major spoke again.

"That was good, lads. Now repeat that for the next two hours and we can move on."

***

By day two each boy was fitted with a parachute rigging harness, with straps that crossed the shoulders and tight up high against the inside of each thigh.

"Kind of bunches up the bits," Henry said, adjusting the straps that were nearest to his groin. "Just a tad," Freddie agreed, pulling at his pinching harness.

"Once you have your harness secure, climb up the ladder to the top." They did as the sergeant major instructed. Waiting there up top were some enlisted men, holding steel cables that reached up to the ceiling high above. The boys climbed the ladder to the 25 foot ledge above. Once there, the enlisted men attached the cables to their harnesses at the metal shoulder rings. They stood abreast, waiting for instructions.

"Lads, this exercise is to simulate how it will feel when our parachute opens, and what you should do to keep your parachute cords from tangling and getting you into a messy situation." He walked the line, only he was 25 feet below it.

"When I give the command, you'll jump from where you're standing now and swing forwards. Do not worry, each of those steel cables can hold an elephant."

Willy and Jack stood next to each other and looked at the floor far below. "It looks a lot higher from up here than it did from down there." Jack said backing away from the edge.

"It's not too bad." Willy said under his breath to Jack. "No, not too bad," Jack said, looking skyward a the cables attached to his shoulders. "I just hope he's right about these cables holding an elephant. They look awful thin, for that."

A nervous Reggie was inspecting the cables that the enlisted man had attached.

"Don't worry mate," one of the privates said. "Everyone survives this part. Well, almost everyone." He winked at Reggie. Freddie smiled. Reggie didn't. He swallowed hard.

"Now. As you swing forwards, you are to place your hands above your head, grabbing each of your risers securely. Pushing them out, away from each other, will keep you from spinning like top." Spinning like a top? Though it sounded fun, just the thought, combined with the height made Reggie start to feel queasy. He started to sweat. His mouth flushed with saliva, as if he were going to throw up. He swallowed fast, trying to keep it all down.

"Be sure your harness is secured properly or you quite possibly could rearrange your testicles, and you don't want to be doing that." They each looked to their midsections and said a silent prayer for protection to St. Michael.

"Right, then. Attendants stand clear. Ready… and JUMP!" The Sergeant Major shouted.

No one moved.

"Goodness me, lads," the sergeant shouted, "did you not hear me? I said… JUMP!" Again, no one moved, they just stood, staring down at the flat concrete floor below them. "It's quite normal to be afraid," he said. "Hell, even I was afraid, once. But hundreds of men have done this before you and been just fine. Now if you don't jump on the count of three, I'm coming up there to throw you off myself."

The boys all looked to Reggie. He nodded reassuringly, though he felt anything but assured. "We can do this," he said, his voice cracking.

"ONE! TWO! JUMP!" The sergeant major shouted. They all jumped. Except for Reggie. He stayed frozen to his spot.

Each of the boys swung down and forwards, feeling the weight of gravity pull and pinch at the harness contact points. Dougie and Willy forgot to reach overhead and grab their risers, and ended up dangling back and forth, whirling like Dervishes. Jack pushed more on the right riser than the left and found himself swinging side to side, bumping into Freddie, causing both to spin. Henry had managed to reach up, grab his risers, control his swing, and avoid crashing into any of the others. Text book, sergeant major thought. One out of six. That's a start. But Reggie was a surprise. He hadn't expected reluctance from his patrol leader.

"Reggie." The sergeant major spoke calmly. "Now I understand it might be a bit frightening, but if you don't jump there can't be a mission. I mean, how can there be an operation if you don't make the jump? The whole mission starts with the jump. Not a bloody thing happens until after the jump."

All the boys were now hanging, swinging, suspended by the steel cables six feet off the ground. They pulled their risers to turn and looked at their leader, Reggie, still perched on the ledge high above. A thin line of sweat glistened on his upper lip. He felt sweat drip down his back.

"Come on Reggie, it's fun!" Dougie yelled.

"Just do it Reg, don't be afraid," Freddie added.

"You can do it, trust your equipment!" Henry shouted.

"It's okay Reggie boy," Jack said to the trembling teenager. "Just let go. Trust me." Reggie locked his eyes closed tight, grabbed the risers and hurled himself off the ledge out into space. He fell straight down until the cables reached their full length and rebounded him forwards in an arch towards the floor. Instantly his eyes were opened, and looking up. He separated his risers as he'd been told, keeping his body from spinning out of control. The sergeant major was very impressed indeed. Text book, if only he hadn't hesitated. But now the boy was swinging and smiling, so the sergeant major knew, as with everyone who tried it, the first time was always the hardest, and it gets easier every time.

"Right, let's do it again. Reggie, a word if you please." Reggie came and stood tall before the sergeant major. "You'll do it on command next time, aye?"

"Aye, Sergeant Major. Sorry for the trouble, Sergeant. I'm not very fond of heights.

"I know, I know, back in line with you. Up the ladder, let's go."

***

Every hour had something new to learn. This hour the lesson was how to leave an aeroplane without leaving the ground. They were led to a field that had several wooden huts built on short stilts several feet off the ground. "Those are some strange loos, if that's what they are."

They climbed up inside one of the huts.

"This is known as a dummy trap." The sergeant major explained, pointing at a hole in the floor. "They are the same diameter and dimensions of the holes in the bottom of the Whitley aeroplanes you'll be jumping from."

"You will be seated on the edge of the trap, as such." He sat down, letting both of his legs dangle over the edge, his hands placed one beside each leg.

"The red ready light will turn on. That means you are *approaching* the drop zone." On the wall across from the sergeant major was a double bulb light fixture. One bulb was red. It flashed on. "That's your signal to get ready." They kept their eyes fixed. "When it changes colour, you are *over* the drop zone. You will scoot yourself forwards and drop from the bottom of the plane, always mindful of the slipstream." The red light turned off and the green bulb lit up. "That light means go. Watch me." The Sergeant Major scooted forwards and instantly dropped out of sight. The light switched back to flashing. He popped up in the middle of the hole. "See? Just like that." He climbed up from the hole back into the shack.

"For this drill, you will always practice in the exact order you will exit the plane during the mission. Freddie first, followed by Dougie, Henry, Willy, Jack and Reggie. Always in that order, learn it, know it and don't deviate from it."

They each took their turn, then took it again and again and again. Whilst certainly not as difficult, STS-51 was proving to be as repetitious as STS-21 had been, and learning was accomplished by the same process, by completing drills over and over and over until they were done exactly the same way, every single time.

***

Within two days, they had become proficient at jumping, and landing, swinging and escaping their harnesses. Unlike paratroopers, who were responsible for packing their own parachutes, the boys were instructed only to watch closely as theirs were being packed. They could help fold the silk chute, but nothing more. Knotting and tying of shroud lines was left in the hands of the skilled men who did it as their profession.

Reggie watched intently. Two harness risers connected to twenty-four silk shroud lines meant twenty-four folds that needed to be made and laid just so, if they were to unfurl and open according to design. The silk went in the pack first, followed by the shroud lines, each bound and gathered, again, just so. Then the lines were rolled up together and tucked inside the main back pack.

When the chute he had packed was ready, the packer made note of it in the official log. He marked the date and time, and marked the book with his initials. He passed the book to Reggie, for the boy to sign. The sergeant major stepped in.

"Private, you needn't his initials. For these six chutes I will sign instead." He took the book and initialled all six spaces, one for each of the boy's chutes.

"Yes, Sergeant Major. Very good."

The boys each grabbed their chute and headed out of the hanger.

"Why didn't we sign for our own chutes?" Freddie asked Reggie.

"Dunno." Reggie replied. "Maybe they don't want any record of us ever having been here."

***

"Blimey, look there." Dougie said as he exited the hanger. In the field before them was an inflated barrage balloon, but down, low, close to the ground. It was as wide as three buses side by side and as long as three, set end to end. It floated in the air roughly thirty feet, and beneath it was suspended a large gondola, with a fake trap in the centre, like the kind they had practised jumping from.

"Are we going up in that thing?" asked Jack. Reggie couldn't keep his eyes off the large silver balloon so close to the ground. It seemed so much bigger than when up at altitude. He suddenly felt sick to his stomach again.

In the past, he hadn't been happy when he ventured up into St.

Michael's bell tower. By this point in his training, especially after jumping in the hanger, Reggie was sure he did not like heights. He didn't like being off the ground, and the idea of jumping out of a perfectly good aeroplane seemed beyond reasonable. As they had been reassured by the sergeant major, the chances of a modern parachute mishap were practically nil, yet it all still seemed like nonsense, trusting your life to a piece of folded up silk.

"Alright lads, fall in." They did. "We've reached the time for your first jump. We're going up in that gondola hanging from that balloon. When we reach altitude, each of you will jump, in the same order that we practised in the fake traps. Is that understood?"

"Yes, Sergeant Major!"

"Do you all remember the order?" he barked.

"Yes, Sergeant Major!"

"Douglas," he barked, "What is the order of exit from the Whitley?"

"Freddie. Me. Henry. Willy. Jack. Then Reggie."

"Very good, lad. Very good indeed."

"Thank you, Sergeant Major." Dougie beamed.

"Right. Let's march. Left right left right left right." They matched his pace and made their way to the gondola suspended under the barrage balloon. They climbed aboard and the tractor's diesel engine revved as the winch brake was released and the balloon slowly rose into the air. The higher it rose into the sky, the more trepidation Reggie felt.

"Blimey, you can see everything from up here." Dougie said, his eyes peering over the wall of the gondola, like the other boys. Reggie was having none of it. He just kept staring at that hole in the floor, knowing he'd soon have to drop himself out of it. His head started spinning.

"Reggie," the sergeant major said. "Are you feeling alright lad? You're looking a little peaky."

Reggie swallowed hard before answering. "No, Sergeant. I'm fine. Thank you Sergeant." As the last word left his lips, he leaned forwards and stuck his head over the fake trap. His morning's breakfast exited the same way it had entered. Upon seeing Reggie throw up, Freddie promptly did the same, as did Willy.

"What's this?" the sergeant major asked frowning. "I sensed that

Reggie was going to lose it, but not you, Freddie, and Willy? You? Now that's a surprise."

"Yes, Sergeant Major," Willy said, wiping his mouth with the back of his hand. "Sorry about that Sergeant."

"It's alright. I should have told you we'd be going up today, before you stuffed yourselves at breakfast." He patted Freddie on the shoulder. "Oh, well, next time, aye?"

"Yes, Sergeant." He swallowed, his throat burning with bile. "Next time."

When they reached an altitude of 600 feet, the winch locked and balloon stopped climbing. The wind was blowing stronger than it had been below, and the balloon was bumping about slightly. It was time.

"Alright, lads, hook up." They took the static lines attached to their parachutes and hooked them to a cable in the gondola. Each boy checked the chute of the boy in front of him, with Freddie then checking Reggie's. Sergeant Major watched as they performed all the checks and rechecks they had been practising for days. Reggie counted each static line as he pulled it, assuring that it was securely attached to the gondola. Six including his own.

"Goggles." Instructed the SM. The boys pulled their goggles down over their eyes.

Freddie took his position sitting on the edge of the trap, just as practised on the ground dozens of times. Those all paled in comparison to this. This was real. This was insane. He was trembling with fear. He knew being first out meant he was to set a good example for the others to follow. Puking hadn't been a very good start. At least he hadn't been the only one. "Just remember lads, if your chute doesn't open, just bring it back inside and they'll give you a new one." No one laughed at the sergeant major's joke, but Freddie did smile nervously.

"The red light in front of Freddie turns on." Sergeant Major says.

"Get ready!" Reggie and the sergeant major shouted in unison. Freddie's heart was beating hard in his chest. St. Michael, he prayed, please see me through this. "GREEN LIGHT." Yelled the sergeant major. "Go! Go! Go!"

Freddie scooted his butt over the edge of the trap and gravity took him. He had gone from sitting safely in the gondola to plummeting towards the ground so fast that there wasn't even time for his brain to register what had happened. Terror grabbed him for a split second before his harness did. In that tiny slice of a second he was sure his chute had malfunctioned and he was plummeting to his death. Almost as instantly came the violent jerk that let him know his parachute had performed as designed and unfurled, slowing his descent to non-terminal. When he looked up, his fully inflated canopy was the most beautiful sight he had ever seen. Jesus, God, St. Mike, thank you!

"Go! Go! Go!" The SM continued to yell. Dougie took his place, and was gone. Henry did the same, with the same outcome, gone. Willy. Jack. All gone from the bottom of the gondola. Reggie planted himself on the edge of the hole and the sergeant major put a hand on his shoulder.

"Hold on Reggie. You can go in one minute. First, I wanted to let you know why we have you jumping last. When you are on the mission drop, if for any reason, any of the other boys decide they can't jump, it will be your duty to make sure they leave that plane."

Reggie froze.

"What?" he asked, stunned.

"Aye, lad. By that time it will be too late for cold feet. The mission requires all six of you, so all six must go. You are to insure they all do," he said.

"So I just throw them out of the plane, Sergeant Major?"

"That's right Reggie. It's your duty as the patrol leader."

"Yes, Sergeant Major. I understand, Sergeant."

"Good lad. Now, *go! Go! Go!"* he barked. Reggie hoisted himself up and out the bottom of the gondola, leaving nothing behind but his static line.

***

After his chute inflated, the relief was instantaneous and left Reggie feeling so giddy he actually started to giggle. It was such an unusual feeling, the flipping in his stomach, and buzzing in his head. He had actually done it, and it had worked. He was falling, not at some deadly speed, but at a very controlled 16 feet per second, towards the ground. He turned his head and could see the other boys. Freddie was already hitting the ground, followed by Dougie a hundred feet away. Henry floated on a breeze that took him into a grove of trees on the far end of the clearing. Willy and Jack were still in the air. It was a nice ride down, but was over almost as soon as it started. The thrill was like nothing Reggie had ever felt in his young life. He wanted to do it again. Right now.

Freddie and the rest of the boys ran to greet him as he came down, legs together, into a crouch and then a roll, just like he'd simulated dozens of times. Then he was up, running forwards to take the wind out of the giant canopy, as not to be dragged across the ground.

"Bloody brilliant that was!" Freddie exclaimed unable to contain his excitement, bunching his chute on the ground behind him. Reggie couldn't agree more, but couldn't get a word in edgewise. Every boy was talking at the same time, all using different words but all conveying the same sentiment. "Bloody brilliant that was!" Freddie repeated.

"When can we do it again, do you think?" Dougie asked.

"Soon, I hope," Henry said. "I've never done anything that exciting, ever."

The balloon was lowered and the sergeant major disembarked. The boys rushed him, all singing the praises of parachuting and asking about the next time.

"Atten-*SHUN!*" he yelled at the group. They dropped their chutes and snapped to attention. "Did you forget where you were on the way down? That's no way for a lot like you to be acting. Is it lads?"

"No, Sergeant Major," they answered. They stood before him, their young bodies literally shaking with excitement.

"Now, you did very good lads, very good indeed. Henry, we need to keep you out of the trees next time." Henry frowned. "Yes, Sergeant Major."

"Now, let's get these chutes back to the hanger and repacked. If we get that done early enough we can do another jump. Now hop to it." They trotted off carrying their parachutes to the hanger for repacking.

***

Early the following morning, they mustered in one of the large

251

hangers, inside which sat a large aircraft. It was a bomber, but unlike any they'd seen before. This one was painted completely flat black.

"Boys, I'd like to introduce you to your jump master. Warrant Officer, if you please."

From the bottom of the bomber dropped a man. He landed on the floor and trotted over. He was a tall, and fit, with a short army regulation haircut. His face was boyish.

"Lads, this is Warrant Officer Matt Jepsen. He will be your dispatcher, or jumpmaster, on the flight over. You should listen to him as if he were me. Do you understand?"

"Yes, Sergeant Major."

"Warrant Officer, if you please. The stick is yours." He turned and left the hanger.

"Lads, I'd like to introduce you to the aeroplane you will be jumping from." He led them forwards and started around the plane. "Bomber Command has graciously provided this," he motioned with his hand. "The Armstrong Whitworth AW thirty-eight Whitley. She's a twin-engine front line medium type bomber and will be used to get you to your designated drop zone."

They walked round the aeroplane to a hatch on the port side. "You'll want to mind your heads inside," Jepsen reminded them. "There's not much room."

They climbed aboard through hatch and moved up the centre of the empty bomber in a sort of 'duck walk.' As they passed through the fuselage, they stopped just short of the hole in the floor. They'd seen this all before.

"Hey, this is exactly like the inside of the fake trap huts. But this one is no fake." Dougie said.

"Correct. This is the joe hole you will use from when that light," he pointed to the ready light fixture on the bulkhead, "turns green. Easy-peasy."

"Joe hole?" asked Jack.

"Yup. You're a joe, that's the hole you jump out of, hence it's the joe hole." Jack just nodded.

"Just like what we drilled out of," Reggie said.

"Well, of course it is. What good would drilling be if you didn't learn to do the same thing over and over again? We're simple creatures of habit, all of us, really." Jepsen added.

"Since there are six of you lads, before we board the plane we will do a final check and count down, with each boy checking the parachute of the boy in front of him. When this is done we start the countdown from the rear."

He looked at the boys. "Who's Reggie?" Reggie held up his hand.

"You're number six, but you check number one's parachute rig. As you do, you yell out 'Number One ready!' Then pat the boy's chute in front of you. That is his cue to check and yell 'Number Two ready!' Then so on we go all the way up until number six." The boys nodded.

"I will be standing here, as such." He took his spot at the front of the bulkhead. Hanging on a hook was a set of headphones. "This will be on my head, so I can communicate with the pilot. He will relay to me when we are near our action station." He put the headphones on his head. "Now, with the sound of the wind blowing and the engines revving, it will be very noisy in here. Therefore," he continued. "we'll be using hand signals to communicate." They all nodded in acknowledgement.

"I will also yell out each command as I give the sign. This," he said raising his hand, "means 'stand up'." They all did the sign together. "This," he raised his hand above his head, "means 'get ready.'" He extended his hands flat, and raised them.

"This," he wrapped his forefinger and thumb of one hand around the forefinger of his opposite hand, "means hook up." They all practised his hand movements together. "That is when you attach your static lines to the cable here." He pointed at it. "And this," he motioned his hand towards the floor, "this means 'go', which is the sign for you to jump. Along with me reminding you to *GO! GO! GO!* " he screamed so loud that in the enclosed space it actually hurt their ears. Each winced at the aural assault.

"Sorry lads, but that's how it will go. Now, let's line up in the designated order and run through it all from the top."

***

They had come to STS-51, No. 1 Parachute Training School at RAF Ringway because there simply was no better place on earth to learn how to exit from a moving aeroplane and survive. In a single week, thanks to Sergeant Major Preston-Downey and Warrant Officer Jepsen, they learned it all.

Even with the countless hanger swings, the sandpit slide drops, the hole jumps and the drilling until battered, bruised and exhausted, the boys still took to parachuting like teenage boys take to parachuting. Even Reggie, despite his acrophobia. By their fifth jump, the sergeant major was quite satisfied the boys could exit the plane and perform the successful landing necessary for their mission to begin.

Chapter 40

Show Time

Reggie sat, legs dangling over edge of the black trap into the dark night sky, watching intently the red light in front of him. His heart raced. His pulse pounded in his ears. The celluloid clicked audibly. The red light flooding his face turned to green. *Show time.* St. Mike be with me! He hoisted himself through the hole and began to free-fall through the cold darkness. Straight as a guardsman his brain screamed the words he had heard so often at Ringway. He instantly started to hyperventilate, which added to his fear. He was helpless to control it.

What he could control was keeping as straight as he could manage. Mind the slipstream, mind the slipstream, his brain barked. Always mind the slipstream! Panic began to overwhelm him, as it had at the beginning of every jump. "One one thousand! Two one thousand! Three one thousand!" He was tugged hard at the shoulders and back, and all was suddenly silent but for the pounding of his heart in his ears. His canopy had deployed.

Reaching over his head, he grabbed the shroud lines, overjoyed. His chute had performed perfectly. Darkness surrounded him, but his chute was open, and there were mere seconds before the ground would come up to meet him. His feet came together as he began to whisper through trembling lips. "Four one thousand! Five one thousand!"

Pressure struck his heels sooner than he had expected. He tucked at the knees and rolled forwards into a ball. He rolled over twice, getting only slightly tangled in his lines in the process. His heart pounded. His mind reeled. I'm alive! Jesus, thank-you! That was brilliant!

Off came his harness in a snap. He quickly gathered his parachute up around him in a heap on the ground. He crouched low, looking at the trees silhouetted against the night sky, waiting, listening for even the slightest bit of man-made noise from the darkness surrounding him. Nothing—just the expected night sounds of the countryside.

Out he pulled a small field shovel from its pouch on his leg. On his left was a high bush with hanging branches. Perfect. It would give concealment. Diving under it, he furiously began to dig a shallow hole.

When it was deep enough, only a few inches, Reggie scrambled to his feet. Freezing in place once more to listen for...anything...and not hearing anything, he unbuckled the chin strap of the camouflaged leather helmet on his head. It was strapped to the suit he was wearing, a single-piece coverall, camouflaged in black, brown, and splotches of various greens. His fingers clasped two identical zippers, each one running full length down the front of the suit from neck to ankle.

In one swift motion, he raced the zips down, and the front of the suit fell away as a single piece of material. He dipped his shoulders slightly, and the back of the suit slid effortlessly off his back to the ground. It took all of two seconds.

Like his harness, he bunched it together in a ball, pulled out a small book bag from the large pouch on the back, and stuck the entire mess into the hole. Fill, fill, fill, make sure everything's covered. He did, just as taught.

After this flurry of activity, he froze again, his ears trained around him. Again, nothing but normal night sounds. Good he thought. Nothing. Exactly what I wanted to hear.

He exited from under the bush, crouching low, to make his way along a tree line, heading southwest. In one hand he held a book bag, in the other he held the shovel.

The shovel! Damn!

There was a the loud *CLICK* of a power transformer switch being thrown and from every direction, spotlights flooded the clearing with light.

"Halt!" came a voice blaring from loud speakers somewhere beyond the light. *"Nicht bewegen!"* He froze. There was nowhere to go.

"Well, now. What have we here?" came the voice of the Sergeant Major through the darkness.

"Blast it," Reggie said under his breath. "The *bloody* shovel."

"Aside from that last bit, well done, Reggie." Still standing, dressed now in his battle dress, Reggie couldn't keep his head up. The floodlights were too bright for his eyes; his shame was too heavy for his head.

"Buck up, lad," the sergeant major said, slapping the boy's shoulder. "Wasn't too bad for your first time. You'll just need to be remembering, the shovel goes in the hole last, and you refill it with your boot."

"Yes, I know Sergeant." He spoke with each heavy breath. "Just, if this had been the real jump—I could have given it all away before it got started."

"That's why we drill, Reggie, to make all the mistakes here, not out there."

The other boys appeared, stepping out of the darkness.

"Lads, do you see what's wrong here?"

"Shovel," they answered together.

"Shovel, *Sergeant Major.*" Freddie corrected them.

"Shovel, Sergeant Major." They corrected themselves.

"That's right. What's the only thing that comes away with you?"

"Book bag, Sergeant."

"That's right, and what do we do with the shovel?"

"Last thing in the hole. Cover it with your sole," they said in unison.

"Right, very good. Let's thank Reggie for his outstanding demonstration."

The boys started clapping. Dougie whistled. Willy hooted.

Freddie stepped next to Reggie. "Shovel," he said with a smirk.

"Shovel off, it was my first time."

The sergeant major laughed. "You did fine, Reggie, just fine indeed. When we do it for real you'll perform proficiently, professionally, and perfect."

Chapter 41

Lethal Lessons

The next day started with a bang. Then a hiss.

The concussion shook their beds, startling them awake.

"What the hell was that?!" Reggie shot up and looked around the dark room quickly. Outside, the sky was dark morning blue.

"What was that?" Freddie asked, shaken from a dead sleep. The hissing noise was coming from somewhere close to him.

Reggie watched as a silhouette rose from the corner against the backdrop of the windows. A growing mass billowed across the room. It enveloped Freddie first. It was like a hammer to his face, a harsh, acidic sting, ripping his nose and lungs simultaneously. He began to coughed, and became unable to stop. His eyes instantly flushed with tears.

"Gas!" he yelled, with the last bit of good air in his lungs. He gasped between coughs. "Make—for the—door!"

Unable to keep them open, Freddie's eyes locked shut, which had little effect on the stinging gas. His eyes were useless, so using his ears as his guide, he moved towards the hissing sound on the floor.

Reggie, his eyes also squeezed shut, knew the door was left of his bed. He dropped to the floor, as they were taught in fire drills at St.

Mike's. He yelled over the loud noise, "Get low! Follow—follow my voice—follow my voice! Stay low!"

Henry rolled onto the floor and grabbed Dougie's foot. Dougie instinctively reached down to grab for his hand, thinking it was in need of a pull; instead it grabbed his leg and pushed him. He had to get out of this choking gas, no matter what it took. "It's me!" Henry yelled. "Just keep going towards—Reggie's voice!"

All were coughing, quickly overcome by the gas. It burned their eyes, throats, sinuses, and lungs with each breath. This is it, Reggie's panicking mind screamed. They're trying to kill us.

Freddie, on a mission to end their torture, searched for the gas canister. On the floor, near the corner, he reached out, making full sweeps of his arms as he blindly zeroed in on the source of the hissing. He force his eyes open and spotted it, a canister a bit like a tin can, perhaps a bit larger spitting the noxious fumes from one end. He grabbed it with his bare hand. It instantly burned and blistered his skin. He screamed in pain.

"Freddie!" Dougie yelled upon hearing the scream.

Freddie, with all the strength he could muster, his hand feeling as if it was on fire, threw the burning can in the direction of where he thought the closest window should have been.

CRASH! Through a window, the canister exited the room as quickly as it had come in.

Hearing the breaking glass, mistaking Freddie's outgoing canister for a second incoming one, Willy screamed, coughing, "Here comes another one!"

Reggie reached the door and tried to open it. It was locked. Buggers! They *are* trying to kill us. This is the door—the only door—we're all dead, he thought.

Reggie jumped to his feet and kicked the door with all his might. It popped open under his bare foot, and cool air rushed in. He dropped back to his knees.

"This way! This way! This way!" he yelled over and over again. The boys began to come through the door. Reggie did his best to count them as they came. Henry, one; Dougie, two; Willy, three. After a long pause, Freddie scrambled out the door on his stomach.

Freddie, four. Thank God.

No Jack. He quickly glanced at the boys through watering eyes, all now coughing, vomiting, and spewing body fluids in all directions. He counted again: one two three four me. No Jack.

"Jackie!" he yelled in the door. "Jack, come to my voice!" There was no response, nothing but the sound of a small boy coughing somewhere in that hellish cloud. Without a second thought, he dived through the door on his knees. Holding the fresh air from outside in his lungs, he scrambled up the centre aisle to Jack's bed. It was empty.

"Jack!" he yelled again. "Where *are* you?" He heard a faint cough from under the bed. That's it, Jackie, he thought. Reaching under the bunk, he felt a piece of clothing and pulled it. It was connected to a body—Jack's. He was on the floor on the opposite side.

Jack wasn't moving and was practically dead weight. Reggie pulled with all his might. As soon as he had Jack, he grabbed the boy's head and blew the air from his lungs into Jack's. Suddenly, he felt someone pulling on his own collar.

"You got him? Let's go!" It was Willy, brave little Willy pulling his collar, trying to get him to the door. Holding Willy's arm was Dougie, who in turn was held by Henry, making a chain to the door. Pulling with their combined strength, they tumbled out the barracks in a heap. But it wasn't over yet.

Reggie dragged Jack's limp body away from the door. They all gathered round. Reggie now had tears streaming down his face, but not from the gas, purely from the thought of losing his Jackie. Reggie started coughing, which led to his vomiting. Dougie and Henry took over, pushing Reggie aside. "See to him!" Henry told Willy.

Henry stretched out Jack's legs so his body was straight, making room for his lungs to expand, as they'd been taught. Dougie had Jack's head tilted back and his nose pinched, and with his lips locked over Jack's mouth, pushed his breath into Jack's congested lungs.

"Come on, Jackie. Don't do this to us." He took another frantic breath and blew it into the boy's mouth. He seemed so small like this, so helpless. "Jack!" he yelled again. "Come on, Jack, *breathe*!" He gave another blast of breath.

Jack began to cough violently, which led to violent vomiting. Dougie rolled him on his side, making sure his airway was clear. Dougie started to cry. "Oh, thank you, God, thank you!" he said again, slowly rubbing Jack's back, wishing there was more he could do to help the struggling boy.

Reggie, having regained his composure, but with tears still running down his face, joined the others around Jack.

"Give him"—*cough*—"some room." They all stood and took a step back—all but Reggie. He was on his knees, next to Jack. He lifted the boy and gave him a deep hug. "I thought I'd lost you, Jackie boy." Jack coughed again, his small face covered in dirt and soot. "Please…"—he struggled with the words, coughing—"don't … call me … Jackie." Reggie smiled and squeezed him closer, never wanting to let him go again.

Freddie was on his knees, whilst a shivering, shirtless Dougie stood and dressed his wounded hand with his own vest he had removed to do the job. Using his other hand, Freddie pulled his own vest over his head. "Here," he said to Dougie, "put this on." Dougie was more than happy to do so even though the shirt smelled like that nasty gas.

From the doorway of the barracks strode three men, each wearing a gas mask. They removed their masks as they walked away, all smiling. "Good show, mates," one said as they passed the group of drippy boys. Their bloodshot swollen eyes still burned and watered, their noses and sinuses still stung and ran, but they were alive. They were all alive … and together.

The last man out of the door was wearing a kilt. He took his mask off.

His pain instantly forgotten, Freddie was up from his knees, bowling over Dougie. Teeth clenched, he was on the sergeant major in a flash, his shin driving at the big man's groin, his arm up fast, and his hand in a claw, ready to palm the jaw and drill its fingers deep into eye sockets. It was a textbook strike, effortless, performed just as he'd been taught, automatic, unflinching. Yet against the sergeant major, it was futile. In less than a split second, Freddie was flat on his back on the ground, the sergeant's knee in his chest. The man's thick hand was squeezing his aching trachea just tight enough to let the boy know who had the upper hand.

"Is there a complaint you'd like to be filing, young man?" he asked politely. He released just enough pressure on the boy's airway to let him speak.

"What are you playing at?" Freddie spat. "You almost killed Jack, and us along with him! If you want us dead, just take us out in the field and shoot us! Now! All at the same time!" His voice started to shake, and tears raced down his cheeks. "At least then ... we'll go together." The sergeant major heard his anger, but he realized Freddie had reached his breaking point. It was a milestone.

"Kill you?" The Sergeant Major smirked. "Oh, laddie, I've spent far too much time and effort on you to do that now. That would be a bloody shame. You might even see me shed a tear." He turned to address them all.

"That was simply a tear gas canister. Unpleasant? Extremely. Deadly? Not even close. That was a little test, and I must say, based on your performance, it was your last." He removed himself from on top of Freddie and offered his hand to help him up. Freddie glared at him through angry tears and took it ... with his good hand. "So we failed?" Freddie asked.

The sergeant major laughed. "Failed? On the contrary, you passed with flying colours."

He slapped Freddie good-heartedly on the shoulder. Freddie was not in the mood. "Oh yeah, what about Jack? Did he pass, Sergeant Major?" Freddie asked. His hand throbbed, as did his anger for this man, this place, this pickle they'd got themselves into.

"Jack?" asked the sergeant major. "Well, he didn't pass away, so I suppose he did pass." He chuckled at his own joke. "Well done, Jack."

"Thank you, Sergeant." Jack, coughing, replied the best he could. He still rested safely in Reggie's arms.

The sergeant major studied at the group. A runny, snotty mess, they were.

"I'm sorry, Sergeant Major, but I don't understand," Reggie said, with gas induced tears running down his cheeks. "Look at us, we're a mess. Not to mention in no condition to do anything, especially fight. How could that be a pass?"

The sergeant major called, "Atten-*SHUN!*" They all stood, even

Jack, with the help of Reggie, and snapped to the best attention they could muster, which was very rough, considering what they'd just been through. They stood, not in their normal order of tall to short or vice versa, but they were all standing, hunching, leaning, so it was technically attention.

The sergeant major spoke.

"Freddie made immediately for the threat and eliminated it while Reggie made directly for the door, not to run, but to secure an exit route for the squad. He also kept track of exiting squad members, and after realising one was unaccounted for, of his own accord mounted a rescue mission to retrieve the missing man. The others"—he motioned to Dougie and Henry—"didn't wait, but followed his lead into danger, without being ordered to do so. Even in his weakened, wounded condition, Freddie mounted a direct assault the instant he made enemy contact." He winked at Freddie. "That's how it's going to go down in my report. Myself and the other three blokes were in there the whole time, observing, ready to pull you out if it got hairy, which, I'm quite pleased to say, it never did. Not in the slightest. Well, except for Freddie's hand there."

He took Freddie's hand, turning it over and looking at the blistered flesh of his palm. Freddie was shaking. "Good lesson for you, lad," he said. "Those cans are filled with a chemical that once lit, keeps burning down the container until it's done. They get glowing hot. You can kick 'em away, or use something to grab 'em with, but from now on, they're bare hands off. Understood?"

Freddie looked up at the sergeant major.

"Yes, Sergeant Major," he said almost in a whisper. "I'm sorry, Sergeant, about the way I reacted when—"

The sergeant major silenced him with the wave of his hand. He put his arm around the boy's shoulder and leaned in close to his ear. "I'm just glad I'm not dead, lad. You must never forget, you're lethal now."

When the sergeant major leaned back, Freddie's entire demeanour had changed. All signs of anger were gone from his face, replaced with an expression of astonished realization.

"It's a lucky thing I've been doing this for twenty-five years, or you'd have had me." Like a camera flash bulb going off in his head, an entire new world of responsibility suddenly hit Freddie like a shot to the gut. "You're human weapons now." The sergeant major said with a wink and a nod. The teen looked with wide-eyed disbelief at his own hands. "If you'd had done that to any other man, I have no doubt you would have killed him." His words shook Freddie to his core.

"Dougie, I'd like you to escort Jack and Freddie to the infirmary and then return. We have a busy day ahead."

"But I thought we were through, Sergeant. I thought we passed." Reggie said.

"Oh, you did. You passed Phase One. Now begins Phase Two."

Chapter 42
STS-31, Finishing School

Special Training School-31, Beaulieu was a finishing school for agents, where they were sent to become equipped with the specific needs for their individual mission. For the boys it meant 'basic' training was now over, and specialized training was about to begin.

"Lads, I'd like you to meet Captain Eric Brown." Before them stood a short man, much smaller in stature than the sergeant major, so much so that the top of his head barely reached the sergeant major's shoulder. He was quite dashing, a very handsome young man of twenty-four years, with wavy black hair and stunningly blue eyes that perfectly matched the blue of his Royal Navy tunic. "We've only got him for a short time, so when he speaks, give him the attention you'd give me."

A pilot from the Royal Navy? Good Lord, Reggie thought, now we have to learn to fly? What's next, submarine school?

"I've asked Captain Brown to join us here because he's one of the few people who has experienced the Boy Scouts and the Hitler Youth first hand. As an invited guest, he spent time at one of their camps and lived with them for several weeks. He knows your advisory better than any."

"Winkle, if you please." He motioned to the captain to step forwards.

Henry looked at Dougie, mouthing the word silently with his lips. "Winkle?"

Dougie just shrugged.

"Good morning, lads," Captain Brown said as he stepped forwards. Based on his heavy brogue, it was safe to assume he was a Scotsman like the sergeant major. "I've been asked here to debrief you, as the Sergeant Major mentioned. I spent time with the Hitler Youth several years ago."

Willy raised his hand.

"Yes, Wilfred?" He's knows our names already, Reggie thought.

"Permission to ask a question, Captain?" Willy asked. The captain turned and smirked at the sergeant major.

"Granted, Wilfred."

"You can call me Willy, Captain. Everyone does," he said politely.

"Well, then Willy, you can call me sir." He winked. "Everyone does."

"Actually, sir, that's my question. Why Winkle, sir?"

The captain and the sergeant major laughed. The captain walked back and stood next to the sergeant major. He tilted his head back, exceedingly far back, to look up at the large man. "As you can see by my physical dimensions, I'm a wee bit lack in the leg. Five seven, and that's on me tip-toe."

"Winkle is short for 'periwinkle.' I guess I'm like a tiny purple flower. My squad decided they liked it, so that's what I got." He walked back over to the boys. "We don't get to pick our own call signs, the senior men do it for us."

Dougie looked at Henry, smirked, and nodded. Henry nodded back.

"I'm sorry, sir. I didn't mean to pry, or mock your name..."

The captain smiled broadly. "No offence taken, lad. Just remember, bigger isn't always better. I'd change nothing about my size, even if I could."

Jack's confused eyes met Willy's equally confused eyes. "Come again, sir?"

"Being able to curl myself into a little ball inside my cockpit saved my skin more than once. Had I been a head taller, or my legs just an inch longer, I'd not be standing here talkin' to you now."

Willy flashed back to the skating encounter he had with the Sister backsides and how tucking into a tight ball had save his skin.

Freddie raised his hand.

"Yes, Fredrick?"

"Freddie, sir, if you please. How did you end up being a 'guest' of the Nazis, sir?"

"Well, it's a bit of a tale but a good one, if you'd like to hear it."

From behind the captain the sergeant major spoke. "At ease, boys, stand easy." They relaxed.

"My father flew as a member of the Royal Flying Corps during the Great War. Years later, during the '36 Olympics, the Germans decided to hold a reunion for all the veterans of the war—no matter which side they fought for—inviting 'em to Berlin for the games. For Hitler, it was just about showing off a rebuilt Germany to his old enemies. No matter. For the veterans, it was a wonderful trip. Hitler put on a good show— grand spectacles and parades the likes of which you've never seen. At least, it was more than a boy like me had seen. Spectacular. It made quite an impression, I must admit." He began to walk the line.

That's odd, Reggie thought. He had never heard anyone speak fondly of the Nazis, especially not someone wearing a Royal Navy uniform.

"You see, this was long before Poland, before all of this now. I was young and impressionable, being about your age at the time. German Ace Ernst Udet had flown against my father. When I met him, he took a liking to me and offered me a ride in his aeroplane. Of course I wanted to, more than anything. He strapped me in tight, and up we went."

The boys listened, fascinated.

"He did things with that machine I didn't think were possible, but darn glad I was he'd strapped me in so tight." He started to get excited, moving his hand around like an aeroplane, his thumbs and pinkie fingers stuck out as the wings.

"It was a biplane, see, open cockpit, and after the war he'd become an aerobatic pilot. We flipped and flopped and then flipped back again"—he flopped his hand plane quickly—"I thought I'd be thrown out of the thing. It was spectacular." He put his hands to his hips. "I was hooked."

"Udet and I became friends. He said, 'You are like a young me,'" the captain said, roughening his voice into the perfect German accent. "He said I had a pilot's instinct and told me to do two things for him: learn to fly and learn to speak German."

"I went to university and did both," he explained, "and when I wrote to tell him I had, he invited me to Germany as an exchange student. Thus began my experiences with the Hitler Youth. That ended when England declared war on Germany. I was sent packing. Any questions?"

"They actually let you go, sir?" Freddie asked.

"Just came to my room, knocking one morning. Told me a state of war existed between our two countries, and it was time for me to leave. They took everything I had except my car. They let me keep that. Said they had no spare parts for an English motorcar, so it was of no use to them. Mighty fine of them, if I do say so, but my guess is it was because I was a guest of a Luftwaffe General and a university student. I think it's safe to say that kind of consideration no longer exists in Germany, so don't be expecting it." He walked the line.

"I'm here to turn you boys into a Hitler Youth squad. You're already British Boy Scouts, so that's a bit of a start, but believe me when I tell you, the Hitler Youth groups are very different from the Boy Scouts. They're much more physical, competitive … and violent."

"Whilst Boy Scouts are taught to work as a team for the good of everyone, they're taught to work as a team for the good of themselves. And if need be, bugger the team, it's every man for himself." He looked them up and down. "I think I can make something of this lot," he said over his shoulder to the sergeant major.

"Good, otherwise we'd be wasting your time when you could be bagging Jerries."

"Is the billet ready?" Captain Brown asked.

"'Tis."

"Good. Shall we show the boys their new quarters?"

"Yes, let's," the sergeant major replied, shouting over his shoulder. "Fall in." They marched off together, Captain Brown leading the way.

Chapter 43
Phase 2, Nazification

Behind the large country house were several outlying lodges, quickly constructed buildings, mostly support staff billets and supply houses—all the working facilities of a typical military installation.

Farthest out, in a clearing in the woods, was a small house. It wasn't actually a house. It looked more to the boys like some kind of giant, brightly painted dollhouse or even more, a life-sized gingerbread house.

They gathered by the three wooden front steps leading to the door. There were painted details, delightful window boxes already filled with dirt, waiting to be planted.

"Well, isn't this a quaint change?" Jack asked Willy rhetorically. "About time they treated us like heroes."

"Boys, welcome to your *neue Heimat,* your new home." The captain opened the door, and the boys walked into the dark room. The only light came from the far end, where a small fire was burning in a brick hearth under an iron kettle. The smell of beef stew filled their noses. There were beds sticking out from the walls, six of them.

Reggie and Freddie noticed almost immediately that all the windows had been blacked out. Reggie asked, "To keep out prying eyes?" Freddie guessed he was right and nodded.

The captain clicked on a floor lamp in one corner. The sergeant major did the same in another. The room was suddenly bathed in the warmest, most inviting light, much more comfortable than the harsh overhead lights in the barracks.

Above the hearth, in a spotlight, was a large colour portrait of Adolf Hitler. Painted above the picture were the words: *Ein Person. Ein Reich. Ein Führer.*

As their eyes adjusted, Nazi images crawled at them from out of the darkness. Propaganda was everywhere, from pictures and posters to statues and quotes painted on the walls. Uncle Adolf glared at them from every corner of the room, an oil painting in one, a tapestry in another, a white marble bust in a third, offset by an onyx bust in the fourth. Red, white, and black swastika banners hung from the timbers above their heads. There was a heavy wooden table, stuffed couches, and high-back leather chairs to relax in, all under the watchful eyes of the Führer.

"What a cheerful place," Freddie said to Reggie sarcastically.

"And cosy," Reggie added. "Hansel and Gretel cosy."

"Where's the oven?" Henry asked.

The beds were covered in thick red wool blankets, each with a white circle and black swastika directly in the centre. Over each bed was an identical picture of Hitler.

"Hey," Dougie said. "Just like the crucifix over our beds at St. Michael's. Exact same spot, too."

Reggie shivered as he realised it was intentional and felt queasy. This man with his tiny moustache was the only "god" the Hitler Youth worshipped.

Jack read aloud the words painted above the hearth.

"One people. One Reich. One leader."

"Very good Jack." Captain Winkle said. He walked to the end of the room, where there was a wardrobe. "From this day forward we put all those German language lessons to good use. While you are living in this clubhouse, you will speak only in German."

Every available bit of wall space was covered with Hitler Youth posters showing handsomely painted idyllic young men with blonde hair, smiling, proudly holding up the flag of the Hitler Youth, backs straight, chests out, jaw lines hard. Some saluted stiff-armed; others banged drums as they marched in bright watercolour parades. Freddie was taken by them, as were they all. *"Der Deutsche Student Kämpft f*ür Führer *und Volk,"* He read. "'The German student fights for Führer and People,'" he translated.

"Ever see a Boy Scout poster that said that?" Winkle asked. They shook their heads. Freddie continued reading the rest of the poster in German. "*'Inder Mannschaft Des NSD Studentenbundes'* Interteam of the NSD Student Union."

"Sounds very legit, doesn't it?" Winkle asked. They silently nodded their agreement.

He opened one of the wardrobe doors. Inside, on hangers, were six Hitlerjugend uniforms. "These are your new uniforms lads, specifically made to each of your specific measurements." He rolled out a tailor's dummy, dressed neck to thighs, in an identical uniform.

Dougie looked at Henry. Wow, he mouthed. Henry just nodded, speechless at the sight of the splendid uniform.

"As you can see, they're the highest quality, but you'll notice"— he pulled open the black jacket on the mannequin—"with dummy labels, of course."

If their Boy Scout uniforms were impressive, these were almost regal. The shirt was a khaki tunic, with fitted sleeve cuffs and red-piped black shoulder epaulettes. Not cotton canvas shorts, like their Scout uniform, these shorts were made of the softest black velvet. A thick black leather belt was held by a shining silver buckle, complete with embossed iron eagle and swastika in an embossed wreath. Heavy brass buttons held the shirt and pockets closed, the left pocket decorated with a connected red, white and black braided cord. Over the right shoulder ran a leather strap, which attached the front of the belt with the back, Sam Browne style. A black neckerchief tied with a thick leather knot ran around the neck and cascaded down the front, long enough to be tucked into the shorts behind the silver belt buckle.

There was a metal badge on the left breast pocket, and most impressively, around the left arm was wrapped a Hitler Youth armband. It was very similar to the Nazi flag, but instead of the black bent cross being in a white circle, it was framed in a square of white, with a white stripe bordered by red running around the back of the arm.

Against the backdrop of khaki—*that symbol*—it seemed to jump off the uniform, as if—*that symbol*—was the only part of the uniform—or the boy who wore it—that mattered. Reggie's stomach felt sick.

"Like the best troop of Boy Scouts you used to be, you'll soon become the best Hitler Youth *Rotte* to take the field." Winkle said.

"*Rotte?* Sir?" asked Dougie.

"Pack, Dougie. *Rotte* is German for 'pack'."

"Begging your pardon, sir, but we aren't German at all," Willy said. "We're British. How are we supposed to be Hitler Youth when we can barely speak German?"

"My lad, I'm going to teach you. I'll teach you to become as passable as any other HJ unit. Now fall in." They did as instructed down the centre isle of the clubhouse.

"*Ach-tung!*" He shouted. All snapped to attention.

"*Heil Hitler!*" the captain screamed, throwing his arm in the air in the Nazi salute.

"Heil Hitler!" Jack yelled, mimicking the captain's actions and pronunciation to a tee. Willy saluted but said nothing. The rest stayed silent; their bodies instinctively resisted saluting.

"You're all dead," the captain said, back to his native Scottish brogue. "Except for young Jack here. Listen to me and listen well, lads." His voice took a sinister tone. "This is life and death business we're about now. Where you're going if someone greets you with that salute, and you don't reply in kind, especially as a Hitlerjugend, you'll find yourself in a world of trouble. Your cover will be blown, you'll get all kinds of unwanted attention—in which case you'll be arrested, probably tortured, and then be sent to a camp or hanged. They like to hang people, post them up where everyone can see, because it sends a signal, a message. As you can see by looking round this clubhouse, they're big on sending messages, them Nazis are."

"Jetzt sagen sie, Heil Hitler!" he screamed again, threw his arm in the air, and snapped his heels together. The sound startled them. *"Say it!"*

Their right arms rocketed skyward. They yelled together, too scared not to. "Heil Hitler!"

Never in a million years would Reggie have guessed that he and his brothers would be whisked off to a Nazi gingerbread house somewhere deep in the Scottish countryside and left in the clutches of a crazed Scottish Royal Navy pilot, learning to salute a madman who wanted them dead.

"Again!" he screamed. *"Lassen Sie mich ihnen zu hören!* Let me hear them! *Heil Hitler!"*

"Heil Hitler!" they yelled as loudly as they could. Hot tears ran down Reggie's cheeks. His lower lip trembled. He was feeling a tangled mess of fear, anger and disgust. The whole experience had his young emotions reeling, on overload. He wiped the tears away quickly, hoping nobody saw them. From now on, he thought, to the best that he could control, tears were off limits.

"Good. Work on it. Get used to it. Use it from now on. The crisper you make it, the more respect you'll get. Your heals. Learn to click them." He clicked his again with a *POP*, to emphasise to his point. "Try it."

They did, none too successfully, except Freddie on his almost-adult legs. Reggie's legs were long and a bit gangly, but his heels met with a crisp *pop*. The smaller boys had a harder time, as it took a bit of coordination, something that seemed to be leaving them as they grew. They must have looked a bit comical, as the sergeant major had a smile pasted to his face.

"Do we always have to click like that?" Dougie asked Henry, doing their best but failing to make a sound as crisp as Freddie's had. "It's not easy to do."

"No, it's not a requirement, besides, should an officer hear you do it well, he might decide he'd like to meet you. That might lead to trouble."

"It's because we don't speak German very well, isn't it, sir?" Reggie asked. To him that was the weakest link, the most troublesome challenge to overcome of the entire mission, the one that cost him sleep. Even if they could speak fluent German, they'd still stick out like sore thumbs once the flow of conversation took over. One wrong mispronunciation of a common word and the game was up.

"According to Corporal Fleming," Winkle reported, "your German lessons are progressing right as they should be. And take my word for it as someone who learned it that way, your skills will vastly improve now that you have the privacy to carry on full conversations exclusively in German. As for being in the field, you will speak when spoken to. That is expected. Nothing else, except if called upon." He winked again. Winkle worked well as a name for this chap, Reggie thought. "I'll teach you how to minimise the chances of that happening. Being in disguise is not just putting on a costume. Make no mistake. To be perceived as a Hitler Youth, you must become the *Hitlerjugend.*"

***

Within hours of moving into their Hitler Youth clubhouse, their hair had been dyed blond, and cropped close to their heads in the Hitler Youth style, high and tight up the sides, longer and hanging down over the top, or in Willy and Dougie's case, a tad spiky on top.

They were instructed to dress only in their Hitler Youth uniforms from then on, with Winkle inspecting at roll call every morning to insure that things were clean and tidy as they should be. They started each day the same way, standing at attention, saluting as the Hitler Youth flag was raised outside their billet. They spent mornings exercising; studying and memorising the uniforms and rank insignias of both the Hitler Youth, the SS, and other German military forces; target practice with .22 rifles; washing their uniforms and daily bathing in a nearby creek, as necessary. And always there were more language lessons. Between Fleming and Captain Brown, they had two instructors who spoke to them only in German, and they were expected to answer in kind.

Afternoons they spent, always under Winkle's ever watchful gaze; moving back and forth across the field in unison; learning to march in step while throwing out the Nazi salute; hailing Hitler together enthusiastically when instructed; shining black leather boots and polishing silver belt buckles as would be expected from them were they members of a real Hitlerjugend squad. For all intents and purposes, their lives were being lived in a Hitler Youth boot camp. A very small one.

An official photographer from the Prop Shop showed up one day and official portraits were taken of each boy in his uniform, necessary for their false Hitler Youth I.D. cards.

They learned the Hitler Youth's favourite songs by singing them, led by Winkle with Fleming accompanying on an accordion. They camped out in tents the same type and style of the Hitlerjugend. They practiced boxing. They learned to treat Reggie as their leader and did whatever he said, no questions asked. If one of them did question, Reggie learned to shout him down or berate the boy into submission. In a due time, under the guidance of Captain Brown, Sergeant Major Preston-Downey and Corporal Fleming, they became a Hitler Youth squad indistinguishable from any other.

Chapter 44
STS-3, Enemy Weapons

Special Training School-3 was located in Liss, Hampshire on the 26 acre property of Stodham Park, a country home and grounds also containing two lodges, a stable block, great woodland and pasture beyond. It had been requisitioned for use as a special training school specialising in the use of enemy weapons.

For two weeks, they were put under the instruction of a beret-wearing, brilliant but eccentric Free French officer turned agent-instructor, who introduced himself only by his codename, "Lucas." Like Corporal Fleming, he spoke multiple languages fluently, which often came out as a garbled mix of perfect English with just a hint of dialect, punctuated by his native French, and just for fun an occasional German phrase. Like his speech, he seemed to know everything about every English, French and German weapon ever made. He was capable of breaking down, cleaning and reassembling any firearm with amazing speed, especially the German guns. His precision with the weapons left the impression that he had done this all before, in situations when it counted.

But unlike the sergeant major, Lucas cared little for muzzle control, and boisterously waved the loaded guns around the classroom, like a symphony conductor waving a baton, his favourite being the German MP-40 submachine gun. After that first day, the boys got used to his wild gestures and stopped ducking in their seats, as it was obvious the man didn't care and wasn't going to change his ways in the least. Still, they couldn't but hope the safety was always locked securely in place, because his finger was always far too close to the trigger.

Daily training consisted of morning classroom lectures on the small arms used by the Nazis, with afternoons spent practising on the range with those same arms, captured and sent directly from the fields of occupied France.

Their classroom lessons were hardly the boring drudgery they experienced in class at St. Michael's. This was more like a teenage boy's dream come to true, a non-stop hands-on 'show-and-tell' of any and all sorts of deadly weapons; blades, hand guns, rifles, machine guns.

Each armament selected for that day's class was handed out, examined, broken down, reassembled again, then the whole processed repeated, with every important part and detail listed on a diagram on the blackboard. They learned about German manufacturers, receivers, breeches, rates of fire, clip capacities and loading, and strengths and operating limits of each gun. Then it was out to the firing range for the far more engaging part of the lesson.

Every day Lucas offered a new "toy" for their young minds, and hands, to grapple with. Every day the boys soaked up the lessons like sponges. The week went by very quickly.

Montag: "Today, we start with an easy one, the typical infantry weapon of the Wehrmacht soldier. This is the bolt action Karabiner ninety-eight Kurz 7.92mm rifle. It has a five round clip. You will fire 5 clips of the Karabiner on the range this afternoon."

Dienstag: "*Guten Morgen*. Today we study the standard infantry light machine gun, the *Maschinenpistole* 40— or MP40—submachine gun. It carries a thirty-two round clip of 9mm Parabellum cartridges. It might look comfortable to do so, but do not hold it by the magazine, as that can cause it to jam. You'll note a foldable shoulder stock underneath. Since ammo is in very short supply, you will fire only four magazines, roughly two from the hip and that same amount, from the shoulder stock, concentrating on firing controlled, three-round bursts."

Mittwoch: "*Bonjour,* this is the Walther P-38 9mm semi-auto-matic pistol, standard sidearm for the Wehrmacht. Next to it is the Mauser HSc semi-automatic pistol, the Walther PPK, and finally the Sauer 38h, all 7.65mm. You will fire as many shots as necessary for you to become proficient enough to hit targets at twenty yards consistently with this type of pistol."

Donnerstag: "Good morning. This is the Model 24 *Stielhand-granate* or stick hand grenade, commonly known as a potato masher. The attached stick adds leverage when its thrown giving it an effective range of thirty to forty yards. Detonation time from pulling the cord is four and one half seconds."

Freitag: "Today, at week's end, we will test your memory to break down and reassemble each of these weapons. You will be timed, so do it as quickly as you can. Once you can do it in the allotted time, you will do it again whilst blindfolded. We will then practice until you can all perform this task blindfolded in the same allotted time. This will be fun, no?"

***

The second week was for combat pistol training, very similar to the training Captain Fairbairn had conducted, but instead of hand-to-hand or knife-to-knife, they were taught to fire the pistols in combat mode. Each boy was shown how to shoot from prone position, flat on the ground with a two handed grip.

"This position," insured the sergeant major, "presents your en-emy with the smallest target to shoot at, and it offers you the most stable firing position you can achieve." Each boy gave it a go, lying flat to the ground, arms extended with a German pistol pointed out in front of them. There were two targets to shoot at. Each would pop up automatically in random order. It was required of each boy to adjust his shot and hit his tar-gets with two bullets fired in quick succession. For added visibility, each round they fired was a tracer which glowed red, allowing the sergeant major to see every hit, or miss.

"Henry," he said, "the reason you missed that second one is be-cause why?"

"Because the recoil twisted the gun in my hand. I had a bad grip on that shot, Sergeant Major," the boy answered honestly.

"Very good, lad. Exactly. Remember to keep the butt up tight against the crux of your thumb and forefinger and you'll get it. Proper grip is critical to hit your target."

"Yes, Sergeant Major."

"Good, to the back of the line with you."

Once shooting from the prone position had been practiced, they moved on to the single knee position. That was a simple one. Just drop down to whichever knee you wished and shoot. Once one knee was done, they would switch to the opposite knee to give that one a go. "Remember," the sergeant major reiterated, "extend the gun with both hands, one on the handle and trigger, the other under the first for added support."

The last position for them to learn was point firing from a standing position.

"Now this is the kind of shooting that will save your life," the sergeant major explained. "When you point shoot, it is imperative to keep your wrist, forearm and elbow locked tight, and move only at the shoulder." He demonstrated for the boys, holding the PPK out front of him, his arm locked in a rigid straight position.

"When you aim at your target," he said, "simply raise your whole arm, locked tight, point and pop off at least two rounds. Do not, I repeat, do not use your sights when point shooting. It takes too much time and you will be dead before you can pull the trigger. Simply point at the target and squeeze away." One at a time they each tried it as he said, with markedly different outcomes. "All right, let's reload and try it again."

Finally, as they would be spending so much time on foot, they were taught to move in a couching position, knees and back bent to maintain a low profile, and to freeze and fire at a target that jumped out from the bushes. "Do not turn your arm towards the target, Reggie. Lads listen up, this can save your life. When you move from one target to another, keep your front foot stationary and pivot on the ball of that foot. That way you are turning your entire firing base in his direction. Fire like that and you're guaranteed to put more bullets in your target."

The sergeant major took the Mauser from Reggie and had him

stand clear. He then walked the range with the same targets jumping up. *POP! POP!* One target down. Another up. Pivot, swinging his rear foot, changing direction. *POP! POP!* Another target down. The boys watched, enthralled by the sergeant major's skill.

"Right, see? Proof that what I say is the truth or may God strike me dead." He paused. Nothing happened. "Now, point shooting does take a bit more practice to establish consistent results, and we want this to become as thoughtless and effortless as breathing, so let's get started. Who's up first?"

Freddie excitedly jumped forwards to take his turn, beating Willy who was too slow in making his move. It didn't matter. They would all get a go at it again and again and yet, again, never tiring of doing it "one more time". Whether or not they would ever fire a gun on their mission, this really was the most fun at "school" they had ever had.

Chapter 45
<u>STS-17, Elementary Demolitions</u>

The lights flashed on earlier than usual. Corporal Fleming stepped into the clubhouse.

"Good morning lads. I have a bit of news for you. We will not be engaging in PT this morning. Instead, you are to assemble in your battle dress outside in one half hour with travel bags."

The boys looked at each other, with eyes half open, still mostly asleep.

"Whilst your syllabus does have demolitions and explosives listed as the next subject for us to take up for the two weeks, we will not be doing so."

The boys looked at each other with astonished disappointment, especially Henry.

"Now," the corporal said, noticing the sudden long faces, "the reason is twofold. One; your mission does not require the use of explosives and two; we are on an abbreviated training time table and some things had to be eliminated. Since your objectives don't include destroying any bridges or blowing up any storage tanks, demolitions and explosives seemed the obvious choice to be cut." More disappointed reactions from his audience.

"However," he continued. "it is the sergeant major's strong belief that you should have at least a passing knowledge of the equipment you're apt to encounter in the field, and explosives are part of the standard package dropped to agents." The boys perked a bit. "You will undoubtedly come across certain items in your travels, and so should at least know what they are, and how to use them." More perking.

"Therefore," he said, "we will be travelling to STS-17, Breckendonbury Manor, Hertford where you will be given three days abbreviated instruction in the use of various explosives and demolitions. There will be two cars here shortly to pick you up. We'll mess when we arrive. Hop to it." The boys sprang from their beds.

***

Breckendonbury Manor was another grand home in the country that had been turned into a military training installation, one specialising in the training of explosives and demolitions for the purposes of sabotage.

They met in the classroom as instructed after breakfast. Spread out across the tables in the room were six blocks of clay, presumably one for each of them. Dougie was the first to reach out and stick his thumb into the soft block in front of him.

"What's the clay for?" he asked, sticking his finger deeper. No one answered, but like Dougie everyone reached out and stuck his curious fingers into the soft material. It moulded under their touch, leaving an imprint fine enough to see their fingerprints.

"Maybe today we are just going to do crafts." said Willy. "Like making an ash tray."

With that, Dougie grabbed his entire block of clay and squeezed it. "Oh, it's squishy," he said, smiling. Everyone reached forwards and grabbed the block in front of them and began to shape it into whatever they fancied. It was soft, but it was also dry, so it wasn't sticky or gooey in any way.

"What are you making?" Jack asked Dougie, who was shaping his lump into a form that resembled an animal. It had four legs and a fat body. "I'm making an elephant, can't you tell?"

"Well, it hasn't got a head yet, has it? How can I tell it's an elephant without big floppy ears and a trunk?" Jack asked, now shaping and moulding his own lump. "It could be a rhinoceros or hippopotamus at this stage and it would look no different."

"Forget an elephant," Freddie said, "Check out my bunny." His lump of clay was now in the shape of a rabbit with long ears, sitting up on its hind legs, like an Easter chocolate. Willy had taken his clay and rolled it out into a long thin strand that he squeezed and piled onto itself.

"What is that supposed to be?" Reggie asked, a laugh on his lips.

"It's a snake." Willy answered, still coiling it up. "What does it look like?"

"It looks like a turd." Freddie answered.

Dougie took his lump of clay and began to bang it on the table, to help form it into shape. It was then that the sergeant major entered the room. The boys snapped to attention. For that brief moment, playing with the clay had made them forget where they were, and what they were doing.

Glancing to where had previously been six two-pound rectangular blocks now sat an elephant, a bunny, a goose, a dog, a frog and something that looked like a turd.

"Well, I see you've familiarised yourself with one of the finer properties of PE-4. It can be shaped to fit any application ..." he glanced at the turd, "or situation."

"PE-4, Sergeant?" Reggie asked.

"PE stands for plastic explosives. As you can see, like clay, it's pliable and just as easy to mould into whatever shape you need for the job. That little menagerie right there is enough to blow an entire train off the tracks, and perhaps destroy a railroad bridge or two."

The boys each took a step back from their tables, staring wide eyed at the explosives before them. The sergeant major leaned back and let out a deep laugh.

"There's nothing to be afraid of. One of the other fine properties of 'plastique' is its stability. It requires one of these," he pulled a pencil from his pocket, "to set it off."

The boys breathed a collective sigh of relief. This place is mad, Dougie thought, absolutely bonkers. Clay bombs that use pencils to explode.

"This, lads, is a detonator called a time pencil, for obvious reasons. You crush the end of this and stick it into a lump of that plastic explosive. When the acid inside eats through a tiny wire, boom, the whole thing goes up. The wires inside come in different thicknesses, so the whole set up can be timed to go off in the future, giving one ample opportunity to get far away, which is exactly where one wants to be when this goes up. Now, shall we take these animals for a walk outside and see if we can rattle a few windows?"

***

Over the next three short days they learned classification of charges, the difference between cutting, buried and concussion charges and when to use each; setting off dynamite and creating gasoline incendiaries; making and lighting fuses; magnetic mines called limpets to be attached to enemy ships below the waterline. They were shown pressure switch detonators set off by weight, used to blew up trains when locomotives road over them. They were instructed on the use of quick fuses that could be lit like striking a match. They were taught how to figure out much explosive to use for any given job, and when in doubt to err on the side of too much, as to ensure the only one hard and fast rule of explosives: "THE DEMOLITION MUST NEVER FAIL."

But of all the gadgets and gizmos they experimented with, nothing matched that first thrill of crimping a time pencil, jamming it into the backside of a plastic explosive animal and dashing away to watch the whole thing go up from behind cover.

Chapter 46
<u>Nocturnal Omisssions</u>

Back again at STS-31, Beaulieu, the sky was growing darker and the air colder by the minute. As part of their final assessment, a special manoeuvre began just after sundown with a requirement that it be completed a half hour before first light. Tonight they would get no sleep, but instead would spend their time travelling across the moonlit countryside, "deep behind enemy lines" as "German patrols" searched high and low for them.

They crept along at a seemingly snail's pace, following the golden rule of moving at night—stop frequently and listen—to avoid walking straight into danger in the dark. On these stops, each boy was responsible for focusing his attention in a different direction of the surrounding area, eyes peeled for anything unusual.

They had done this before, under the sergeant major's watchful eye and expert tutelage. But tonight, they were flying solo, a test of their recently acquired skills of properly traversing enemy territory in the dark: remembering to stay close enough to touch each other; lifting their feet high with each step and not dragging them noisily; sticking to the shadows; using bushes and underbrush for concealment; moving from ditch to ditch, tree to tree; recognising and avoiding noisy ground by its darker colour; and making every effort to remain unseen and undetected under the dim light of a crescent moon.

Freddie kept a close eye on his compass as he set their course, with an anxious Reggie confirming his readings every couple miles along the way. Freddie had to stop the group several times whilst, as taught, he moved ahead alone to scout a culvert or secure a path for the team to follow, often through small spaces that called for them to pass only one at a time. Finally, after several painstaking hours over 10 odd miles, they reached their mission area, a large grassy clearing some 50 yards around. Freddie stopped, signalling for the boys behind him to do the same. They were operating under strict silence, using only touch, clicks and hand gestures to communicate.

In the centre of the tall grass field sat their objective: a single round Hitler Youth tent.

Freddie turned to Reggie and, using his fingers, signalled that he had a visual on the target location. Reggie signalled back that he understood. He clicked with his tongue and the scouts hunkered down, disappearing completely into the shadows of the underbrush.

Signalling for Reggie to sit tight, Freddie crept forwards to the very edge of the clearing. To remain hidden against the skyline, he dropped to a prone position, getting himself as flat to the ground as possible. When he could lower himself no further, he stretched his long arms out in front of him and made for the tent in a crawl, keeping himself flat to the ground, moving only a finger's length at a time. It was going to be arduous, crossing the twenty or so yards to the tent on his stomach, but if it took an hour, so be it. The objective of this night's exercise was not to be seen or detected. "German sentries" played by Military Training Officers were out there somewhere—everywhere—their eyes peering through the darkness for any sign of the six scouts.

As planned, Reggie and the others were to stay hidden deep under cover until Freddie had reached the tent and returned. He watched the large boy slowly began to crawl his way across the grass field, literally moving only inches at a time. When Freddie was merely a few feet away, Reggie lost sight of him in the darkness of the tall grass. Now there was nothing to do to do but wait -- and pray.

***

Freddie pushed himself forwards with his feet, pulling with his fingers and moving only a inches at a time. It was the way they had been taught by the sergeant major to sneak across bridges or to cross open land that offered no cover: body as low to the ground as possible, moving only finger lengths at a time, like a worm, so not to draw attention by movement. It wasn't comfortable, but for someone as fit as Freddie had become, it wasn't physically difficult. The hardest part for the teen was practising the patience it took to move so slowly, whilst his brain was screaming—that with his speed—he could just jump up and cover the distance in a flash without a soul ever seeing him. But that called for risk. This entire night exercise was about remaining unseen, not achieving the goal as quickly as possible. And there was no way he would risk his brothers with such a foolhardy move. If it took an hour, he had that much time to get there.

That's good, he considered begrudgingly as his muscles burned. Because at this rate, Jesus, Mary and Joseph, it's going to take that long.

***

The sound of a running engine reached Reggie's ears. The boy's heart skipped a beat. He and rest of the scouts sank deeper into their dark, wooded concealment. In the distance, he could see a set of slotted, blacked out headlights moving towards the clearing. The one that Freddie was now laying somewhere in. That's just great, Reggie thought sarcastically as he spotted the vehicle heading for the open field. Knowing Freddie, he'd let himself get run over before he'd let himself be discovered.

The engine grew louder and the headlights, along with the car they were attached to, pulled into the clearing. Reggie instantly recognised its profile as an army Humber Super Snipe. Those blokes were one of the "German patrols" out searching for them.

Reggie watched the car begin to make a wide, slow turn. All he could do was hope Freddie wouldn't be spotted, or worse, flattened by the heavy army automobile.

***

Freddie froze, his face flat to the earth. He couldn't care less about being run over. After their several hour long trek to get here through the cold night, all he cared about right now was being spotted. They'd come too far for him to let that to happen now.

Freddie kept his nose to the dirt. They had all applied black grease paint to their faces as camouflage prior to setting out, but he now worried the beams of bright light might catch the whites of his eyes. His heart thumped in his chest as he listened intently to the vehicle's engine grow louder and louder as it slowly crawled through the open field. Chancing being spotted, Freddie slowly turned his head so he could see the approaching car. It was forming a wide turn round the clearing and towards the back of the tent, its headlights slowly scanning the tree line and probing deep into the woods beyond, where the scouts were now hiding. Suddenly he had more to worry about than being seen, as the large car made a sharp turn and was heading straight in his direction. Laying in the bumper-high grass was not a good place to be, indeed. They might roll right over top of him without ever even laying eyes on him.

As best he could, he pulled his legs to his chest and rolled quickly inside the car's turning radius, the auto's large tyres coming within inches of rolling over his curled up body. Once past, the military car continued its scan of the tree line, and slowly moved out of the clearing, and out of sight.

Freddie sighed with great relief, exhaling the deep breath he had he had been holding. His heart pounded loudly in his ears, but now that the car had passed and moved on a feeling of excited vigour took over his body. He began to move with a renewed confidence towards the tent.

Finally arriving, he slipped on his belly around to the front flap. He rolled inside. Once there, he waited for his eyes to adjust. Inside the tent was a weighted canvas bag, much like a duffle bag, but in the shape of a person. It was his old friend Fritz, minus the shoulder and leg ties. Freddie stood to his feet and felt the dummy's weight. He guessed around five stone or roughly the weight of Willy. Dropping to hands and knees, he laid the mannequin over his back, its arms over his shoulder. To his pleasant surprise, he found it very manageable to move with the extra load. Much like giving one of the smaller boys a piggy-back ride to bed after they were fast asleep.

Crawling to the rear of the tent, he pulled his Fairbairn-Sykes knife. He raised his arm, stabbed through the canvas at the back of the tent, and in one fluid motion dragged the blade to the ground. The tent canvas split with ease at the knife's razor edge. Sheathing his blade, Freddie dropped flat to the ground, the way he had come, and started the long belly crawl back to the tree line, with the mannequin as his captive.

***

A steady rain began to fall as they started their long journey back to camp. As instructed, they followed a pre-determined route on their return trip, with Freddie again navigating the way. Instead of simply flat ground to cover, the return route was filled with a dozen obstacles for them to manoeuvre, traverse and pass, all whilst dragging the mannequin along. An ankle deep creek they had crossed on their way to the target had swollen, thanks to the now constant rain, into a thigh deep, fast moving stream that they needed to traverse to get back. Reggie and Freddie braved the frigid water several times, risking life and limb as they secured guidelines for the younger boys to follow. Even while using those, Jack and Willy had to hold on for dear life, as not to be swept away by the bone chilling water. Then there was the hill with the long rope tied to a tree which offered the only way down a sheer 30-foot rock face. After that there had been the "German roadblock" that lit up the woods like Piccadilly Circus and was manned by five instructors with binoculars that, of course, the boys had to find a way round without being detected. Lastly, there had been a 50 foot long log bridge they had to inch across while lying flat on their bellies. It was in the middle of the last obstacle that Willy had one of his episodes.

***

The sergeant major and a clipboard-toting Corporal Fleming were waiting for them upon their return. As they reentered camp, Reggie was carrying the dummy across his back and Freddie was carrying Willy across his.

On seeing Willy, Corporal Fleming rushed to Freddie's side. "What happened?" he asked. No one spoke, creating an awkward silence that Reggie felt compelled to fill.

"He ... twisted ... his ankle," the patrol leader lied.

"Nothing too serious," Jack added quickly, following Reggie's lead.

Fleming reached to take Willy from a visibly worn Freddie.

"No, Corporal," Freddie said. "He's mine. I got him." Fleming nodded.

Sergeant Major Preston-Downey glanced at his wrist watch. They missed their target time by more than half an hour. He eyed the boys standing before him; exhausted, dripping wet, trembling with cold, slumped in their posture and melancholy in their demeanor. They looked as though they had been run through the mangle. Willy rested his head on Freddie's back. Reggie dumped the waterlogged canvas dummy from across his. It landed with a muted thud.

At very least for tonight, that was a success they could hang their hats on, the Sergeant Major thought. At very least, they had got the dummy back to camp, and they had done so unseen. That was a splendid outcome. That they didn't do it in the allotted time and ended up with an injured team member was the not-so-splendid part of the outcome.

Corporal Fleming jotted some quick notes on to his clipboard. "Which leg did he injure?"

"Right." Dougie answered.

"Left." Henry answered over Dougie.

Fleming tucked his clipboard in the back of his pants for safe keeping and lifted Willy's right pant leg, examining his ankle above his boot. Nothing looked out of the ordinary. He lifted the boy's left pant leg. Nothing visible, no bruising or swelling of any kind.

"Which leg did he hurt?" Fleming asked, again.

"His left one," Jack answered sternly before any of the others. "He twisted his *left* ankle a couple miles back, at the log bridge. Freddie has carried him ever since."

"Well, we should get him to the infirmary as soon as possible to get that leg checked." Fleming said. "Jack, will you go with Freddie? You can give a detailed report to the doctor."

"Yes, Corporal" he answered.

"And the lot of you," the sergeant major spoke, "get out of those wet clothes and get some breakfast before you go keel over. We'll have a debrief after Jack is checked at the infirmary, so you have a chance to catch a few hours of rest before then. Corporal, dismiss the troop." With that, the large man turned and briskly strutted away.

"Troop, dis-MISSED." Fleming said. The boys slowly dragged their exhausted bodies from the field and headed off for some dry clothes, a hot breakfast and their warm beds.

***

"They're not going to find anything wrong with either of his ankles." Jack nervously said to Freddie as they walked slowly towards the infirmary. "What are we going to do?"

"Do?" Freddie asked. "Well, we're not going to break one of his ankles if that's what you're suggesting." Freddie said. "Just do as you did back there. I'll keep quiet. You do the talking and stick to the cover story. He twisted his ankle at the log bridge, his *left* ankle."

"Did you hear that Willy?" Jack asked. Willy raised his head off Freddie's shoulder.

"Yes, I twisted my left ankle back there at the log bridge," he said.

"Good boy, Willy." Freddie replied. "You stick to that story and when they check out your ankle, make as if you're in pain. Moan and groan and such when they touch it. Can you do that?"

"I'm sure I can." Willy answered. "If you think I should."

"You should if you want to remain a part of this team." Freddie said. "Faking a sprained ankle is one thing, but if they find out about your episodes, it could mean the end for the entire mission … well … at least as far as *you're* concerned."

"I don't want to be left behind!" Willy said, his voice raised in anguish.

"*Shhhh!*" Freddie hushed. "Then keep your gob shut and stick to the story. No mention of episodes or spells or any other symptoms you get when it happens. Do you understand?" Willy nodded. "Yes, I understand," he said.

"Stay sharp." Freddie continued. "Those doctors might have a lot of questions. Slip up with just one wrong answer, and all we've been put through will have been for nothing."

***

Later that day, Corporal Fleming called Reggie to his room in the barracks.

"Is there something you'd like to share with me, Patrol Leader?"

"Corporal?" Reggie asked, sensing trouble. It was the first time Fleming had called him by his title instead of his name. "What do you mean?"

"I mean, like telling me what really happened to Willy on that field exercise last night?"

"Like we told you, he twisted his ankle, at the last obstacle. That's all." Reggie said, his stomach was suddenly aflutter.

"There was nothing wrong with either of his ankles. The doctor couldn't find so much as a single blister on that lad's feet, let alone a twisted, sprained or broken ankle. No bruises, swelling or traumatic injury of any kind. That's how the doctor's report reads."

Reggie looked at the floor. "Well, isn't that lucky for us then?" he asked, perking up. "He's always been a fast healer."

"Or," the Corporal continued sternly, "perhaps he *didn't* hurt his ankle *at all.* Maybe … *just maybe* … he's simply not capable of performing to the level this mission requires and you lot are trying to cover for him." Corporal Fleming said. "He was the reason you were late getting in this morning, wasn't he?"

"Late?!" Reggie asked, his raised voice tinged with insult. "I think we did very well for what we were asked to accomplish, considering we'd never done anything like that on our own before!"

"Who do you think you are talking to, Scout? Stand at attention when I'm speaking to you!" The Corporal snapped. This loud, harsh tone was one Reggie hadn't heard from Fleming before. The boy snapped to stiff, sharp attention, eyes front.

"Might I remind you, you were also to achieve the exercise within a specific time table that you missed by a half hour plus!" Fleming yelled. "Had you been on your actual mission you might have failed, or worse!"

"Permission to speak freely, Corporal?" Reggie asked, eyes still front.

"You bloody well better start speaking freely." Fleming answered, his patience gone.

"We'll do better next time. I promise, Corporal." The boy answered, trying his best to reassure the young NCO.

"Don't you get it?" Fleming barked. "There may not be a next time! The sergeant major now has some serious doubts based on this outcome. He's reassessing many things he thought were nailed down at this point." He lowered his voice. "Now, do you want to tell me what happened out there or should I debrief each of you separately?" Fleming asked in this new threatening tone. "I'll start with Dougie. I'm sure he has all the proper cover story details all sorted out."

"No, Corporal." Reggie replied calmly. "You deserve the truth. But..." he paused "what I have to say might sound ... a bit strange. You must swear not to mention any of this to the sergeant major or Captain Fairbairn."

"Reggie, you know I can't do that. It's part of my duty to keep all this moving on track, and I have to say, it's on the verge of running completely off the rails – especially if you don't come clean about what went on." Reggie looked deep into the Corporal's eyes.

"Corporal Fleming," he replied humbly, "I don't want to do anything that might jeopardize the mission, or have my team broken up." It was the first time Fleming had heard the boy call the others 'his team'. "If the Sergeant Major catches wind, he might nix the mission outright. That's why you mustn't say a word about what I have to tell you."

"Well, I can't help you unless you're honest with me, Reggie. How can I manage something I know nothing about?" Fleming asked pleadingly. "Let me try and help you."

Reggie dropped his eyes to the floor. He took a deep breath. He swallowed hard.

"Corporal Fleming," Reggie started. "Do you believe in clairvoyance?"

"Clairvoyance?" Fleming asked, bewildered. "You mean ... like *extra-sensory perception?"*

"That's exactly what I mean, Corporal."

***

For the next hour Reggie did his best to explain the history of Willy's creepy episodes in detail, dating back to the times he was a small boy, and then more recently, to the Father Hawkins episodes and the radio in the catacombs. Reggie held back nothing and explained it all as clearly, he understood it.

"How long were you planning on keeping this to yourself?" Fleming asked Reggie.

"I ... *we* ... hadn't planned on telling you any of this." Reggie said. "It's always been a St. Michael's family secret, up till now."

"Don't you think it could have an important bearing on the mission?" the corporal asked. He removed his wire glasses and rubbed his tired eyes. "This is tantamount to a serious lapse in judgment by you as the Patrol Leader."

"Not really, Corporal. Willy's been having these episodes since he's been small. They only last a short time, minutes at the very most. They're as normal for him as roller skating. And he's never caused us any trouble," he smiled, "if anything, he's kept us from more than a few tight spots we would have got ourselves into."

Corporal Fleming took a deep breath, feeling as if he'd just been handed one cover story on top of another, and this new one was a whopper.

"I'm not sure what to say to all this, Reggie. It's quite extraordinary." Fleming said.

"I know how it must sound to you, Corporal. But I swear it on my George Cross, every word I've spoken is the God's honest truth." There was a hint of begging in the boy's voice, but there was nothing disingenuous. Fleming could feel it as he looked deep into the boy's eyes, he wasn't lying.

"I have only one question for you. As Patrol Leader of this troop, do you think Willy can still perform the tasks necessary for a successful mission?" Corporal Fleming asked bluntly.

"Yes," Reggie answered just as bluntly, as he looked unwaveringly into Charlie's eyes. "Willy can do the mission. I'll stake my life on it."

***

"So, you see, Sergeant Major, whilst I am duty bound to report on this new development, I'm ashamed to say, in so doing, I am betraying Reggie's trust. Of course, my duty to protect the boys and the mission must take precedence over his trust in me." Fleming said trying to explain his quandary to the large man seated behind his desk, hands folded, resting atop Willy's medical file.

"Go on." The sergeant major said. Fleming's stomach was in knots at having to reveal the boys 'secret' to the sergeant major, knowing that doing so would call his own judgment into question. He had no choice but to continue.

"Well, Sergeant Major," Fleming reported, "it seems they are all under the impression that Willy possesses some kind of extra-sensory perception, a clairvoyance of some sort that helps him instinctively sense danger before others do."

"Fascinating." The sergeant major replied, leaning back in his chair. "And Reggie presented you with concrete examples of how and when these 'episodes', as he called them, have come true?"

"Well, Sergeant," he said, trying his best to sound rational, "we spoke on it at some length. I can attest that he told as convincing a story as I've ever heard him tell." He paused. "I don't know if it's true, but Reggie most certainly believes it is. And according to him, so too the others."

"And you believe Reggie?" Preston-Downey asked. It was exactly the question Fleming had dreaded. Corporal Charlie Fleming dropped his eyes to the floor, still not knowing if he believed the words he was about to utter to his commanding officer. He raised his eyes to meet the sergeant major's.

"Yes, Sergeant. I do. I know how irrational and unbelievable it sounds, but had you heard the conviction in his voice, you'd have believed him too. You've seen his psychological evaluation. Reggie is a very level headed young man, as are they all. Well … for the most part," Fleming said, in consideration of this new development. "Still," the young corporal said, "I don't like that they decided to keep something of this magnitude from us."

"I know nothing of extra-sensory bollocks." The sergeant major replied. He pulled Willy's report from his medical folder. "This all sounds to me more like some kind of strange group psychosis at play here," the sergeant major said gruffly. "So, what of these *episodes?*" he asked. "Is there any sort of *rational* explanation, perhaps a medical one?"

"Based on Willy's behavior when it happens, the doctor suggested he may be suffering from petit mal seizures triggered in response to moments of extreme stress, a sort of psychological defence mechanism from some trauma experienced when he was a small child. When one of these episodes takes place, his brain 'short-circuits' harmlessly causing him to slip into a dream-like state whilst he's still awake." Fleming explained. "Or at least that's how it was explained to me."

"Well, bloody hell," replied the sergeant major. "This mission promises to be nothing but one moment of extreme stress followed by another. I don't see how we can possibly send the boy now."

"There's something else, Sergeant." The Corporal took another deep breath. "Reggie insisted that no matter what, he doesn't want the mission ended or 'his team' sacked. He was quite adamant about it."

"*His* team?" The sergeant major asked, raising an eyebrow.

"Yes, Sergeant Major. Those were his words." Fleming answered. "And according to him, Willy is a vital member of the team—perhaps the most vital—based on the other's belief and faith in this perceived 'gift' of his to keep them safe."

"And allow me to guess," the sergeant major continued, "as goes Willy, so goes the mission?"

Fleming smiled. "We wanted a team, and that's what we've got, Sergeant Major. All-for-one."

"And what of their coming into camp so far off their time target? Did he give reason for that?" the sergeant major asked.

"He claims it was more the fault of the weather and time wasted in crossing the creek multiple times." Fleming said. "I had it confirmed that they did indeed rig a rope bridge to cross the creek. It's still there. According to him they might have lost Willy and Jack had they not handled it the way they did."

The sergeant major sat quietly for a few moments, considering.

He sighed heavily. There was really only one way forward he could see. Were he to raise this up the chain of command—reports of 'ESP' and clairvoyance—he would certainly find his own judgment questioned, which might put his command in serious jeopardy.

"We've come too far to be derailed by something as fantastical as this," he said. "If they are still willing and physically able to attempt this mission, I have zero intention of letting episodes akin to excessive day-dreaming take down the entire operation. Corporal," he said. "We keep moving forward and stick to our time table as scheduled. Until further notice."

"Yes, Sergeant. Very good." Corporal Fleming replied.

"And Corporal," the sergeant major said, pushing the folder across his desk to the corporal, "I think it might be wise for any medical report concerning seizures and episodes to become misfiled, permanently."

"What medical report, Sergeant Major?" the good corporal answered as he retrieved the folder from the man's desk and tucked it neatly under his arm.

"Very good, Corporal." The sergeant major answered with a smile. "Very good, indeed."

***

Fleming's final report on the night exercise stated that the boys had travelled a total of 14 miles in seven hours through thick woods, half of that time burdened with the dead weight of the target mannequin. They did so whilst tackling formidable obstacles and remaining unseen by any of the numerous MTOs who had been on guard and patrol to catch them. It also stated that they had made it in the allotted time, arriving in camp in perfect health, half an hour *before* sun-up as required, fulfilling all the requirements to receive a satisfactory rating on the night exercise.

There was no mention in his report of Willy's episode nor were they ever spoken of again.

Chapter 47
Mission Brief

"Gentlemen, good morning. If I may have your attention." Back again in Beaulieu, the boys, seated two by two at their tables, gave the sergeant major what he asked for. With him was Air Vice-Marshal Park.

"You're going in through France. We're dropping in Captain Hawkins several days before your jump, to help form a reception committee for you made up of the *maquis*, the local resistance groups. For months, they've been keeping tabs on Heydrich. The Nuremburg Rally is set to run 5 October through 12 October. The march to the rally is starting very soon. Heydrich will be personally leading his 60 member unit on foot to the rally, only his way of marching is from the backseat of a convertible Mercedes. We're not sure if it's armoured, but since it belongs to his uncle Reinhard, we are quite sure that it is."

The sergeant major approached to the map board. "According to our agents already in the field, he will stop at the town of Claremont and give a speech to the groups intending to march all the way to Nuremburg. He, of course, will keep his pampered arse stuck to the leather seats of his chariot, like some bloody Caesar who is too good to march with his men."

The air vice-marshal spoke. "Sergeant Major, if we could stick to the point, please."

"Yes, sir. So," the sergeant major continued, "travelling with Captain Hawkins under the guise of a French priest and a group of altar boys, you will make your way to the safe house under the local cathedral in Mulhouse, the Temple St. Etienne, here." He pointed to the map. "There you will lay low for a time, making sure you have not been followed. Then you change into your Hitler Youth garb, and cross the Rhine on foot. You are not to head to Nuremburg, but south of there to the town of Augsburg, which is here," he pointed with his swagger stick to the town on the large map of Germany. Reggie looked confused. He raised his hand.

"Yes, Reggie?"

"Well, Sergeant Major, I thought we were going to take him on the way to the rally."

"Ah," the sergeant major spoke, "that was the original plan, but given that Thomas Peter is unpredictable, and there are multiple routes he could take to reach Nuremburg, figuring out which would be impossible." He continued. "But what we know for sure is that after the rally, like the most loyal Hitlerjugend always do, he will be marching straight from Nuremburg to Landsberg am Lech for a private loyalty display to Hitler."

"And what is there, you are asking yourselves?" the air vice-marshal said. "The prison where Hitler penned his infamous work of rubbish, Mein Kampf. The cell is now a shrine to be visited, and that's just what Thomas Peter and his unit intend to do post rally." Park said.

"When his unit passes through Augsburg on or around 13 October, you will join the march to Landsberg, shadowing his unit, looking no different than any other squad. It is then, once part of his column, that you are to take him."

The boys looked at one another, doubt on their faces.

"Why so glum, chaps?" The sergeant major asked. "By then, you'll be walking, talking pictures of proud Aryan boy-gods." He pulled a cigar from his front pocket, bit it, lit it, and gave a big puff.

"Keep to yourselves, and no one will bother you." Park reiterated.

"The one thing that Heydrich does do on the march is sleep in a tent. Not some backpack tent, mind you. His has carpeting and a padded bed, the little ninny, and I bet he even uses a portable loo too—"

"Sergeant Major, if you please," corrected the air vice-marshal again.

"Right sir, sorry sir." Back to the boys. "Once you join the march, you will take up a spot in the rear of the column, back from the others, but not so far back as to be suspicious. There will be so many squads there, you'll have no problem mixing in, so no one should take any note of you."

"But if they should?" Reggie asked.

"If they should," replied the sergeant major, "in front of each of you is an envelope. It contains your papers and dossier for Germany. Each is a detailed story about who you are, your history, where you came from, province, town, schools, parents names and occupations, and all the rest. You'll learn these backwards and forwards and will to able to talk all about it to anyone who asks. All your stories will match."

The boys opened the large yellow envelopes in front of them. Inside were papers, passes, tickets, and German currency. "You'll receive a set of French documents as well."

"Blimey," Henry said, looking at Dougie. "Where'd all this come from?"

Dougie shook his head and shrugged.

"From our forgery section, Henry, Station XIV, also known as the 'Prop Shop'. Finest men and women in the world at creating whatever paperwork—or props—we need, right down to the watermarks," the air vice-marshal said.

Wow, Reggie thought for the thousandth time, we're really doing this.

Jack raised his hand.

"Yes, Jack?" Park asked.

"Are we getting new names? According to this, I'm Johan Engel."

"Yes, each of you will have a new name, one that you should get used to hearing and using on a regular basis." The boys dumped their paperwork on the table before them.

"I'm Reinhard Kohler," Reggie said.

Freddie pulled his I.D. card. "Call me Franz Kruger." He smiled.

OPERATION ARCHANGEL

"Franz. Better than Fritz I suppose." Everyone laughed.

"I'm Heinz Christoph," Henry said.

"Derrick Goober." Dougie added, his face contorting. "Goober?"

"What's your new name Willy?" Reggie asked.

"It says on here I'm Waltham Kohler. I guess we're still brothers." He smiled.

The sergeant major spoke, "Your HJ identity card must be carried with you at all times. Be ready to present it if asked. That probably won't happen when you're dressed in uniform, but you may need to show it to pass a checkpoint. In all reality, your Hitler Youth uniforms and swastika arm bands are the only real passes you'll need once in Germany."

"What's this?" asked Willy, holding up a small brass piece that looked like a large spring loaded nail clippers. "Push it," the air vice-marshal said. Willy did.

Click! He released the pressure. *Clack!* It was like a party noise-maker, from what he could tell. "That, my dear lad, is known as a cricket, because that's the sound it makes." The rest of the boys were now holding theirs. "Try it again, only faster." The sergeant major picked one off the table and did it fast, as it should be done. *Click-clack!*

With that, the room erupted in clicks and clacks as each of them gave it a vigorous go.

"All right, they all work." The sergeant major said.

The sounds continued. "Gentlemen, enough," the sergeant major said louder this time.

Click-clack! Click-clack! Click-clack! As if they didn't even hear him. This thing was fun.

"Enough!" The Sergeant shouted. "That's an order!" Instant silence fell and five pairs of wide eyeballs moved in his direction.

Click-clack! Everyone turned and looked at Dougie, his head down, still transfixed by the little brass device in his fingers. He looked up. Seven pairs of eyes glared at him from their sockets.

"What?" he replied. Henry elbowed him in ribs, jerking his head towards the sergeant major and air vice-marshal.

"If you're quite finished, Douglas."

Dougie nodded. "Sorry, Sergeant Major."

"This little device, as I said, is known as a cricket. After you land, you may be separated, and possibly fine yourself alone." He watched as trepidation wash over their faces. "But not to worry. This clicker is going to be there to help you find one another."

They again looked down at the small devices in their hands. "When you land in enemy territory, first you must hide. Then you get your bearings and figure out just where you are so you know in which direction you need to go. You'll each have a map and a small compass to help you along, but the most important thing to do is find each other. That's where this comes in." He held it up.

"When you're hiding in the bushes, or wherever you can find, if you hear someone near, use this."

Click-clack.

"If you don't hear—*click-clack*—in return, stay silent and stay put until they pass. If you're out there, and you hear this—*click-clack*—you respond in kind—*click-clack*—then move in the direction of the sound. When you get close, you can use the password. That way, should one of you have the bad luck of not making it and a German gets hold of your clicker, you can keep from being lured in. Got it? No yelling, no calling out, do nothing that would let anyone know you're there. At this point, you'll be acting as true scouts, so blend in with your surroundings and leave no trace of where you were. Move so not to be tracked."

"Sergeant," Reggie spoke up. "I don't think we'll be needing these."

"How's that?" the air vice-marshal asked, sceptical of the answer he hadn't even heard yet.

"Well, sir, we can already do that." He whistled, and it sounded exactly like a songbird. When he finished, each of the boys returned a whistle, yet each was separate and individual from the other.

"We can tell who's who and where we are, all based on our whistles, and each is an actual bird call so they can't be identified as coming from people," he smiled.

"So you can." The air vice-marshal was more pleased than impressed, and he was impressed to high Heaven. "What else can you do with those whistles?"

"It's not just whistles. It's glances, tongue clicks—"

302

"And grunts too," Henry added. "When you live in a home full of adults who always have their noses in your titbits, you find a way to keep secrets. We can hold full conversations right under their noses, and they don't even know it." The boys smiled proudly at their ingenuity.

"Well, that's all well and good, but you will also have these crickets with you, as songbirds tend not to sing at night, and that's when we're dropping you." Park added.

"The whole mission hangs on your being able to capture Heydrich and smuggle him back here. If it becomes necessary during the return trip to eliminate young Thomas Peter, then you are to do so—but only as a last resort. If it comes down to him or any one of you, don't hesitate." The air vice-marshal said.

No beating round the bush, Henry thought looking nervously at Reggie.

"Yes, lads," sergeant major said, "you'd best be ready to kill at any moment on this mission. There's just no way round it. But don't fret. You'll do it fast and efficiently so you walk away, because you've been trained for this game, and that's how it's won."

***

The sergeant major reached up with his swagger stick, stuck it through the handle, and pulled down one of the many map scrolls that hung above the blackboard, revealing a three images taped to a typographical map of Germany with routes marked out in black wax pencil.

"Lads, I'd like to introduce you to someone you're going to get to know very well." He walked past the hanging scroll to stand next to the largest picture.

From what Reggie surmised, they were looking at pictures of the same boy at different ages.

Dougie leaned close to Henry. "Who's that?" he whispered, getting the answer he knew Henry would give, punctuated with a shrug. "Dunno. But I have a guess."

There were three photos, the first a blurry shot of a boy dressed in the black uniform of the Jungvolk, the kindergarten version of the Hitler Youth. Adolf Hitler himself had his arm around the boy's shoulder.

The next larger picture looked like a blow-up of a Hitler Youth I.D. card photo, as it had a large embossed swastika and some lettering across its corner. The angelic looking boy in the picture was several years older. He was very handsome, dressed in the lighter uniform blouse of the Hitler Youth, and he was smiling proudly, arms tucked behind his back. His blond hair was thick on top, with long strands that probably bounced when he walked.

In the third image was that of a teenager in the black uniform of a Senior Unit Leader, standing before a line of uniformed boys at attention. He glared menacingly towards the camera, as if he intended to smash the skull of the photographer. All the softness and warmth of his younger face, the things that made that second picture so pleasing, were gone, replaced with raw rage, hard lines, and stark edges; the tall peak of a sharp nose, the rigid musculature of a locked jaw.

And then there were the eyes. Any light or allure that spilled from them in that second picture was gone, replaced by a depthless, dark glare. Something had happened to this boy between the taking of the second and third photographs, and based on the way he looked in the third, whatever it was, it hadn't been good.

"Gentlemen," the sergeant major continued, "This is Ober-stammführer Thomas Peter Heydrich. This, my dear lads"—he slapped the image with his stick—"is your target."

Chapter 48

The Target

And so it went for the rest of the day. Who he was, what he was, how he came to be. His father, his uncle, his place in the scheme and why they had to go get him. All with that attractive smiling boy and the angry young man he had become staring them in the face.

"If we get him, we disrupt the minds of keepers," said the air vice-marshal, "and his keepers include his godfather, Hitler himself. If we get him, we get in their heads."

"Right you are," the sergeant major concurred. "We also end a reign of terror that needs ending. Though not yet an adult, he's already a top knob in their plans, and he gets right down in the muck and the blood. Whilst his father, Heinz is an SS-Obersturmführer, basically a first Sergeant Major, he ingratiates himself more to his uncle, SS-Obergruppenführer Reinhard Heydrich, Supreme Leader of the SS, and in turn, he gets treated like some kind of prince, which, indecently, is his nickname: 'the Nazi Prince.'"

The boys eyed at each other apprehensively. Any mention of the *Schutzstaffel*, the *SS*, was enough to make them shudder. The sergeant major noticed the chill immediately. "Not to worry, lads, you'll be able to handle them."

"This one"—the air vice-marshal pointed to the image with Thomas Peter standing next to a smiling Hitler who has his arm around the boy—"was taken on Adolf's birthday, April 20, 1934, the year Peter turned ten." That makes sense, Reggie thought. In the picture he was still a small boy, wearing the black uniform of the Jungvolk.

"On Hitler's birthday, he gets all the boys and girls who turned ten years old that year, as a present."

"Blimey," Dougie said quietly. "Where does he put them all?" Henry shook his head and rolled his eyes.

The air vice-marshal stifled a laugh and looked directly at Dougie. "I know it sounds bizarre, but it happens every year. In Germany, on the twentieth of April, every ten-year-old is required by law to take the oath of the Hitlerjugend. Like it or not, for worse, never better, when you're ten, you're in and you are his." The air vice-marshal dragged out the last word, reminding Reggie of a hissing snake. The boy's blood ran cold.

"As you can see"—the sergeant major's pointer moved to the creepy image of a smiling Führer—"Uncle Reinhard has some pretty important friends. As leader of the *SS*, he's fourth in command of the Nazis behind Hitler."

"Just four?" Jack asked. "Who's in front of him?"

"Goering, Himmler, Goebbels then Uncle Reiny."

"Those are some bad blokes," Reggie said.

"The worst," Freddie added.

"Yes, Freddie, the worst indeed. But remember, you're not going after any of them. Here"—he moved his pointer to the picture of the handsome boy, the boy they'd all like to be friends with—"is Thomas Peter at a later date. This was what he looked like when he turned fourteen and graduated from the Jungvolk to become a full-fledged Hitlerjugend."

"As you can see, this is one of the reasons he's his uncle's pride. He's a living example of *SS* ideals, all that Aryan rubbish: the blond hair, the blue eyes. No doubt—even if he doesn't deserve it—he's got a high Nazi rank waiting for him once he comes of age."

"Not if we can do anything about it," Reggie said.

The sergeant major grinned. "Let's hope you're right, Reggie"—

he pointed to the third picture—"because this is the bloke you'll be facing. Not that little blondie who makes all the schoolgirls blush when he smiles at them."

I'd blush if he smiled at me, Dougie thought. He looked at Freddie.

Freddie smiled.

Dougie blushed.

"This is the most recent picture we've got of little Thomas Peter. We believe it was taken two months ago inside Czechoslovakia, whilst on a visit to his uncle. As you see, he already wears the uniform and title of a Senior Unit Leader, yet he's just sixteen."

"Is that normal? I mean, to move up so quickly, sir?" Henry asked.

"No, it's not. It's because of who he knows, Henry, *not* what. Intelligence reports from the field tell us he's a poor leader. He's prone to emotional outbursts, has a ruthless temper and likes to throw violent tantrums as a way of flexing his muscle and showing his unit who's in charge."

"Hey, Jack, sounds a bit like you," Willy said, sticking him in the arm with a pencil. The others chuckled.

"What are you talking about? I'm a *very* good leader. It's you lot who don't know how to follow orders properly." He folded his arms in faux disgust.

The air vice-marshal laughed out loud, as did Reggie and Freddie. In three seconds, the entire room, including Jack, was awash in laughter, albeit of the nervous sort. Still, it was enough to break some of the tension.

"You're a fine leader, Jack. We all know. But make no mistake, lads, this boy is no laughing matter. He's ruthless, impulsive, unpredictable, and he commands thugs in the field."

He paused and pointed again at the picture. "Whatever good that was in the smiling boy in this photograph up here is dead in this scowling boy in the photo down here. This is the face believed responsible for the burning of houses and synagogues; mass kidnapping of entire villages boys; grotesque, systematic abuse and torture; and even suspected of mass murder. Dozens of boys have gone missing and are presumed dead because of this bloke right here, including members of those boys' families who tried to get in his way." He stopped speaking and glanced at the fading light of the setting sun outside the window.

The room fell silent. Thomas Peter Heydrich just glared at them from eyes set deep in his skull, behind rocklike cheekbones.

I'm looking into the eyes of the devil's apprentice, Reggie thought. I don't want to see that face in my dreams tonight. But deep down, he already knew he would.

"And on that happy note," the sergeant major said, "What say we all trot over to the mess tea time, aye?"

Chapter 49
A Hard Pill to Swallow

The following morning, when they arrived at the classroom the sergeant major was already waiting. As they entered the room, he handed each a small ring for their finger. The top of the ring was silver with a swastika stamped into it, like every other Nazi accessory.

"G'morning lads. This little gift comes by way of Station IX, as all the best gifts do. This little gadget looks like an ordinary ring, however, it's hollow. Remove this cap here," he twisted the small silver cap with the swastika on it, revealing an open space which was filled with four tiny white tablets. "These are fast dissolving knock-out tablets. Drop them into a subject's drink, and in 30 minutes, they'll be out like a light."

"30 minutes? That's not a very fast knock-out." Dougie said as he looked at the tiny pills.

"Aye, Dougie, unfortunately not. Because they enter the bloodstream the same way as food, the sleep agent takes time to be digested. But once they're asleep, you can be assured they'll stay that way for a good long while." The boys each slipped on their rings.

"Now the key to using these is to make sure you are not spotted dropping them into your target's drink. The utmost discretion is advised.

Or in other words, be bloody careful not to get caught or seen by anyone."
He removed one of the tablets and dropped it into a glass of water on the
table before him. The tablet began to bubble furiously and before they
could blink, fizzled away to nothingness, like magic.

"Now, that was fast." Dougie remarked.

"As you can see, in a glass of liquid or a canteen it will dissolve
instantly. It's also tasteless and odourless." He passed the glass among
them. Each stuck his nose inside, smelling nothing.

Reggie upended his ring and held the tiny tablets in his palm.
They sure were awfully small. He raised his hand.

"Yes, Reggie?" the sergeant major asked.

"What kind of dosage do we give, Sergeant? I mean, is one pill
going to be enough or should we use all four at once?"

"An excellent question, Reggie. Mind you now, you don't want
to give the lad an overdose, or he might never wake up again. We don't
want that," he said. "One tablet at a time is enough to put someone his
size under. Best not to slip him another until he wakes up again."

"Now, this," he removed a small tube from his pocket, "is a much
faster way to administer the sleep agent." He held up the tube for all to
see. "This is a called a syrette. It is a disposable tube with a tiny needle
attached, allowing you to inject the sleep agent directly into the subject's
bloodstream." He demonstrated how it worked by cracking the tip off,
exposing the needle beneath. "Once the tip is broken off, it's ready to use.
Just stick it in, and squeeze the tube." He squeezed and liquid squirted
from the tip of the tiny needle. "This will render your subject unconscious
in roughly 30 seconds."

"Wow, now *that* is fast-acting." Dougie said.

"Yes, very fast." The sergeant major replied. "The only draw-
back is you need to get close, very close to use it, and once stuck, you
might find yourself in a jam if not administered correctly. Also, be good
and sure you're prepared to handle a sleeping boy, because once you use
that, in seconds a sleeping boy is what you will have to contend with."

"Where are we supposed to hide those Sergeant Major? They're
not as easy to hide as tablets," Henry asked.

"These? We're not going to hide these at all, not really. As the squad medic, Jack will carry a supply of these in his medical bag, tucked away to look like a box of bandages." Jack's look turned to one of concern. "Don't fret Jack, a medical kit is standard equipment carried by every Hitler Youth unit marching to Nuremburg. There will be a lot of blisters to contend with, so medical supplies on the march will be plentiful. Chances that someone will go rummaging through your medical kit are very slim indeed. Especially if you carry it on your person."

Jack nodded.

"If someone is in need of something, they'll just come out and ask for it. Remember, you will be just another Hitler Youth unit on the way to the grand celebration, just like the thousands of other boys marching across Germany. When people see you, they'll be happy and cheering for you. You will be one big happy Hitler Youth family." The sergeant major reminded them. "They won't suspect you don't belong, as long as you act as you do."

"Now that we've talked about the sleeping tablets, there is one more tablet we need to address." He reached in his pocket and pulled out small box. Opening it, he removed one of the round capsules inside. "This is something we give to every agent who is dropped behind enemy lines, as you boys will be." He held up the clear capsule for them to see. "This is a lethal pill that will cause death in one minute." Reggie was again bewildered at the idea that something so small could kill a man. "It is filled with liquid cyanide."

"Who are we supposed to use that on?" Dougie asked. "I thought you wanted us to capture him alive, Sergeant?"

"This capsule, Dougie," he answered, "is for you. And Reggie, and Freddie, and rest of you will have one as well." They looked at one another with blank stares. "These are suicide capsules for you to use as a last resort." A dark mood descended upon the room.

"Suicide capsules?" Reggie asked. "Why in heaven's name would we need those?"

"I'm sorry lads, but this is just part of the brutal truth of what you are getting into. If you are discovered and captured, you will very likely be tortured, as in finger and toe nails being pulled out with pliers, or white hot pokers applied to bare skin. We give these to our agents as a way out when they've had enough, or to avoid it completely, if they so choose."

"Where," Reggie asked, having trouble forming the words, "are we to hide these?" He guessed they would need to be carried on their person at all times.

"Your Hitler Youth uniforms have brass buttons. Whilst the real versions are solid, yours—like the ring—are hollow." They each began to play with their buttons. "They unscrew similarly, with enough room for a single pill inside. A single pill is all you will need. Stick it between your rear teeth, and bite down. Then, in a few seconds, it's all over." The Sergeant Major handed them each a single pill.

Reggie sat heavy in his silence, looking at the small pill in his hand, thinking of how horribly wrong things would have to go, how hopeless a situation he would have to be in to use that capsule. Of course he had considered, and accepted, that he might never see home again, that he could be killed during this operation, but he had never once considered that he might have to end the mission by ending his own life. As a young man feeling the most invincible he'd ever felt before, that outcome—the very idea of it—had never even crossed his young mind.

***

They were gathered in the clubhouse preparing for bed.

"I don't get it." Freddie said. "They tell us with every breath to keep living and then issue us suicide pills." He shook his head. "Now I know for a fact these blokes are seriously off their heads."

"Strange, innit? They've spent all this time building us up, and then give us a pill that'll drop us in 30 seconds," Henry said,

"All that training and hard work for nothing." Dougie concurred.

"See? Bonkers," Freddie said. "The whole place."

"There you go again," Reggie sighed, "trying to make sense of something that hasn't got any. This whole business we're caught up in is beyond ridiculous." It was finally becoming clear to him. "The military doesn't operate under the same rules as the church, and the SOE surely doesn't operate under the same rules as the military," he said. "Even war is supposed to follow codes of conduct and be governed by agreed upon rules. But apparently that doesn't hold true for this kind of war or for this place. I guess in this covert war, the battlefield is everywhere with no out of bounds, and everything is permitted with no holds barred," Reggie said.

"I don't think I could do that," Henry said. "Take that pill, I mean. It's the worst sin—to kill one's self."

Willy spoke and said what was on all of their minds. "You go straight to hell, for that."

"Although, I suppose by the time that pill becomes an option, you'd already have one foot in hell as it is, so it probably makes no difference at all," Freddie said, trying and failing to belay Henry's fear.

"Yes, but we've never been tortured." Jack added. "If it comes to that, I guess all we can do is our best and hope to hold out as long as we can." He then quoted Captain Fairbairn. "Pain is temporary," he said, "but defeat is forever."

An eerie quiet settled over the room.

Reggie spoke. "If our lives together have taught us anything, it's that suffering is real—but it's also temporary—and if we hold on just long enough—the situation always changes—usually for the better."

"Nothing doing." Freddie said defiantly. "That pill is nothing but the coward's way out. If Jerry catches me, I'm going down like a soldier. If they're going to try and take me prisoner, I'm going to fight and keep fighting until they're forced to shoot me. That way, at least, I have a chance of taking a few of them with me."

"But what if they knock you out and tie you up?" Dougie asked, sounding genuinely concerned for Freddie's welfare. "A pill won't help unless you can get to it."

"I don't care about that pill. As long as I'm alive and kicking, I'm going to find a way out of the jam I'm in and suicide is no way out of anything." Freddie stated emphatically. Willy and Henry nodded.

"Listen to me. We're going to make sure it never comes to that." Reggie reminded them. "We perform as they've taught and we keep our wits about us, and those pills will never come into play. Understood?" All nodded their agreement, but the resolution did little to ease Dougie's concern.

Chapter 50
Sinful Seams

It had been decided that Captain Hawkins would drop first, to lay the groundwork with agents already active in France. He would form a reception committee for the scouts and help guide their plane into the drop zone. When dropped at such a low level, one after another, from a single aircraft, they would land close to each other, in a single field if done correctly. And, with Captain Hawkins and a reception committee awaiting their arrival, crickets, it was decided, weren't necessary.

Overalls, however, were another story. Even the smallest sizes were still too large for Willy and Jack, and the extra material on the way down could lead to disaster. Once again, the Sisters' skills were perfect to construct workable replacements.

Prior for his leaving for France, Captain Hawkins secured two samples from the Thatched Barn and brought them to the London shop to explain his need to the good Sisters.

"You'll be needing what now?" Sister Noreen asked.

"You see this?" He held up an adult-size version. It was a baggy, ugly thing with zips and all sorts of pockets. "Striptease suits, in sizes for

Willy and Jack, specifically."

"What'd he say?" Sister Doreen asked, suddenly hard of hearing.

"I said, dear Sister, I need *two*"—he held up two fingers—"of these, one for Willy, the other for Jack," he repeated, now that he had her attention. Concern washed her cheerful expression.

"I don't know, Father, if we can help you with something that sounds so ... *so sinful,* " Sister Doreen said, a tone of sincere questioning in her voice.

"I'm not too sure those kinds of items are allowed under our sacred oaths," Sister Noreen added, scratching her coif in befuddled contemplation.

"Oh Sisters, for Pete's sake," he said, "see here." He held up one of the suits. "It's simply a set of overalls that are quickly shed, as in a burlesque striptease. There will be no nakedness of any sort, I assure you. That's simply the nickname given by the agent instructors for these types suits."

"Oh, agents instructors," Noreen whispered, glancing left, then right, checking for rogue ears. "For the *mission*, eh?" He winked at her as he raised his index finger to cover his pursed lips.

Sister Noreen locked her lips with her imaginary key and tucked it into her ample brassiere. Her hand went to her heart. "On sacred vow. We'll have two new suits for you before you can say Jack Robinson."

"Actually, I was hoping you'd be up for a bit more," he said, raising his eyebrows.

The Sisters looked intrigued. "What kind of more do you mean, Father?" Noreen asked.

"I'd like you to be there for their final fitting."

"Oh, their final fitting!" Doreen cried. "What an awful thing to say!"

"Listen, do you want to see the boys or not?" Father Hawkins asked, his patience wearing thin.

"Wait, what did you say?" Doreen asked at mention of her boys.

"That's right, Sister Doreen. I want you ladies to be the ones to fit their mission clothes before they set off. That means taking a trip to see them."

Both ladies faces broke into huge smiles at the prospect of seeing their boys again.

"Whatever they need, Father." Sister Noreen answered. "We're here for them."

Chapter 51

Team Thimble

The automobile turned into the dark courtyard of the St. Michael's at 0427 hours, exactly three minutes early. The RAF driver got out, loaded the two waiting suitcases, opened the back door to an empty backseat, and waited for his passengers.

From inside the home, the Sisters emerged, covered not in their usual habits, but both wearing matching black greatcoats. Their coifs remained over their heads, but atop of them now sat matching black felt hats. Although the sun had yet to come up, both were wearing dark round sunglasses, actually, a bit too dark, as Sister Noreen stumbled onto the first step from the top one because she couldn't see the edge. Doreen grabbed her so she didn't go down, but Noreen shoved her sister away, as to not draw attention to themselves.

"Oh, crikey, get a load of this," the driver said to himself in a whisper, trying his best to stifle his snigger at the two enormous ladies trying their best to be inconspicuous, and failing miserably.

They walked slowly to the car, glancing quickly left, then right, then back left again, their eyes peeled behind their dark eyewear for any trace of enemy agents.

"Good morning, ladies," the driver said.

"Good morning," Sister Noreen answered curtly, with just a hint of suspicion in her tone. Captain Hawkins said they might try to test them, so she was ready for anything.

"It's just a short trip to the aerodrome, and then you'll be in Corporal Fleming's good hands."

"Aerodrome? Why would we go to the aerodrome?" Noreen asked.

"Well, how else do you think you're going get to your destination?" he asked. "It's a long way from here."

"Aerodrome? No one said anything about airfields and aeroplanes!" Doreen shouted. She had never flown and decided long ago that she never would. "If it doesn't have wings given it by the good Lord, then it shouldn't be flying around. Birds, bugs, and angels. Nothing else."

"Shhh Sister," Noreen hushed, "it's most secret! This is for the King, the very one you embarrassed me in front of. Now if you want to see those boys, hush up and get in the car."

***

The small aeroplane presented a tight squeeze for the two over-sized ladies. Sister Doreen kept her eyes closed for the entire duration of the flight, saying prayers to calm her nerves. Though she never looked, she was thankful for the black curtains that hung on the inside of the small black plane's windows.

Sister Noreen, on the other hand, was practically wanting to wrest control of the Lysander away from the pilot. She watched the gauges, the artificial horizon, the altimeter, the compass, airspeed gauge. It was her first time in an aeroplane, and she was loving every second. Maybe I should learn to fly one of these things, she thought. If that Amy Johnson can do it, why not me?

When their plane landed, Corporal Fleming was waiting with a car to shuttle them to their final destination. He, too, had to stifle a snigger when he saw the two extra-large would-be spies come climbing out of the plane. "Oh, good heavens," he said quietly upon seeing them dressed in their matching spy get-ups.

"Corporal Fleming, I presume?" one asked.

"Yes. I'm Corporal Fleming, it's a pleasure to meet you both."

"Are you here to take us … *you know where?*" she whispered.

"I know where?" Charlie asked, confused.

"Yes. You are here to take us to our … *final destination.*"

Oh my, this is going to be amusing, he thought. He lowered his voice to a hushed tone. "I am. Are you ready for your … *final destination?*" he whispered.

"Lead on, good Corporal Fleming. Duty waits for no one," Sister Noreen said.

He led them towards the car and opened the rear door.

"It's finally nice to meet you, Sisters. I've heard so much about you."

"From whom? Who told you about us?" Noreen asked, fearing her cover had been blown.

"The boys, of course. I'm their batman."

"Oh," Sister Noreen said, impressed. "We know all about those, don't we sister?" Sister Noreen asked.

"Aye, we do," Sister Doreen answered. "Daddy had a batman, you know."

***

The boys were dressed in their Hitler Youth exercise kits: a sleeveless vest emblazoned with the Iron Eagle, black shorts, and soft-soled slippers for their feet. After spending the first part of the morning boxing their appropriate size partner, Winkle was showing them how to run as a human chariot team. That was a favourite game of the Hitler Youth. It was a simple exercise to orchestrate better teamwork and allowed them to show off their physical prowess, making it a perfect activity for the Hitler Youth. If they were going to the rally, there might be chariot racing in their future. He wanted them to at least seem familiar with the event, if not become somewhat proficient.

Freddie and Reggie were the big rear horses, tied with the black belts from their uniforms as harnesses. A wobbly, shoeless Jack rode with one foot on each of a larger boy's shoulder, holding the leather strap reins of Dougie, Willy and Henry, who acted as the front three of the five horse team. They were having trouble keeping track of their own legs whilst trotting together, tripping and regaining their footing as they moved forwards.

A black car rode across the field and stopped near their Nazi clubhouse. Winkle called the boys to attention. The boys stopped, Jack jumped off and they unharnessed each other.

Getting out of the back were two large people. Greatcoats, glasses, hats. On seeing the boys, one of the oddly dressed visitors put their hand to their mouth. Reggie instantly recognised Sister Doreen's gesture.

The two ladies suddenly broke away from the corporal and ran full tilt for the boys, throwing away their hats and quickly discarding their glasses.

"Sisters!" Dougie yelled.

"Lads, dis-MISSED!" Winkle shouted with a smile. The boys broke into a sprint towards the two ladies.

The reunion was a bit rough, with boys and busts all crashing into one another at speed, but none were injured so none cared.

"Oh, boys!" Sister Noreen cried as she hugged them all in a great huddle. "Look how you've grown! And that blond hair! Look at it! Dougie, you've faded away to nothing!"

"Don't they feed you here?" Sister Doreen asked as she hugged away. By squeeze gauge, Dougie felt like half the boy used to, and his previous softness was now replaced with hard points and sharp corners.

"All the time!" Dougie answered. "All we can eat, too."

Corporal Fleming let them have their moment. He hadn't seen the boys this happy since they'd been here. Even their trips under canopy at parachute school hadn't inspired so much excitement.

"When did you arrive?" Reggie asked. He was literally being held at arm's length by Sister Noreen, who was looking him over from head to toe, surveying all of his pieces, taking note of any bruises, cuts, or other blemishes.

"We *flew* in this morning! Think of it! Sister Doreen and I flew in an *aeroplane* to get here. Just like the RAF lads! We didn't run into any Luftwaffe captains, thank goodness, so it was a grand time," she said with a giggle of pride.

"It was wonderful, really," Sister Doreen added with a girlish nod.

Sister Noreen shot Reggie a glance and whispered, "Never looked out the window once—and whimpered all the way through our final landing procedures, that one."

Reggie laughed. Same old Sister Doreen.

"Folks, I hate to break up this little reunion, but we do have a time table we need to stick to, so if you please."

They all fell in line, facing Corporal Fleming. The Sisters were in line with the boys, holding the hands of the boys standing next to them.

"It's was so wonderful to be together again." Sister Doreen said.

Chapter 52
Final Fitting

"I've been instructed to let you know that the good Sisters will be joining us as a special, vitally important addition to our team." He walked up and down the line as he had seen so many officers do before, but he had never done.

"Are they coming with us?" Dougie asked.

"Heavens, no," Corporal Fleming answered, drawing a rebuking sideways glance from Sister Noreen. "No offence, Sister, but your skills are far too valuable here at home." Fleming said, humouring her. She nodded in confident agreement.

"Leave field work to the boys," she said, "I'm more brass material anyway."

"Sisters are joining us by way of a special unit, helping to make sure your uniforms and clothing are up to snuff for the task ahead." He stopped in front of the line. "Your bodies have changed quite a bit since your uniforms were completed. The Sisters are here to give your mission clothes one final fitting. So if you would, please go and put on your Hitlerjugend uniforms, complete with all pieces. Sisters, if you would please join the boys in their quarters, we can get started."

Together, they walked to the gingerbread looking clubhouse in the clearing.

"Oh, they gave you your own little house. Isn't that lovely?" Sister Doreen said, admiring the quaint exterior. "Sister, look at the lovely detail of the place. They even have flowers in painted flower boxes,"

"We did those ourselves," Willy said proudly. "We started a vegetable garden in the back, too."

"You've been busy little bees," Sister Noreen commented. "And this is the most adorable little house I've ever seen. And the way you've dressed it up out here is just lovely. I can't wait to see what you've done with the inside."

***

The door creaked open. Upon seeing the interior Sister Noreen lost her balance and stepped backwards down the stairs, her right arm grasped at her chest, as if she'd been struck by an arrow, her left arm flailing wildly in an attempt to keep the ship afloat. She stumbled, almost fell, and then finally grabbed the railing to catch her balance. She was struggling for breath.

"Sister, sister!" Doreen darted to her side. "Are you okay? Breathe!"

Sister Noreen couldn't seem to catch her breath. Her heart was beating like an artillery barrage.

"Did you—can you—is there—how did—what the—?" was all she could manage to get out. The corporal rushed to her aid and grabbed her arm to help steady her. "It's all part of the mission, Sister. It's to help get the boys accustomed to what it will be like to live as the Hitlerjugend, ah, the Hitler Youth do."

"But—but—but—" she said, sounding like an old Morris Six with a shoddy exhaust.

"It's okay, Sister," Freddie said reassuringly. "It's all for show. We still say our prayers at night just like you taught us. There's a lot of fluff in there, but we know who's in here." He pointed at his heart. "You put Him there."

Sister Noreen reached out and grabbed Freddie. She hugged him harder than ever before. "When I saw that," she said, "it just reminded me that in many ways, I've already lost you. You're already gone." She started to cry.

He squeezed her hard. "Come now, Sister, you aren't getting rid of us that easily."

"Yeah," Dougie added with a wink. "To get rid of us, you'd need an army."

***

Inside, the boys dressed in silence. Not too unlike their Official Boy Scout uniforms, these Hitler Youth uniforms made by the Sisters had just as many pieces and parts. Unlike their homemade scout uniforms, there was nothing individual or varying about these. Each was exactly alike in form and function, the only difference being Reggie, who had a Patrol Leader pin stuck on his pocket, and Jack and Willy, who at their young age wore the dark uniform jackets of the Jungvolk. The other boys were dressed as regular Hitlerjugend members. Uniformity was a big deal to the Nazis, as Winkle had so aptly explained. Variation was not encouraged or tolerated, as their warped ideology was based on racial purity and genetics. Sameness, perfect exact sameness was the goal of the Nazis, and their identical uniforms were an outward projection of that principle.

Once dressed, they stood in line for the Sisters to get a first-hand look at their handiwork. To Sister Noreen they looked like the most handsome group of boys she'd ever seen, minus that red armband with the crooked sign of the devil at its heart. The perfect metaphor for the perfect evil, she thought—those black twisted crosses. To her eyes, the boys never looked better … or worse.

"Hmmm," Sister Doreen said, glancing over the line in front of her. "Sister, you take notes."

"Aye," Noreen responded. She pulled pencil and clipboard from seemingly out of nowhere.

Sister Doreen spoke as she surveyed their work. "We need to re-measure and adjust all their waistlines. All sleeves need to be finished. Elastic for the armbands, which need to be made to size for each boy. We need new holes for Dougie's and Henry's belts, they're smaller now.

Jack's jacket needs to be taken in at the back, but sleeves stay the same. We want it to be big so it looks like a hand-me-down from Reggie." She looked at their black neckerchiefs. "Let's finish these with a thread, I don't like how they fray."

"Um-hmm, fray," Noreen repeated, frantically jotting the instructions from Doreen on her clipboard. She looked puzzled. "Whistles. We have cords but no whistles."

"Oh, yes," Fleming answered, referencing his own clipboard. "Those are on order, should arrive in a day or two."

A quick nod from Doreen to Noreen, who jotted a quick note. "Two days, eh?"

"Shoes, these need some work of their own. They're a bit to shiny and new looking. They should look shined, but also used." Doreen said.

"Right. I think that's everything. Sister?" Doreen asked, offering up the boys to her. Sister Noreen stood with her list and began to do her own singular inspection, from nose to toes.

"Corporal Fleming. Do you have the striptease—overalls—for the jump? We'll need them to try their schoolboy uniforms, and then the overalls on top of them, for proper fit."

"Yes, Sister, they're in the boot of the car. I'll go and get them. Please excuse me."

"Lads," Sister Noreen said, "I want you to put on your French schoolboy clothes. It's time to check the pockets, and make sure they are empty of everything. Also we will double check to make sure there are no labels, pins or zips that could destroy the mission."

"Zips? How could a zip destroy the mission?" Dougie asked. Sister Doreen spoke. "That zip has a name inscribed in it, the name of an English maker."

Sister Noreen finished her sister's explanation. "If Jerry catches you all he has to do is look at that zip, and that's it, your cover is blown, and the mission is over."

Dougie was suddenly grabbing at his pants zip, pulling out the tab. Where an engraved name had once been was now nothing but a smooth surface.

"Did that pair myself, I did." Sister Noreen said. "Used the tiniest of drills you'd ever see in your lives to scratch out the name." He looked at Sister Noreen with a new found understanding. "That's what it means to have the right kind of disguise." She said, winking at the boy. "Every last detail needs to be considered," she said, sounding like an expert.

Corporal Fleming returned from the car and passed each boy his set of overalls. Once their French school clothes had been checked, and re-checked, measured and marked for alterations, they dressed in their jump-suits, helmets and goggles. They stood outside the clubhouse looking iden-tical in their new overalls, covered from helmet to boot in green, brown and black patterns that were to act as camouflage and mix in with their surrounding once they'd landed. The Sisters noted size and fit for each.

"Okay, lads, let's give your striptease suits a try." Corporal Flem-ing instructed. "Fall in."

They did as told. "Okay, on my count, just grab your zips and run them all the way down in a single pull." They each found the two zip tabs at their necks and held them, awaiting the word.

"One, two, three." Fleming counted.

ZIP! Down they ran the zips all the way to their ankles, and the front half of their suits fell away, revealing their schoolboy clothes be-neath. As each stood, the back half fell off, just as designed. Sister Nor-een's eyes opened wide, after seeing how quickly the overalls fell off. Striptease? There was no *tease* about it, she thought. All were now stand-ing, minus their bulky striptease suits. All but Jack. His suit was teasing him, as he wrestled with his right zip. It was stuck at the neck.

"That was splendid." said the corporal, looking at the pile of shed overalls at their feet.

"Splendid?" asked Jack. "Not for me. I'm stuck," he said, still tugging at his neckline.

"Right." said Sister Noreen. "Sister, make a note. Oil all the zips for the striptease suits, especially Jack's. We can't have that happen in the field." Corporal Fleming nodded his agreement.

***

Fittings, alterations, and more fittings were time-tabled to take several days, and the Sisters and the tykes were glad for it. They hadn't realised how much they were all missing one another until they were able to enjoy each other's company once again, and it felt wonderful. Even in the Nazi decorated clubhouse, Hitler's evil stare seemed to fade into the walls after a time, and all they could see were each other's smiling faces filled with joy.

***

Days later, when all the sewing was done and their various disguises were complete, the Sisters' part in the epic play was over. It was time for them to leave the stage and head back home. Unlike their previous parting, this time there were not only tears, but broken hearts and new doubts. Sister Doreen said not a word as her slow stream of tears flowed unabated, and she did nothing to wipe them away. Her heart was shattering, and if she spoke, she was afraid she'd lose the pieces out of her mouth, so she said nothing.

To think that this might be the last time she would see any one of these boys was gut wrenching, to think it might be the last time she'd see all of them was too much to bear. Sister Noreen and all the boys joined Sister Doreen in her tears and her silence, for much the same reason. No words were needed. Simply hugging was all they wanted to do, to hold onto this feeling and one another for as long as possible.

Corporal Fleming looked at his watch. It was time. "I'm so sorry, Sisters. Your driver is waiting."

One last giant squeeze, one last deep inhalation of their smells, one last kiss of their soft skin. Sister Doreen grabbed her sister's arm and pulled. Sister Noreen, their rock, let out a cry of pure torment, a wail so deep from her soul that she collapsed to her knees. Fleming and the boys jumped to help her up, to slowly walk her to the waiting automobile. Once in, they closed the door, and the automobile pulled away. Sister Doreen looked back, placed her hand flat on the rear windshield, and with that last gesture, it rolled out of sight.

Fleming gathered the silently weeping boys in his arms and led them back inside.

***

The team's newly altered Hitler Youth uniforms, along with all the assorted accessories including ruck sacks, canteens, sleeping rolls, tent pack, cooking gear from production Station XII, and their false German papers from the Prop Shop, Station XIV, were immediately rushed to and collected at STS-61Audley End, Saffron Walden. That was yet another stately home requisitioned by the army used as a packing station for the thousands of specially designed parachute supply canisters destined to be dropped into France.

Their mission mandatories were packed promptly into two specially marked supply canisters. Along with their Hitler Youth gear, the canisters contained their FS daggers, Sten Guns, Webley pistols, extra ammunition, plastic explosives, and time pencils from weapons acquisition at Bride Hall, Station VI. Extra rations and medical supplies were also included, as agents in France were constantly requesting resupply of those items. Once packed, the two canisters were secured then loaded on a waiting lorry and rushed immediately back to a secret RAF station for loading into the belly of the Whitley bomber that would be dropping them, along with the boys.

25 September 1940

FROM: DR. HUGH DALTON, D.O.O.

TO: PRIME MINISTER WINSTON CHURCHILL

RE: OPERATION ARCHANGEL

Prime Minister,

Please be advised that weather permitting, Team Archangel is set to launch for their designated drop zone just past dusk this evening.

If all goes to plan that will allow 18 days for them to travel into Germany then 176 miles to the town of Augsburg.

They should be in position awaiting to rendezvous with the target on or about October 13.

May God go with them.

Chapter 53
Last Arrangements

The day they had so long worked for had arrived much sooner than they thought it would. During those long painful months of torturous training it felt so far away. Now that the day was here, time seemed to have passed in the blink of an eye.

Just past supper, two camouflaged Humber Super Snipe motor-cars arrived for the boys. They were loaded three each into the cars, with the sergeant major in one and Corporal Fleming in another. Both drove in separate directions, but both ended up on the same long side-road closed to public vehicles. It ended at the entrance of a secret RAF station from which they would take off for their mission across the Channel.

In the centre of the station was an old farmhouse surround by several barns. Both cars pulled into the courtyard of the farmhouse where they were met by Warrant Officer Jepsen standing in the doorway.

Inside the barn, laid out on a long table were their six overalls, all lined up with various supplies next to them.

"Each of you will find a pile of gear with your name on top of it."

Reggie instantly recognised his neatly folded French schoolboy clothes and striptease suit beside it.

"Now," instructed Warrant Officer Jepsen, "you are to remove all your clothes and pile them next to your name on the table. Redress in your French clothing. When you are finished, pick up your battle dress clothes and come back inside to the house, so we can have a look at you." With that, he left and went inside.

The boys did as instructed, stripping naked and piling their army issued clothing next to their jump suits. Each took their pile of French schoolboy clothes and began to dress in the chilly barn. All around them were stacks of parachutes, with several open ones hanging from the ceiling. To Dougie it felt as if he were walking inside a cloud.

Once dressed, they returned to the house. On another table were piles of supplies, as well as their envelopes from the prop shop that contained more false papers and documents. "Here," said Jepsen, stepping up to Reggie. "Let's have a look at you." Reggie stood, wearing trousers, a baggy shirt and a light jacket over the top. On his head sat a cap. He looked exactly as he should, like a school aged French boy. "Hold open your jacket and let's see the inside." Reggie did as told. French labels, good. "Now turn round please." Reggie did. Warrant Officer Jepsen pulled at his belt and looked at the label on the inside of his trousers and underpants. All there, the specially made tags. He turned Reggie around and shoved his hands inside the pockets of the boys jacket. Empty, as it should be.

"Turn out your pockets please." He did as instructed. Nothing in either. Very good.

"We just did this the other day with the Sisters. Is this necessary again?" Reggie asked.

"This," Warrant Officer Jepsen answered, "is part of *my* job. I do the final check to make sure nothing that isn't supposed to get on the aeroplane does. One old candy wrapper and the game is up."

Reggie nodded.

"Now, here are your papers." He handed Reggie a small wallet. "Inside are your French papers, necessary whilst you are in France, including I.D. and ration card. Check to ensure that it's your photograph, and that other personal details like height and weight are correct." Freddie placed the item inside his jacket pocket. "Here," Jepsen said, handing Reggie some colourful banknotes. "French currency, just some small money, as would be expected." Reggie put the paper bills into the front pocket of his trousers. "Do you smoke?" he asked Reggie.

"No." the boy answered. "Why?"

"Because if you did you'd need a French pack of cigarettes, not English." He showed Reggie the pack of French cigarettes.

"Can I have those anyway? They could come in handy for trading or making friends." The Warrant Officer took the package of French cigarettes and shoved them into the front pocket of Reggie's shirt. "Suit yourself. But be careful not to smoke those things yourself. Once started, it can be a nasty habit to kick. And you're still awfully young for picking up nasty habits."

The scene was played out six more times, with each boy, with each costume, and with every label and pocket. Once Jepsen was satisfied with their state of readiness, he sent them back to the barn to put on their jump suits. The boys dressed in silence, each helping the other into the baggy overalls.

Back inside the house they trudged, each feeling extra bulky with all this clothing on. When they stepped inside, Corporal Fleming had gathered their battle dress uniforms and was taking inventory, making sure all parts and pieces were accounted for, paying special attention to Dougie's pile. It would be just like him to wear his army issue undershorts and blow the whole mission by the seat of his pants.

"Right," the sergeant major said. "There are a few things you will need for the trip. Here is a torch." He handed to each a small square battery-operated light. "That goes in your front top pocket. Along with your compass."

"Here are two cans of emergency rations. These, along with this bandage pack, should go in your other chest pocket."

"Finally, here is your spade and handle. These go in the pockets on your jumpsuit leg." That was it.

"Very good. You're ready." Jepsen walked to the door. "Now if you lads will follow me to the rigging barn, we can get you all set up with your parachutes. This way."Each carried with them their soft leather helmets and goggles.

The rigging barn was used for packing and storing parachutes. Six had been selected and lined up against the wall. "Select any chute you prefer. They're all the same. Packed each one myself." He reassured them. Corporal Fleming and the sergeant major stepped forwards and helped the boys secure their parachutes, paying special attention to helping Jack and Willy, as theirs harnesses needed the most adjustment to the fit their small frames properly.

When they had finished, the boys slipped on their helmets, and rested their goggles on top, or let them hang around their necks. "Alright lads, fall in."

They did as commanded, now standing tall to short. A fine looking group indeed, if I do say so myself, thought the sergeant major. He looked at Warrant Officer Jepsen. Jepsen smiled and nodded his approval. "They're as ready as they'll ever be."

***

After a short ride across an airfield filled with parked bombers, they stopped and exited next to their assigned black bomber, Whitley Z 7508, the very kind they had seen previously in the big hanger at Ringway.

This was it. Mission time had arrived. The sun was beginning to set. Standing outside were the plane's six crew members, each dressed in full leather flight suits, parachutes, life preservers and pilot caps. As no smoking was allowed in the bomber, each was enjoying a final preflight cigarette.

"Good evening, sir." Warrant Officer Jepsen said to the pilot with a curt salute. "Good evening," replied the captain. Jepsen turned to the boys. "Lads, this is your pilot, Wing Commander Hansen. Wing Commander, I'd like you to meet your team for the evening."

The Wing Commander smiled. "Pleased to meet you, team." The dashing pilot walked the line and shook the hand of each of the boys. "Well, we've got a great evening for flying, so it should be a rather uneventful trip, and an easy drop, just as we like them."

"Very good." Warrant Officer Jepsen said. "Now if you'll follow me, we can get aboard." He led the group to the rear of the plane where a small side hatch opened in to the fuselage.

"Team, fall in." Jepsen said. The boys did as instructed. "Commence parachute check." The boys did a right turn in place and began to check each other's chute.

"Team, left face!" The boys turned in place again, facing forwards.

Corporal Fleming stood by silently and watched the boys. He had prepared them the best he knew how. There was nothing more he could teach, nothing more he could do but see the boys off and let fate take their course. It was something he was now dreading. Although he was aware he wasn't to get close to the men under his command, he couldn't help but have a feeling of melancholy at seeing these boys off. He had grown very fond of them, indeed.

The sergeant major spoke.

"Good-bye, lads. God bless you. May St. Michael protect you on your mission." He extended his hand to Freddie. Freddie took it, and shook the man's large hand. He so had to resist the urge to hug the big man, the one who he had grown to trust and care for as much as he had Father Hawkins. Even at fifteen, he thought a hug would feel right as rain about now.

He got his wish as soon as he finished shaking the SM's hand as Fleming reached out and gave him a tremendous hug. He hugged just as hard back. So it went down the line, a curt handshake from the sergeant, a bear-hug from the corporal. Both send-offs were as different as the men who were giving them, yet both right in their own regard.

Warrant Officer Jepsen opened the hatch, and Freddie, first as always, climbed aboard, with a helping shove from behind. The rest of the boys followed in their jump order, Dougie, Henry, Willy, Jack and finally Reggie.

When the sergeant major took Reggie's hand he squeezed it gently, warmly, yet firmly. Now it was the sergeant major's turn to pull the boy forwards and give him a very un-sergeant major-like hug, with two quick pats on the back. "Good luck to you lad," he said in Reggie's ear. "Remember your training and I will see you again. May St. Michael protect you." Reggie had to blink hard to keep his tears from running. The sergeant major let go of the boy and patted him twice on the shoulder.

Now Fleming, his own eyes brimming with tears, grabbed Reggie and squeezed with all his might.

"You've done well Reggie. Be proud of yourself and your brothers. I'll see you all when you return." A tear rolled down his cheek. He made no attempt to hide it. Reggie smiled at the young man and his bright green eyes. "Thank you for all your help Corporal. I'll never forget you."

Corporal Fleming nodded and turned Reggie away from him, pushing the boy towards the hatch. He felt on the verge of breaking down completely, and it was the last thing he wanted Reggie to see before heading off on a mission he probably wouldn't be returning from. As a final act of support, he gave the boy a boost into the hole, then helped Jepsen up before he closed and secured the hatch behind him.

Reggie climbed aboard, followed by Warrant Officer Jepsen, who had all the boys move forwards to get the weight right for take-off. He then immediately began to dress in his leather flight suit, helmet and parachute. The boys were now under his command until they were safely out of the joe hole. Wing Commander Hansen pushed the throttle forwards, the twin engines of the Whitley roared to life and the heavy plane began to taxi across the airfield.

***

The black Whitley lumbered through the dark, moonless sky. The flight, as the pilot had anticipated, had been uneventful, even offering them enough time to try and get some sleep. Of course, none of them could. They were also served sandwiches and tea on the long journey across the Channel. Warrant Officer Jepsen made sure each ate and drank his share. That had been a couple of hours ago. They were ever nearer to the jump zone.

Now, the Warrant Officer stood at his position by the bulkhead, headphones on his head. Suddenly, the steady red glow of the jump signal lit his face, causing a slight glare from his goggles. He put his hands to his ears, as the pilot spoke. Turning, Jepsen relayed the message to the jumpers. "Hook up!" The boys did as told and attached their parachute static lines to the inside of the aeroplane. "Running in! Action station one! Get ready!" He raised his hand over his head.

They were dressed in their heavy striptease suits, helmets, and goggles, but could still feel the chill of the night air rushing around them. First in line, Freddie dropped to the edge of the joe hole, his legs dangling in the cold night air. Behind him stood the stick of Dougie, Henry, Willy, Jack, with Reggie bringing up the rear. Reggie was busy thinking only of his duty to kick them out if they developed cold feet. Which was all well and good, unless he was the one to develop the cold feet. What then? He looked at large Warrant Officer Jepsen. Jepsen eyed the boys coolly. Reggie assumed the big man probably had secret orders of his own.

He also knew all that wouldn't be necessary. They'd sworn to see out their duty, and that time was finally here.

Chapter 54
Greenlight

The Whitley's twin engines grew audibly quieter as Wing Commander Hansen pulled back the throttle to reduce the planes speed, beginning its decent. They were approaching the drop zone. All the training was over. All the lessons were learned as well as they were going to learn them. Reggie's stomach rolled twice as the plane hit an air pocket and tossed them about. Everyone had passed muster when the prime minister came calling on his visit. He had already seen all the assessment reports from the boys four days of competency testing. He laughed when he heard about Freddie's answer of "girls" to every word association question he was asked. He was impressed by the quality of their uniforms and their patrol unit; even the German they spoke was excellent, or so it sounded to his ears, and they were getting better. Reports stated that their language lessons had gone so well that for the last five weeks at Beaulieu they had spoken with their commanders and each other exclusively in German.

They had even, whilst the PM was seated in the officers' mess for lunch with them, managed to excuse themselves and return one at a time, and whilst distracting the PM's driver, used a bag of flour, a detonating time pencil they had 'requisitioned' from demolitions, and some axle grease to set up a surprise for the prime minister. The entire set up took just four minutes.

PFOOF! The time pencil in the flour bag went off just as the PM's driver opened the rear door, exactly as planned, throwing flour over the poor unsuspecting driver from head to toe. Good discipline the chap had. He didn't flinch at all; just brushed the flour off the PM's seat and stepped back to allow his passenger to enter.

"Splendid! Bravo! Good show, lads—very good show indeed!" the proud prime minister commented through his laughter. "I wish I had six thousand more like you." The general and the air vice-marshal weren't exactly with him on that sentiment. Perhaps after a successful mission they might be, but not simply by an ill-advised lunchtime flour bomb. Whilst the prime minister was impressed, the sergeant major was not. They paid for that bag of flour with two extra miles the following morning.

***

They were all anxious for the jump. Each handled it in his own way. Reggie looked over the squad, as him mind raced with dozens of things to remember. Freddie fidgeted in his seat, biting his nails, his lips moving as he mumbled a prayer to himself. Dougie and Henry were holding hands. Jack was busy checking his harness, again. And Willy? He was standing, oddly staring at the fuselage of the plane. Reggie looked at him hard. The boy didn't look right.

Between the wind blowing through the plane and the roar of the engines, it was useless to speak. To get Freddie's attention, Reggie blew an ear-piercing blast of a whistle. It worked. Freddie looked. Reggie extended his middle and forefinger in the shape of a 'V'. He swept his hand from his eyes to Willy, meaning that Freddie should take a look at the boy. Freddie looked, instantly seeing what Reggie was concerned about. Willy was sweating, staring, not like he was scared to jump, but like he was—*oh no, not now*—like he was—

Reggie got his confirmation from watching Freddie's face turn. His eyes got as big as roundels and he blinked twice. He nodded to Reggie. Willy was having an episode.

The jump-warning light flashed from red to green.

Jumpmaster Jepsen lowered his arm. *"Go! Go! Go!"* His shout, once taken by the wind, sounded as a whisper.

Freddie turned back around and with a blast of wind was suddenly gone. Dougie dropped to the lip of the hole and he too was gone in a blast. Henry's turn came and he went. Willy stood in the way of Jack, oblivious to the happenings around him. Reggie pushed Jack forwards past Willy, giving a thumbs-up signal for Jack to see. The boy did as told, dropped to his butt, then out the hole he fell. Good Jack. It was just he and Willy. He turned the boy and looked deeply into his eyes. A blank stare glared back.

"Come on, Willy!" he yelled. "Not now! Come back to me!" He shook the boy slightly, to no avail. He shook harder. Nothing.

Jumpmaster Jepsen stood watching, more than anxiously waiting for Willy to take his seat and make his exit. He ripped off his headphones in a rush, letting them fall and swing against the bulkhead. He was tethered to the fuselage by a long heavy strap and hook, just in case, but remained ready and able to 'assist' his jumpers out the hole -- if need be.

With no other option Reggie grabbed Willy, turned him round, shoving him down to a seated position on the lip of the hole. "I'm right behind you!" he yelled into Willy's ear and nudged him out.

Jepsen watched as Reggie pushed his little brother out the joe hole and into the cold dark sky rocketing past at 125 miles per hour. The smaller boy seemed to be in the grip of shock, probably brought on by fright. His brother performed his expected duty, as instructed. Jepsen gave him a wink, a nod. The boy plopped himself on the edge. Jepsen snapped a salute then pointed at the hole. *"Go! Go! Go!"*

With a last glance at the Warrant Officer and the words "St. Michael, be with me" on his lips, he closed his eyes tight, and dropped from the aeroplane into the cold night sky over occupied France.

ACKNOWLEDGMENTS

This book would not have been possible without the help,
encouragement and support of the following people.
I am eternally grateful.

Kevin Kinert, Chris Heinz, Mark Jepsen, Mick Prodger, Diane
Prodger, Richard Bradburn, Connor Steeves, Jesse Tomaras,
Matt Jepsen, Ethan Heinz, Erich Heinz, Mason Malkowski,
Aimee Jepsen, Debbie Fleming, Jill Malkowski

VERY SPECIAL THANKS TO

Marilyn Morales

ABOUT THE AUTHOR

Dan Morales is a writer who lives and works in Chicago. A graduate of Columbia College, Dan's degree in marketing and advertising has served him well at ad agencies great and small. His copywriting work has earned praise and numerous awards, including an Effie and a FAB Award. More about Dan can be found at his web site, dmoralescopy.com. This is his first novel.

CPSIA information can be obtained
at www.ICGtesting.com
Printed in the USA
LVHW04s1242140518
577104LV00001B/78/P